"I'd prefer to keep our relationship businesslike in nature, Aiden. I think it would be for the best."

"I couldn't agree more," he answered even as he gently threaded his fingers through Darcy's hair.

A deliciously tingling wave swept her from head to toe, taking her breath. Then her mind recognized the danger and her heart skittered. She leaned back as she said, "This isn't my understanding of how business—"

"You have so much to learn." He drew her toward him.

She couldn't breathe, couldn't resist the gentle pull. "I don't want to learn," she heard herself whisper. It was a tiny sound and she knew it would make no difference.

"Let's see," he answered just as quietly, his lips brushing over hers in prelude.

She started to protest again, but the parting of her lips served only to invite him to kiss her in earnest. This wasn't at all like the kiss before, in the Lion and Fiddle. That one had been hard and then possessive. But this time . . . The gentleness of Aiden's lips made her shivery, then warm. Reason argued for resistance. Something else urged surrender. . . .

DARING
THE
DEVIL

LESLIE
LAFOY

BANTAM BOOKS

*New York Toronto London
Sydney Auckland*

DARING THE DEVIL

A Bantam Fanfare Book / September 1999

ISBN 0-553-58042-6

Published simultaneously in the United States and Canada

Bantam Books are published by Bantam Books, a division of Random
House, Inc. Its trademark, consisting of the words "Bantam Books"
and the portrayal of a rooster, is Registered in U.S. Patent and
Trademark Office and in other countries. Marca Registrada. Bantam
Books, 1540 Broadway, New York, New York 10036.

PRINTED IN THE UNITED STATES OF AMERICA

WCD   10 9 8 7 6 5 4 3 2 1

For the Ladies of the Lounge

DARING THE DEVIL

DARCY O'KEEFE PAUSED on the front porch. The morning air was cool and damp, held close to the city streets by the thick blanket of gray clouds overhead. Around her swirled the sounds and scents of a community awakening to a new day; hawkers' cries were beginning to rise on the next street over, the whiffs of coal smoke not yet strong enough to overpower the aromas of meat pies and pastries. Darcy lifted her face to the meager sunlight and smiled at the feel of the fine mist on her cheeks.

Her mother's voice drifted downward, and she glanced up at the second-story window to her left. They were doing their morning rosaries, her mother and Bridie, the girl who stayed with her each day. Darcy smiled ruefully. Mary O'Keefe couldn't tell you what year it was, but she remembered to begin each day with a rosary, close each day with another. Darcy shook her head. Bridie O'Shaunessy had the patience of a saint and was easily worth twice what Darcy paid her in wages.

The thought of money, as always, shifted Darcy's gaze back to the streets around her. Today was the first true autumn day. The people bustling in the street weren't yet accustomed to wearing an extra layer of clothing. The moisture in the air had their heads down and them focused only on getting their tasks completed so they could find the warmth of a hearth fire. Darcy grinned. It was a fine, fine day for picking pockets.

She checked to be sure her hair was completely tucked into her woolen cap and then pulled the collar of the man's coat up around her neck. The heavy square heels of her boots made little noise as she skipped down the wooden steps into the stream of people moving along the cobblestones. With her hands rammed into the pockets of her trousers, she listened to the voices around her.

Not a one from anywhere but Charlestown and Boston. She reminded herself that wealthy visitors weren't likely to be wandering this street of boardinghouses; that if they were here for the fleecing, they'd be found just around the corner, on the merchants' way. *If* . . . It was still early in the day. Visitors didn't usually emerge from their lodgings until midmorning. And if the mist turned into actual rain, they wouldn't come out at all, and the day would be for nothing.

Darcy turned the corner into the bustle of Charlestown's street commerce.

"Eggs! Fresh eggs here!"

Darcy separated herself from the pedestrians. "Good morning, Maisey," she said, slipping behind the young woman's makeshift counter.

Maisey grinned, the expression brightening her copper freckles and lighting up her green eyes. "How are you this mornin', Darce? And your mother?"

"Mother's hoping that Nelson survives the 1805 Battle of Trafalgar. She's saying a rosary for him, I think."

"Poor dear. It must be so terrible to be lost in your own mind."

Darcy shrugged. "Mother doesn't know she's lost, so she isn't the least bit concerned by it. Proof, Maisey, that God is merciful to the simple and the innocent."

"And where did you hear that bit of comfort? Sounds like something Bridie would say."

"Or Mrs. Malone down the hall."

Maisey turned her attention back to the street and shouted, "Eggs! Fresh eggs here!" A quick succession of paying customers kept Maisey busy long enough for Darcy to note the absence of fine tailoring in the crowd moving past her.

"Looks to be a slow day for you, doesn't it?" Maisey observed, pocketing coins. "I suppose that's why we haven't seen Patrick yet. The air's a wee bit thick for the fancies to come out. Might sog up their hat feathers and spot their kid gloves."

Darcy was about to agree with her friend when a splash of mulberry wool caught her attention. "Things just looked up," she said. "Over by Mrs. Boyle's stand. Just to the right of the salted cod. Do you see him?"

Maisey craned her neck for a clear view and then gasped. "Lord, how could a girl not notice that? What do you make of him, Darce?"

Tall, very tall. Massively built. Broad-shouldered and well dressed. Bareheaded; ebony hair, silken and unfashionably long. Patrician features carved in granite by a master. Very much a man of the world, and very self-assured. "Not young, not old," Darcy said aloud. She moved to the end of the counter, her gaze never leaving the stranger. "He's from elsewhere, to be sure. Judging by the finely tailored coat and shiny Hessians, it'd be my guess that his money outweighs his common sense."

"He's a good-looking man, isn't he?"

"Are you asking me or telling me?"

"I'm checking to be sure that you've still got some hope in you, Darcy O'Keefe. The day you don't recognize a breathtakin' man is the day I truly begin to worry about the end you'll come to." Maisey grinned. "Not that I'm trying to hurry you toward any end in particular, mind you."

Darcy stepped outside the stall. "Well, if he asks me to marry him . . . should I say yea or nay?"

"Are you goin' to fan him? You might as well. Even if he doesn't have much money, it'd be worth the checkin'." Maisey made a soft clicking sound with her tongue. "My, my. If you've a brain in your head, Darce, you'll say *yea* if he asks. I do believe those are the most wonderful shoulders I've ever seen."

Darcy grinned. "I'll be back in a whistle."

"Be careful, Darcy. He's big."

"But I'm good," she countered, watching the man move away from the fishmonger's stand. "If Patrick shows up, tell the slacker that I started to work without him."

AIDEN TERRELL STEPPED into the tide of humanity making its way along the cobbled street. Out of the corner of his eye, he saw the tall, thin, fair-skinned youth fall in behind him. Knowing how pickpockets generally worked, Aiden scanned the crowd ahead of him, searching for the one who'd create a pretense for stalling him and allow the other to empty his pockets from behind.

He frowned. Either the boy's accomplices were especially good at blending with the crowd, or he was working the street on his own. Aiden's frown became a scowl. Being alone meant the boy was confident and therefore probably good at his work. Or an overconfident, inexperienced fool. Aiden hoped for the former.

Aiden swore beneath his breath. Time had grown far too short on him. He needed an entrée to Charlestown's criminal underworld, and he needed it now. He'd left his hotel room that morning determined to attract the larcenous attention of one of the children who scurried like rats along the edges of Charlestown's streets. The boy coming up on him from behind was older than he would have liked, but desperation made any opportunity acceptable.

Desperation also made him impatient. He stopped in the middle of the street and gawked at his surroundings as though he'd never seen bricks and mortar. The brush was light and quick, on his left side. Because he knew he was supposed to, he turned in that direction, an apology tumbling from his lips.

The touch on his right might have gone unnoticed had he not been expecting it, had he not been hoping for it. The boy *was* good. Very good.

Aiden whirled to his right, but his hand encountered only

the shoulder of a middle-aged woman who censored him with an indignant huff. And then he noticed a quick movement in the pale shadows of an alleyway.

Darcy tossed the empty leather wallet into the first ash bin. The stack of paper was incredibly thick. Her stride faltered. She quickly fanned out the bills to see exactly what she'd netted. Sweet Jesus, Joseph, and Mary. She held three hundred dollars in her hand; more money than she'd ever seen at one time. And all of it American dollars. Not a franc or a pound in the bunch.

"I believe you have something that belongs to me."

Darcy spun about. Her mark stood between her and the entrance to the alleyway, close enough that his shadow fell over her and chilled her blood. She'd been a fool twice over. The first mistake had been to work alone; the second to count the accursed money. The pause had been enough for the mark to catch her.

He took a step forward. Dark brows. Square jaw. His lips would be full when they weren't compressed by anger. Darcy shoved the money into her pocket and took a step back. Judging by the look in the man's gray eyes, her disguise remained intact. There was no leer, no lust in his expression. She could outrun him. Easily. His legs were longer and definitely well muscled, but she knew the twists and turns of Charlestown; he didn't. She just had to get past him and back out into the street.

"A proposition, boy," he said slowly. "You can keep a hundred of it for a favor."

"I can have it all for nothing, too," she answered, careful to keep her voice low.

"That's based on the assumption that you can get past me with it, lad. I bet three hundred dollars that you can't."

A shiver raced down her spine. This man was dangerous. It was more than the width of his shoulders, the size of his fists. There was an intensity about him, a depth of reserve that resonated with tightly leashed power.

As though he'd read her thoughts, he said, "We can do this the simple way or the hard way. The choice is yours. I'd recommend the former. I have no real desire to pound you into cooperation."

"As if you could," she retorted defiantly.

"Before you step forward for a battering," he countered, "you might want to consider the favor I'm asking."

She quickly appraised him from head to toe. Nothing about him so much as whispered of unnatural tastes. Masquerading as a boy as long as she had, she'd developed a finely honed sense about such matters. No, this man definitely preferred women. She'd bet all three hundred on it. She'd also bet that the suggestion of perversity would anger him beyond reason.

"I've seen the likes of you before," she sneered. "You're not the first nancy man who's come down here looking for his sick pleasures. I'm not interested, mister. Not for all the money in Boston."

He laughed quietly and her stomach knotted. Nothing had gone right since the moment she'd touched this man's pockets. She should have waited for Patrick. She shouldn't have gone after this one alone. If she got out of this mess without losing some skin, she'd count herself damn lucky.

Aiden studied the defiant figure in front of him. For a pickpocket, the boy had an unusual degree of pluck. Any other would have bolted by now. And to stand there with stolen money in his pockets and taunt a man easily twice his size . . . The Irish grew them tough in Charlestown.

"Who do you work for, boy? Who takes a cut from your earnings?" The boy squared his shoulders and Aiden added loyalty to the young man's list of better qualities. "Two hundred's yours for an introduction."

"I've got three hundred already. Can't see any reason to want another two. Greed's a mortal sin."

"And thieving isn't?" Aiden countered, his patience weakening. "I'll give you two seconds, boy. Take me to your boss or I'll haul your ass to the first constable I can find."

The young man slowly reached into his pocket and brought out some of the paper money. "It'd be your word against mine," he said quietly as he lifted up the two bills.

"Especially when there's no evidence," he added, tearing them into pieces.

As they fluttered to the ground, Aiden sprang forward. The boy laughed and darted to Aiden's left.

Darcy heard his curse as she ran for the light at the end of the alley and the open street beyond. And then, without warning, her feet went out from under her and she fell head-long onto the pavers. Fear drove her back to her feet before she could take a breath. But even as she focused again on the end of the alleyway, sensation and awareness collapsed into each other, tearing an angry sob from her throat.

Blinded by the mass of dark curls tumbling over her face and snarling every curse she'd ever heard, Darcy pried franti-cally at the iron band clamped painfully about her waist, kicked her legs with fierce determination.

"Sweet Jesus Christ."

His soft declaration sliced through her anger and she pan-icked. He knew her ruse, knew he held a woman's body hard against his own. She threw her head back with all the force she could muster and counted the pain of impact worth it when he loosened his grip. Darcy didn't pause to think. The instant her feet hit the cobblestones she drove the heel of her boot onto the vamp of one of his well-polished Hessians.

Aiden gasped and swore as the world went red. He snatched handfuls of whatever he could grasp and jerked it toward him. He heard her squeak, felt her struggle in his hands. He willed the haze before his eyes to clear, hoped that he could control the girl without truly hurting her. But con-trol her he would, one way or the other.

He felt his left shoulder strike something solid and in-stantly, he whirled the girl about and pinned her against it, held her there with the full length of his body.

"Get off me you goddamn bastard!" she snarled, strug-gling to escape.

"Your manners were better as a boy."

"You son of a bitch! I'll scream rape."

She would and he knew it. Aiden pressed against her just hard enough to drive the air from her lungs, then clamped a hand over her mouth, being careful to cup his palm to keep the minx from biting him.

It was then, standing with his body pressed against hers, that he got his first good look at her. Eyes the color of dark chocolate and fringed with silken lashes of the same hue. Eyes that flashed with a fire that caught his breath. And her hair . . . It cascaded over her shoulders, a riot of loose ringlets—for the most part dark brown, but touched with streaks of warm golds and vibrant reds. Her cheekbones were high and delicate. Far too delicate to be mistaken for a boy. Aiden cursed himself for his earlier lack of awareness. If he were to make a habit of it, he'd be dead before the week was out.

"Hey, there!"

The girl renewed her struggle but Aiden held her firmly as he turned his head toward the alley opening and the male voice. "The matter's a private one," he snapped. "Leave us be."

The man stopped in his tracks and tilted his head to the side. "Aiden? Aiden Terrell? Could that be you?"

The accent was Irish, but he remembered it and a brief, alcohol-soaked friendship in the shadows of Liverpool. "Patrick Gallagher," he acknowledged with a slow smile. "It's a small world."

The girl went absolutely still.

"Indeed it is," Patrick seconded, stepping into the alley. "I see that ye've met me partner. Mornin', Darce."

CHAPTER 2

W E HAVEN'T BEEN formally introduced," the man replied without looking at her. The resonance of his voice awakened her to other sensations . . . the warmth of his body, the hammering of his heartbeat. All of it in stark contrast to the cold, hard bricks at her back.

Patrick chuckled. "Well, considerin' your circumstances there, we'd best be about remedyin' that oversight, wouldn't ya say?" He didn't pause to let either of them answer. "Darcy O'Keefe, the monster pinnin' ya to the wall be Mr. Aiden Terrell, late of Liverpool. Aiden, that comely bit of Irish womanhood you're claspin' be Miss Darcy O'Keefe, who until this mornin' would have been described as one of Charlestown's best pickpockets."

"A pleasure, miss," the stranger said. His dark gray eyes belied the assertion. Without looking away, he asked, "If I let her loose is she going to act civilized?"

"Hard to tell." Patrick shrugged. "I suppose we can ask Darce what she's of a mind to do. She does tend to have one of her own."

Terrell eased the pressure of his hand across her mouth. "Miss O'Keefe?"

"Get off me, you clod," she demanded, trying to push him away.

"Ah, such honeyed words of civility." One corner of his mouth quirked upward as he slowly eased his weight off her.

Darcy shot a quick glance toward the alley opening. The money was still in her pocket, and if she could slide away while the two men resumed their acquaintance . . .

"What brings you to Charlestown, Aiden? 'Tis a long way from Liverpool."

As Patrick spoke, she started to ease her way down the wall.

"You're not going anywhere," Aiden Terrell said, drawing her back with such speed that her feet slipped on the wet cobblestones. If he noticed her near-fall, or the effort it took him to haul her upright, he gave no indication of it. Holding her at his side, he continued his conversation with her partner. "I'm here on much the same business as took me to Liverpool, Patrick. And then Edinburgh and Dublin after that."

"Still haven't found the man, huh? 'Tis likely that he's long ago sold the jewels."

"But I won't know for sure until I find him."

"I gather that you've reason to believe he's come to Charlestown?" Patrick asked.

"My task would be more quickly and easily accomplished if I had a bit of assistance," Aiden answered. "I was hoping to convince your friend here to introduce me to someone who might be in a position to provide it."

" 'Twould be Mick O'Shaunessy you'd be wantin' to meet, then. I think I can arrange it. Mick'll expect a fee for any help he gives you, of course. Most likely a hefty one."

"Of course. How soon do you think you can put together the meeting?"

"Don't see any reason why we can't head over to the Social Club now, an' see if Mick's handy. If he's otherwise engaged at the moment, we can carve a time out for later in the day."

Oh, wasn't Mick going to be pleased by this turn of events? Darcy mused. He'd have Patrick's head for it. No one was allowed to bring nonmembers into the Social Club without Mick's prior approval. She wouldn't have a chance to exact revenge on Patrick Gallagher for ignoring her and letting

Terrell manhandle her. Mick wouldn't leave any hide for her to flail.

Of course, she wouldn't have much hide left either, if Mick learned she'd violated the rules and gone after the mark alone. With any luck she could send the two men off without her and escape three hundred dollars richer. Of course luck wasn't something she'd had in spades so far that morning. . . . Darcy took a deep breath and committed herself to making some.

"I can see from the shape of your plans, gentlemen, that there's no place in them for me. So, if you've no objections, I'll be leaving you to relive your old times together. Do tell Mick I said hello."

Aiden Terrell's smile didn't warm the color of his eyes, and he didn't release his hold on her arm. "I'll have my money back before any of us leave here."

"I need my hand free to get it," she replied icily, wresting herself from his grip. Only after she'd stepped beyond his immediate reach did she think about sticking her hand into her pocket. She winced with pain. Darcy looked down at her hand. She couldn't have said how or when it happened, but her fingers were swollen and stiff. Odd that she hadn't even noticed the throbbing pain until now.

Patrick leaned closer to look and whisper, "Can you move your fingers, Darce?"

"Aye," she answered, checking. "No bones are broken. They're just a bit bruised is all. They'll mend before the week's out."

"But 'tis your right hand. You'll not be poking pockets for a while. Mick's not goin' to be happy when he hears about it. How'd you do it?"

She said nothing, but gave Terrell a steely look.

"It was not my intention to hurt you, Miss O'Keefe," Terrell said coolly. "If you'll recall, I made several attempts to negotiate for your cooperation."

"Darcy—negotiate?" Patrick laughed outright. "Oh, won't Mick enjoy that!"

Darcy clenched her teeth and, despite the pain in her fingers, separated two bills from the wad in her pocket before pulling it and handing it to Terrell.

"There's forty dollars missing," he stated, holding the fanned bills out for inspection. "I'm sure it's merely an oversight."

Darcy met his gaze squarely. "I tore it up, remember?"

"Ya shredded money?" Patrick asked, obviously appalled.

"You tore up two fives," Terrell said. "I've accounted for those. There's still forty missing."

Patrick muttered, "I suppose that fivers is the best choice possible, if you're desperate enough to commit the sacrilege."

"Give it over, Miss O'Keefe." Terrell extended his hand and snapped his fingers. "I'll check your pockets myself if I have to."

She knew he'd do it just to goad her. She gave up his money, retorting, "It's well worth forty to keep your hands off me."

Patrick laughed. "Now there's a twist, huh, Aiden? A woman not wantin' yer touch."

Terrell replied dryly, "I'm deeply wounded. I don't know if I can survive the rebuff."

She wanted to kick him in the shins and wipe the smug smile right off his handsome face. Darcy controlled the impulse, telling herself that pulling the lion's tail would only prolong their unpleasant association.

"We'll have Darcy's ma pray for your speedy recovery," Patrick said, whipping his hat off his head and clutching it over his heart. His eyes belied the solemnity of his words. "Mary O'Keefe whispers in God's ear, ya know. Has a special in, she does."

"Leave my mother alone, Patrick. Or answer to me for it," she said quietly.

Patrick winked at Terrell. "And our Darce is just a might tender-skinned about it."

"Be that as it may, if we could proceed to the Social Club and a possible meeting with Mr. O'Shaunessy . . . ?"

She disliked Terrell too much to be grateful to him for changing the subject, but she was willing to accept the opportunity it gave her to make an escape. She scooped up her hat from the cobblestones. "Enjoy your jaunt, gentlemen," she offered, slapping the hat on her head.

"Now, now, Darcy girl," Patrick said, cutting off her exit. "Where do ya think you're off to? If ya can't work the markets, then Mick'll likely expect ya to work another job while ya heal. There'll be no holiday just 'cause yer hand's hurt. You'd best come along an' present yourself. He'll be more inclined to give ya something easy if he doesn't have to send someone lookin' for ya."

Damn and double damn. Patrick was right. And there was no point in making matters any worse than they already were. Darcy stared at the ground and tried to swallow back a rising sense of dread. She told herself that Mick was basically a fair man and that he tended to have a soft spot where she was concerned. There was really nothing to fear in going with Patrick and his friend to the Social Club. She'd just make it clear that it was Patrick's idea to bring Terrell along.

"I can't go out of here with my hair down," she said, but her fingers refused to cooperate as she tried to shove her hair under the fabric of her hat.

"Here," snapped Aiden Terrell, pushing her hands aside. "We'll all grow old waiting for you to get it done."

Her breath caught in her throat. Darcy had no real choice but to endure his hands in her hair, and the blush creeping over her cheeks. To his credit, he was gentle and capable, almost as though he were accustomed to tucking curls out of sight. Darcy scowled down at the pavers, unable to understand why his touch heightened her senses. It was a most curious thing.

"Thank you," she murmured after he completed the task.

Without a word, he went to stand beside Patrick. Terrell's gaze traveled down the length of her and then just as slowly upwards. He shook his head. "How could anyone think you're a boy?" he asked derisively as he turned away and started toward the end of the alley.

"You did," she retorted evenly, falling in behind the two

men. Terrell's shoulders momentarily stiffened and she
smiled.

DARCY LEANED AGAINST the end of the bar with
her arms folded over her midriff and one ankle crossed casually over the other. The low buzz of conversation swelled
around her, but none of the words were clear enough to be
understood. It didn't matter anyway. It was a given that Patrick was scrambling to explain; equally clear that Mick
wasn't the least bit happy about the presence of an unexpected visitor.

She focused on the scratched wooden floor, her face in the
shadow of her hat brim. Halfway to the Social Club she'd discovered that her hand wasn't the only injury she'd incurred in
her scuffle with Aiden Terrell. Somehow her lip had been cut.
How she hadn't tasted the blood before that point baffled her.
Never in her life had her perceptions been so disconnected
from her thinking.

The only reasonable explanation for it seemed to be Aiden
Terrell himself. She shifted so that she could study him out of
the corner of her eye. He stood well apart from her, his attention fixed on the table in the back where Mick sat and listened to Patrick rattle on.

She decided that Terrell was a man who didn't like to ask
for permission. He'd probably never had to. He stood over six
feet. If she had to guess, she'd put him at about two hundred
and twenty pounds. But he wasn't one of those giants who
didn't quite know what to do with his size. He moved like a
cat, purposefully and with easy grace. There was a wariness
about him as well, and a tension that vibrated in the air
around him and cleared the sidewalks ahead of him.

And if his physical size wasn't enough to make most men
think twice about opposing him, one piercing look from his
slate gray eyes would quell them. Darcy turned slightly to see
him better. He stared straight at her.

Caught in the act, she abandoned her surreptitious study.
His cheek was red and swollen where the back of her head

had connected during their struggle. It had to hurt just as badly as her hand did. All things considered, Darcy decided that he'd gotten the worst in their fight. At least *she* hadn't limped halfway to the Social Club. With great effort, she held her smile in check. *I'm not afraid of anyone or anything. Including you, Aiden Terrell.*

For an instant his brows furrowed. And then the seemingly impossible happened: He smiled. His eyes lightened in color and sparkled like the Charles River on a sunny day. Her breath caught low in her throat.

In that moment she understood that it wasn't just men who gave Aiden Terrell whatever he wanted, when he wanted it. Darcy deliberately turned her back on him. Sweet Jesus, Joseph, and Mary. To think that twinkling eyes, ebony hair, and an inviting smile could send her blood pounding through her veins. She must have hit her head hard on the bricks in that alley.

She looked up to see Patrick motion and Terrell start toward the table. Mick was silently ordering her to come with him. She obeyed, but stopped well behind Terrell and out of Mick's direct line of vision.

"Mick, this be the Aiden Terrell I've told ya about before," Patrick began. "From me Liverpool days. He's come to Charlestown lookin' for a man, an' wants our help findin' him."

"And just how is that you knew to be a-lookin' for Patrick among us, Mr. Terrell?"

"I had no idea he was here in America. Our meeting this morning was purely by chance."

Patrick grinned and bobbed his head. "Broke up an alley fight 'tween him an' Darce, I did."

"A fight now?" Mick repeated, cocking a sandy-colored eyebrow. He leaned to the side and looked around Terrell. "Did I hear him right, Darcy O'Keefe?"

"You did," she answered demurely. There was nothing even remotely demure about her silent curses as she stepped up beside Terrell.

"And would ye be about to explain the particulars of how ye came to be a-throwin' punches with this brute?"

Damn. Damn. Damn. "He took issue with having his pocket picked." She glared at Terrell. "Obviously he has no sense of public charity."

"And how was it that he even knew he'd made a contribution to the Widows an' Orphans' Fund, girl? Were ye workin' alone? Were ye careless?"

"She's fairly good, actually," Terrell answered. "If I hadn't set myself out as a mark, if I hadn't been waiting and expecting it—"

"Set yourself out as a mark?" Darcy repeated as her hands went to her hips and she turned to him. "Are you implying that I'm fool enough to let you sucker me into fanning your pockets and lifting your wallet?"

He smiled disdainfully. "You're not as good as you think you are, Miss O'Keefe. Not nearly."

"Oh? And an expert on pocket picking, are you?" she retorted hotly. "I rather thought your expertise lay in assaulting women in alleyways."

His eyes instantly darkened, and she felt the twin pangs of triumph and regret. Somehow, she knew he'd make her pay for that barb.

Mick quietly cleared his throat and asked, "An' why is it ye wanted yer pockets reefed, Mr. Terrell?"

As Terrell smoothly gave him the same explanation as he had Patrick, Darcy eased away.

"Darcy, girl! Don't be a-wanderin' off. We're not near done yet."

First Patrick and now Mick; both of them seemed determined to make her suffer. She winced when she tried to shove her hands in her pockets.

"What's the trouble with yer hand, Darce?"

She knew full good and well that Patrick had already told him every detail of what had happened in that alley. Mick's asking didn't bode well. "It's just a slight battle wound, Mick," she answered with a quick shrug. "It's a tad swollen and sore, but it'll be fine in a day or two. There's no cause for worry."

"An' yer lip? Another wee battle scar?"

She glanced at Terrell. "Bridie was flipping hotcakes this morning. I forgot to duck," she supplied.

Mick laughed. "Norm'ly, Terrell, I'd take offense that ye'd scuffed up one o'mine, but 'tis clear that ol' Darce gave as good as she got. Ye'll be lucky if that eye don't blacken 'fore the afternoon's done."

"And he'll be limpin' for a while yet, too," Patrick contributed with a chuckle.

"Would ye be a-thinkin' yer foot's broken, Mr. Terrell?"

"God isn't that benevolent," Darcy muttered.

Everyone laughed. Except Terrell. He shot her a murderous glance before giving Mick a tight smile and saying, "It's fine."

"We've a doctor or two here'bouts who'd be glad to see to it if need be."

"It's fine. Thank you," he said tersely. His tone was more conciliatory when he added, "But it's most kind of you to offer."

"Well," Mick said, easing back in his chair, "now that we've dispensed with the explanations all around, an' civil enough pleasantries, I suppose we should be about the business that brought ye here. What is it ye want of me exactly, Mr. Terrell?"

Darcy wondered if anyone else noticed the slight shift in Terrell's stance, in the set of his shoulders and jaw.

"I'd like to hire one of your men to assist me in my search for the man who stole some valuable property from my father."

"And what manner of assistance do ya see this man providin' ye?"

"I need someone who knows the streets of Charlestown. Someone who knows the people of the city. I need a man adept at asking questions and collecting information. He need be involved no further than that. I'll act alone on what he brings me."

"So, 'tis pretty much a guide ye'd be a-lookin' to hire, correct?"

"Essentially. A knowledge of who works the streets and back ways would be equally valuable to me."

"And what would ye be willin' to pay for such valuable services?"

"The price is negotiable. Depending, of course, on the man's experience, contacts, and talents."

Mick tapped the pad of his forefinger against his lip. "Well, a-seein' as how Patrick vouches for ye an' assures me ye're a man who deserves to be met halfway . . . 'Twould be less than decent of me to offer ye anyone but me best. Twenty dollars a day until yer business is concluded."

"Ten."

"Fifteen, an' we don't start the tallyin' 'til tomorrow. Today's on me."

"Done."

Darcy expelled a breath, only then realizing that she'd been holding it through the quick negotiation. Done was right. Now she could be on her way. Why she'd had to be present for this bit of business was beyond her, but strange were the workings of men's minds.

"Darcy."

She started and blinked at Mick. "Sir?"

"Dead men don't pay their bills. So see that nothin' unfortunate happens to Mr. Aiden Terrell here, an' five a day is yours, girl."

Her stomach dropped to her feet. Her and Terrell? *Teamed?* She sputtered, unable to force a coherent word off her tongue.

"You can't be serious. *Her?*" Terrell exclaimed. "That's the most ridiculous—"

"Mr. Terrell," Mick interrupted. "I'm giving ye the best in me organization. Darcy O'Keefe knows the streets and the folks that works 'em like no one else. An' a good head she has on those slim shoulders o' hers."

"If today was any indication of—"

"I'm not interested in doing it, Mick," Darcy blurted out. "Pick someone else. Patrick and Terrell—"

"Ye don't have a say in the matter, girl. Yer hand makes ye of no use reefin' for at least a week. Yer lip's too puffed to make ye suitable for doin' an inside over in Boston. Ye need to be a-doin' something, an' it might as well be escortin' Mr. Terrell here. A bum hand an' a split lip won't hinder the task in the least way."

"I don't like it," she pressed. "I don't like him."

Terrell snorted. "The feeling is mutual."

"Then ye'll be about the completin' of the task with all due speed, girl. Which is for the best, since it's poor enough wages ye'll be a makin' at it." Mick smiled at Terrell. "An' 'tis a very good thing you're not a-fancyin' Darcy. Her services as a guide is all ye be a-payin' for. I hear word that ye've taken a liberty with her, an' I'll see yer hands served up on a silver platter. Do I make meself clear?"

No one said anything to ease the tension.

"Good," Mick pronounced with a curt nod. "Her abilities aside, Mr. Terrell, 'twas at yer hands that she's come to be of no other use to me this week. 'Tis the least ye can do to see that the girl earns something with which to feed herself an' her mother."

Terrell stood there like an overstoked stove waiting to explode. Darcy stared at the floor, cursing the luck of the Irish and the impulse that had sent her after Aiden Terrell's pockets.

"Well? What are the two of ye a-waitin' for?" Mick demanded. "I'm not a-goin' to walk ye to the door. I'll bid ye good huntin' from right here." And with that pronouncement, he turned back to the table.

Darcy couldn't remember the last time she'd felt this powerless. She didn't bother to look at Terrell. She headed for the door, saying as she went, "Keep up. I'm not looking back."

CHAPTER 3

SHE WAS OUT the door by the time Aiden reached her. Pain shot up his leg with every step he took, but he refused to give her the satisfaction of seeing him favor his injured foot. Damn her long legs and furious stride. If her intent was to kill him before the day was done, she might very well succeed.

"Where are we going?" he asked through clenched teeth.

"Back down to the market. I haven't eaten today and I'm hungry."

"There's a dining establishment on the corner ahead. I noticed it as we came this way earlier. Perhaps—"

"Suit yourself," she said. "I'll be in the market when you're done. Find me if you can."

"Are you always so obstinate? Or is this behavior something you've adopted just for me?"

She stopped in her tracks. An angry fire flashed in her dark eyes. "We're shackled ankle and elbow, Terrell," she said, poking him in the chest, "and there's no way out for either of us except to find the man you're looking for. I'm of a mind to get it over and done by nightfall. Now, you can go sit in restaurants and order food off printed menus if you like, but I'm not wasting the time. I want you out of my life as quickly as you came into it."

Before he could reply, she marched away again. He

watched her go, considering his options. Not going after her appealed to his pride. Why did Mick O'Shaunessy assign this creature to him? Why didn't Patrick Gallagher step forward and insist that he'd be his guide? Spending God only knew how many days and nights in Darcy O'Keefe's company wasn't something he was looking forward to at all. *She* wanted it over and done? Not nearly as much as he did. If he hoped to see his home before yet another Christmas passed, he needed to be on with the search. He caught up with her a half city block later. They passed another in tense silence.

"Why don't you have accented speech like every mother and child down here?" he asked, not because he wanted to know but simply because the sooner they talked about something, the sooner they could talk about the hunt itself.

"It's a long story, Terrell, and not worth the time it'd take to tell it." Her gaze touched him for a scant second. Her pace slowed to a merciful saunter. "Now, if you'd be so kind," she said, "as to tell me the name of the man you're trying so hard to find, it would make my work just a bit easier."

As it always did, his pulse quickened. "In Liverpool he went by the name of James Packer. In Edinburgh he was Liam Stewart. In Dublin, Joseph Ryan."

"Do you know his real name?"

"No," he lied. To assuage his conscience, he added, "Not that he's at all likely to use it."

"Do you know what he looks like?"

"Tall, just under six feet. I'd judge him to be two hundred pounds. Maybe more, maybe less, depending on how well he's eating these days."

"Well, so far you've described most of the men in Charlestown and three quarters of those in Boston. What color is his hair? His eyes? Is he fair or dark?"

"He changes his appearance as often as he does his name. But his eyes are dark like yours. And before you ask, he has no scars or other distinguishing marks that I'm aware of."

"He's a professional pennyweighter?"

"A what?"

"Jewel thief, Terrell," she clarified, obviously amused at his ignorance. "Your man—he's a professional jewel thief?"

"No."

"Of course not," she said on a sigh. "That would have made it relatively simple." She took three strides before she asked, "And just exactly what was it that he stole, Terrell? What's worth your haunting the streets of Liverpool, Edinburgh, Dublin, and Charlestown searching for him?"

Another lie slipped smoothly off his tongue. "He stole a family heirloom of considerable monetary and sentimental value."

"You've far more money than sense, Terrell. Do you know that?"

"Your opinion of both myself and my quest is immaterial, O'Keefe," he countered. "You're being paid to find a man, not pass judgment on the wisdom of the search."

She turned on him, her eyes ablaze.

"Mornin' to you, Darce! Will you be havin' your breakfast now?"

Together they turned to the sound of the voice. An old man settled his wheeled cart into the cobblestones and then tipped his hat to each of them in turn. The scents of warm bread and spicy meat wafted around them and made Aiden's stomach growl.

"And a good morning to you, Jack," Darcy said. "I will indeed. The pork today, I think."

Aiden stepped to her side. "Make it two, if you'd please."

"You've a new friend, Darcy," the man observed, opening a door in the top of his wagon box. "Don't know that I've ever seen him here'bouts before."

"I'd introduce you, but he's not staying long enough for a proper handshake."

"Aiden Terrell," he offered as he extended his hand.

"Jack Trehune," the other replied, wiping his hand on his apron before shaking Aiden's. "I'm the pie man. Best and freshest pies in Charlestown. Mornin', noon, and night. The missus brings 'em to me regular-like, hot from the hearth. These came not more'n ten minutes ago."

Out of the corner of his eye Aiden saw Darcy struggle to reach into her right pocket with her left hand. "Leave your money there, O'Keefe," he said quietly. "I'll pay for the food."

"I pay my own way," she replied brittlely.

The pie man's gaze darted between them. Aiden decided that now was as good a time as any to be clear on the nature of their relationship. "If you'll excuse us a moment, Mr. Trehune," he said. "We'll return shortly. If you'd be so kind as to ready our purchases?"

He got her ten feet from the pie man's ears before she jerked her arm from his grasp and snapped, "I'll not be beholden to you for anything, Terrell. I'll earn my daily wage and thank you most politely when it's warming my pocket. But you'll not spend another cent on me beyond that."

"Let's be clear, O'Keefe," he replied crisply. "I'm not the least interested in your being beholden to me. You're eighteen months behind me in the search for this man, and I've tolerated your impertinence only because I've a need to have you informed of the basic facts as expediently as possible.

"I want to be shackled to you only slightly less than I want the pox. Mick O'Shaunessy may have a hold over you sufficient for you to do his bidding against your will, but he doesn't hold claim to me. I can and will walk away from our association at any point in time that I decide to. I can and will easily hire another to take your place." He cocked a brow. "Now," he said slowly, "unless you want to go back to Mick and explain why you've lost him the money from my pockets, I'd suggest that you tuck away your pride or whatever it is that prompts you to behave like an imperial gutter rat."

"I am a gutter rat," she retorted coolly. "And Mick wasn't lying. No one knows the streets better than I do. That makes them mine. And grants me the right to be imperial. Go ahead. Hire someone else, Mr. Terrell. Hire anyone else. They may bow and scrape at your feet, but they won't get you within a mile of the man you're looking for."

Good God, the woman certainly had confidence enough.

Before he could think of something beyond that, she said, "I pay my own way. I don't accept charity—from you or anyone else."

"It's not charity," he countered. "It's a recognition of practical realities. My pockets are a helluva lot deeper than yours. When yours are empty, your stomach will be as well. I'm not going through this . . . misadventure . . . listening to your stomach rumble. I'm not going to have your attention wandering off to pastry wagons when it should be focused on the task for which I'm paying good money."

"I pay—"

"Then go back to Mick O'Shaunessy," he said bluntly.

Her jaw tightened. "Give Jack his money and let's be on with our accursed business."

Victorious, Aiden left her with a curt bow and went back to Trehune's cart.

"Don't let her see you smile, lad," the pie man whispered during the exchange. "Pride's all the girl's got for her own in this world."

He was tempted to tell the man that Darcy O'Keefe was going to have to stow a good measure of her pride in the course of their association, but something in the man's manner told him the words wouldn't be well received. Instead he offered a noncommittal grunt to acknowledge the warning, and started away with their food.

"Oh, an' Mr. Terrell?"

Aiden looked back over his shoulder. "Yes?"

"She's a good girl with a big heart. Don't be a-tramplin' it, or you'll answer to me an' every other man in Charlestown."

Ire shot through him. "Not to worry, Mr. Trehune."

He found her sitting on one of two barrels beneath the overhang of a dilapidated building. Handing her one of the paper-wrapped pies, he settled himself on the other. For several minutes they both watched the passersby without a sound except for the occasional rustle of paper.

Deciding that the ploy had worked well enough the first time to warrant a second use, he asked, "So why don't you have an Irish lilt, O'Keefe?"

She took her time before replying, "My mother's lace-curtain. Her family dropped the O from the Riley and hired tutors to erase all traces of Ireland from their speech. Escaping the taint was the most important thing in the world to them. My mother made sure my diction, among other things, stayed above the street."

He mentally added logical pieces to the information she'd given him. But just to be sure he had it right, he asked, "What do the Rileys think of you?"

"They don't know me." She shrugged. "But then you'd probably already figured that out, right?"

"It's a reasonable conclusion. I can't see lace-curtain allowing one of their own to pick pockets for sustenance. It would tend to undermine their concerted efforts at social climbing."

"That it would. I gather you know something of what goes into climbing?"

"It was, for the most part, done before I was born," he admitted. "My sole responsibility in life is to amass wealth for the continued maintenance of the illusion crafted by my forebears."

"And how is it that you go about doing that, Terrell?" she asked, wiping her fingers on her pant leg.

"I make money through trade, my principle operations being out of St. Kitts. And then I spend that money on material goods that tend to impress people."

"And the man you're after put an embarrassing hole in your social facade."

"I suppose that's the essence of it," Aiden answered. He eased the grip with which he held the meat pie. He didn't know all that much about Darcy O'Keefe, but he knew that the woman had a quick mind and even quicker eyes. She missed nothing. He didn't need her probing into the darker corners of this mess, and the less temptation he gave her for doing so, the better.

"St. Kitts is a British possession," she said out of the blue. "But you don't have a British accent to your speech. It's more southern. Virginia or Maryland."

Impressed at her accuracy, he explained, "My father was originally from northern Virginia, but he removed himself to St. Kitts as a young man. There's a colony of sorts there, of ex-patriots. I'm an American citizen."

She nodded, apparently satisfied with his answer, then drew her long legs up to sit cross-legged on the barrel, saying, "Look, it was obvious that Mick doesn't care what happens once you find this man, but I want to know."

"It's really none of your business, O'Keefe." As she turned to fix those bright brown eyes on him, he hastily added, "I say that not to be rude, but with the certainty that the further removed from the matter you can remain, the better for all parties concerned."

"You don't live down here long without developing instincts for reading people and situations. My instincts say there's a lot you're holding back, Terrell. I don't think this is about stolen jewelry."

His nape prickled, but he managed a smile. "It's reassuring, in an odd way, to know that you're so perceptive. What you need to know, you will. What you don't . . . you won't."

She took a bite of her pie and studied him. "So," she began after a long silence, "if you don't think I'm being too imperial to expect it, tell me what you know about this man. Does he have any particular vices? Any peculiarities we can use to narrow the search?"

Aiden shifted on the barrel and carefully ordered his response. "From time to time he drinks heavily."

"So does most of Charlestown and a full two-thirds of Boston. Does he favor one drink over all others?"

"Not that I'm aware of."

"Jesus, Terrell. I've no interest in or patience with parlor games, especially Twenty Questions. This will go much quicker if you just tell me what you know and let me sort through it."

Part of him stood in awe of her boldness. Another part of him saw the danger that it could pose for them both. It crossed his mind to give her the money in his pocket and send her on her way. "He's young, only twenty, and of English and French descent. He speaks both languages and has traveled Europe extensively," he answered. Then, watching her carefully, he added, "But for our purposes, the most important thing you need to know is that we're looking for a man who enjoys cruelty."

Her eyes narrowed just the slightest bit. "How sick is he?"

"Very."

"You should know that I don't go into those deep shadows, Terrell. I know they're there, but I'm careful to stay well out of them. I'll hunt around the edges for you, but I won't go in with you."

The tension in his shoulders ebbed away. "Finally, something we can agree upon."

"What makes you believe he's here in Charlestown?" she asked. "Couldn't he just as likely be over in Boston? For that matter, what's to have prevented him from traveling on to New York or Philadelphia?"

At last a question with a simple answer! "Money. He traveled steerage to Charlestown. He hasn't the funds to go anywhere else. He's here."

She nodded and went back to eating her pie. "You'd best move your things into my apartment."

He nearly choked on a bite. "I beg your pardon?"

"Your man travels in the darkest circles which, in and of itself, means he's accustomed to living as a shadow. And if he's escaped your pursuit three times already, then he's wary and prepared to move quickly. We have to be just as ready as he is. If word comes of his whereabouts, there won't be time to hunt you down to pass along the information. By the time you get there, he'll be gone."

"The same preparedness could be had," he countered, "were I to rent us separate but neighboring rooms at a hotel."

"My mother and I live in a respectable house, Terrell," she countered icily. "There's no pleasure-trafficking, no rats, no drunken melees."

Lord, her pride was easy to bruise. If he didn't need her help . . . "I wasn't implying any such thing, and I meant no offense. I was merely suggesting an alternative which would prevent the negative consequences that my living in your home would have on your public reputation."

She arched a brow. "Have you always been such a slave to propriety?"

"And do you disregard it completely?"

"Look, Terrell, considering the opinions of others is all well and good, but, in this matter, its cost is too high. Do you think the kind of people that would be bringing us information are the kind who'd want to march into the front room of a hotel? If you want them to find you, then you have to be someplace they're willing to go. Not that where my mother and I live has gone to seed, but it's not fancy enough to scare off snitches, either."

"I have deep reservations as to—"

"Set them aside," she interrupted. "It's a matter of practical realities. If I can bend, then by God, so can you."

He leaned back against the building. He'd never encountered a woman even remotely like her. "You're a very odd girl," he heard himself say aloud, not recognizing his own voice.

"I'm two-and-twenty, Terrell. I left girlhood a long time ago."

Only six years younger than himself. "Twenty-two?" he scoffed. "You don't look to be much over seventeen."

"Then you'd be admitting that maybe these clothes of mine are more effective than you'd thought?"

He wasn't going to admit anything if he could keep from it. "Do you know a person who can serve as a reliable messenger?"

"I know several. Which I'd choose would depend on the nature of the errand."

"I need to send word to my valet to bring my things to your mother's rooms."

"You have a valet?" she asked mockingly. "You don't strike me as the sort who'd allow that sort of pandering."

For some unfathomable reason, her amusement rankled him. "Appearances are important in my world, O'Keefe. I tolerate a lot for the sake of conducting my business. I play by the rules and meet expectations when I must. But only when I must."

She seemed to think about the import of his words and the smile faded. "There are a few things you should know, a few *rules* I'll expect you to honor while you're my mother's guest." She waited until he'd nodded his acceptance. "Her mind is often in another place, and so she says and does things that don't make much sense to us but seem perfectly reasonable to her. As long as what she's doing and saying doesn't pose any danger to herself or others, we allow her to go along as makes her happy. I won't tolerate your laughing at her or baiting her. She can't help it."

This was twice in their brief acquaintance that he'd seen her defend her mother's absent person. Aiden wondered if Mary O'Keefe knew how passionately or how frequently her daughter protected her. He nodded his understanding of the terms. "Who do you refer to as *us* and *we*?"

"Bridie O'Shaunessy, Mick's daughter, stays with my mother when I'm out during the days. Mrs. Malone, a widow who has a room down the hall, comes to sit with her if I'm out for the occasional evening."

She took a long breath. "And another thing . . . Bridie knows what I do to put bread on the table and coal in the stove. If Mrs. Malone knows, she's never said anything. But my mother believes I work for a lace-curtain family as a day nanny and tutor. I'll ask that you keep the truth to yourself and not blink overly much when I spin my yarns for her."

"A day nanny and a tutor?" he repeated, dropping his gaze to her lumpy jacket and the grease-stained, woolen pants. "And she finds this believable?"

"We'll make some sort of suitable and acceptable sleeping arrangements," she said evenly. "Purely as a concession to your already bruised sense of propriety, you understand. How to explain your presence to my mother and the neighbors will require an acceptable story. Would you have any suggestions for it?"

"Perhaps we can extend your facade to cover me. We'll tell

them that I'm a tutor newly hired by your employer and, having just arrived in the community to take my post, have found myself without lodgings. You've taken pity on me and offered me a roof over my head and a pallet on the floor until I can find rooms of my own."

"You don't look poor enough to need pity, mine or anyone else's," she countered, quickly measuring the length of him.

He gave her what he considered a fair warning. "Appearances can be deceiving, O'Keefe."

"What subjects would you have been hired to teach?" she asked. "You sometimes have to give credible performances for my mother. Her mind may not always follow the world as ours do, but there are unexpected times when she's button-bright."

"I think that I can decently carry discussions on mathematics, geography, botany, and chemistry. Just out of curiosity . . ."

"Languages, penmanship, drawing, and deportment."

"Deportment?" The image of Darcy O'Keefe teaching anyone the finer social graces—He choked on laughter.

She flashed him a look clearly meant to wither his amusement. When it failed to do so, she made a quick, most unladylike gesture, dissolving the last of his restraint.

CHAPTER 4

AIDEN STARED AT the clothing in his hands and muttered, "I'm going to look like a dockworker with far more aspiration than good taste."

"You'll look fine," Darcy said from her perch on the dry goods counter. "As I said, the point is to make you a bit less noticeable than otherwise. It's to your advantage to look like you belong in Charlestown."

Aiden studied the cut of the jacket disparagingly. "Your rather transparent way of saying I need to look impoverished?"

"Did you wear your fancy suits in Liverpool?"

He slanted her a dark look. "I'm not completely inexperienced in the matter of blending with my fellows, O'Keefe. But I've found that when offering money for information, looking like one can afford to do so is a great advantage."

"Sweet crimeny, Terrell, it's no wonder you've chased this man across the world. You really should try thinking from time to time. Clothes say much about a man. In your case, and in your circumstances, far too much." Darcy shrugged. "If you want people to know you're wealthy and cultured, then by all means parade around in your tailored best. If you want something from them beyond envious stares and blatant efforts to empty your pockets, then you might want to reconsider. If they think you're a man of modest means trying to

right a wrong, then they're going to be more willing to help
you."

"You're a rather mercenary young woman."

"I survive, Terrell."

"By manipulating what people think."

"And you don't?" she scoffed. "You don't wear your expensive suits and shiny Hessians to meet the expectations of the
people with whom you do business?" She pointed to the
clothing in front of him. "Would you consider wearing that
to your next business meeting?"

He didn't answer; there wasn't any point in it.

"The only difference between us, Terrell, is where we play
the game. You play your part in exclusive gentlemen's clubs
and teak-paneled offices. I play mine in the streets and in
smoke-filled pubs. You've chosen to come into my world, and
if you want to succeed at your unholy quest, then you're going to have to play by the rules that govern here."

"I'm no stranger to back ways and pubs and dark haunts,
O'Keefe. I've seen far more of them than you ever will. But
you've made your point, and I'll accept your reasoning if for
no other reason than to still your tongue."

"Then why are you still standing there? The sooner you're
changed, the sooner we can be about our task."

"And the sooner we can be rid of each other."

"Nothing would make me happier," she said brightly.
"The fitting rooms are back through the curtain and on the
right."

Darcy watched him stride to the rear of the dry goods
store. While she knew precious little about Aiden Terrell, she
was certain clothes off the shelf weren't going to magically
transform him. His bearing was of the upper classes and a
world beyond Charlestown. He could wander the streets in
rags and it wouldn't make a difference. People would know
he wasn't one of them.

God. She couldn't decide who was the craziest in this
whole mess—Terrell for thinking he had a chance of finding
his quarry, Mick for assigning her the responsibility for helping him, or herself for agreeing to it. And if, by some miracle,

something actually did come of her efforts, it wasn't going to be anything good.

Selia McDonough poked her head around the end of a shelf. "So what's the tale of the gent, Darce?"

"I'm trying to make him less of one," Darcy answered, shaking off the sense of foreboding. "Not that I have any hope of making it happen."

The store's proprietress stepped closer, absently brushing dust from her skirt. Her eyes were on the curtain at the rear of the store as she asked, "How'd you get hitched to his wagon?"

"It's a long story, Selia." Darcy sighed. "Suffice it to say that Mick thinks it's a good idea and sees a profit in it."

"You're working for Mrs. Higgins now?"

The suggestion was jolting. "Good God, no! Whatever made you think—I know it's been a few months since we've had a proper conversation, but I haven't changed *that* much. Nothing's bad enough to consider prostitution."

"Well," drawled Selia with a sly smile, "if ever there was a man to make a good girl consider crossing to the other side of the street, it'd be that one. Handsome he is. And looks to be one of God's more generous pieces of handiwork, if you ask me."

"I didn't ask," Darcy retorted dryly. "And I have no intention of judging either God's creative abilities or His generosity."

Selia shook her head. "You amaze me, Darcy O'Keefe. I think a smart girl like you would see the advantages of giving it over to a man like that. He's got the money to set you up and dress you fancy. And it wouldn't be such a horrible thing having to repay him for it from time to time. As earnin' wages go, it seems like it wouldn't be all that hard of work."

A few months had apparently seen a great change in Selia McDonough. "Selia," Darcy whispered, "if your ma could hear you, she'd pin your ears to the counter."

"Ma's going deaf," the other young woman answered with a dismissive wave of her hand. "And her sight's failin', too. She doesn't much notice what I do or say these days."

Darcy cocked a brow. "Is Jimmy going deaf and blind as well?"

"Jimmy's eyes and ears are just fine. As for other parts of him . . ." She looked back at the curtain. "I'll wager my drawers that man's got twice what God gave Jimmy. And he probably doesn't fumble with buttons and laces like Jimmy does. I'll bet he takes his time with the doin', too."

Darcy hopped down off the counter. "From the sound of it, it would appear you and Jimmy have gone a bit past hand-holding. So when are you getting married?"

"Don't know that we will," Selia answered smugly. "It seems to me that a girl shouldn't settle for the first man to come around. I don't buy the first merchandise a salesman lays on my counter, and I don't buy everything he's got. And I sure don't buy from just one. Being with a man shouldn't be any different. I'd fancy seeing what a man like that could offer me. What's his name, Darce?"

For some unfathomable reason Darcy hesitated. Irritated with herself, she replied, "Aiden Terrell."

"And you're sure you're not interested in him?"

"Interested? Only in getting rid of him as soon as I can," she answered. Then, feeling morally bound to warn her child-hood friend, she added, "Something tells me that he's a man with dark secrets. I'd think twice were I you, Selia."

"Well, thank the Good Lord I'm not you, Darcy O'Keefe. Virgins squeak when they walk."

"I hadn't noticed," Darcy shot back.

"Of course not." Selia grinned and moistened her lips. "But I'll bet Mr. Aiden Terrell has. And I'll bet he'd be interested in making a girl squeak in other ways if the opportunity presented itself. Wonder how far he's gotten in the changin' of his clothes, and if he needs any help. It's my duty as proprietress to assist customers any way I can."

"Be my guest, Selia. You're braver than I am." *And more the fool.* Darcy turned, unwilling to witness the encounter. The bell over the door jangled as she passed through and closed it behind her.

She barely had time to look up and down the sidewalk

when the bell jangled again. She turned to see Aiden Terrell storming out of the store, his old clothes in a jumble under one arm, his new coat under the other, and a boot in each hand. She took a step back.

"You needn't have hurried on my account, Terrell," she said, eyeing his untucked shirttail. "We've time enough for you to finish dressing in private."

He dropped his boots to the sidewalk and shoved his clothes into her hands. "I suppose that was your idea of great amusement."

Darcy barely contained her smile. "Buying clothes has always been a rather practical matter for me," she said blandly.

"I'm talking about your friend." He leaned back against the storefront and rammed a foot into a Hessian.

"Selia? I don't think I'd describe her as friend. More as someone I grew up with and see only—"

"Was it your idea to send her back to the fitting room, O'Keefe?" He pulled the second boot on and then vaulted upright to glare at her. "I'll have you know that I am perfectly capable of procuring . . . services . . . on my own."

She was losing the battle to keep her smile contained. The corners of her mouth were twitching. "Actually, I tried to discourage her, but she's consumed by some recent discoveries she's made about men. She seemed quite determined. I hope you weren't injured."

"Hardly," he snarled, snatching his new jacket from her.

"She didn't embarrass you, did she?"

"More herself, I should think," he answered while shoving his arms into the sleeves. "Are all your friends so brazen?"

"Most of my friends are male. As for brazen—" She grinned. "More hopefully bold than anything, I suppose. From what I can tell, it appears to be a fairly common male characteristic."

He considered her for a long moment. "There are exceptions."

The iciness of his voice surprised her. "You being one of them, of course."

"I believe in selectivity and discretion."

"Selia meeting neither requirement, I take it. I can assume that I don't either?"

"You most certainly do not."

"That's the first good news of the day," she said, shoving his old clothes back at him. "Now that my luck seems to have turned for the better, perhaps we should get on to our task? I'm thinking we should go talk to Seamus O'Hearne at the Lion and Fiddle. Not much happens in Charlestown that ol' Seamus doesn't hear about."

"You are the guide."

"I am indeed. And it's in that capacity that I suggest you get rid of those clothes, stuff your hands in your pockets, round your shoulders, and shorten your stride. Try to look like the weight of the world is on your back and you can't remember the last meal you ate."

He didn't move. "Is this properly pathetic?"

"Insolence doesn't contribute to the effect, Terrell. You might want to work on that aspect of your performance, too."

Aiden watched as she walked away, his anger swelling when she glanced back over her shoulder to see if he was obediently following. Aiden clenched his teeth, remembering one of his childhood toys, a stuffed horse on wheels he'd pulled behind him on a string. He felt like that horse.

Darcy O'Keefe stopped and shaded her eyes with her hand. She looked past him and called, "Maisey! I was going to go find you in a bit!"

"Oh?" said a soft voice behind him. Aiden turned to find a slightly pudgy redheaded woman standing in the shadows of the dry goods store. Darcy O'Keefe swept the clothing from his arms as she went past him.

"These belong to Mr. Terrell," she said, thrusting them at the woman she called Maisey. "They need to be taken to his hotel room and a message delivered along with them. There's money in the errand, Maise."

Maisey turned big green eyes on him, and her freckles darkened as a blush spread over her cheeks. "I—I—" she stammered.

Darcy ignored her friend's obvious reluctance. Turning to

Aiden, she said, "Where are you lodged, Terrell? And what's your valet's name?"

"The Presidential Hotel," he ground out. "And his name is Chandler."

Darcy nodded. To Maisey, she said, "Tell Chandler that Mr. Terrell is staying in other quarters for the time being. He'll need his shaving kit and some of his less dandy clothes. The simpler, the better. Wait while he packs it up, Maise, and then take it all to the cubbyhole."

The young woman looked between the two of them and then managed to whisper, "Why are you with him, Darce?"

"It's an ugly story," she answered. "And hopefully a short one. I'll tell you the tale later."

"If you want me to take his things to the cubbyhole—" She darted another look in his direction. "Does that mean he's stayin' with you an' your ma?"

"I said it was ugly," Darcy replied with a heavy sigh, "but it's the best of the courses available."

Being talked about as though he weren't present added to Aiden's annoyance. Reaching into his pocket for money, he stepped forward and shoved a five-dollar bill into Maisey's hand. "Tell Chandler that he's to consider himself on holiday until my return."

"Yes, sir."

"Thank you, Maise," Darcy said, turning away. "I'll see you later this afternoon."

Aiden caught Maisey's eye. "Does everyone always do as Miss O'Keefe bids them?"

" 'Tis easier that way, sir. She has a mind of her own, an' when it's set in one direction or 'nother, she can't be pulled back. Better to go along an' save yourself the effort of a tussle. She's goin' to win anyway."

"She *always* wins?" Aiden asked skeptically.

"I can't remember the last time she was swayed to anyone else's way of thinkin'."

Aiden chuckled. "I saw it happen not more than two hours ago."

Maisey's gaze shot in the direction of the departing Darcy

O'Keefe. "Then I can well imagine that 'twas ugly indeed." She smiled at him shyly. "A word of caution, Mr. Terrell? Give Darcy a bit of room for the next day or so. Don't, an' she'll lop your head off. She has a temper, an' she's not terribly forgivin' when her pride's been bruised."

It was the second time that day someone had thought to warn him of Darcy O'Keefe's pride. "I'll take your warning under advisement," he replied, turning to go. "And it's room two-thirteen at the Presidential, Miss Maisey." She murmured an acknowledgment as he strode after his surly companion. If O'Keefe thought he was going to kowtow like every other person in her world, she had best think again. He didn't know how to be subservient, and he wasn't about to learn for her.

AS PUBS WENT, it was typical of lower-class establishments the world over. The tables were scarred and sticky from years of spilled ale. The air was thick with smoke and the odors of old food and sweaty bodies. It took several pints of brew to grow accustomed to the smell. Aiden scowled into his fifth—or maybe it was his sixth?—glass of ale, listening to the voices swell around him. Darcy had deposited him at a table in the darkest corner while she had gone off to speak with the barkeeper and the various denizens of the pub. *Like a child being punished,* he inwardly groused. He looked up and watched her tip back her mug for a long drink. She certainly wasn't the first woman he'd ever encountered who drank spirits, but the cultured patterns of her speech had led him to expect her to order a sherry and sip daintily. Hah! She'd been welcomed by a rousing chorus as they'd entered the tavern, and the barkeep, Seamus, had drawn a pint at the sight of her.

"So how'd you come to be with Darce?" asked a wiry young man as he dropped onto a chair to share Aiden's table.

Aiden snorted. "Miserable luck."

The man laughed and stuck out his hand. "My name's Rusty Riordan."

"Aiden Terrell," he responded, grasping the man's hand briefly. Rusty's red hair and freckled complexion prompted him to ask, "Are you a relation of a young lady named Maisey?"

"A cousin on my da's side. How'd you meet Maisey?"

"Miss O'Keefe introduced us a while ago. Maisey is running an errand or two for me."

Rusty took a long pull from his mug and wiped his mouth on his shirtsleeve. "Maisey's a good girl. No doubt because she's a little shy. Not at all like Darce."

"Are you telling me Darcy O'Keefe isn't shy or that she isn't a good girl?"

"If you've spent any more than five minutes with her, you already know there isn't one shy bone in her body. As for being a good girl—" He grinned. "You wouldn't need to ask that if you'd tried to kiss her."

"And you have?"

"Most every man hereabouts has been the fool at least once."

Aiden narrowed his eyes and studied Darcy as she stood at the bar. She leaned forward, resting her weight on her elbows. One foot was casually propped on the brass foot rail. Her stance pulled her trousers tight over her hip. It was a very attractive curve.

"Darce doesn't take well to it."

"Take to what?" Aiden asked, bringing his attention back to Rusty.

"Being kissed." Rusty leaned forward and added in a whisper, "There's a standing wager. Five dollars to play. Seamus holds the pot. First one that gets a kiss from Darcy O'Keefe, without being slapped senseless, gets it all. Last count there was a hundred dollars to be had for some brave soul."

"That's a great deal of money," Aiden observed. "I'm assuming that more than a man's word is required to make the claim for it?"

"There's got to be witnesses. Reliable witnesses."

"Are you considered a reliable man, Rusty Riordan?"

"I am indeed."

Aiden shifted, pulling his money from his pocket. He peeled off a five-dollar bill and dropped it on the table, saying, "I'm in."

"Would you be expectin' me to follow you around until you make your move on her?"

"You can sit right there, Mr. Riordan," Aiden answered, rising. "This won't take but a moment."

"Here and now?" Rusty laughed. "You're a crazy bugger, Terrell. She'll tear your throat out."

Aiden shrugged. He didn't care at this point. He'd spent the better part of the day being publicly put in his place by the uppity Miss O'Keefe, and the prospect of bringing her down a few pegs appealed to him. Experience had taught him that a woman's sense of power over a man could usually be tempered with a thorough kissing. It occurred to him as he moved toward her that he might not be so ruthlessly determined if he hadn't spent the last several hours drinking. But, he'd warned her of his weakening patience at the pie cart. It was her fault she hadn't heeded it. He'd had all he was going to take of being ordered about and shoved into dark corners.

Darcy turned her head as Aiden strolled up to stand beside her at the bar. "Terrell, this is Seamus O'Hearne. Seamus, Aiden Terrell."

"It's a pleasure," Aiden said, sparing the man a brief look and an even briefer nod.

"Same," the barkeeper said, wiping the counter with a stiff rag. "Can I get you another pint?"

"Thank you, no. Six is quite sufficient. But in just a moment I'll have the money in the betting pool."

Darcy vaulted upright, her eyes flashing, her breathing hard and quick. He didn't give her time to think or move, as he grabbed her upper arms and jerked her against him, seizing her lips with his own. She held her mouth hard against his, her back stiff as steel, and her hands shoved between their chests. She tried to twist away, a desperate, angry cry strangling low in her throat. At the edge of his awareness, Aiden heard cheers of encouragement and glass mugs banging on

tabletops. The sound penetrated the cloud of drink and re-
sentment to stab his conscience. Silently swearing, he released her just as abruptly as he'd pulled her to him.

The full magnitude of his transgression came to him as he
looked down into her furious face. Hurt and humiliation
shimmered in the tears rimming her lower lashes. He opened
his mouth, intending to apologize. She didn't give him a
chance. Before he could blink, her left hand connected with
his cheek in a blow that set his face on fire. Peels of laughter,
wild applause, and shouts of "Attagirl, Darce!" followed in
its wake. His own sense of dignity rebelled, trampling the
compassion he felt only a moment before.

He met her defiant gaze and smiled. "What say you to trying that again, O'Keefe? More gently this next time,
though."

"You've lost the wager," she ground out through clenched
teeth.

"No one said anything about the number of attempts being limited. I'm of a mind to keep trying until we get it
right."

"I'm of a different mind."

"True enough. I've never known a woman quite like you."

"And you're a man very much like all the rest, Terrell," she
retorted caustically. "You think everything's yours for the
taking."

He traced the line of her jaw with a slow fingertip as he
whispered, "I can give, too. Generously. I'd like to show
you."

She stepped away from his touch, but not before he saw the
telltale flicker in her dark eyes. He closed the space she'd put
between them, slipping his arm around her waist and quickly
drawing her to him. She gasped and stiffened as he pressed
his lips to her ear.

"I'll give you every cent," he promised. "And match it.
Two hundred and ten dollars, O'Keefe. All yours if you surrender gracefully."

Darcy's heart lurched. Two hundred and ten dollars! What
she could buy for her mother with that kind of money. . . .

It was only a kiss. And it certainly wasn't the first to be inflicted upon her. If she handled her exit from the Lion and Fiddle with aplomb, she could salvage the essence of her reputation. And once she had the money in hand, Aiden Terrell could be made to understand just how repulsive she found him and that he was never to take the liberty again. Was it worth taking the risk? Worth enduring the laughter and the cheering and the joking sure to accompany her surrender?

She was still considering the merits and costs when he took gentle possession of her lips. She heard a soft chorus of oohs and aaahs. Stacked against two hundred and ten dollars, half from Terrell's own pockets, the appreciation of the audience didn't count for much. Darcy willed herself to relax, to endure for the sake of the money to be had at the end of it. Even as she did, she realized it as the mistake that it was. A molten heat flooded her veins and she gasped at the heady pleasure in the sensations. No other kiss had been like this one. This one could so easily lead to more.

On the verge of panic, she pushed herself from Aiden Terrell's embrace. He let her go, meeting her gaze as she pressed the back of her hand to her mouth. He knew the effect his kiss had on her. She could see the satisfaction in his eyes. Anger washed away the lingering warmth of pleasure. He cocked a brow in silent reminder of their bargain.

"You insufferable son of a bitch," she snarled, jerking her jacket back into place. Then, without another word, she stepped around him and stormed toward the door. It rattled in the frame as she slammed it behind her.

She marched down the sidewalk, her hands fisted. Of all the foolhardy things she'd done in her life, this one was the corker. Damn Mick O'Shaunessy for tying her to Aiden Terrell. And she wouldn't have been at Mick's beck and call if her father hadn't died and left her with the responsibility to put food on her mother's table and clothes on their backs. And if her mother's mind hadn't drifted away, she wouldn't—

Darcy stopped and gulped a deep breath, ashamed of herself. She had no right to blame her parents for her circumstances. They hadn't chosen their courses, hadn't consciously sent her out to make her way as she had. The decisions she'd made were her own. If they came around to bite her, then she had no one to hold accountable but herself. She had agreed to submit to Aiden Terrell's kiss for the money. That it had been far more than she expected was a fact she didn't have to admit to anyone but herself.

As for Terrell . . . She'd learned a valuable lesson in the exchange. He hated to lose. Scruples weren't his long suit. He'd gotten the best of her in the Lion and Fiddle, but now that she knew how he approached contests, it wouldn't happen again. She didn't like losing, either.

"Are you all right, Darcy?"

She looked up to find Terrell standing not more than an arm's length away. "I'm fine," she replied, smiling brightly and holding out her hand. "The money, if you please."

"Two hundred and ten dollars," he said, laying the stack of tattered bills in her palm, and then matching it with crisp ones of his own. "You might want to know that amidst the congratulations there were murmurs of collusion."

"I don't care," she said.

Aiden gave her a quirked smile. Who would have expected the little mercenary to be a complete innocent? "There might be requests for a repeat performance so that they can feel assured of our honesty."

"They can go to hell."

"Am I supposed to go with them?"

"You can if you think I'm going to let you kiss me again," she shot back, shoving the bills into her pocket with her uninjured hand.

Aiden considered pointing out that she hadn't been wholly unwilling the second time, but decided that he'd be pushing his luck. His cheek still stung from her slap. Thank God she'd chosen to hit the side of his face she hadn't hit in the alleyway. He didn't relish the idea of inviting another blow so soon. The wiser course lay in offering her platitudes, even if he didn't mean them. "I should probably apologize for putting you in the position I did," he said smoothly. "I let anger and drink get the better of my good judgment."

"I don't want your apologies, Terrell. I wanted the money. It was a fair bargain."

He chuckled. "Two hundred dollars for a kiss? You don't know much about the exchange rate for feminine favors, do you?"

She studied the twilight sky. "There are some things I deliberately avoid learning."

Aiden was tempted to tell her that if she ever wanted to know about carnal pleasures, he'd be more than willing to teach her. She'd be a good student . . . and an interesting diversion. He kept the offer to himself. Instead, he started down the sidewalk, saying, "Speaking of learning, did Seamus or the others know anything about the man I'm looking for?"

For once she had to catch up to him.

"No. Nothing."

"What do you suggest we do next, O'Keefe?"

"He's got to be sleeping somewhere. The logical place would be a boardinghouse. There are hundreds of them in Charlestown. If, as you say, he's down on his luck, we're more likely to find him in one of those that have already gone to seed. We'll start there and work our way up through the lot of them. It's going to make for a long day, Terrell."

Aiden shrugged. "I like to feel I'm getting my money's worth for the wages I pay."

"I'm easily worth four times what Mick's charging you," she countered, shaking her head. "God only knows why Mick let you off so easily."

"Maybe he's playing matchmaker," Aiden countered with a dry chuckle.

Darcy countered with a most unfeminine snort and said, "Mick doesn't *play* at anything. And, if you'll recall, he threatened to serve your hands up on a silver platter if you so much as touched me. I don't think he has any romantic notions about us. I sure as hell don't."

"Neither do I," Aiden replied honestly. With equal honesty he silently admitted that, where Darcy O'Keefe was concerned, his notions were likely to be purely physical and decidedly, wonderfully hedonistic. All Mick's threat would accomplish would be to add a very nice edge of danger to the temptation. If the man had intended to place an obstacle in his path, he'd gone about it all the wrong way.

CHAPTER 5

THE ROOFTOPS TO the west were silhouetted against the last pale light of the day when Darcy O'Keefe led Aiden up the steps of the brick apartment house owned by Maisey's father. As she closed the thick, oval-windowed door quietly after them, Aiden surveyed his surroundings. The entryway was small, no more than five feet square. An umbrella stand stood to the side of the door. On his left there was a small closet, no doubt for brooms. A long flight of narrow wooden steps led up to the individual living quarters.

"Maisey's not here," Darcy said.

He could see that for himself. "I gather she's supposed to be?"

Darcy turned slowly about as though she thought Maisey could be hiding somewhere in the small, spartan space. "She helps me with my laces and buttons. It's almost impossible to get them by myself."

Aiden instantly understood the dilemma. It intrigued as much as it amused him. A mental image of Darcy wearing only a chemise and stockings came to his mind. Amusement quickly faded, replaced by a sudden, intense desire to make his imagining reality. "I could assist you with both," he offered. He saw the slight stiffening of her spine and how she edged away from him, the perfect picture of studied nonchalance.

"You have experience in dressing women, Terrell?" she asked dryly without looking at him.

"More in undressing them," he admitted, grinning, "but it seems as though the task this evening would simply be a reversal of the process. Being a reasonably intelligent man, I think I can do that."

She scanned the sidewalk through the window glass as she answered, "I'm sure you could. But if it's all the same to you, I'd rather not suffer the indignity of letting you develop your skills on me. Maybe if you change first, Maisey will be here by the time I need to dress."

"And if she's not?" he pressed. While her eyes were averted, he slowly appraised the length of her legs and the sweeping curve of her hip. Her skin would be creamy white, he knew, and feel like warm silk on his fingertips.

"I'll just have to manage dressing on my own." She pointed offhandedly to the small, narrow door on the left side of the entryway. "In there. It's cramped, but it suits the purpose well. I'll wait for you out here."

Aiden set aside his fantasies for the moment, opened the door, and peered inside. His most travel-worn valise had been placed inside. "It's nothing more than a broom closet," he observed. "And a damn short and dark one at that."

She wheeled on him, her eyes bright with umbrage. "It's sufficient for its purpose, Terrell. We can't all have elegant suites at the Presidential Hotel."

Aiden smiled, lifting his hands in mock surrender. "I'll wedge myself in somehow. If I need assistance, may I call on you?"

She turned away, barely nodding. As he stepped inside the closet, he heard her mutter, "Not that I have any intention of answering." He grinned and opened his valise, removing what clothing he needed before pulling the door closed.

Darcy sat on the bottom step to wait. The very thought of letting Aiden Terrell assist her in dressing! she fumed. She'd die first. Actually, she reluctantly but honestly amended, she'd likely die if she let him touch her so intimately. The second kiss he'd given her in the Lion and Fiddle still throbbed on her lips. The long hours since that moment hadn't faded the sensation in the least. All she'd had to do was look at him in the course of their day and she'd remembered. And damn if her gaze didn't have a way of constantly drifting over his face to linger on those incredible lips of his. The worst of it was that he recognized the direction of her thoughts, and his smile was always so gentle and wantonly inviting. Turn her back on him and ask him to pull her laces? Darcy chuckled darkly. Aiden Terrell would never pass up the opportunity for seduction. And she wasn't all that sure that she'd have the wherewithal to muster much of a protest. Not if he kissed her first.

A hard thud came from the cubbyhole, followed by a string of gruff curses. Darcy smiled. She'd hit her head more than once on the stair riser. A flash of red on the other side of the window glass caught her eye, and she watched Maisey bounce up the front steps.

"I'm sorry I'm late this evenin'," her friend offered, quietly slipping inside. "I hope I haven't kept you waitin' long."

"We just got here. Did you have any problems getting Terrell's things?"

Maisey dropped down beside her on the step. "None at all. Chandler is . . . His real name is Nathan, you know."

"Oh? Nathan, huh?" Darcy cocked a brow in mock reproach. "You're calling him by his Christian name already, Maisey? Rather forward of you, don't you think? On such short acquaintance and all."

She blushed prettily. "He's very nice. Very much a gentleman. He insisted on havin' tea served while I waited for him to ready Mr. Terrell's bag."

Darcy wiggled her brows and asked, "And did he share your scones and crumpets?"

"You're a fine one to be askin' me that, Darcy O'Keefe," Maisey retorted with good-natured indignation. "I'm late because I ran into my cousin Rusty, an' he wouldn't let me go until he'd told the whole tale of you an' Mr. Terrell at the Lion an' Fiddle this afternoon."

"That couldn't have taken any longer than two minutes,"

Darcy rejoined, her pulse skittering. "It's not much of a tale, from Rusty's side of it."

"And from your side, Darce?" Maisey prompted.

Darcy shrugged and said indifferently, "Terrell promised me the money—and to double it—if I'd go along with him." She rose and fished into her pocket, drawing out part of the money. "Here," she said, dropping forty dollars into Maisey's lap. "Tuck it away somewhere for a rainy day."

Maisey's eyes were huge when she looked up. "I can't take your money!"

"Yes, you can. There's been many a day when your eggs were the only thing I had to eat. And Lord knows I couldn't keep Mother's illusions going if you didn't help me every evening. Consider it a payment for your services. A long overdue payment."

"Darcy, if my da were to find this money, what could I tell him? He'd think the worst."

"Tell him the truth," Darcy answered, sitting down beside her friend. "By tomorrow morning all of Charlestown is going to know Terrell won the betting pool. I'd like to think your da knows me well enough to believe I'd give you some of my winnings."

Maisey stuffed the money into her apron pocket, then leaned close to whisper, "Was he any good at the kissin'?"

Maisey was her friend, true enough, but Darcy had limits on what she would share with anyone. "I can't say that I have all that many men to compare him against," she said.

"Would you do it again?"

"I don't think so."

Maisey chuckled softly. " 'Twas that good, huh? Did your knees go weak? Selia McDonough says your bones should melt."

"And Selia seems to have become an authority in these matters, hasn't she?" Darcy answered smiling.

"Quit tryin' to evade my question, Darce. What was it like?"

Knowing that Maisey wasn't going to give up, Darcy decided to tell her just enough to end the torment of her questions. "I suppose it was pleasurable enough as kisses go. It was the afterwards, Maisey. There was a look in his eyes that said he had some kind of leverage over me. I didn't like that at all."

Maisey considered her for a long moment. "Was it like the look Mick O'Shaunessy gets when he's tourin' the stalls an' collecting his rents?"

"No, that's business. This was personal. I can't explain it any better than that."

Maisey smoothed her apron. "Maybe he saw that you liked kissin' him. Ma says that once a man knows you like it, you can't beat him off with a sharp stick."

"I didn't kiss him," Darcy retorted sharply. "It was the other way around. And it didn't last long enough for there to be any opinion formed on whether I liked it or not. It was done and over in a single breath." *Albeit a very long breath.*

"Maybe *he* liked it."

"Then he might as well kiss a lamppost. It'd give him the same pleasure and take a lot less effort on his part."

The latch on the broom closet swung up. Darcy winced when her elbow connected with Maisey's as they both thought to warn the other of Aiden Terrell's imminent intrusion.

AIDEN STOOD ON the sidewalk with his valise at his feet, studying the lamppost on the corner. If Darcy O'Keefe thought kissing her was a close approximation of pressing his lips to cold iron, then she was even more inexperienced than he'd originally thought. The first kiss he'd stolen from her had been everything he'd expected, a hard-hearted spinster's caress. But the second . . . Aiden scowled. Her Majesty, the Imperial Gutter Rat, had been startled by her response. The most disturbing truth was, so had he. That didn't speak well of his perceptions. The realization that he wanted to sample more of Darcy O'Keefe disturbed him to a far greater degree. He needed his attention elsewhere. Jules was somewhere in the vicinity. Seducing Darcy wasn't a pastime Aiden could afford at the moment.

"I'm ready if you are, Terrell."

He turned toward her voice. She came down the stone steps, holding the hem of her dress just above her ankles with gloved hands. A little beaded reticule hung from her left wrist. Her hair had been piled atop her head and a small hat pinned onto the nest of curls. And her dress . . . Aiden sucked in a hard breath as his gaze swept over the well-tailored garment and the enticing feminine curves it displayed. He hoped she intended to wear her loose-fitting boys' clothing for the larger part of their association. She was entirely too attractive dressed as a woman.

"Is there a problem?"

He picked up his valise. "No. Why do you ask?"

"You're scowling."

Aiden shrugged, and unwilling to share his baser thoughts with her, gave her a more general truth. "I'm reluctant to stop my search for the day. It seems to me that hunting at night might well produce results."

"I'm willing to consider any suggestions you have to offer as to how to go about doing that while preserving my mother's illusions."

Aiden looked at her askance and said dryly, "I don't suppose you've considered telling her the truth of what you do for a living?"

"Once or twice," she replied with a shrug.

"So why haven't you?"

"I enjoy the challenge of living separate lives," she answered flippantly. "It makes it interesting."

"I think it's more a matter of your enjoying being a petty thief."

"You've found me out," she replied. "It *is* ever so entertaining to go through a day hoping that you don't get beaten up or arrested. I can't think of any other thing I'd rather do with my life."

"You're educated. Picking pockets isn't your only recourse. You could easily find legitimate employment."

"Oh, I could, Terrell. But working at legitimate jobs makes me a slave to the man who pays the wages. There are days when I can't leave my mother and employers tend to frown on coming to work on an occasional basis." She met his gaze squarely and smiled. "Most importantly, Terrell, being a store clerk or a teacher or a nanny doesn't pay half as well as reefing does. It costs money to have someone stay with my mother while I'm gone and it's nice, after paying those wages, to have something left with which to buy food and coal. Selfish of me, I know, but. . . ." She shrugged, not the least bit apologetically.

For some reason her refusal to be serious irritated him. "Have you given any thought," he asked brusquely, "to what we're going to do if a message comes in the middle of the night giving us a chance to catch my quarry?"

She answered him in the same breezy manner as before. "Actually, I have. Mother can't be left alone, and pounding on Mrs. Malone's door in the wee hours would be an imposition on an older lady who truly needs her sleep. Maisey would be willing to sit with Mother if the need arose, but it would take time to stop by and roust her. I've been wondering if maybe Bridie would be willing to live in for the duration of your stay. That would simplify matters greatly." She cocked a brow and added, "Not to mention ease your over-propriety-burdened conscience."

Aiden swallowed a fiery retort and instead said flatly, "I'll pay this Bridie person's wages if you'll propose the arrangement."

"I have the money to pay her, Terrell," she said, starting up a set of stone steps. "We've already discussed the financial aspects of our association."

"We have indeed," Aiden agreed, opening the door for her and then following her into the small entryway. "And I thought I had made myself very clear on the matter. I'll see Bridie paid and your mother cared for, so that you can focus on my business without distraction. I expect you to be at my immediate disposal around the clock."

She froze on the steps. "At your *immediate disposal*?"

He stopped once he reached the top and turned back. She looked up at him, her skirt gathered in her fists and fire blazing in her eyes. "Yes," he answered coolly, for some inexplicable reason pleased to so easily ruffle her feathers. "I'm paying for your services. When I snap my fingers, I expect you to move without hesitation."

She glowered at him, her lips pursed. Then she marched up the remaining stairs saying, "It'll be a cold day in hell. I'm not your underling. Neither am I your paramour."

He laughed quietly as he fell in behind her. "Time will tell on the latter, O'Keefe. As to the former . . . I'm paying Mick O'Shaunessy for your services and he, in turn, is providing your daily wages. You may not like it and I truly don't care. You *are* my employee. You *will* do as I expect."

She paused with her hand on a doorknob and glared at him again. "We'll finish this conversation later."

He deliberately waited until she'd pushed the door open and started across the threshold before offering his rebuttal. "There's nothing further to say, O'Keefe."

He saw the catch in her stride but she didn't pick up the gauntlet. Instead, she pasted a cheery smile on her face and swept toward the middle-aged woman knitting at the kitchen table and the younger blond woman keeping her company.

"Hello, Mother. How was your day, Bridie?"

" 'Twas a good one," the blond woman replied. "We read the newspaper a bit this morning, and then started to knit stockings in the afternoon before our nap."

"General Jackson has called for winter stockings for the southern army," the older woman said earnestly. "We must each do our part in the defense of our country, Darcy. I expect you to spend some time with the needles and yarn this evening."

The girl named Bridie shrugged and quietly said, "There was an article in the paper about the effects of President Jackson's western land policies. I tried to explain, but she thinks Jackson's still defending New Orleans from the British."

"Thank you, Brid," Darcy whispered. She laid her hand on

her mother's shoulder and smiled. "Mother, I want you to meet someone." She motioned for Aiden to step closer, saying as he did, "This is Mr. Aiden Terrell, Mother. The Sinclairs have hired him to tutor the boys in more advanced subjects. He arrived to his post just today and needed a place to sleep until he could find rooms of his own. I said he could stay with us for a few days." Darcy straightened and met his gaze squarely, a flicker of defiance in her eyes. "Mr. Terrell, this is my mother, Mrs. John O'Keefe."

Aiden offered the lady a courtly bow. "It is a pleasure to meet you, Mrs. O'Keefe. You have a most generous and compassionate daughter. I promise that I will impose on your hospitality no longer than necessary."

She smiled sweetly, glanced back and forth between him and her daughter, and then said, "The pleasure is mine, Mr. Terrell. A gentleman is always welcome in our home." She made a genteel gesture toward the chair opposite her. "Please have a seat. Have you eaten your evening meal? Bridie made an excellent lamb stew."

"It's beef," Bridie corrected quietly. "There's biscuits ready to go into the oven, Darce. When you weren't here at your regular time, I held the rest of the meal."

"We were delayed in leaving the Sinclairs'," Darcy supplied. She glanced over, and seeing Terrell engaged in conversation with her mother, took Bridie by the arm and drew her aside. "Your da's put me in a mess, Brid," she explained softly. "I need to ask a favor of you. A big favor."

Bridie grinned. "If it's taking Mr. Terrell off your hands, I'd be happy to oblige."

"I need you to stay here 'round the clock, Brid. Terrell's hunting a man and your da says I have to help him. If word comes in the middle of the night, I need to be able to leave, knowing that Mother isn't being left alone. You'll be paid for the extra time, of course. It's only fair."

"You'll be wanting me to start tonight?"

Darcy nodded.

"I'll need to go home for just a while and pack a few necessary things. I could be back within an hour or so."

Darcy felt the tension in her stomach ease. "I truly appreciate this, Brid. I'll try to get this business over and done as fast as I can. I don't want Terrell around any longer than he has to be."

"Where's he from? Not here'bouts."

"From St. Kitts, down in the Leeward Islands."

Bridie nodded, but Darcy knew that her friend hadn't the foggiest notion of where the Leeward Islands were or which of them was St. Kitts. Bridie's knowledge of the world didn't extend beyond Charlestown, and she was perfectly content with its narrowness.

"What does he want with this person he's hunting?" Bridie asked. "Money?"

"He told me it was about stolen jewelry. Family treasures and such. That might be part of it, but I have a feeling that it's not the whole story."

"And Da wants you to help him?"

"Wants isn't the word I'd choose. More like *demands*."

"But if you have to be shackled to someone for even a day or two, a handsome, rich man would be the best."

"How do you know he's rich?"

Bridie snorted. "I'll go get my things and be back shortly. Rusty said he'd walk with me this evening. He's eating with the family tonight. He and Da have business to discuss."

Rusty again. Bridie would know about The Kiss before she was ten steps down the sidewalk. Mick would have the story—if he didn't already—before he sat down to his soup. The money was already looking like insufficient recompense. "Want me to save you some of the stew and biscuits?" Darcy asked.

Donning her cape, Bridie shook her head. "I'll eat at home. It won't take long. You know how Ma is about dashing in and out without sitting at her table."

Darcy did know. No one so much as knocked on the O'Shaunessy door without being fed. Everyone knew that Bridie's mother had been only days away from taking her final vows as a nun when Mick had come into her life and swept all thoughts of a cloistered life from her mind. To

Darcy's way of thinking, Maureen O'Shaunessy's determination to feed the world was a daily act of contrition—and one that Darcy had deeply appreciated many times in the first few weeks following her father's death. She'd have starved without Maureen's meals. But, more importantly, she'd have lost her mind without those precious, brief glimpses of normal family life within the O'Shaunessy household. She owed them—Mick and Maureen—for nothing less than the salvation of her mind, body, and soul; it was a debt that could never be fully repaid.

She smiled and returned Bridie's jaunty wave as her friend left the apartment. Behind her, she heard her mother inquiring into Terrell's feelings regarding the current war between Britain and America. Darcy sighed and stepped into the kitchen. Tonight her mother's mind appeared to be wandering about in 1815. Heaven only knew where it would be tomorrow. She heard Terrell make a polite attempt to correct her mother's misperception. Darcy waited, listening as she eased the glove off her injured hand. When his effort failed to have the least effect, Terrell accepted it and managed a diplomatic evasion, claiming to be above taking sides in the military fray. Darcy sighed in relief, and, thankful that he'd displayed grace and kindness, popped the biscuits into the oven.

BLOOD SPATTERED THE *plastered ceiling, the Persian carpet, the French silk wallpaper, the curtains that had been finely woven white linen. The droning of flies reverberated around him. Hundreds of thousands of big black flies. The heat of the Caribbean summer was crushing. There was no air to breathe. Only the thick stench of days-old death cloying his lungs. Bits of flesh and broken bone . . . arranged on fine china plates around the table, skewered to the walls with silver flatware. The severed, faceless head hanging from the dining room chandelier . . . His father's head. He staggered and gagged.*

Aiden frantically clawed his way from sleep, vaulting upright on his pallet, his heart racing as he desperately gulped air. He reached for his valise, tearing open the bag and snarling as he swept the inside with both hands. Chandler would have known . . . His fingers touched the silver flask, and a sob of relief caught low in his throat. He pulled it out, unstoppering it as he did, and instantly brought it to his lips. The whiskey burned his throat, searing his insides and letting him pretend, once again, that it was what brought the tears to his eyes. He choked and gagged and poured more of the numbing potion onto the hideous memories.

"Terrell? Are you all right?"

He only then remembered that Darcy O'Keefe had made her sleeping pallet on the other side of the parlor. He didn't let himself look in her direction, but took another deep drink before he said gruffly, "I'm fine. Go back to sleep."

"It seems to have been a nasty nightmare."

"Aye," he answered. "Go back to sleep."

"Would you like to talk about it? Sometimes that helps you realize that it wasn't real."

"No," he replied sharply. Talking couldn't make it unreal. It had happened. His father had been hideously butchered. So had the foolish French doctor. And the doctor's silly wife. Aiden hadn't been there to prevent the brutality, the inhumanity. He'd come home to find it waiting for him . . . it and the burden of tracking down the madman responsible. He hoped that once justice had been done, the nightmares would end. Until then, he could only drink them away. Aiden sloshed the remaining whiskey around in the flask. He swallowed another mouthful, reminding himself to get more tomorrow.

Darcy watched him from across the room. He eased himself around until his back was against the parlor wall and his legs were drawn up before him. He drank hard from the silver flask, using it, between draughts, to aimlessly trace a pattern over his knees. His hair was rumpled and shaggy, his clothing askew, but he didn't seem aware of it. His vision was focused elsewhere. His mouth was a hard, thin line; his jaw granite. She wondered if he might at any time lean over and retch into his valise. Part of her wanted to make it better for him. It bothered her conscience to see someone suffering so and to make no effort to ease their pain. But another part of her sensed that the demons of Aiden Terrell's sleep were especially vicious, and that if she ventured close enough to help him, they'd come to haunt her, too. She shuddered and drew the blankets up around her neck. She couldn't fall back to sleep until Aiden's head dropped to his knees, and the empty flask slipped from his limp hand and rolled across the hardwood floor.

CHAPTER 6

GOD, HIS HEAD hurt. Thinking that perhaps the pain would lessen if he tried to focus on something other than the pounding of his head, Aiden blotted his mouth with the linen napkin and noticed that Mrs. O'Keefe had paused in the course of eating her breakfast to study her daughter. He wondered if Darcy was aware of the scrutiny. If she was, she presented the perfect picture of casual indifference.

"Darcy?" Mrs. O'Keefe began.

She looked up from her eggs and toast. "Yes, Mother?"

"What happened to your lip?"

Her fingers went to the slight tear in her lower lip, and she shrugged with a smile. "Ellen threw a tantrum yesterday afternoon over having to redo her letters. She flung one of Samuel's wooden blocks and I dodged in the wrong direction. It will be fine. It doesn't hurt much at all."

"I hope she was disciplined."

Darcy nodded and went back to eating, saying, "She had to write her alphabet twice."

Aiden silently congratulated her. If he hadn't known better, he would have thought that Darcy did indeed spend her days tutoring ill-tempered children. She lied exceedingly well.

"Forgive me for saying so, Mr. Terrell, but you look as

though you didn't sleep well. Were you perhaps troubled by thoughts of taking up your academic duties?"

Aiden started at the realization that Mary O'Keefe had turned her attention to him. If Darcy could spin stories for her mother's benefit, then so could he. "I think it more a matter of having traveled so long and hard yesterday, and the strain of being in new surroundings," he replied. Ignoring Darcy's knowing look, he smiled at her mother and added, "I'm sure tonight will see more restful sleep."

"No doubt. John, my dear departed husband—God rest his gentle soul—always said that a man didn't properly rest unless he was in his own bed, in his own home. I hope that you will come to consider yourself at home while you remain with us."

He hoped he didn't have to be in Charlestown long enough for the possibility to even arise. Diplomatically, he answered, "I'm sure I shall, Mrs. O'Keefe. You are a most gracious hostess."

"We should be heading on to our posts, Mr. Terrell," Darcy said. "It wouldn't do to be late on your first full day."

Mary O'Keefe smiled. "Which of the boys will you be instructing, Mr. Terrell?"

"He's to have Joseph and James for the better part of the day," Darcy supplied quickly, rising to her feet. "I'm attempting to convince Mrs. Sinclair that Caroline would also benefit from instruction in the advanced sciences. At this point, however, she's hearing none of it."

"Something about the horrible social consequences of being a bluestocking, I believe," Aiden added, feeling quite pleased with his ability to so easily contribute to the web Darcy was weaving. She rolled her eyes in appreciation of his effort.

Her mother didn't see the gesture. "And what are your feelings on the matter of fully educating women, Mr. Terrell?"

Darcy left the table and snatched her cape from the peg by the door as Aiden answered, "It seems to me that any woman capable of advanced studies, and inclined to pursue them, shouldn't be denied on the basis of her sex."

"Then what do you say, Mr. Terrell, to those who argue that excessively educating a woman makes her wholly unsuitable for marriage?"

Mary O'Keefe sat back in her chair and waited for his reply. It occurred to Aiden that he was witnessing one of those "button-bright" moments Darcy had warned him about. He glanced over to see if Darcy might be about to rescue him, but she seemed to be preoccupied. "I should think a man would be grateful for an intelligent conversational partner and a wife capable of managing his household with mental acuity."

"I assume then, that you'll someday wed an educated woman?"

His heart tripped as it always did when he and the suggestion of marriage were combined in the same sentence. Hoping his smile didn't look as tight as it felt, he answered, "I can't say that I've given the matter much thought in any personal sense."

From the door, Darcy said sternly, "I really must insist that we be going, Terrell."

As though her daughter hadn't spoken, Mary said, "Darcy is very well educated, you know. Her father and I thought it important, and worth the expense of tutors. Among her other accomplishments, Darcy reads, writes, and speaks six languages."

"Indeed?" he countered, suddenly understanding Darcy's determination to see them on their way out the door.

"I'm leaving now," Darcy said, coming back to the breakfast table to kiss her mother's cheek. "I hope you have a good day, Mother."

Mary patted her hand, apparently oblivious to Darcy's wince. "I will, dear. Bridie and I will pray this morning for the health and wisdom of General Jackson. Then we will take up our knitting again. I understand that the winters near New Orleans can be quite chilling."

Darcy moved toward the door, saying over her shoulder as

she went, "Are you planning to teach today, Terrell? Or do you think the Sinclairs intend to pay you for visiting with my mother?"

Aiden chuckled softly and rose from his chair. Darcy swept out into the hallway as he was reaching for his coat, leaving him alone to offer his own polite farewell to Mary O'Keefe. Darcy was already in the tiny foyer of Maisey's apartment building when he caught up with her. She kicked the heeled slippers off her feet and into the open closet, while he closed the door behind himself.

"Six languages?" he said, leaning back against the jamb.

"Ignore my mother's obvious attempts at matchmaking, Terrell. I do," Darcy said as she flung her cape off.

"Should I heed her subtle ones?"

"Let's be clear on this," she said, stripping white gloves from her hands. "I have no intention of marrying anyone. I'm quite satisfied with my life as it is." She hastily began to unbutton her short jacket. "I cannot understand why some women actually search for the chance to be chained to cookstoves, or why they'd choose to spend their days with children clinging to their aprons and worrying about their husband abandoning them. I'll not be at a man's beck and call, and I won't be dependent upon one for my very sustenance." Her jacket landed atop her cape and gloves.

"A rather dim view of marriage," he offered, wondering if she intended to strip naked right in front of him. It was an intriguing prospect. She had wonderful curves, and he wasn't the least opposed to seeing more of them. "I had formed the impression that your mother and father had been happy together."

"They were each other's world," she answered, reaching behind herself to work at the buttons holding her skirt closed. "And when my father died, something within my mother did as well. I'll not go down the road she chose for herself. The price at the end is too steep."

With a disgusted sound she whirled about and presented him with a view of her back. "We're late, and Maisey's had to go on to the market," she said hotly. "My fingers hurt and I can't get the buttons myself. I have no choice but to ask for your assistance."

He felt the warmth of her body through the fine linen of her blouse and ruthlessly tamped down the impulse to glide his hands over the curves of her hips. The buttons gave easily, and he quickly stepped away once the task was completed, his mind scrambling to remember what it was they'd been discussing before she'd distracted him. "Your rationale for being opposed to marriage is, of course, based on the assumption that all couples share a grand passion," he observed as she at last stepped into the cubbyhole. "That isn't necessarily so. In fact, I've observed that most marriages are based on mutual practical benefit."

She spoke through the door left ajar. "Usually financial?"

"For the most part." He caught a flash of white petticoat and then of a long, lean, bare leg. Aiden's pulse quickened. Disturbed by his reaction to such a simple sight, he turned his back and removed his own coat.

"I can earn my own way," Darcy said from the closet. "I don't need to shackle myself to a man to be assured of eating or a place to sleep."

"Might I point out that you're presently dependent on Mick for those very things?"

"Circumstances required the arrangement. But I won't always be." She stepped from the closet, if not entirely dressed, at least for the most part covered. Her shirttail needed to be tucked in and her feet were bare. In her arms she carried socks, shoes, and her boy's hat and coat. Her cheeks were flushed and her auburn tresses tumbled in a curly riot over her shoulders. She looked like a lover dashing off lest she be caught in her paramour's bed. Aiden wanted to thread his fingers through the silken strands and kiss her into staying.

"I've been saving my earnings," she went on, unaware of the direction in which his thoughts had wandered. He blinked and headed for the closet as Darcy added, "And with the money from yesterday . . . I'll not be beholden to Mick much longer, Terrell. Come spring, I'll buy train tickets for my mother and me. We'll go west. We'll go where it doesn't matter that I'm Irish, where it doesn't matter if I'm lace-curtain or shanty. And when I find that place, I'll become the teacher I've always pretended to be. I'll buy my mother a house with a fancy parlor, a flower garden, and a picket fence in any color she wants."

"You certainly have ambition." As Darcy had done, he left the door ajar.

"I hope you noticed that finding a husband isn't one of them."

"I feel reassured," he countered dryly.

She made a most unfeminine snorting sound. "As though you were worth having. All that drivel you served up to my mother about appreciating an intelligent helpmate. You don't want an equal, Terrell. You want a woman who will be happy tucked among your other pretty possessions and content with helping you maintain your precious social facade. You want someone who will coo at the sight of you and then let you wander off to your own amusements without so much as a whimper of complaint."

It was precisely the kind of woman he'd always thought to someday marry, but he refused to be drawn into the fray and forced to defend sensible realities. He pulled on the cheap pair of trousers he'd purchased the day before, saying, "Clearly you don't meet those essential wifely characteristics. We may both sleep easily."

There was a long silence. "I suspect you don't ever sleep easily, Terrell," she said evenly from just the other side of the door. "Do you drink yourself into oblivion every night?"

Aiden quietly swore. Of all the fool things . . . He firmly answered, "I hardly think the nature of our relationship requires a discussion of either my sleeping or my drinking habits."

"Who's Jules?"

He straightened too fast and cracked his head on the stair riser. For a moment the world was a haze of white and red. When it cleared, something between desperation and panic forced him to ignore the pain and nonchalantly ask, "I beg your pardon?"

"You heard me," she calmly replied. "Who's Jules? You called out his name just before you bolted upright last night."

"He's someone from my past," Aiden answered, hoping the simplicity of his words and the ease of his manner would mollify her.

"I've already figured that much out for myself," she countered, a slight edge in her voice. "Why do you have nightmares about him?"

Aiden gathered up his workman's boots and pushed open the door. Darcy leaned on the other side of the jamb, fully dressed, her arms folded across her midriff. It occurred to Aiden that, had she been so inclined, she could have been watching him dress. The determined glint in her eyes, however, said her mind was elsewhere. Aiden stepped past her and through clenched teeth asked, "Have you given any consideration as to how we're going about the search today?"

"Are we hunting for this man Jules?"

Without looking at her, Aiden sat down on the steps to put on his boots. "Jules is my brother. Son of my father's second wife."

"Is he the man we're searching for? And I want an honest answer, Terrell. I'm not budging from this spot until I get one."

The evenness of her inquiry and her dogged persistence were maddening. Combined with the pounding in his head, it was too much to bother resisting. "Yes, his dammit," he growled, vaulting to his feet. "We're looking for Jules. And you don't need to know anything beyond that. Satisfied, O'Keefe?"

"You're going to kill your brother?"

"I've never said anything abouthis planning a murder," he shot back, heading out into the street.

"You don't have to," she said from his heels. She caught him by the arm and pulled him around to face her, seemingly oblivious to both the disparity of their sizes and the scene they presented on a public walkway. "I can see it in your eyes,

Terrell. In the way your lips thin when you think about catching your quarry. You're going to kill him, aren't you?"

"Christ, O'Keefe," he snapped, jerking his arm from her grasp. "If I have to, yes."

She took a step back. "You're crazy, Terrell. Stark raving mad. Even if you don't get caught and hanged for it, your soul will burn in hell."

Something deep inside Aiden gave way. He closed the distance Darcy had put between them. "I know all about hell, O'Keefe," he ground out. "I've spent every moment of the last eighteen months in the hell of Jules's making. His death is the only chance I have of ever escaping."

"I won't be a party to it," she said, shaking her head and backing away again. This time, however, she didn't stop. "Mick couldn't have known what you really wanted. Once he does, he'll let me off the hook."

"I gather that's where you're going?"

"I don't care what story you make up to explain it, but get your belongings out of my mother's apartment. Our association is over, Terrell." She whirled around and headed off down the sidewalk, not even bothering to look over her shoulder. "Over!"

He watched her march down the sidewalk, an odd, empty feeling sliding over him. Was Mick going to be surprised by what Darcy would tell him? Patrick had been in Liverpool; he knew what had happened there. It was logical to assume that Patrick had shared that knowledge with O'Shaunessy. Yes, he'd lay money that Mick O'Shaunessy had known the particulars of his quest when he'd assigned Darcy O'Keefe to assist him. Aiden frowned. Mick had claimed that, injured as she was, Darcy was of no other use to him for the days ahead. It had seemed like a sound rationale at the time. But, now in the cooler light of another day . . .

Darcy's concerns over being caught and hanged for cold-blooded murder were well founded. Mick certainly knew the danger existed, and yet he'd consigned her to the risk. Why? And if Mick had even the slightest understanding of the depth of Jule's depravity, he had to suspect that he was plac-

ing Darcy in grave physical danger. Why had he been willing
to do that?

The pounding in his head intensified. Aiden snarled and
turned on his heel. He was in no mood for solving inconse-
quential riddles. Darcy O'Keefe's life didn't matter one way
or the other to him. He needed a drink.

IT TOOK EVERY ounce of her self-discipline to halt a
half dozen paces from Mick's table and wait for permission to
approach.

"Where's Terrell?" he asked without looking at her.

"I left him standing outside Maisey's apartment house.
Where he goes from there, I don't give a goddamn."

His gaze snapped up to meet hers. "Watch yer tongue,
Darcy girl. Keep it civil. Ye were raised better."

Ignoring the censure, she took a half step forward. "Do you
know why he's here, Mick? The *real* reason?"

"I think so," he said, motioning her over to the table. "But
if ye'd like to tell me what ye think 'tis, I'd be willin' to listen. Have ye had yer breakfast yet, girl?"

"Even if I hadn't, I would have lost my appetite." She
dropped down onto the chair at his right. "The man he's
hunting isn't a pennyweighter, Mick. He's his brother. And
when I pushed, Terrell admitted that he intends to kill him. I
won't be a party to murder, Mick. I won't."

Mick buttered a biscuit. "It seems to me, Darcy girl, that
ye're in no position to decide on the matter. I pay yer wages,
an' ye'll do as ye're told."

His nonchalance stunned her for a moment. "You can't seriously expect me to help Terrell commit murder!" She
slammed her fist on the marred tabletop. "Dammit, Mick. I
told you when we began that I had limits on what I'd do in
repayment for your help. You agreed to respect those limits."

To her surprise, Mick didn't react to her display of temper.
Instead he took a thoughtful bite of the bread. Only after he'd
washed it down with a long pull of coffee did he reply, "I'm
not expectin' ye to shoot the man or help Terrell bludgeon

him to death, Darce. Ye're to do everything within yer power to find Jules Terrell. An' once ye do, ye're to back away. Aiden Terrell will mete out the justice required."

Darcy sat frozen in her chair. Mick already knew the identity of Aiden Terrell's quarry. That meant—"You know the whole story!" she accused. "You knew yesterday, didn't you?"

Mick picked up his knife and fork. "Aye. Do ye know why Terrell's intent on killin' his brother?"

"No. And I don't care. It's as wrong as wrong can be."

"The brother's insane."

Her heart pounded. "So's Terrell if he pursues this. And I would be, too, if I went along with it."

Pushing aside his plate, Mick turned in the chair and faced her squarely. His voice low and even, he explained, "Jules Terrell is a butcher, Darce. He murders for the thrill of it. He mutilates his victims, hackin' an' tearin' 'em to bits. There's some that says he eats parts of 'em. I don't know the truth of it, but it seems not too much to believe. Patrick was in Liverpool when Jules struck there. 'Twas a minister who provided a soup line for the down an' out. What was left of him was found about the kitchen the next mornin', simmerin' in a stockpot."

Darcy stared at Mick, her blood running cold, her mind numb.

"Word is he committed other ugly murders, in towns near Edinburgh an' Dublin, after he left Liverpool," Mick finished. " 'Tis obvious Terrell thinks he's here now, in Charlestown or Boston."

Darcy managed to shake her head. Shoving her hands into her jacket pockets, she looked blindly at the tabletop. "How does Terrell know it's his brother? How can he be sure?"

"Patrick says Terrell, deep into his cups, told him that Jules's first victim was their father."

"And you knew all this yesterday and didn't say anything to me." She looked up to search Mick's face. "Why, Mick? Why have you put this in my hands and on my shoulders?"

Mick sighed long and hard. "Jules Terrell has to be found an' stopped, Darce. He'll kill again. An' the next time 'tis likely to be someone we know. Ye've got the brains 'twill take to find the butcher. An' once ye do, let Aiden Terrell do what he must. 'Tis a big man who can walk up to the line an' step over it for the sake of others. Seems to me ye might want to take a leaf from his book Darcy girl."

Her conscience rebelled at the suggestion. "Can't Jules just be captured and locked away where he can't hurt anyone? Does it have to end in murder?"

Mick shrugged. " 'Tis Aiden Terrell who's in the best position to judge. If he thinks there's only one end, then I'm inclined to respect his opinion on the matter."

She swore softly and clenched her fists tighter in her pockets, only vaguely feeling the pain of her injured hand.

"I'll allow ye that one, Darce. I've put a burden on ye, I know. But 'tis not any more than ye're able to carry."

"I think you're wrong, Mick. I can't do this."

"I was hopin' ye wouldn't come to the truth of Terrell's task until ye were a wee bit further down the road with him, till you trusted him, till ye were well past the point of bein' particular 'bout the means of endin' the terror." For a long moment he simply looked at her, and then he reached into the breast pocket of his coat and withdrew a folded sheet of parchment. "But since ye've balked an' I'm not a man given to hopin' an' waitin', I'll use what leverage I have to hold ye to the task," he said, sliding the paper across the table to her. "Open it an' read what it says."

Darcy did as instructed. It was a fifteen-year-old loan contract, signed by her late father. In exchange for his signature, Mick had given John O'Keefe a thousand dollars. She looked at Mick over the top edge. "Was it ever repaid?"

"No."

"Do you know what he did with the money?"

"Do ye think a bricklayer's wages were enough to pay for nice clothes an' fancy tutors, Darcy girl?"

She couldn't tell which felt worse, the guilt and shame or the certain knowledge that a trap was about to be sprung around her. Darcy laid the document down on the table and slid it back to him, determined to keep her poise. Arching a brow, she asked coolly, "Why are you showing me this now, Mick? Why haven't you mentioned it before?"

"I haven't needed the leverage on ye before this. Ye've always been a sensible girl an' done what needed to be done without being nudged along. Help Terrell find his brother, an' I'll tear it up an' give ye the pieces, Darce. The slate will be wiped clean."

"And if I don't?"

"Then the balance is due, in full, in ten days. Ye'll pay it or I'll seize everything ye an' yer mother own for repayment. An' don't think I haven't heard about the bettin' pool money, Darcy. I can well imagine into whose pocket it went. I'll have it, too. Ye'll do as ye're expected, Darcy O'Keefe, or ye an' yer mother will be a-standin' in the street with nothing but the clothes on yer backs."

He'd do it. She'd seen him wield a heavy hand before. What Mick wanted, Mick got—one way or the other. He was the ward boss. It was his responsibility to protect the community. That came before friendship, before money. It came before all else. "When I'm done with this, I'm through, Mick. I'm going west on the first train."

Mick slowly smiled, took a cigar from his breast pocket, and bit the end off. "We'll see," he said just before spitting the bit of tobacco onto the floor. "Life takes strange turns from time to time."

A cold lump formed in the pit of her stomach. She forced herself to calmly ask, "Do you have any more promissory notes from my father?"

"No." He sighed and studying his cigar, added, "Yer da was me friend, Darcy. We went back a long ways together. When ye were born I promised him I'd watch over ye if he couldn't. He pledged the same for me when Bridie came into this world. The good Lord saw fit to take yer da first, an' I've done me best by ye ever since. I'd not have used his note against ye if there'd been any other way to see that ye stay with Aiden Terrell."

Darcy rose slowly to her feet, saying, "Then make me a promise as you made my father, Mick." She waited until he looked up at her before continuing. "If something happens to me, swear that you'll see my mother cared for to the end of her days. Swear it on Maureen's soul."

"Many a man's come through the doors of this club, Darce. I've become a good judge of 'em, good an' bad an' the whole run of 'em between. Aiden Terrell's a good man, a most capable man. Tell me ye haven't noticed how other men move aside for him. Tell me ye haven't noticed how he faces the world square on, an' a-darin' it to come at him. We both know a man can't do that if'n he's ever lost a battle." Mick grinned and cocked a brow. "Nothing's going to happen to ye, Darcy girl. Work with him just as ye did in the Lion an' Fiddle yesterday, an' ye'll do fine. Mighty fine bit of playing that was, hear to tell."

Darcy refused to be sidetracked. She leaned forward, putting her fists on the tabletop between them and resting her weight on them. "Swear it, Michael O'Shaunessy," she demanded. "Swear that you'll take care of my mother or the sight of my backside leaving here will be the last you ever have of me. Hell will freeze before you'll collect so much as a cent of what my father owed you."

"I swear it, Darcy," Mick replied, pressing his hand over his heart. "On Maureen's soul. Yer mother will be cared for as though she were me own." He dropped his hand and his expression hardened. "Now get gone an' back to Aiden Terrell."

Darcy turned on her heel and left him without another word. Outside, she paused to look up and down the street. She had half expected to find Aiden waiting for her, a satisfied smirk on his handsome face. Darcy pushed her hands into her jacket pockets and ambled along, her face angled down but her attention far from the cobbles passing beneath her feet.

Despite all that life had thrown at her in recent years, Darcy had never doubted either her ability to survive or the likelihood of her triumph over circumstances. In the days following her father's sudden death, there had been wracking grief and confusion, and an occasional blessed numbness. When she'd realized that her mother's mind would never recover from the loss, there had been a sense of aching hollowness. Necessity had seen it quickly filled with grim resolution and employment. There was a certain exhilaration to be found in picking pockets. It was an adventure; a game of wits and daring. And while there were risks inherent in the contest, she had never been afraid of what—or who—waited around the next corner.

Dread now gnawed at her insides. The weight of it urged her to run to the furthest corners of the earth and hide. She tamped down the impulse, sternly reminding herself of the responsibility she bore for her mother, and for the safety of all those whose lives had been placed in jeopardy by the presence of Jules Terrell. Running away wasn't the answer, tempting as it was. She could never live with the guilt. Jules had to be stopped.

She thought about Aiden Terrell and his unholy quest. Would she have done any differently if someone had butchered her father? If it were her brother leaving bloody bodies in his wake, would she feel the same sense of responsibility as Aiden did? She knew the answer to both questions. But could she live with knowing she'd helped a man kill his brother? Was ending brutality with brutality the only way? With a sigh, Darcy lifted her face toward the sun. The autumnal morning light warmed her skin, but it couldn't reach the cold deep within her.

CHAPTER 7

AIDEN BLINKED INTO the light of the Lion and Fiddle's open doorway and wondered whether a half dozen shots of whiskey had been too much or too little. Darcy O'Keefe stood silhouetted in the frame, her woolen hat in her hand, her hair cascading over her shoulders and her womanly curves tantalizingly obvious despite her boyish clothing. Aiden quickly looked away, his gaze going to Seamus just in time to catch the man's puzzled expression as he returned the ale glass to the shelf behind the bar.

The scraping of chair legs brought Aiden's attention to his own table. Darcy dropped down into the seat across from him, her dark eyes solemn.

"I gather Mick sent you back here," he said, pouring another shot from the whiskey bottle and sliding the glass toward her. "A cause for drinking if there ever was one."

She shoved it back. "How much have you had already?"

He shrugged and tossed the whiskey down his throat. "Was Mick the least surprised by what you had to tell him?"

"No. Patrick had spilled the story about Liverpool. Mick knew the whole of it yesterday when he set us up."

Aiden poured himself another shot. "No offense against your sainted Mick O'Shaunessy," he said, the glass halfway to his mouth, "but he knows precious little of the story."

"What will it take to get you to tell me all of it?"

Aiden chuckled darkly and reached for the bottle again. "At least a full one of these."

"Then start drinking, Terrell. I have to know everything you do."

As he trickled more amber fluid into the glass, her hand shot out to clasp his wrist. He stared down, thinking that her grip was surprisingly strong for a woman. And delightfully warm.

"But," she said, "you need to know that once you're done with the telling, you're done with the drinking, too, Terrell. After we've found your brother, I won't care if you climb into a whiskey barrel and nail the lid shut from the inside. But until then, I need you sober and clear-headed."

He was clear-headed enough to appreciate the feel of Darcy O'Keefe's bare skin against his own. There wasn't enough of her against enough of him of course, but that could be remedied. Aiden slowly smiled at her. "I don't think you're going to like the sober Aiden Terrell. He tends to be a rather humorless fellow. He borders on morose, actually."

She released him and settled back in the chair. "I'm not the least interested in your sense of humor, Terrell. Drunk or sober. I need your brawn at my disposal, and you can't wield it effectively if you're clutching a whiskey bottle and holding up a wall."

"It's certainly not the most poetic offer I've ever gotten." He grinned. "But given your lack of experience in such matters, I suppose it will do. Still, I feel honor bound to tell you that it's been a helluva long time since I made love stone-cold sober."

She shot forward to grip the edge of the table and glare at him. "I'm not talking about that kind of brawn, Terrell. I'm not interested in becoming your lover."

"You'd be better at it than you are at picking pockets."

"I'm the best reefer in Charlestown," she ground out.

"I didn't say you weren't," he replied, watching the light spark in her eyes. "I'm simply saying that, with the proper instruction, I think you could very well add 'damn fine lover' to your list of skills and accomplishments."

She wished him to the fiery depths of hell. He could see it in her eyes. She had the most amazing eyes. And lips, now that he took the time to really notice. Aiden's gaze slipped along the delicate curve of her jaw, back and up to her earlobe, and wondered what sound she would make when he nibbled at it.

"Tell me what you know about Jules. Does he choose one kind of person over another? Mick said the man murdered in Liverpool was a minister. Does Jules always kill clergymen?"

He blinked at her through the twin fogs of fantasy and whiskey. While her words slowly sank into his brain, he didn't find them of any particular importance. "Why have you taken off your hat?"

It was her turn to blink. "What?"

"Yesterday you said that you didn't go anywhere with your hair revealed. Today you come in here with your hat in your hand and your hair loose. Why?"

She glanced down at the woolen hat she'd cast on the table as though she expected it to supply the answer to his question. After a moment she looked up to steadily meet his gaze. "My days of picking pockets are over. Once we're done with this, I'm done with Mick. I'll wear these clothes until then, though. They're better suited for what we have to do than my skirts and blouses." She shifted in her chair. "Now answer my questions about Jules."

"You have the most beautiful hair," he said, reaching out to take a strand between his fingers. "Colors a man finds himself wanting to touch."

He heard her breath catch and her lips part as she watched him play with the strands of her hair. He smiled, was still smiling when her gaze lifted back to his. A dusky rose colored her cheeks. "You're trying to evade the issue, Terrell," she finally said, swatting his hand away. "And wasting time while you're at it."

Of course he was. If she had any manners at all, she'd have let him get away with it. No woman of genteel breeding pressed an issue a gentleman clearly wanted to avoid. But since she wasn't a woman of genteel breeding, he wasn't obligated to behave like a gentleman. Aiden found himself feeling incredibly liberated by the realization. "There are the most fascinating lights in your eyes when you're angry. Makes a man wonder what they'd look like in the throes of passion."

"Goddammit, Terrell. Stop this!"

"Such kissable lips, too," he pressed, knowing that Darcy was wondrously susceptible to the mental images he created for her. "Not at all like a lamppost, Darcy. Not at all. You taste sweet, like ripe cherries and cream."

He watched her bite back a reply and then, in the same instant, she slipped behind a mask of cool disdain. The speed and ease with which she'd set them apart stunned him. Darcy O'Keefe was a shanty Irish gutter rat, but she had somehow managed to learn the dismissive arts of an experienced courtesan. Aiden eased back in his chair, knowing that, for the moment, the game was done, and silently vowing to make her pay for having declared him unworthy of a contest. Maybe not today. As they said, vengeance was a dish best served cold.

"Mick said the first victim was your father. Is that true?"

Her prodding unleashed memories. Horrible memories. Aiden poured himself another shot of whiskey, saying, "Knowing is going to change you, Darcy O'Keefe. Forever and not for the better."

"If you think I want to do this, you can think again. Mick told me enough to give me gooseflesh. But I'm determined to be done with this business as quickly as possible and that requires that I know everything I can about the man we're hunting. You're the only one who can tell me. I don't much care how you go about that telling. Start wherever you like and go at any pace that suits you."

The only pace that suited him was a dead stop. Aiden studied the tavern doorway through the amber of the whiskey.

"I'm not going away and I'm not going to stop pestering you, Terrell. So screw up your courage and get it over with."

Aiden resisted the impulse to swing his fist at her. He

might be a lot of unsavory things, might be guilty of using poor judgment more often than any man wanted to admit, but he wasn't a coward. Not by a long shot. "There were three that first time," he retorted, his anger suddenly greater than his reluctance. "The order in which he murdered them, I can't be sure. My father was the most butchered." Aiden poured another shot of whiskey, hoping to dull the sharpness of the images playing across his mind. "The French doctor and his wife seemed more an afterthought. Almost as though Jules was methodically disposing of witnesses. There was more precision with them. Less savagery."

She pursed her lips and then asked, "How do you know it was Jules who did it?"

Did the damn fool woman think he'd tracked his bastard brother halfway around the world on a mere *maybe*? Aiden gritted his teeth and took another drink, willing himself to tolerate the naive inquisition. "*I know.* But I suppose *you* won't be certain unless I assure you that the die was cast long before that one day. Jules was born different, O'Keefe. Destructive. Call it bad blood or whatever you like. He was that way when my father married his mother and they came to live with us. Jules was ten then. As he grew older, his penchant for destroying things took on a vicious edge. He was thirteen when he dismembered Blanche's cats and my father began calling in doctors to cure him."

She hadn't so much as winced about the cats. Or, he admitted, sloshing whiskey past his glass rim, she might have and he just couldn't tell. The liquor was finally beginning to work.

"Who's Blanche?"

He looked into soulful brown eyes. It took him a moment to find the answer she wanted. "Jules's mother, my stepmother."

"Why didn't Jules kill her? And you?"

Because God isn't that merciful. He pushed the bottle away and sagged back into the chair. "Blanche was in St. Croix at the time, at her brother's wedding. My father was at home with Jules and Dr. LeClaire and his wife."

"And where were you?"

Too far away to make any difference. "I was in Nassau, picking up a cargo of lumber."

"How did the doctor and his wife come to be there? Was the doctor one of those your father brought in to help Jules?"

God, he was tired. Bone-deep weary. Too tired to fight the persistent waif on the other side of the table, too beaten to bother with trying to evade her questions. Maybe if he told her what she wanted to know, he'd finally be free enough to close his eyes and die. "When he was fifteen, Jules attacked his tutor with a hammer, and my father decided that it was time to let the European doctors have a crack at him. Dr. LeClaire assured my father that he could help Jules, and so he was tucked away in LeClaire's very expensive asylum in the French countryside."

"How did Jules get back to St. Kitts? Did your father bring him home?"

Aiden snorted. "After several years of 'treatments,' LeClaire pronounced Jules cured, hauled him across the Atlantic and presented him as a triumph of French medicine."

"Did you think he'd been cured?"

"Frankly, I think Mme. LeClaire wanted to sail the Caribbean, and escorting Jules home was a convenient way of getting my father to pay for her and her husband's passage. I think they knew damn good and well that Jules was still as crazy as a privy rat, but they thought they could control him. I told them they were wrong." He picked up his empty glass. Turning it slowly around in his hand, he added, "And in case you're wondering . . . there wasn't any satisfaction in discovering I'd been right."

There was a long pause before she quietly asked, "Do you have any idea why Jules murdered your father?"

Aiden shook his head, remembering the years Jules had lived in the house on St. Kitts. There was no telling which of the stormy exchanges had been the one Jules had chosen to avenge. There were so many of them, too many to count.

"Who else has Jules killed?"

"Besides the minister in Liverpool?" Aiden asked, cocking

a brow, his gaze never leaving the whiskey glass in his hand. "Outside Dublin, it was his landlady. She was stabbed to death and her tongue cut out. Near Edinburgh, there were two, a moneylender and a hack driver. Both came to the same end as the landlady."

"Do you have any idea why he chose those people to kill?"

He wondered if Darcy O'Keefe would be so dispassionately dogged in her pursuit if she'd had to look at the bodies. Darkly, he realized that he'd probably know the answer before he left Charlestown. Given her life, the odds were the next body would be that of someone whose path had crossed hers since childhood. And just as likely, her dispassion would be replaced by utter loathing for him, for bringing that kind of evil into her world. His stomach clenched. "I suspect Jules's victims were simply poor souls who happened to be in the wrong place at the wrong time," he answered. "There might be more of a reason in Jules's mind, but I can't fathom it."

She nodded and then asked, "Does Jules strike at any particular time of the day? Any particular time of the week or month? Is there a pattern to be found in it at all? Something we can look for and anticipate?"

"No to the first two questions. As for the other two, the only pattern is that I arrive in a city behind him, and that I haven't been able to prevent him from killing before he moves on again." *He performs for my benefit,* Aiden silently added, *and only when he knows I'm there to see his work.*

Darcy O'Keefe tilted her head and knitted her brows as she studied him. "How do you know where he's going next? How do you know he's here in Charlestown?"

He wondered why she hadn't asked the question long before now. It was the first one he'd have asked were he in her shoes. Obviously, their minds didn't work at all alike. He couldn't tell whether it was a good sign or a bad one. "Jules tells me where he's going. Or at least he gets me close. After the murder of our father, Jules fled to London. I had to deduce his destination from the port records. From there, I tracked him to Liverpool. After the minister was murdered, a package was delivered to my hotel." He paused and waited, almost hoping Darcy O'Keefe wouldn't ask the obvious. And fearing that she wouldn't.

"What was in the package?"

"The minister's tongue." She flinched and for some reason the reaction satisfied him. He waited to let the image take root in her mind and then added, "And with it came a note in Jules's hand, consisting of a single word: Dublin. After Dublin, another package arrived, leading me to Edinburgh."

"And after Edinburgh came one that said Charlestown."

"Boston," he corrected. "But his pattern has been to name the larger city and to murder in a neighboring one. That fact, combined with his present indigence, tells me it's Charlestown this time."

She watched him worry the glass for a long moment. Her words were gently spoken and touched him like a lover's caress. "This hasn't got anything to do with the actual finding of Jules, but I want to know for myself: Why haven't you gone to the paddies with what you know? Why are you taking justice upon yourself?"

"I went to the authorities in Liverpool and warned them, asked them to help me find Jules. When he murdered the landlady, they arrested me. I was held for trial, and it wasn't until my barrister arrived from St. Kitts that I was released and free to take up the chase again. I haven't made the mistake of seeking the assistance of the authorities since."

"You've answered my first question, Terrell," she responded, just as gently as before, "but not my second. Why are you the one responsible for finding Jules and seeing him stopped?"

"He's my brother and my responsibility," Aiden answered simply. "No one else can do what must be done." *No one else has the right.*

There was another long pause. "Do you think Jules knows you're here yet?"

He cocked a brow and said dryly, "Since no one's found a mutilated body, I rather doubt it."

"Might Jules stop killing if you stopped pursuing him?"

How many times had he asked himself the very same question? He could only give his companion the same answer he gave himself. "If I give up the search and he kills anyway, then I've got to live with the certainty that I made no attempt to protect innocents from a madman I knew to be loose among them. I already have enough difficulty sleeping."

"Speaking of sleeping," she said, taking the glass from his hand and pouring a tiny bit of whiskey into it, "I don't think we should go back to my mother's apartment. It's just a feeling, Terrell, but I don't like it." She tossed the liquor down her throat, shuddered, and then set the glass before him, empty. "If Jules watches for you, then he may see us going in and out of her apartment. I don't want her put in danger. Bridie either. I think we should stay elsewhere until we find your brother."

"My rooms at the Presidential?" he offered, his brain filling with images of her hair fanned across his white linen-covered pillows, her naked upon his sheets and waiting for him.

"The objections I raised yesterday to the Presidential still stand," she answered crisply, rising from her chair. Her tone and abrupt movement shattered his carnal fantasy. "Seamus has rooms to let upstairs," she went on. "We could take two of them. We could explain our absence to my mother by sending word that Mr. Sinclair has unexpectedly decided to take the family on a short holiday and asking her to send your valise and a trunk of my belongings with the messenger. I'm thinking that perhaps your man Chandler would do as the courier."

Two adjoining *rooms upstairs,* he mentally amended. "You have a quick and devious mind, Darcy O'Keefe." *Not quite as quick and devious as mine, but you'll learn. I'll teach you.*

She cocked a brow and studied him quizzically. "Can you stagger out of here?"

Aiden laughed and rose smoothly to his feet. "I haven't had that much to drink. Yet." With a confidence born of years of drinking and walking, he started toward the bar, saying as he went, "I'll pay Seamus for the whiskey and see to letting the rooms." He heard the bell on the door jangle as she left him to the tasks.

Darcy waited outside for Aiden to conclude the transaction with Seamus. She'd hated having to put him through the torture of telling her of Jules's crimes. His shoulders had knotted, and the look in his eyes . . . She'd wanted so much to put her arms around him and hold him close, to promise him that the ghosts could be defeated. It had taken every measure of her self-control to keep her seat, to press logically and dispassionately for the answers she needed. Comforting Aiden would have been so easy to do, so satisfying to her own heart and soul. Resisting the urge to touch him was the hardest thing she'd ever done.

What she had guessed in the middle of last night, she now knew for certain. Aiden Terrell's soul was haunted by memories. And they were the memories of what he had seen in Jules's murderous wake. She'd held her fear in check, too, only once slipping. The boxes Jules had sent him, the ones containing the proofs of his depravity and crime . . . If she somehow managed to survive this excursion into hell with Aiden, it would be nothing short of a miracle. Darcy realized her hands were cold and she stuffed them into her pockets, wishing Aiden would hurry.

She had a quick and devious mind, Aiden had said. Darcy frowned and studied the toe of her boot, reminding herself that she hadn't been hired to heal Aiden's emotional wounds. It was far better, far safer, to keep her thoughts focused strictly on the task of finding Jules. She didn't like the conclusions her mind was drawing from all that Aiden had told her. It seemed as though Jules was playing a gruesome game of tag with his older brother. Why? And did Jules send the packages because he wanted Aiden to catch him? Or because he intended to catch Aiden? Her pulse raced cold at the thought, at the image of Aiden lying bloody and dead in a dark alleyway. She shuddered and deliberately forced her thoughts back into objective logic of the puzzle.

Was Jules as crazy as Aiden thought? Or were the mutilations done simply to give the impression of a mind diseased beyond the control of reason? A cunning and vicious sane man would be infinitely more dangerous than an insane one.

Aiden emerged from the Lion and Fiddle, casting her a sidelong glance before moving past her down the sidewalk and toward the docks, the quickest of the routes to his hotel. She caught up with him and asked, "Is there any possibility that Jules may be saner than he appears on the surface?"

"Would a sane man murder and mutilate?" Aiden responded.

She offered him one of the easiest of her suspicions. "He might if he wanted people to think he was insane."

"I understand the tack of your thinking, O'Keefe," he said, "but remember, Jules has always been fascinated by cruelty. Even as a child he enjoyed it. I might be inclined to consider the possibility you're suggesting if not for that fact."

Lord, Aiden Terrell had long legs. She didn't have to hurry to keep up with anyone but him. "How does Jules support himself?" she asked, scampering along at his side and hating that she had to do so. "It costs money to buy passage between cities and across the Atlantic. And of course there's rent and food and clothing."

"I might have attempted to avoid telling you the whole truth at the outset of our association, but I've never lied to you," he answered without even so much as glancing at her. "Jules did indeed steal valuable family jewelry before he fled St. Kitts. Patrick was right in suggesting that it was long ago pawned to see to Jules's daily needs. Once those monies were exhausted, he took up gambling and petty thievery. His victims have all been stripped of their personal possessions."

"What kind of games does he prefer?" she asked, her mind racing even faster than her feet. "Have you been able to learn what kind of den he usually plays in?"

"There's a type of lizard in the islands called a chameleon. It can change its coloring at will to blend in with its surroundings to avoid predators. Jules is very much like the chameleon. In London and Liverpool he lived in the tenements without drawing attention to himself. In Ireland and Scotland, he associated with the upper classes. He was a guest at some of the most exclusive gentlemen's clubs in both Edinburgh and Dublin."

"Boston has gentlemen's clubs," she mused aloud. "Charlestown has them, too, of course, but they don't have the same reputation for exclusivity."

"I don't think he has the resources at the moment to make his way through the haunts of the wealthy. Remember, he traveled steerage from Edinburgh to Boston. If he's here, he's in Charlestown."

"And looking for a way to acquire the money he needs to wheedle his way into Boston society."

Blessedly, he slowed and then stopped, turning to face her, his brows knitted. "What makes you think that?"

"If you'd stop to think, you'd see that it makes sense," she answered. At his cocked brow, she impatiently explained, ticking the points off on her fingers as she did. "He stole the jewelry in St. Kitts and then went to London and Liverpool. In both places he lived like a poor man. But when he went to Ireland, he lived in luxury. I'm inclined to think that he could do that because he'd fenced the jewelry between Liverpool and Dublin. When he went to Scotland, he continued to live among the upper classes. So either there was money left from the jewelry, or he'd won some gambling. Obviously, he prefers to live well rather than poorly. Who wouldn't? And all of that makes me think that he'll try to move himself over to Boston as quickly as he can."

She saw surprise flicker in his gray eyes, surprise mixed with some other emotion she couldn't readily identify. She didn't have the time to puzzle it out, either, because in the next instant, both it and the surprise were replaced by the bright light of anger. "Allow me to save you the exertion of explaining the next part to this feeble-headed male," he drawled sarcastically. "It would behoove me to end our association and make my own way through Boston's gentlemen's clubs in search of Jules. You want out, and this is the best way to accomplish it short of helping me."

He'd all but outright called her a coward. The tender thoughts and compassion she'd felt for him only minutes earlier were trampled beneath his words. "I think searching for Jules in Boston might be worth the time, effort, and aggravation," she answered with a dismissive shrug. "But I'm sure you'll do exactly as you think best."

He spoke through his teeth. "Aggravation?"

She deliberately arched her brow. "I don't have much patience with wealthy men and their grand sense of self-importance."

"I'm a wealthy man."

The dare was obvious. Darcy refused to back away from it. "And you'll be happily among your own, won't you?"

He slowly measured the length of her, crossed his arms over his chest, and replied, "I refuse to apologize for enjoying well-dressed, polite, and intelligent companionship. And I'll make no pretenses about preferring clean linen sheets in a first-class hotel over a ratty blanket and a lumpy mattress in a dingy room over a tavern."

Darcy's blood heated at the verbal slap to her and hers. "Some us have enough humility to be damn thankful for what we can get," she retorted.

"Well," he replied, a hard smile coming to his lips, "since you appear to take great pride in being able to endure hardships with dignity and humility, *you* can have the floor tonight, with my blessing and appreciation."

Her mind whirled—and toward a conclusion she didn't like in the least. "The floor?" she repeated warily.

"Seamus had only one room to let," he supplied, his continued calmness further infuriating her. "Rather than waste time searching for another place with two, and given your oft-stated disregard for propriety, I took it for us to share."

"You didn't!"

"I did."

"There are degrees of disregard, Terrell," she countered. "I'm willing to bend the strictures a bit in the name of practical necessity, but this is going too far. After our performance yesterday in the Lion and Fiddle, everyone will assume the worst about our sharing a room."

His smile turned mocking. "I'll make a public announcement every morning proclaiming your continuing good virtue."

"You'll do no such thing!" she declared, stepping toward him, her hands fisted at her sides.

The mocking smile turned sardonic. "Then perhaps you'd prefer that I bed you and make the talk truth?"

She leaned toward him, "The hell you will!"

He unfolded his arms and reached out to trace the curve of her jaw with a fingertip. His touch drained the anger from her as though he'd pulled a plug. Darcy held her breath, her skin tingling and warmed, her mind issuing commands her body refused to heed. His eyes darkened and softened as his smile eased. The tension that had tightened his shoulders ebbed away. God, he was a handsome man. Tall and broadshouldered, with strong massive hands that could be surprisingly gentle. In that moment he looked far younger, more vulnerable, than he had before. If he leaned forward, if he tried to kiss her . . . Darcy let out a ragged gasp with the realization that she hoped he would.

His words came on a gentle whisper. "If I decide to take you to bed, Darcy, I rather doubt you could stop me. Or that you'd want to." The smile he'd given her yesterday after kissing her in the Lion and Fiddle returned as he added, "Admit it, Darcy. You're drawn to the notion."

She was, but admitting it to herself was horrible enough. Admitting it to him . . . Darcy acted without conscious thought or decision, bringing her hands up between them and shoving him with all her strength. To her shock, he stumbled backward, swung his arms once, and then disappeared.

Darcy blinked and rubbed her eyes. The edge of the dock and the dirty water of the bay came into focus. Her heart flipflopped. How could she have been so caught up in Aiden and their exchange that she hadn't given the slightest thought to their whereabouts? How could she not have smelled the tang of the water or been aware of the reek of the wharves? It was a damn dangerous state of mind to be in, considering the task they—

"I can't swim!"

She started, the sound of Aiden's distress breaking through her wonderment with all the force of a fist. Good God! What had she done!

"Darcy! Help!"

She threw her hat down, swearing at herself and then at him. Aiden Terrell wasn't the first sailing man she'd encountered who couldn't so much as tread water. Why in the name of all the saints did men go to sea if they couldn't swim? Cursing the stupidity of it all, she dived into the bay. She knifed through the water and quickly surfaced, shoving her wet hair off her face. She found Aiden no more than a foot from her, grinning.

"I lied," he said, reaching for her.

"You son—" was all she managed to snarl before he pushed her under the surface.

CHAPTER 8

I F SHE'D HAD any strength left she would have refused Aiden's outstretched hand. It was galling to have to accept his help, even more humiliating to know that he'd been so little taxed by their struggle that he'd easily hoisted himself up onto the dock and then magnanimously offered to help her out of the water. The cocky bastard. She grasped his hand and pulled. He chuckled, grabbed her collar with his other hand, and hauled her upward, plunking her down on her bottom beside him on the planking.

"You're a son of a bitch," she declared, shoving her hair off her face and glaring at him.

"I know," he replied, pulling off his boot and pouring out water. "You, too. The way I see it, we're an even match."

God, she couldn't remember the last time she'd been so frustrated. "I hope I hurt you."

He laughed and shot her a sideways glance. "You missed and hit my thigh."

"Damn shame," she said, gaining her feet. "I'll do better next time."

"Aren't you going to empty your shoes out?" he asked, pulling off and emptying his second boot.

"There's holes in the soles of both," she retorted, jerking her sodden jacket away from her body. "They'll drain on their own as we walk."

Aiden heard her stomp down the dock and frowned. She had holes in her shoes? Why? She made decent money working for Mick; she could afford to buy a new pair of shoes. The mental puzzle soon faded from his thoughts, however. Walking behind Darcy O'Keefe had been irritating yesterday. But today it was an entirely different matter. She was soaked, and her trousers were plastered to her lower half like a second skin. It was a fascinating sight to behold. Inspirational, in fact, and for the first time in years he was tempted to offer the good Lord a bargain. It was the thought of what he might have to offer God in exchange for Darcy O'Keefe naked in his bed that stopped him. He suspected it would have to be a mighty big sacrifice on his part, and he wasn't sure whether he was ready to pay it just yet.

His musings on God's commodity exchange rate were brought to an abrupt halt when a dockworker stopped to openly leer at Darcy. She had no sooner passed, when the man chased after her. Aiden clenched his teeth, balled his hands into fists, and lengthened his stride. He had almost closed the gap when Darcy spun around and kicked the man in the groin.

Her eyes widened and her mouth formed a tiny *O* as she watched the dockworker wordlessly sag to the walkway, his hands clutching his abused member. Then she looked past his prostrate form to meet Aiden's gaze. The *O* twitched into a smile as her hands came to her hips.

"I thought he was you," she said.

"Missed again," he countered, walking past her with a wide grin. Lord, he thought, he had to be insane. Too many years of drinking too hard had pickled his brain. Darcy O'Keefe was a dangerous little creature with a short temper and penchant for revenge. Taunting her was like daring the devil. He should have known better. Actually, he did know better. He just couldn't resist pulling her tail. As sport went, none other quite equaled the thrill of it.

Darcy quickly came up to walk beside him, her hands stuffed into her trouser pockets. He found himself wishing she'd storm ahead so he could see the full effect of the extra pull of the fabric across her backside.

"I suppose I should thank you," she muttered after a moment.

"For what?"

"You were going to intervene. I saw it in your eyes."

"Well, you saw wrong," he corrected. "I had no such intention. I was going to encourage him."

"Encourage him?" she scoffed. Darcy shook her head. Why couldn't he admit that he wasn't the complete bastard he pretended to be? She made her living reading people; the way they moved and the look in their eyes told her all she needed to keep her skin intact and her pockets full. She had read Aiden Terrell like a book back there. She'd seen the ruthless determination in his eyes. She'd also seen the appreciation for the speed with which she'd dispatched the lech who'd fallen in behind her. But could Aiden Terrell accept her thanks with any grace and honesty? Hell, no. Well, she fumed, if he wanted her to think he was a cad to the bone, she'd be more than happy to oblige him.

They walked together in silence and, despite her anger, Darcy was acutely aware of Aiden at her side. Damn if he didn't look handsome even dripping wet. God knew she didn't look any better than a wet wharf rat. It rankled to know that every passerby had to be wondering where Aiden had gotten such an awful creature and why he wanted her company. She hoped that they could reach their destination without someone actually pointing a finger.

Her luck, of course, went as it had since the moment she'd laid eyes on Aiden Terrell. When they reached the Presidential Hotel, the doorman opened the heavy door for Aiden, and then made a choking sound as he reached out to block her progress.

"She's with me," Aiden declared, taking her by the arm and drawing her forward. The doorman instantly stepped back, his vision deliberately glazed.

"That was a bit proprietary," she muttered as they crossed the threshold.

"I don't know why you're put out," he quietly retorted with a knowing smile. "I'm the one he considers to have exceedingly poor taste."

His teasing prodded her already bruised pride. She sputtered and tried to pull her arm from his grasp.

"Don't create a scene, Darcy," he warned blithely, his grip tightening only slightly. "Or they'll never let you work the Presidential again."

"I'll get even with you for this," she whispered. "I swear I will."

Aiden only chuckled, and steered her around the red velvet circular couch in the center of the lobby.

"Mr. Terrell?"

Darcy started at the sound of another person's voice. Chastising herself for again having let her focus narrow to only Aiden, she looked for the other occupant of the room. She found him, suited and pinch-nosed, standing behind the lobby desk. He shot her a look of utter disdain.

"Yes?" Aiden queried offhandedly on their way up the carpeted stairs.

"Nothing, sir," the young man answered, curling his lip as he continued to inspect Darcy. "I simply wanted to be sure it was you. Shall I have . . . ahem . . . a bath sent up to your room?"

"Send two of them," Aiden replied as they reached the second floor. "Immediately."

"Yes, sir," the desk clerk answered, his smile salacious. "I understand. Right away."

The tight-assed clerk understood nothing. Darcy flashed him an age-old hand gesture of heated sentiment and instruction. He tilted his nose into the air and sniffed like an offended old biddy before turning his back on her.

"That was hardly ladylike," Aiden observed dryly as he drew her down the hallway. "Can't you behave yourself even for a bit?"

Darcy jerked her arm from his grasp, retorting, "He expected it, and I didn't want to disappoint him. If you'd let loose of me, I'd have punched him in the nose."

He paused with his hand on a doorknob and waited for her to face him before quietly saying, "How about this? If he looks at you the same way on our way out, I'll punch him for you. Will that make your bruised pride feel any better?"

"I appreciate the offer and the sentiment behind it, but I'm perfectly capable of defending myself."

"You're a bloodthirsty savage, O'Keefe," he observed, turning the knob and pushing open the door.

"Sir!"

She stepped into the room behind Aiden to find a man of Aiden's age dressed in an impeccably ironed black suit. He was standing beside an ironing board, obviously attempting to press the same neat creases into a pair of trousers. She couldn't readily guess who the trousers belonged to, since there wasn't all that much difference between his height and Aiden's. He was considerably slighter than Aiden, though, and much fairer. As the man quickly assessed her in return, she had the feeling that, like Aiden, he didn't miss a thing.

"Chandler," Aiden acknowledged with a crisp nod, closing the door behind them.

Chandler put the iron on the rest and came around the ironing board, his gaze full of dismay as he took in his employer's state of disarray. "Good Lord, sir! What has happened to you?"

"Darcy O'Keefe," he said as he took off his coat.

Chandler accepted the sodden jacket with two fingers and then turned toward Darcy, a smile tickling the corners of his mouth. "I presume that madam is the Miss O'Keefe to whom you refer?" Darcy nodded, and Chandler's smile broadened as he gave her a slight bow. "Miss Maisey mentioned you yesterday. Allow me to say how very relieved I am to know that you will be assisting Mr. Terrell in his quest. Miss Maisey spoke most highly of your skills and resourcefulness."

"Maisey's a kind soul," Darcy replied with a smile, deciding that she liked Nathan Chandler. Maisey apparently had good taste in men.

"And Maisey's obviously blind," Aiden added.

Chandler pulled his smile inward and turned back to his employer. "Were you waylaid by thugs, sir?"

"I was waylaid by Miss O'Keefe."

Chandler shot her an inquiring look and she shrugged. "He deserved a tumble into the bay. I, unfortunately, believed him when he said he couldn't swim and went in to save him from drowning. If I'd taken the time to think, I'd have seen that he drowned and done the world a favor."

Chandler grinned, then with obvious great effort, sobered. "Shall I have a bath brought up for you, Miss O'Keefe?"

"Thank you, Chandler, but the nasty little desk clerk offered to see to it as we trailed puddles across the lobby and up the stairs," Darcy explained.

"We have a more important task for you at the moment, Chandler," Aiden said, tossing his boots onto the carpet. He opened the front of a small secretary. "Here's paper, pen, ink, and a blotter, Darcy. Write the note to your mother while I explain our plan to Chandler."

She was suddenly conscious of the water dripping from her pant legs and the cuffs of her jacket. It was pooling around her feet. If she crossed the room, she'd ruin not only the finely finished wood flooring, but the carpet as well. There didn't seem to be much else she could do, though. She didn't have a change of clothes. Darcy went reluctantly, pushed the velvet upholstered chair out of the way, and hovered over the desk as she took up the task Aiden had assigned her. It wasn't easy, especially while trying to keep her soaked jacket sleeve off the paper.

She didn't notice the low murmured conversation on the other side of the room until there was a pause in it. Chandler quietly cleared his throat just before Aiden gruffly said, "For God's sake, Darcy, take off your jacket, roll up your shirt-sleeves, and sit down."

My shirt's got a hole in it and it's worn too thin to be decent when dry, much less wet. "I'll manage as I am," she retorted. "If I sit, I'll ruin the upholstery."

"If you do, I can afford the cost of recovering it," he quickly countered. *"Sit down."*

"Here, Miss O'Keefe," Chandler said, coming toward her with a folded sheet of linen. He spread it over the seat cushion, then stepped behind the chair, saying, "Please allow me."

"Thank you, Chandler," she murmured flashing him a smile of appreciation for his understanding. Aiden could well take a lesson or two from his valet on courtly behavior.

"My pleasure, miss. If you require anything else, you have but to ask."

From the far side of the room, Aiden practically snarled, "*I* require something, Chandler."

"Always," Chandler muttered dryly, then added normally, "at your service, sir."

AIDEN HAD TAKEN the note from her and was sending Chandler on his way when Darcy picked up the small oil painting that had been placed atop the secretary. It was a portrait of a family: A husband and wife and their two sons. The man was tall and powerfully built. His eyes were piercingly black, and he wore an expression that made Darcy think of thunderstorms. Something about him said that he was never satisfied with what life served him. The woman beside him looked exotically dark and delicate, and much younger than her husband's years. She could have easily been his daughter, but the hand the man pressed to her shoulder said that he claimed her in a far more intimate way. Darcy found herself feeling sorry for the woman, and wondering if it was a ghost of fear and regret that she saw in the woman's dark eyes.

Disturbed by the feelings stirring in her, Darcy focused her attention on the two boys. A span of perhaps as much as five years separated them in age. And beyond the color of their hair, neither of them looked like the other. The younger of them clearly favored the woman. The older didn't look like anyone but himself. Darcy smiled. The older one was Aiden; she recognized the tilt of his head and the ease of the stance. She studied the younger boy, knowing she was looking at Jules, and an idea began to take shape in her mind.

"This is your family, isn't it?" she asked turning around in the chair and holding out the portrait as Aiden closed the door behind Chandler.

"Yes," Aiden whispered.

"Judging by the change in your appearance, it was painted some years ago."

There was unmistakable tension in his voice when he replied, "It was done in the earliest days of my father's marriage to Blanche, when it was still possible to publicly maintain the illusion of being a happy family."

"You haven't changed all that much over the years."

"The die was cast early and deeply."

She remembered that he'd said the same thing of Jules, and wondered if it was a characteristic of the people who inhabited the Caribbean. "While you're considerably taller and your shoulders are much wider, the angles of your face, your features, are still yours. Harder, certainly, but still yours. Has Jules changed very much over time? Or would I recognize him as I do you?"

"The last time I saw him—the day before he murdered my father—Jules looked like an older version of the boy he was. It's difficult to say for sure, however. The life he's lived since he fled St. Kitts is bound to have put a few lines on his face. If he had a conscience, I'd suggest that his eyes might look less sharp and a bit haunted, but since he doesn't . . ."

Darcy hesitated, not wishing to make his tension any greater than it already was. Still, she told herself, there was a task to be done, and Aiden's being uncomfortable for a few moments was a small thing to ask of him. "Would you describe Jules's appearance to me in detail?"

"Why?" he demanded, looking over his shoulder at her, his eyes accusing.

Darcy refused to be daunted. "Wouldn't it be much easier in making inquiries after him if we had a drawing to show people? Asking after a dark-haired newcomer to Charlestown isn't being terribly specific. A boat docks every day and spills them down the gangplank by the dozens. If we could show a drawing of the individual we are searching for—"

"It would greatly expedite finding him," Aiden finished. He looked back into the embers of the hearth. "Can you draw?"

"I told you that drawing is among the subjects I teach the Sinclair children."

"The Sinclairs and their ill-tempered children are wholly fictitious. I assumed that you had just as freely defined your areas of instructional expertise."

Darcy set the portrait before her on the desk, angling it so the midday light fell fully across it. "Mother would know better. With her, it's always prudent to stay with the essence of truth. One of my earliest memories is of a drawing lesson. Have you any charcoal pencils?"

He patted his trouser pockets. "It would appear not."

"Then I'll make do with pen and ink," she replied, unstoppering the inkwell and selecting a pen.

Aiden suddenly crossed the room with long strides and flung open the door. "The task can wait; our baths are arriving."

Over the huffing and puffing of several servants and the clang of a long brass tub coming none too expertly through the door frame, she said, "This won't take unduly long, Aiden."

If he heard her or not, she couldn't tell. His full attention was on directing the parade of servants filing into his room. "Fill the tub behind the screen, and cover it to preserve the warmth of the water. Place and ready the other tub before the fire."

While they did as he bid and while he carefully supervised their work, Darcy sketched the basic structure of the adult Jules's face, using the boy he had been in the portrait as her guide. When Aiden tipped the servants and closed the door after them, she was ready to press him for the details she needed to finish her work.

"Is Jules generally a charming or a brooding man?"

He sighed and ran his fingers through his already tousled hair. "He can be both, depending on the circumstances. Remember the chameleon?"

"I've never seen a live lizard of any sort," Darcy admitted as she worked on Jules's eyes. She made them distant-looking, detached. "Only in picture books. Well, there was a stuffed lizard in a traveling exhibit that once visited the lyceum, but it was old and dusty and one leg had fallen off, so it was difficult to imagine it as being real."

"Have you never been outside Charlestown?" Aiden asked from the hearth.

Darcy glanced over to find him gripping the mantel with both hands. Determined to make his suffering as brief as possible, she went back to work. "I've been to Boston a time or two. Mick took me over."

"Were they profitable journeys?"

"I didn't go there to steal, if that's what you're implying. How does Jules wear his hair? Parted down the middle or on the left or right side?"

"Left, I think. So why did Mick take you to Boston?"

"To see my grandmother," she supplied, quick strokes of the pen defining Jules's crown. "What length does he prefer to wear it? Is it straight or does it have a tendency to curl?"

"Last time I saw him, he'd been under Dr. LeClaire's tutelage and it was short. I can't say for sure now. My guess would be that it's largely unkept at this point. And it curls. What did your grandmother think of you?"

Darcy added curls around Jules's face and collar. "Grandmama thought I lacked sufficient experience to scour the pots in her kitchen." She studied the look of her work to that point, nibbling on the end of the pen. "Does Jules wear a dressing on his hair?"

"If he could afford it, I suppose he would. You didn't tell her you were her granddaughter, did you?" He didn't so much as pause for her to answer. "Why not?"

"It would have been a bit like begging to be taken in, don't you think?" Darcy pointed out, making Jules's hair darker.

"So why did you go in the first place?"

"I just wanted to see what she looked like, what kind of

person she was, what kind of house my mother grew up in. Nothing more than simple curiosity."

"What did you find?"

Darcy felt a pang of regret. While her first reaction was to ignore the question, she knew that if Aiden could bear talking about his murderous brother, she could well find the courage to speak of her own family disappointments. "The house is big, the furnishings are expensive, and my grandmother is an ordinary-looking woman who lives in a very narrow world."

"She probably didn't see the decrepit lizard at the lyceum then."

She heard his amusement and it lightened her own spirit. She looked up to smile at him. "No. I suspect there's a lot she hasn't seen."

He cocked a brow. "Including her own granddaughter standing in front of her."

"My grandparents were opposed to my parents' marriage and disowned my mother. I doubt it's ever crossed my grandmother's mind that I might exist."

"It's a shame your grandmother doesn't know how very much she's lost."

His words warmed her, gently wrapping around her like a soft wool blanket on a cold night. They fell into a silence that Darcy found comfortably companionable. In it she added the final touches to the picture of Jules and then announced that it was completed to the best of her ability. Aiden crossed the room to stand behind her chair and look over her shoulder. His nearness sent a warm shiver over her flesh, and Darcy set about cleaning the pen in an effort to distract herself.

"You're very good, Darcy," he said softly. "Actually, you're exceptional. If you ever decide to give up your life of petty crime, you might consider doing portraits for a living."

She ignored the flush of warmth his compliment sent through her, and put the stopper back in the inkwell, saying, "The people I know don't have the money to pay for portraits."

"People like your grandmother do. If you're interested, I could make some introductions."

"And when the paragons of polite society asked after my training?" She shook her head. "I'd rather not take the beating, thank you."

"You might be pleasantly surprised, Darcy."

God, she'd never known that a voice could be so caressing. Her heartbeat was dancing beneath it. It had to be because he was so close, she decided, and resolved to place some distance between them as quickly and discreetly as she could. She pointedly glanced at the rear chair legs and then up at him, adding, "If you wouldn't mind moving, I'd like to have my bath now."

He pulled back the chair for her, whispering as she rose, "If you need assistance in washing your hair, I'd be happy to oblige."

"I'll manage," she assured him, moving with deliberate speed toward the screen in the far corner of the room.

"I might need my back washed."

Darcy stepped behind the partition before she had the breath to retort, "Then I suggest you wait for your bath until Chandler returns." She listened intently, trying to decide whether it was safe to disrobe and throw herself into the tub. If Aiden came after her, she didn't want to be found in any state he might deem as inviting his attentions. She heard only the sound of her own rapid breathing and after a long moment, stripped her clothes away with a speed that sent buttons bouncing over the floor. In the next second she immersed herself up to her neck and prayed that Aiden would leave her to peacefully enjoy the wonder of warm water and rose scented soap.

Aiden fingered the drawing she'd left on the desk. He hadn't lied. Darcy O'Keefe was a very talented artist. Could she work in other media? he wondered. She had asked for charcoal pencils, so those were obviously her preference. Even so, her pen and ink work showed experience and a confident hand. Had she ever worked with pastels, watercolors, or oils? Could she capture the wild beauty of the Caribbean seas? The glorious splendor of the sunset? The exotic tangle of the foliage? Had she ever sculpted clay?

His mind filled with an image of Darcy, her hair pinned haphazardly atop her head, errant tendrils framing her oval face as she intently fashioned a male torso, her long fingers graceful and deft and sure. Aiden sucked in a hard, silent breath as his blood warmed, then shook his head to dispel the fantasy. The disappearance of the image did nothing to soothe his ardor, and he decided that immersing himself in his cooling bath might be the only way to quench the fire. Unless . . . He studied the screen in the corner of the room, and wondered what Darcy O'Keefe would do if he stepped around it and joined her in her bath. Swear, no doubt. And it somehow seemed just as likely that she wouldn't limit her resistance to verbally bashing him. Good judgment suggested that it probably wasn't at all wise to invite her to assault him with a cake of soap. She wouldn't even try to resist the temptation.

Still, the temptation she presented him made turning away an act of great self-denial and self-discipline. Aiden told himself he was a better, more intelligent man for doing so, but his libido grumbled anyway.

Darcy breathed a long sigh of relief when she heard the water splash over the rim of Aiden's tub. She'd heard his soft footfalls on the carpet and for a wild, heart-thundering moment, she'd imagined him coming around the corner of the screen to renew his offer to wash her hair. He wouldn't have stopped there, of course. She hadn't known him long, barely a full day, but she had seen time and time again that restraint wasn't one of Aiden Terrell's stronger virtues. It wasn't one of her better ones either—at least when it came to her temper. And he seemed to have a way of sparking it that no one else did.

Anger isn't the only thing he sparks. Darcy quickly set about soaping her sponge. Determined avoidance, however, didn't make the truth go away. By the time she climbed from the tub and reached for the linen sheet, Darcy knew she had to face it in order to have any hope of resisting it. Aiden had said she was curious about bedding him, and part of her was. It was his knowing, his having seen what she thought she'd hidden so well, that had prompted her to shove him away as she had on the dock. It was one thing to be curious, another to act on it, and yet entirely another to have someone daring you to cast aside all common sense.

And the last man she should consider as a sensible candidate for her deflowering was Aiden Terrell. He was unapologetically upper-class, insensitive, rude, domineering, and . . . and . . . well, frighteningly forthright about wanting the honor. Yet she couldn't deny that something about him appealed to her. It wasn't anything she could see, but rather something she sensed. What, precisely, it was, she hadn't the faintest notion.

Having finished toweling her hair and drying her body, Darcy faced a dilemma more immediate than the puzzle of Aiden's appeal. She didn't have clean or dry clothes. Hiding behind the screen until Chandler arrived with a proper set of clothing would be cowardly. Darcy studied the damp linen sheet she held in her hand and wondered if it would be a sufficient cover. Given the alternative, it would have to be, she decided, wrapping it tightly about her body and carefully tucking the corner over the upper edge and between her breasts. Then she took a deep breath, squared her shoulders, and stepped boldly around the screen, prepared to face Aiden's certain and equally bold advance.

He was asleep in the tub. Sound asleep; his head lolled back, his neck cradled on the rolled edge of the brass tub, his arms resting along the sides, and his legs dangling off the far end. She moved closer, stopping when she stood with the fire to her back and Aiden before her. He'd washed before sleep had overtaken him. His hair was dark and damp, a thick lock of it tumbling over his forehead. His lips were softly parted, his face relaxed in repose. Darcy smiled, happy that his dreams weren't troubled as they'd been last night. He needed to sleep, and sleep well and easy. She suspected that it didn't happen often for him.

Her gaze slid slowly down over his shoulders and chest, her

artist's eye drinking in the strong lines, wondrous ripples, and hard planes, her woman's heartbeat quickening at the contrast of the satin smoothness of his shoulders and the dark, rough furring of his chest. He had a jagged-edged scar on his right forearm, a longer, even more jagged one across his left ribs. They had whitened with age and stood out starkly against his sun-bronzed skin. Aiden clearly didn't live a particularly safe life, and it appeared that a large portion of it was spent wearing only minimal clothing.

Darcy forced herself to swallow. She inched away from the fire, its heat too intense to bear, but she couldn't make herself look away from Aiden. The water, made milky by a floating cake of soap, protected his most private regions from her shameless perusal. But his legs, from the tips of his toes to his upper thighs, were bared for her visual feasting. They were as bronzed as his upper body, and similarly scarred. Darcy battled the impulse to trace her fingers over the contours of corded muscles and sinew.

From the recesses of distant memory came her mother's voice: *Ladies don't look, Darcy.* Darcy grinned guiltily and turned away from Aiden, promising herself that she wouldn't leave him to chill and wrinkle in the tub. In a little while—after Chandler returned and brought her some decent clothing—she'd have the valet wake Aiden and encourage him to sleep in his bed. But until then . . . What was she to do to amuse herself and pass the time? Spying the paper and ink on the desk, she shrugged and decided it was a better alternative than gawking at Aiden or staring into the flames of the fireplace.

She gathered up the artwork supplies, settled herself on the carpet at the edge of the marble hearth, and began to sketch.

A MOVEMENT AWAKENED him. Years of wariness had taught Aiden the value of feigning sleep while quickly surveying his surroundings through his lashes. He slowly turned his head toward the motion that had called his attention from sleep. The sight almost undid his careful act.

Darcy, wearing only a finely woven linen sheet, sat cross-legged on the floor between him and the fire. She was twisting her hair into a loose knot atop her head, using a single ink pen to secure it in place. The firelight illuminated the sheet from the back, shadowing the dramatic curves of her waist and hips. Her efforts to secure her hair thrust her breasts forward and pulled the sheet taut across them. He'd thought he'd had a fairly good idea of what she'd hidden under her boyish clothes and her modest lady's attire. Now he knew he'd been woefully underestimating Darcy O'Keefe's attributes. She'd been fashioned by a very generous god with an eye for beauty and a soul filled with lust.

Aiden's conscience reminded him that gentlemen didn't ogle ladies. He countered its admonition with a reminder that Darcy wasn't a lady, and he wasn't much of a gentleman, either. And because his conscience was used to being ignored, it quieted and allowed him to settle into watching Darcy sketch with her pen and ink. She either finished the one she was working on or decided to abandon it, because she set it aside and began another. He couldn't see what it was she drew, but her hands worked quickly and surely, the lines she put on the paper smooth and free-flowing. After several long moments she looked up at him and arched a brow.

"You might as well open your eyes."

He smiled and complied, knowing he'd been caught and wondering how long she'd been aware of his regard.

"Ah, just like that," she said, blindly dipping her pen, intently watching his face.

He frowned. "Are you drawing me?" he asked, for some reason agitated by the possibility.

"Imagine me joining you in your bath," she replied.

It took only a second for his blood to sing through his veins and he smiled. "Climb on in. I'll make room."

"I wasn't serious. I just wanted to see that smile one more time so that I can get it right."

He sighed, rebuking himself for having jumped so quickly at her offer. He hadn't been that blindly eager in a long time. "I'll let you get away with it this time, O'Keefe," he offered with what he considered true gentlemanly virtue. "But don't make the offer again if you're not willing to see it through."

She nodded but didn't look up from her work. "A lady doesn't tease, Darcy."

"What?"

She winced as though she hadn't realized she'd spoken aloud until he'd asked her to explain. "It's one of my mother's lessons on life and proper deportment," she supplied hastily. "A lady doesn't tease. She doesn't look, either."

Aiden grinned, knowing. "But you looked anyway, didn't you?"

"I'm an artist," she countered. "It's rather difficult to sketch someone with your eyes closed."

She didn't look up, but she didn't have to. Aiden saw the blush pinkening her shoulders. He couldn't resist teasing her. "Did you like what you saw?"

She cleared her throat before saying, "You're nicely constructed and well proportioned."

"How much did you see?"

"Enough."

Aiden looked down at the milky water. "I doubt that." He grasped the edge of the tub, pulled in his feet, and rose. "But that can be easily remedied."

She squeaked and threw her hands over her eyes. It was such an innocent, girlish gesture—so at odds with the tough Darcy O'Keefe of the streets—that he couldn't help but laugh. He picked up the drying sheet and wrapped it around his waist before he stepped from the tub. "I'm decent," he promised, heading toward his bedroom. "You can look without endangering your delicate sensibilities."

"Not until you're fully clothed," she retorted.

He laughed again and whirled around, catching her peeking between her fingers. She dropped her hands to reveal twinkling brown eyes, rosy cheeks, and an impish smile. The sight tightened the muscles across his lower abdomen, and his manhood stirred to life beneath the damp sheet. With a silent groan, he turned back toward his room. He needed to find Darcy something to wear other than that thin sheet, or she wouldn't even have that for very much longer.

Darcy watched him disappear into the other room and slowly released the breath she'd been holding. Where the hell was Chandler, and what was taking him so long?

HE STOOD IN the shadowed doorway of a shop and watched. Nathan Chandler hadn't changed all that much in the last few years. He'd have recognized his brother's man-servant anywhere. And Chandler escorting a cart of trunks through the streets of Charlestown, Massachusetts could mean only one thing. Aiden was finally here.

He smiled. It was time to begin the game again. It had been too long.

He turned, grasped the doorknob, and went inside. The jangling bell announced his arrival. A girl came from the back of the store, her gaze moving up and down the length of him. She stopped just a few feet in front of him, put her hands on her hips, and sneered, "Whatever it is you want, it's not leaving here without being paid for."

"Payment will be rendered in full," he said, reaching into his pocket.

She paled at the sight of the knife, and he grinned in satisfaction as he quickly set to work.

CHAPTER 9

H E'D BEEN A fool to think that putting Darcy in one of his own shirts would help matters. He'd thought that ordering the noon meal brought to his room would serve as a distraction. He'd been wrong about that, too. Darcy sat across the table from him, chatting and eating, but mostly being a delectable enticement in rolled-up shirtsleeves. He heard only about half of what she said, his mind having a tendency to drift into appreciating the drape of the linen over her breasts. He suddenly blinked and ran her last words over in his mind. "The Rat?"

Darcy quickly chewed a bite of ham, nodding. She blotted her lips with the linen napkin and swallowed. "Yes, Timmy the Rat. He lives in a hole in the wall down along the wharf. Literally. You have to crawl into it on your hands and knees."

Aiden cut a bite of the steak he'd ordered for his lunch. "If you believe the effort would be worth it, I'm willing to do whatever leads to results. But I am curious as to what it is that you think Mr. Rat can do for us."

"Timmy scurries the edges, hence one of the reasons for his name. He has a unique ability to see without being seen. If you want to know anyone's secrets, it's Timmy you ask. That's how he makes his living. Vampiring."

Aiden cocked a brow and she quickly replied, "People pay him to forget what he's seen." She scooped a dainty portion of candied yams onto her fork as she added, "And Mick's employed him from time to time, too. Along with his other remarkable abilities, Timmy's also the best budge in Charlestown."

"Budge?"

She ate, again nodding. "He slips into a place—usually a business, but houses can be budged, too—and then hides. When everyone is gone or abed and the place is locked up, he slips out of hiding and opens the door for the knot. For his part, the knot gives him a whack from the Family Man."

A whack from the family man? It sounded slightly obscene. He studied her, trying to decide whether the bright expression she wore came from the enjoyment of her meal or from taunting him with his ignorance. In the end he couldn't keep from asking, "Are you enjoying this, Darcy?"

"It's excellent food," she quickly answered. "Simply delicious. I see why you chose to stay here. Thank you for thinking of ordering it sent up."

"I'm not talking about the food—although I'm glad to see you eating with such enthusiasm. Most women pick at their plates like wounded birds. I'm asking if you enjoy speaking in a language I don't fully understand. Are you trying to make me feel foolish?"

Her eyes widened in realization. "I'm sorry. Truly I am. Sometimes I forget and slip into jabber, especially when I'm speaking of the people who live and work on the streets. I'm very careful with Mother, of course, but other times—" She took a quick breath. "A knot is a group of thieves, a whack is a share of the proceeds, and the Family Man is the fence, the one who—"

"I know what a fence does," he interrupted, holding up his hand. "I haven't spent my entire life in a teak-paneled office."

"I know that," she retorted mildly. "I saw your scars earlier when you were . . ." Her cheeks grew pink as she sought the right word. "Well, you know when," she finally said with a dismissive wave of her empty fork. "The ones on your arm and left side were nasty wounds. If I were to hazard a guess, I'd say they were from broken bottle glass."

The incongruity wasn't lost on him. She sat there, the perfect picture of sweet virginal innocence, discussing the types of scars left by broken bottles. There could of course be only one way she knew of such things, and imagining Darcy in a tavern brawl was somehow both amusing and horrifying. Aiden shook his head to dispel the image and answered, "You're basically correct on the arm; it was a broken crystal decanter. The side wound was from a dull machete."

"I've seen sailors carrying the latter. Good that it was dull. If it hadn't been, you'd have been cut in two."

He remembered the speed and power behind the strike. "Definitely."

"I suppose the other fellows came out of it worse for their effort?"

"Not at all. And it was the same fellow both times, actually," he answered. "Jules slashed my arm when he was eleven. The machete attack came some fourteen months later."

Darcy frowned. "But your father didn't think to take him to doctors until he attacked his tutor? Didn't you tell me that was when he was fifteen?"

"He had local doctors in before that—after Jules dismembered the cats at thirteen—but, because the tutor was an employee and the attack on him demanded a serious reaction, my father decided at that point to haul Jules off to Europe."

"And the attacks on you didn't matter as much to your father as the attack on the cats?" When he shrugged, Darcy pressed. "Did he know about them?"

"He was a keenly observant man," Aiden supplied. "I assume he deduced the connection between the servants cleaning up the blood, my being a bit slow to get around for a few days, and saw Jules's role in the two. But it's only an assumption on my part. We never actually spoke of it." At Darcy's puzzled expression, he added, "My father and I had a . . . unique relationship."

"Apparently."

"My mother died in giving birth to me," he said, the truth being so old that he'd long ago become accustomed to the pain. "It was the first significant stone in the foundation on which we endured as father and son."

"There had to be other, better ones, Aiden," she said softly. "No man wholly and forever resents his son, no matter how much he cherished the wife who died in giving him birth. Surely you reminded him in some ways of the woman he loved and lost so tragically. That had to bring him a measure of happiness from time to time."

He chewed the meat slowly, trying to decide how best to approach the matter. By the time he swallowed, he'd realized that he might as well tell her the plain truth. She'd pester him with questions until she got it anyway and there wasn't any harm in her knowing. "I'm reluctant to shatter your romantic illusions, Darcy, but my mother and father weren't a love match. Their marriage was a practical matter of profitably merging two families' businesses."

"How do you know that?"

"I was raised by servants. Servants whisper, and little boys have sharp ears and too much curiosity for their own good."

"Still, it shouldn't have mattered," she said sadly. "You were his son."

Aiden shrugged. "The servants said otherwise. I'm inclined to think they're right."

"I'm so sorry, Aiden," she whispered. "So very sorry. It must have been awful to have grown up estranged from your father."

It had been, but it was in the past and couldn't be changed. Darcy's sadness was in the present moment, however, and Aiden didn't like to think of himself as responsible for having doused the bright lights in her eyes. "It isn't all bad," he countered, giving her a reassuring smile. "In fact, it's best if a man learns to make his own way early on. That way he's beholden to no one for what he has or achieves."

His words had no outward affect on her. Her eyes remained clouded and her expression troubled. "There's no need to look so bereft," he said, widening his smile, determined to keep her from slipping into pity for him. He'd rather face a hurricane than anyone's pity. "Unless, of course, you're on the verge of offering me tender consolation for a life of tragic loneliness and paternal deprivation."

She laughed, the sound so bright and magical that it instantly shattered the cloud that had fallen over them. "You're a hellion to the bone, Aiden Terrell."

"As long as you know that from the start . . ." Aiden said, grinning. He glanced at her plate. "Have you had enough to eat? I'll order you more if you like."

"Thank you, but I couldn't possibly eat another bite," she said, rising to her feet and taking both their plates from the table.

He watched her carry them over to the rolling cart on which the waiter had brought them from the kitchen. When Aiden had given her his shirt, Darcy had wrapped the sheet tightly around her waist to form a makeshift skirt. He knew that she intended it to preserve her modesty but its effect was the opposite. When she walked, it pulled as invitingly across her hips as her wet trousers had. Aiden found himself wanting very much to trace those curves with his hands and wondering what she'd do if he tried. Then he remembered the slap she'd delivered for the kiss he'd taken.

As Darcy turned and walked back toward the table, the tucked end of the sheet slipped out of place. She caught it with a gasp, then laughed as she quickly pulled it back around her waist and said, "I hope Chandler hurries and brings some clothes for me. If he doesn't, I'm going to embarrass myself in this sheet." Her quick movements loosened the ink pen holding her hair atop her head and, as she worked to secure the sheet, a cascade of long ringlets tumbled down over her shoulders. Aiden's ability to resist temptation fell with them.

"Cinnamon gold sunset."

Darcy started at the caress she heard in his voice, then froze as he came to stand in front of her. The hunger in his eyes was unmistakable. With her hands clasping the sheet around her waist and her heart racing, she lifted her chin and met his gaze. "I'd prefer to keep our relationship businesslike in nature, Aiden. I think it would be for the best."

"I couldn't agree more," he answered, even as he gently threaded his fingers through her hair.

A deliciously tingling wave swept her from head to toe. She leaned back, trying to ease her hair from Aiden's grasp. "This isn't my understanding of how business—"

"You have so much to learn." His fingers burrowed deeper and drew her toward him.

She couldn't breathe. "I don't want to learn," she heard herself whisper. It was a tiny sound, and she knew it would make no difference.

"Let's see," he answered, his lips brushing over hers in prelude.

She started to protest again, but the parting of her lips served only to invite him to kiss her in earnest. This wasn't at all like the kiss before, the one in the main room of the Lion and Fiddle. That one had been hard and then possessive. But this time . . . The gentleness of Aiden's lips made her shivery and warm. Reason argued for resistance. Something else urged surrender. His arms slipped around her shoulders and drew her closer. The instant she felt the heat and hardness of his body against hers, the battle of wills within her was done. Darcy vaguely felt the sheet slide down her legs and puddle around her feet. Her arms encircled Aiden's waist and he moaned against her lips, the sound sending another wondrous wave of exhilaration through her.

His hands slid lower, caressing the sweep of her back and pressing her even closer to him. She gasped at the sensations that followed Aiden's touch. His arms gently tightened around her, and the slow touch of his tongue to hers sent a molten current spiraling into the center of her being. When his hands slid lower to hold her hips against his own, she could only revel in the exotic and heady promise of the contact.

He groaned again, but this time a note of frustration rippled through the sound. His kiss deepened with a speed that left her gasping when he abruptly set her from him. His eyes glittered with wanting and his breathing was as labored as

her own, but his lips were compressed in a stern line of resolve.

God, what had she done? What must he think of her?
Darcy quickly looked away as she felt the heat race up her
neck and suffuse her cheeks.

There was a knock on the outer door of the room and from
the other side of the heavy wood panel came a familiar voice.
"I do say, sir, are you there?"

"Chandler," she heard herself whisper.

"And growing impatient from the sound of it," Aiden replied. "God only knows how long he's been knocking." He
bent down, grabbed the sheet, and handed it to her, saying,
"Perhaps you should retire to the bedroom to compose yourself."

He didn't have to offer twice. Darcy took the sheet and
ran. The door slammed behind her but the sureness of its clo-
sure didn't settle her nerves in the least. She'd barely had
time to draw a quick breath and wrap the sheet back around
her waist when there was knock on the panel. Darcy gasped
and spun to face it, instinctively bringing her fists up before
her.

"It's Chandler, Miss O'Keefe," Aiden's valet said quietly.
"Miss O'Shaunessy suggested that you might appreciate having these items brought directly to you."

When she opened the door, Chandler stood there soberly,
her small battered cardboard valise in his hand. "Thank you,
Chandler," she said, taking it from him with what she hoped
passed for a relaxed smile. "How did you find my mother? Is
she well?"

"Yes, miss. She insisted I remain for luncheon." The corners of his mouth lifted into the gentlest of smiles. "Your
mother is a charming hostess. She asked that I convey her
best wishes for your holiday and assure you that you've no
need to worry about her in your absence."

"Is she still knitting socks?" Darcy asked warily.

His expression didn't alter. "Yes, Miss O'Keefe. I had an
opportunity to view her work. She is a very talented needle-
woman."

"Thank you, Chandler. For everything." *For not finding amusement in Mother's confusion.* "I'd best change now."

Aiden stood at the window, watching over his shoulder as Chandler bowed and turned away and Darcy eased the door closed.

"You took your sweet time in getting here," Aiden observed, refocusing his attention on the street below and willing the hardness in his loins to ease.

"You didn't seem to lack for a pastime."

Aiden grinned. He'd long ago accepted the fact that Chandler could not be bullied into absolute servility. It had drawn them together as boys, had become a central feature of their relationship as men. "And then you managed to arrive at the most inopportune moment possible."

"I very much doubt it was the *most* inopportune," Chandler said dryly, "but I strive to do my best, sir."

"Did you have any problems with Mrs. O'Keefe?" Aiden asked.

"None, sir. She didn't seem the least suspicious."

"Did you have any with Seamus O'Hearne?"

"None," Chandler answered, beginning to clear the table. "I did, however, endeavor to leave your lodgings slightly more hospitable than when I found them."

"And in what way would that be, Chandler?"

"I should say they're considerably cleaner at this point, sir. I secured new bedding and saw that the floor was scrubbed. You need not be concerned about vermin of the insect variety."

Aiden chuckled and, now sufficiently composed, turned to face his employee. "The human variety being another matter entirely, of course."

"I do have my limits, sir." Chandler deposited the remaining silver and the table linens on the serving cart. Then his gaze slid to the closed bedroom door, and Aiden saw the tight-lipped expression that always preceded one of Chandler's lectures on "the proper thing." Aiden braced himself. He was spared by a sudden, rapid pounding on the outside door of the room. He and Chandler both turned at the sound, but it was Chandler who cast a quick look about the room and then went to answer it.

Maisey Riordan stood in the hallway, wringing her hands and breathing hard. Tears rimmed her eyes as she looked up at Chandler.

"Miss Maisey! Whatever is the trouble?" Chandler exclaimed, catching her hands in his and drawing her across the threshold.

Words tumbled out of her. "Is Darcy here? Bridie said you'd come for her clothes, and I was hoping . . ."

"Have a seat, Maisey," Aiden said, pulling out a chair for her. "Tell us what's happened. Is it Darcy's mother?"

She didn't move, but clung to Chandler's hands. "It's Selia McDonough," she finally managed to choke out. "She's been killed. Murdered. They say it's hideous."

Aiden's heart jumped and his blood shot ice-cold through his veins. Over his shoulder, he shouted, "Darcy! Get out here!" and then turned his attention back to Maisey. "Where did it happen, Maise? When?"

"In her sh-shop," the girl stammered. "They say just a while ago. They say the blood's—" She gagged, and when Chandler quickly gathered her in his arms she sniffled and bravely finished. "The blood's still wet."

Chandler looked at Aiden and cocked a brow. "I do believe a bit of brandy is in order, sir. If you'd be so kind . . ."

Aiden nodded and quickly went to the armoire where Chandler had stored his personal stock. A moment later Aiden pressed the glass into Maisey's chilled hand.

"Please drink it, Miss Maisey," Chandler cajoled. "It will make you feel much better."

Darcy lost all thought of her trouser buttons the moment she emerged from the bedroom and saw Maisey, standing in Chandler's courtly embrace and clutching a glass of brandy as though it were a lifeline. Darcy darted forward. "Are you all right, Maisey? What—"

"We have to go, Darcy. *Now,*" Aiden interrupted, roughly shoving his arms into his coat sleeves. "Jules knows I'm here." He was already on his way out the door when he said, "Take care of Maisey, Chandler. See her safely home."

Darcy glanced between Aiden's back and her friend, uncertain.

Maisey nodded and offered her a feeble smile. "Go with Mr. Terrell, Darce. I'll be fine."

Darcy paused just long enough to snatch the drawing of Jules off the desktop and then ran after Aiden.

CHAPTER 10

AIDEN QUICKLY SCANNED the crowd assembled in the street, gawking through the display windows of McDonough's Dry Goods Store. He couldn't find a bob of cinnamon gold hair amongst the ghouls, and he grew anxious and worried until he saw Darcy ease her way around a cluster of gray-haired women. He shook his head, reminding himself that Darcy was perfectly capable of protecting herself in a crowd. It was how she made her living.

" 'Twould be reasonable to assume this be yer brother's handiwork?"

Aiden recognized the voice and turned, finding Mick O'Shaunessy and two huge brutes standing behind him. "An assumption is always dangerous," Aiden observed.

"Then we'd best be a-makin' certain. Come with me." Mick motioned to the crowd before them, and the two brawlers—with forearms the size of hams—stepped forward to clear a path. A hush fell over the assemblage as Mick led the way toward the front of the store. The uniformed constable guarding the door wordlessly opened it and stepped aside as Aiden and Mick neared.

Six feet into the dim interior, Mick stopped. "Holy Mary, Mother of God," he whispered, slowly crossing himself.

Aiden swiftly assessed the scene. He'd seen too many others, too similar. Familiarity, however, didn't make it any easier. As always, his stomach twisted and heaved. Uniformed constables stood as close to the walls as they could get, their hands clasped behind their backs and their gazes fixed on the tin ceiling. The detectives wore suits and stood only marginally closer, furiously writing in their notebooks and glancing up only occasionally with cold eyes.

There was blood everywhere. On the floor, on the counter, on the shelves. The smell of it filled the air, ladened with the reek of death itself. What had in life been Selia McDonough lay sprawled in a deep pool of crimson midway down the center aisle. Her body had been slashed and gouged, her face hacked beyond recognition.

A priest knelt beside her, heedless of the blood, his earnest prayers his only concern. Aiden nodded. The priest would do far more for the peace of Selia's soul than all the constables in Charlestown.

"So, Terrell?" Mick asked. "What do ye think?"

"It's Jules's work." Through the ceiling came a piercing wail. Aiden clenched his teeth, hoping that the family upstairs wouldn't be permitted to see what had happened to their child. From behind him came a gasp and a churning gag. Aiden turned and found Darcy, her face colorless, her eyes closed, and her hand blindly searching for something to grasp.

Aiden took it and pulled her into the curve of his arm. "Christ, O'Keefe," he ground out as he moved her toward the door. "Don't faint. You'll embarrass yourself."

"I don't faint," she said weakly as they emerged into the afternoon sunlight. "I may hash lunch, but I won't faint."

He steered her through the crowd and down the sidewalk. When they were past the throng he gave vent to his anger. "What possessed you to go in there, Darcy? Of all the foolish things!"

"I d-don't know," she stammered. Her step faltered, and Aiden caught her arms with both hands before she could collapse. "I saw you go in and—"

"Take a deep breath, Darcy," he commanded. "And open

your goddamn eyes. Fill your mind with something other than what you saw back there."

She obeyed, looking up at him and taking a shaky breath. A hint of color came back into her cheeks as she swallowed.

From behind him came Mick's voice. "I don't want to be a-seein' anymore of me people like this, Terrell."

And I do? Aiden didn't bother to look over his shoulder when he replied, "The services for Selia, Mick . . . see that they're done right. Send the bill to my man at the Presidential."

" 'Tis me responsibility, not yers," Mick countered as he walked past with his henchmen in tow. "I'll see to it. *Ye* see to catching yer madman brother."

Aiden watched him go, thinking of imperial feudal lords and quaking vassals. Obviously Mick considered himself the former and Aiden the latter. Darcy interrupted his thoughts.

"We should find Timmy straight away," she said, attempting to ease away from his grasp. "He might have seen something."

"It will have to wait, Darcy. You're still too pale," he replied. He drew her toward a bench on the walkway. "Sit down here a minute, Darcy."

She locked her knees and wrenched herself from his hands. Tears pooled along the base of her lashes. "I can't sit. Selia's dead because I've been sitting around with you instead of doing the job I've been hired to do."

"It's not your fault," he countered, not as gently as he'd intended. "The only one who bears any responsibility for Selia's death is Jules."

"You don't believe that any more than I do, Aiden." She spun on her heel and crossed the street. "Now, let's be on with it."

They wound their way through the streets and alleyways, neither of them speaking, both holding private their devils and regrets. Aiden thought once to ask after her thoughts and decided against it. In time he would, but for the moment, Darcy needed to find her own way of living with the images of Selia's death.

They turned from a narrow back street into an even narrower dark alley. Midway down, Darcy halted in front of a large pile of broken barrels, discarded planking, rusted buckets, and rickety crates. She pushed a stack of the crates aside to reveal a man-sized hole at the base of the wooden wall behind, then dropped to her hands and knees and stuck her head and shoulders inside.

"Timmy! Are you in there?" she called. "It's Darcy O'Keefe. May I come in?"

Aiden tore his gaze from the curve of her backside and considered the trash heap. "Would he answer you if he were . . . home?"

"I'll go check."

Aiden watched her disappear and then, deciding that he looked like a fool standing in an alley fascinated by rubbish, he went in after her. He navigated by feel until a light suddenly flared ahead. It had settled into the glow of an oil lamp by the time he reached the end of the tunnel. Emerging into a chamber of sorts, he rose to his knees and stared about. The room was no more than six feet in diameter, and less than that in height. It would have been impossible for anyone but a child to stand upright in it. The lamplight was sufficient for him to decide that the pile of discards outside were those things Timmy the Rat hadn't been able to drag inside. Aiden saw untold numbers of everything stacked everywhere around him. China basins and pitchers, thunder mugs, books and newspapers, boxes of every size and material, pieces of shattered wood and twisted, rusted metal. The odor of old food and unwashed human hung in the air. "Lord Almighty, Darcy. Someone actually lives in this?"

"We call him the Rat for a number of reasons," Darcy replied, sitting cross-legged beside the crate on which the oil lamp rested. "I think we should wait for him. At the moment, he's the best avenue we've got for finding Jules. If we wandered the streets showing Jules's picture to everyone so soon after Selia's . . ." She swallowed and brushed dirt from her pant leg. "Well, we'd attract the attention of the constables, and it's for the best if we don't. You might have another experience like Liverpool and, given my profession, the further I stay away from them the better. Timmy should be back shortly. He doesn't usually go out at all in the day. The excitement of the—" She cleared her throat. "He must have gone out to see what it was all about."

The lamplight fell softly over her face, but Aiden saw the haunted look in her eyes. She'd had long enough to beat back the memories, and done as best she could. From his own experience he knew that she could have forever and a day more, and it wouldn't make any difference. What she needed now was to discover that the memories could be blocked out, that she could sometimes pretend it hadn't happened, that she hadn't seen.

Aiden made himself a place to sit across from her. "Does your mother have any idea you know people like Timmy?"

As he'd hoped, her eyes brightened. "I sincerely hope not. Her heart wouldn't take it. My father probably spun in his grave the first time I crawled in here. This wasn't what they envisioned for my life."

"What did they want for you?"

"Oh, I was supposed to become the wife of a well-to-do businessman. I was to manage his household efficiently, entertain his business associates when necessary, bear and raise his children without expectation or complaint, and in general be a lovely and docile adornment to his life."

"Docile?" Aiden chuckled. "Your parents believed there was a possibility of this actually coming to pass?"

"There was a time when I might have been able to do it," she countered, grinning.

"But then you learned to walk and talk and all hope was gone."

Her smile slowly disappeared. "Then my father fell dead, and necessity suggested that the course of my life change. I had to choose between starving to death in a most ladylike fashion, or learning how to scrap in the streets. I felt fifteen was too young to die, so I picked the latter."

She adjusted the wick on the lamp. "Maureen O'Shaunessy—Mick's wife—says that all things happen for a reason. I suppose she's right. My mother was raised to be a wife, and her entire world revolved around my father. When he was gone, so was her universe. Mother didn't know what to do with herself. She had no idea how to go about making her own way in the world. It was so difficult for her that twice she had 'accidents' that nearly took her life. It was after the second time that her mind truly started slipping away. I don't know if she'd try to end her life now, but it's better not to take the chance."

"And that's why you don't leave her alone," Aiden supplied.

Darcy nodded. "But I'm digressing. What I started out to say was that if my father hadn't died, I'd have blithely gone down the same path my mother did. If there's a silver lining in it all, it's that I was fortunate enough to see the danger and consequences in time to avoid them."

Aiden considered mentioning that not all women surrendered their minds with the advent of widowhood, but it occurred to him that to do so would be perilously close to asking Darcy to reconsider what appeared to be a healthy loathing of marriage. Women who weren't actively trying to ensnare a man were rare indeed. If it were ever discovered that he'd talked a female *into* thinking of matrimony, he'd be whipped and pilloried by his kind. He decided wisdom lay in changing the course of their conversation.

"Timmy has the most interesting articles lying about," he observed, sorting through the pile of smaller objects he'd earlier pushed aside to make himself a place to sit.

"He's something of a pack rat."

"And that's something of an understatement." Aiden pulled a hefty piece of yellowed ivory from the heap. A long steel blade was anchored to the other end of it. "This is especially deadly looking, don't you think?" he asked holding it up. Darcy nodded and an idea shot to the forefront of his brain. "Are you armed, Darcy?"

"I have two perfectly good ones." She lifted them from her sides with a smile. "See?"

"Very amusing. You know what I mean," he countered,

picking through the pile in search of a scabbard or sheath for the knife. "Do you carry a weapon of some sort?"

"I've always thought that men who carry knives tend to rely on them more than their wits. That, in turn, leads them into trouble where they're compelled to use the former rather than the latter. Generally speaking, men who carry knives have short lives that come to violent ends."

He found the leather case and looked back at Darcy as he slipped the blade into it. "Is that a long way around of saying you don't have one for yourself?"

"No." She pulled up her right pant leg and drew something from the top of her boot. Turning it so the lamplight fell over it, she showed him a stubby blade no more than two inches long.

It was the poorest excuse for a knife he'd ever seen. "Are you hoping to tickle someone to death with that?"

"I'll have you know that it's quite sufficient for its purpose."

"And what would that be, Darcy? Peeling apples?"

"Cutting purse strings," she replied matter-of-factly. "And intimidation if I ever find myself needing to fight my way out of a corner."

"So then why didn't you use it on me when I trapped you in the alley? I had you in a corner."

"Honestly?" She grinned. "I didn't even think about it. I forget I have it most of the time. And besides, you didn't *actually* have me in a corner."

"No, *actually,* I had you up against a wall. How's your hand feeling?"

"Fine," she said, flexing her fingers. "How's your foot? You didn't limp for very long."

"I limped only for the effect of it. I didn't want you to feel ineffectual."

She rolled her eyes, and her lips parted to offer a retort. Suddenly she looked toward the tunnel opening. "Timmy's here." She waited a second and then called, "It's all right, Timmy. It's me, Darcy O'Keefe, and a friend of mine."

A head and a thin set of shirt-clad shoulders popped from

the darkness of the tunnel, and then the head snapped up to look around. Aiden couldn't determine the man's age. Not old, not young, but somewhere in the long stretch between. The man's eyes were black, his gaze darting. His nostrils flared as he glanced between Aiden and Darcy. Aiden had never seen a human being who looked, and acted, so . . . well, ratlike.

"If you come to ask me about Selia," the Rat said, scrambling the rest of his body into his den and abruptly hunkering down on his haunches, "I'll tell ya the same thing I told Hamlet: I didn't see no Capt. Hackum."

"We know who Capt. Hackum is," Darcy said while reaching into her jacket pocket. She withdrew a folded piece of paper, opened it, and handed it to the Rat. "Have you seen this man anywhere about, Timmy?"

"Can't say that I have," the Rat admitted, his gaze darting over Jules's likeness in a way that Aiden thought the man might also eye a hunk of cheese. "But can't say that I haven't either. Didn't know I was supposed to be lookin' for him." His nose twitched as he handed back the drawing. "Want me to find him for you?"

Darcy nodded and tucked it away. "Only if you're careful about it, Timmy. He's very dangerous."

He stroked his jaw with long thin fingers. "How much you payin' for the touch, Darce?"

She leaned her shoulder against the wall of debris with a wary smile. "What did Hamlet offer you?"

"Amnesty for my past crimes." The Rat grinned broadly, revealing four chipped front teeth and otherwise toothless gums. "But only if I'd tell 'im what they were."

Darcy shot Aiden a glance, and he understood. "Would ten dollars be enough?" he offered.

The Rat turned toward him and his nostrils flared again. "Who be you?"

"My name is Aiden Terrell. The man in the drawing Darcy showed you is my brother. I've tracked him for the last eighteen months. Selia isn't the first he's killed. I want her to be the last."

The Rat looked him up and down. "Twenty. In American coin. No paper money."

"Twenty it is, then," Aiden agreed. "When you locate him, send word to the—"

"Lion and Fiddle," the Rat finished.

Aiden frowned, and Timmy the Rat flashed him a smile. "Everyone's heard. No whack in it for me to know that you've made Darce a lady bird there."

Darcy countered evenly, "I'm not a lady bird."

All of Timmy seemed to twitch. His smile was wide and his eyes bright. "Play it right, Darce, and you could end up being his left-hander."

Aiden wondered if he were interpreting the jabber correctly. He guessed they were speaking of the nature of his and Darcy's relationship. It was perfectly clear that Darcy didn't like whatever it was Timmy the Rat said about it.

She smiled thinly and made for the tunnel opening. "I don't want to be his left *or* his right-hander."

The Rat waited until she'd started out before saying, "Not much chance of going right, is there now?"

Darcy popped back in just long enough to say, "Find Capt. Hackum, Timmy. Preferably before dawn tomorrow. For every day you waste, you lose a fiver."

When Darcy disappeared from sight Aiden and Timmy looked at one another. Aiden held up the knife. The Rat instantly tensed. "Not to worry," Aiden assured him. "I've another transaction to negotiate is all, Timmy. Would you be willing to part with this?"

"What you offerin' for it?"

"What do you want?"

"Sure is a fancy coat you're wearing. It warm as it looks?"

"Even more so," Aiden replied, seeing the direction Timmy intended to go. "It's merino wool."

"How about a trade?" Timmy offered, stroking his chin with his fingers. "Your coat for the knife. Fair enough?"

"Deal." Aiden shrugged out of the coat and handed it over. To his surprise, Timmy didn't immediately put it on. Instead, he cradled it against his chest and brushed his hand over the fabric with something akin to reverence. It was the first motion Aiden had seen the man make that looked human. It also made him look very young.

"Timmy?" Aiden said gently. He waited until the other's gaze came up to meet his. "Stay well distant from my brother. Darcy's right. He's vicious, and not terribly particular about who he hacks up. No heroics. Just find his hole and then come tell me where it is. I'll take the hunt from there."

Timmy nodded and went back to stroking the coat.

Darcy stood at the end of the alley, watching as Aiden emerged from the wall and put the crates back into place to conceal the opening. She wondered which would come first, his observations about Timmy or his questions about the jabber that had swirled around him. She scuffed the toe of her boot against the cobblestone. She knew she'd defend Timmy's peculiarities as best she could. As for the jabber . . . Darcy decided there was no point in trying to evade the matter of their physical relationship. If he brought it up and pressed the issue, it would be best to face it square on and be done with it. She'd tell him straight out that her conduct in his room after lunch had been an appalling aberration, that her acceptance of his kisses had been a mistake, and that she wasn't going to let it happen again.

Aiden came to stand beside her. "Here," he said, handing her the knife he'd extracted from the pile in Timmy's den. "Now you have a weapon that amounts to something."

"I don't need this," she protested, trying to hand it back. "Where's your coat?"

He shook his head. "I traded it for the knife. And you do need it, Darcy. Selia might be alive if she'd had a way to defend herself."

Darcy considered the weapon for a long moment, and then looked up at Aiden. "Have you ever known one of Jules's victims to survive?" The sudden hardening of his jaw answered her question.

"I'd feel better about having dragged you into this mess if I knew you were carrying the knife," he replied solemnly.

"Please keep it, Darcy. Even if it's only to quiet my conscience."

She acquiesced with a sigh, but when she made to tuck the weapon in her coat pocket, Aiden shook his head. "The scabbard has bands, Darcy. It's made for strapping to the underside of your forearm, beneath your coat and shirtsleeve."

"And I suppose that's how you think I ought to haul it about?" He nodded, and she gave in just to avoid the inevitable argument. "This is ridiculous, but all right. Hold the damn thing while I get out of my jacket and roll up my shirtsleeve."

It was while she was adjusting the straps around her left arm that the dreaded question finally came.

"What's a lady bird?"

"A kept woman, a mistress," Darcy supplied, nonchalantly rolling her sleeve down and buttoning the cuff. "And before you ask, a left-hander is a mistress a man marries. The expression comes from the fact that the man takes her left hand during the vows instead of the usual right one. It's a slap, a public declaration that she isn't of the same value as a chaste, respectable woman."

"Blanche was my father's left-hand wife," he mused, holding out Darcy's jacket, clearly intending to help her into it. She hesitated and then complied, murmuring her thanks and making quick work of the courtesy.

"I don't recall that he actually deviated from tradition in taking her hand during the ceremony," Aiden continued, stepping away, "but then again, she'd been his mistress for years and everyone knew."

Surprised but thankful that the conversation hadn't included any mention of her being Aiden's lady bird, Darcy observed, "Blanche must have been very special to your father. I've noticed that men don't usually marry their mistresses if they can possibly avoid it. Especially successful businessmen concerned with their public reputations."

Aiden chuckled dryly. "My father was a complicated man, and Blanche is a shrewd woman."

It struck her that where Aiden had been concerned, his father had been a mean man. "And Jules is their child, right?"

Aiden nodded. "Jules was born illegitimate, but his legal status was changed by the marriage."

"And if Jules's mind had been normal—"

"My father would have disinherited me in a heartbeat. It just didn't turn out as he'd hoped."

CHAPTER 11

MOONLIGHT ILLUMINATED THE back stairway of the Lion and Fiddle. Darcy trudged up it in Aiden's wake, relieved that he'd fallen silent six blocks back and spared her brain the effort of trying to assemble coherent sentences. She couldn't remember the last time she'd walked as many miles or talked to as many people as she had that day. Her boots felt as if they weighed more than she did, and her legs were trembling with exhaustion by the time she reached the top of the narrow wooden stairs.

Aiden unlocked the door and, saying he'd light the lamp, preceded her in. Darcy stood on the threshold listening to him and studying the room in the moonlight. A rope had been secured to the far side of the door frame and then stretched the width of the room and fastened on the other end to the window frame. Two blankets hung from it, side by side, effectively dividing the space into two. Her trunks had been put on one side, the side with the iron bedstead. The bedding had been folded down and her nightgown laid out. A washstand sat in the darkest corner. On the other side of the partition, the side with the window, a thick pallet had been fashioned on the floor. It, too, had been turned back, and Aiden's nightshirt lay across the bedding. His bag sat on the floor in the corner. Another washstand had been set beneath the window, Aiden's mirror and shaving kit beside it.

There was the noxious smell typical of lucifer sticks. The light flared and steadied, the glass clinked into place.

"Well," she drawled, "if I hadn't already decided I liked Chandler, this would have been the corker."

"Interfering fussbudget," Aiden muttered, glaring at the makeshift partition.

"He's only looking out after both our best interests," Darcy said, moving into her side of the room. "And don't you even consider taking down that blanket, Aiden Terrell." She snatched her nightgown off the bed and walked back across the room.

Aiden stepped into her path. "What are you doing?"

"Chandler laid out our bedclothes on the wrong beds. I'm putting them right. We'll change the trunks to the right sides in the morning. I'm too tired tonight."

"Leave them as they are. You can have the bed. I'll take the pallet."

She gave him a crooked smile. "It's rather late in our association for you to attempt being a gentleman, Aiden. I've seen your true stripes."

"Be that as it may," he said, pushing through the blanket and disappearing, "leave the arrangements as they are."

Darcy stood there staring at the gray wool wall. "I'm also too tired to argue with you about it. It's time to call the day a good one."

"Not that it was in the least," he shot back.

"No, it wasn't, was it?" she admitted, dropping down on the edge of the mattress, intent on being rid of her boots. "But we did the best with it that we could. No one can fault us for lack of effort."

"No, indeed. But they certainly could for lack of result."

She heard the frustration in his voice. "Tomorrow will be a better one, Aiden," she gently assured him. "We'll get some sleep, and things will at least look brighter."

There was a long pause. "You don't talk in your sleep, do you?"

She wiggled her liberated toes as she replied, "I don't know. Why do you ask?"

"Because if I have to suffer your optimistic platitudes all night long, I may strangle you well before dawn."

There was more in his voice than just simple frustration, but she was too tired to puzzle it out. Saying, "Get some sleep, Aiden," she forced herself back to her feet and undid the buttons on her jacket.

Darcy didn't bother to arrange her discarded clothing beyond tossing it across the foot of the bed. She didn't even bother to button the bodice of her nightgown before crawling between the sheets. Sleep came only seconds after her head hit the goose-down pillow.

AIDEN CLAWED HIS way from the blood and gore, vaulting upright on the pallet. His heart thundered and his chest heaved. Aiden grabbed his valise and plunged both hands in. The flask was there, and full. He blessed Chandler as he pulled the stopper and poured liquid fire down his throat.

"No!"

He lowered the flask to blink in the direction from which the voice had come. *Darcy.* He'd forgotten she was there. She stepped through the parted blanket wall, coming at him with all the fury and speed of a runaway horse. His mind warned him but couldn't force his body to react.

When she snatched the flask from him and darted to the washstand, his stupor snapped. Aiden scrambled to his feet and stepped toward her, his hand outstretched in silent command.

She threw open the window and upended the flask, saying, "Drinking won't drown the nightmares, Aiden."

Amber gold poured forth in the moonlight, a travesty of waste. Aiden darted toward her. "Give me that, Darcy."

"No." She tossed the flask into the night.

He heard it strike the walkway below. "Goddammit!"

She closed the window sharply, then faced him with her hands on her hips and her chin up.

"Do you think that's the only whiskey in Charlestown?"

he demanded, turning on his heel and striding toward the door. "I'll find more." A flash of fluttering white gave him pause. Seeing Darcy place herself between him and the door ended his momentary consternation and pricked his anger.

"Get out of my way, Darcy," he said.

She backed up. "If you'd just face the demons, they'd lose their power over you." Her body encountered the door and she flung her arms across the frame.

"What the hell do you know about my demons and my nightmares?" Aiden demanded, his voice a lethal whisper of warning. "You haven't seen what I have, as many times as I have. Now, get out of my way, Darcy, or I'll move you aside."

"No." She widened her stance. "I need you sober. If you want out of here, you're going to have to knock me unconscious and step over my body."

His anger flashed. "I warned you." He grabbed her upper arms and jerked her away from the door. She was feather-light, the task easily accomplished. His satisfaction ended when his head hit the floor.

Darcy sat across his midsection, her eyes ablaze, her hair tumbling over her shoulders, and her new knife pressed against his throat. "Sweet Jesus," he whispered.

"You're not going to drink yourself into oblivion or an early grave, Aiden Terrell. At least not on my watch."

God, was she beautiful. Deliciously, sinfully beautiful. Her hair in the moonlight, the shadowed swells of her breasts. . . . His body responded to the press and warmth of hers, and all thoughts of whiskey were instantly gone. "Calm down, Darcy," he whispered. "I don't want my throat cut. You win; I surrender. I won't go."

She smiled. "Well, at last good sense prevails," she said, sitting up straighter and taking away the knife. "It's nice to see that you're capable of it."

"I'm not." It was all the warning he gave her. The knife flew from her hand, clattering across the wooden floorboards. In the same instant he rolled her beneath him.

"Aiden, don't do—"

He silenced her with his mouth, his kiss insistent and

deeply possessive. His hands pinned hers to the floor above her head, his hips rested in the cradle of her parted thighs, the bulk of his weight borne by his knees and elbows. She squirmed beneath him, trying to turn her head away from the assault of his lips, arching her back in an attempt to throw him off. The effort pressed her closer. Aiden groaned, silently cursing the clothing that lay between them. She went still, and a sob caught low in her throat.

He gentled his kiss, brushing her lips with his and whispering, "I'm sorry, Darcy. I won't scare you again. I promise I won't hurt you."

"Aiden."

It was a plea. "Make me forget, Darcy. Just this one night, be my sweet angel and make me forget."

"Aiden."

There was understanding in the whisper. He heard compassion, too, and it was enough for him. He kissed her again, gently, slowly, and she relaxed beneath him. He traced her lower lip with the tip of his tongue and her lips parted for him, inviting him to taste her. Darcy tugged at his hold on her hands. He released them and sighed when she slipped her arms around his neck and her tongue sought to explore him in return.

She was sweetness and delight, her touch, her kiss sending wave after wave of heat through his body. The pleasure built too quickly, threatening to undo the promise he'd made her. Aiden eased his lips from hers and pressed a kiss to the corner of her mouth, then to the smooth curve of her jaw. She arched her neck with a soft sigh as he trailed kisses down the length of her throat. Her shoulders went back when he kissed the gentle hollow at the base of her throat, and her breasts pressed against his chest. The inducement seared his restraint.

Shifting his weight onto one elbow, he freed a hand and pushed aside the open bodice of her nightgown. Darcy tensed. Aiden lifted his head and gazed into her eyes as he cupped her in his palm. "It won't hurt," he said, slowly brushing his thumb over the taut peak.

Her eyes widened and she sucked in a hard, shaky breath.

Still holding her, still brushing her nipple, Aiden shifted his weight again and eased himself downward. The sight of her in his hand sent a burning tightness through his loins. "So beautiful. So tempting. Do you taste as delicious as you look, Darcy O'Keefe?"

She couldn't answer. Sensation, wondrous and overpowering, swept through her. The tremors deepened and turned her insides to molten liquid. She twisted her fingers in Aiden's hair and arched upward, compelled by the inner fire to press her breast against his mouth. She heard his name tear past her lips and he answered it with a groan.

His kiss deepened and the sensations became exquisitely demanding, possessing her. She struggled against it, its wildness and power too much to bear. It swirled around her, mocking her, sweeping her forward into an oblivion of flaring stars. And abandoned her there.

She heard Aiden's voice, but his touch no longer anchored her. Darcy panicked.

Kneeling between her thighs, Aiden saw the terror in her eyes and froze, his hands on the last button of his trousers. "It's all right, Darcy," he murmured, reaching down to stroke her legs in reassurance. "It's all right. We'll start again."

A sob caught in her throat, and she scrambled away from him as though he were the devil himself. He tried to catch her, but she moved too quickly and the effort left him on all fours, his throbbing manhood jutting from the top of his open pants. Humiliation slapped him. Anger forced him to his feet.

"Aiden." Her voice quavered.

He ignored her anguish, wrenched the door open and then slammed it closed behind him. Fastening his buttons, he stormed down the hallway, took the stairs two at a time, almost hoping he'd miss one, fall, and break his goddamned neck. With his usual luck he reached the bottom and the main room without reward.

Rusty Riordan leaned against the bar, appearing to be at

least two sheets to the wind. He chuckled as Aiden came toward him. "Darcy put up a bit of a fight, did she? No doubt it made the pumpin' all the sweeter, though."

There was the satisfying crunch of bone and the ripple of impact up the length of his arm. Rusty didn't so much as make a sound as he flew backward and hit the floor. There was silence in the bar.

"Get up, you son of a bitch," Aiden demanded, his hands still fisted. "Get up and say it again."

Rusty didn't move. Seamus leaned over the bar and peered down at him. "Don't look like he's gonna. Leastwise not for a while." He eased himself back and smiled at Aiden. "Have one on me, Terrell." A low buzz of conversation swelled to life in the room again.

Aiden ignored the glass of whiskey the barkeeper slid across the counter. "Do you have a loaded pistol behind that counter, Seamus?"

The man's brow shot up. "I might."

Aiden made his way to the front door. "If anyone goes up those stairs after Darcy, shoot him."

"Would in the leg be all right with you?" Seamus called after him.

"I don't care where you shoot him as long as it stops him."

"What about you, Terrell? Should I shoot you when you come back?"

Aiden paused on the threshold, remembering how close he'd come and how much will it had taken to walk away. "Use your own good judgment," he answered, stepping into what remained of the night.

HER WHOLE BODY trembling, Darcy flung off her nightgown and jerked on her clothes. Once dressed, she flattened herself against the wall beside her bed and stared at the moonlit door on the opposite side of the room. She couldn't stop shaking. *If he comes back . . . If he comes back . . .* She bolted forward, suddenly and desperately needing light. She fumbled with the lucifer stick, but somehow managed to drag it between the sheets of glass paper to get the lamp lit. The steady glow settled her enough for her breathing to ease. Her gaze slid to the door again, and she considered locking it. The thought of Aiden tearing it from the hinges, and the public scene that would create, made her decide against throwing the bolt.

Darcy quickly put her bed between herself and Aiden's possible return. And then she began to pace, trying to calm the chaotic chatter of her thoughts. She couldn't. Above all else in her mind was the plaintive chant, *Ai-den, Ai-den.* Darcy couldn't hold back the tears. She collapsed onto her bed and curled into a ball, hugging her pillow to her, not knowing why she sobbed so hard into it, and too overwhelmed to care.

After a long while the crying played itself out, leaving her physically exhausted and mentally battered to numbness. She remained curled in a ball on her bed, staring at the woolen blanket and hugging the pillow to her. Slowly snaking through the silence came an undeniable truth: Aiden had a kind of power over her. He could make her forget everything but him, could get her to surrender every bit of her awareness to the feelings he stirred in her. When he pressed, she seemed to lose all sense of control.

She shot out of bed and paced furiously up and down the width of the room. No one but Aiden had ever been able to push her past the brink of self-control. No one. Not her father in dying. Not Mick in bullying her. Not Maureen's acts of kindness. Not her mother's attempts to end her life. Not a single one of the leches, cons, and belligerent victims that peopled her world. She'd faced it all without letting anyone or anything get through her shell. How had Aiden managed it? And so easily! What was it about him?

Determined to mend her defenses, she ignored the thumping of her heart and the racing of her pulse. She marshaled what she knew of him, and ticked through it from the first thought that came to her. Aiden Terrell had a quick temper and was ruthless in exacting revenge. She'd seen it in him time and time again. He'd resisted in some fashion or another

her every effort to impose control over their hunt. He'd been thoroughly consistent, however, in the manner in which he'd opposed her efforts to define and limit their relationship. He was a son of a bitch who couldn't accept no for an answer.

The niggling voice of fairness reminded her that she'd never actually given Aiden a clear and resounding *No!* She'd resisted, and then capitulated. Every time. Every damn time. Darcy sighed and dropped down on the side of the bed. Staring blindly at the floor, she puzzled the why of it. She sensed that a myriad of reasons went to explaining her acceptance of his physical advances, but only one was clear enough to identify. Aiden, at his innermost core, was a decent man; the most decent and honest man she'd ever known.

His decency had been manifested in his offer to pay for Selia's funeral, in having traded his coat to Timmy because Timmy needed the coat and Aiden thought she needed a knife. As for honesty, Aiden had never made any secret of wanting her in his bed. He'd come right out and said it. She, on the other hand, hadn't been as honest in her refusal. Part of her wanted very much to go—why else would she surrender so easily?—and Aiden was experienced enough in carnal matters to see right through her denial. She couldn't fault him for calling her bluff.

But she knew his wanting, his decency, and his honesty weren't all of his appeal, and she searched further within herself for the answer. Aiden was certainly handsome. There was no denying that. But, just as certainly, he wasn't the first handsome man to cross her path and beckon. She'd ignored the others, so why did she go when Aiden called? It wasn't because of his size or any fear that he'd hurt her if she resisted.

Darcy remembered the tenderness of his touch, and his promises as he'd held her to the floor and soothed her fears. She'd believed him, trusted him. Her instincts had told her she would be safe with him. Why had she thought that?

She raked her hands through her hair, tossed her head back, and exhaled at the ceiling. God, what was it about

Aiden? What made her cast aside common sense and good judgment where he was concerned? What drew her to him?

The answer came with simple clarity. Aiden needed her. Darcy fell back on the bed with a strangled sound. It wasn't that, she assured herself. The world was full of people who needed her. Mick needed her skills and the money she made him. Her mother needed her to keep what remained of her world together. Maisey needed her friendship. So did Bridie and the social castoffs like Timmy.

The answer refused to be denied. It flared again and clarified itself. Aiden needed her in a way no one else did. That was why he affected her as no one else did.

What did Aiden need that she could give him? Darcy snorted. It sure as hell wasn't money and social connections. Lovemaking he could get anywhere, and it would undoubtedly be of better quality than anything she could provide him.

"So just what in hell's name would a rich, handsome, self-assured man want from a gutter rat like me?" she demanded, throwing her arms up in frustration. "Oh, yes, sex of course! He begged me to—" He'd begged her to make him forget.

"Oh, God," she whispered, deluged with the fullness of understanding. Aiden wanted to block out the memories of Jules's viciousness, and of his own failure to stop the murders from happening. But his plea had come from deep inside him, and she knew that Jules wasn't all he wanted to forget. Aiden wanted to erase the memories of his childhood, too, of always being resented and ignored. He needed someone to make him whole.

How could she do that for him? How could anyone? The enormity of his need, the justice of having it met, overwhelmed her.

Darcy was still wrestling with her options—the most attractive one being on a train bound for St. Louis—when the door opened and Aiden filled the frame. Darcy froze, then quickly looked him up and down. He'd been fighting; his clothes were askew, torn, and smattered with blood. She looked him over again, and breathed a silent sigh of relief when it appeared that none of it was his. His face didn't have a mark on it; his eyes were bright and focused sharply on her. If she had to guess, she'd had to say that he'd resisted the urge to wallow in the solace of whiskey. She'd also guess that it had been a big step forward for him.

"Don't look like such a scared rabbit," he said with cold derision. "I can find women I don't have to force."

The thought of Aiden with a prostitute set her teeth on edge. The idea that he'd sought one out after he'd left her made her blood boil. After all the kind thoughts and tender feelings she'd dredged up for him. . . . The ungrateful son of a bitch. "I'm *not* a rabbit," she hotly retorted.

He snorted, muttered, "Christ, don't I know that," and then stepped to his side of the blanket partition.

Darcy wanted to follow him and tell him just what a despicable human being he was. *Not that it will be the first time he's been told that,* she silently fumed. She froze. No doubt his father had said it to him often enough. Enough to last for the rest of his life.

Darcy didn't know what to say, what to do to make it better, and so she turned around, blew out the light, climbed into bed. She curled around her pillow, searching the darkness for answers until sleep mercifully put an end to her torment.

CHAPTER 12

THE KNOCKING WOKE her. Darcy stumbled to the door, feeling as if she'd been beaten with a big stick. It took her brain a long second to remember how to open the door, another to find the name of the man who stood on the other side of it. "Seamus? What time is it?"

"Just past nine," the man supplied. "Will Mahoney just brought this for Terrell."

She extended her hand, only afterward noting that Seamus held a small rectangular box wrapped in brown paper and tied with twine.

Darcy's stomach rolled over as Seamus deposited the box in her open hand. "Th-thank you," she stammered, feeling the room close in on her.

"Get some more sleep, Darce," Seamus advised, grasping the doorknob. Pulling the door closed, he added, "You look like hell."

Darcy swayed on her feet, her every instinct urging her to fling the box as far as she could, but unable to do anything but stand there and stare at it.

"Give it to me, Darcy," Aiden said gently from over her shoulder.

When she didn't move he reached around her and took it.

"It's from Jules, isn't it?" she asked. "It's Selia. . . ." The room tilted crazily and her head threatened to roll off her

shoulders. At the very edge of awareness, she felt the power of
Aiden's hands, felt herself moving and dropping onto the
bed. Then her head did roll from her shoulders. It landed between her knees.

Above her, Aiden said sharply, "Sit there just like that and
don't move."

Darcy took a deep breath and the world steadied. "I think
I'm going to be sick," she muttered.

Aiden went around the end of the bed and returned a second later with the washbasin. "If you are," he said, "for God's
sake do it in this." He shoved her shoulder up and back just
enough to thrust the bowl into the curve between her legs
and torso, then pressed her head back down to her knees.
"Chandler will kill us both if we dirty the floor."

Then, as though satisfied that he'd made her as uncomfortable as he possibly could, he stepped through the blanket
wall without another word. Darcy sighed and, one inch at a
time, began the task of sitting upright without fainting or
being sick.

With clenched teeth, Aiden put the package on his washstand and pulled the ends of the twine. The paper fell open.
As always, the folded note lay atop the box lid, his own name
scrawled in Jules's handwriting across the parchment. Aiden
stared at it a long moment. Inside would be another city, another destination. He would have no choice but to go. *And
leave Darcy behind.* Telling himself it was the best thing that
would ever happen to the both of them, Aiden picked up the
note and opened it.

She wasn't as pretty as the one you found.

Ice tore through his veins. The note shook in Aiden's hand
and he focused his attention on it, determined to keep his fear
and anger contained. It was cheap paper, not the vellum that
Jules had used in Ireland and Scotland. It was grimy from
handling, the edges fuzzy and the corners knocked around.
He turned it over to look at the back and found the faint rem-
nants of a partial column of numbers, and a portion of what
he guessed to be a name: *garty.*

It was more of a trail than he'd ever had. Aiden put the

note into his coat pocket, then gathered up the box, paper, and twine, and shoved them between his washbasin and the wall. Stepping away from it, he pushed his fingers through his hair. What should he do about Darcy? Show her the note from Jules and let her draw her own conclusion? Just tell her? Assure her that she'd be all right, that he'd protect her? Aiden swore softly. What he most wanted to do was send her far away where Jules couldn't find her. Paris. He could buy her paints and brushes and canvases and send her to Paris to study art.

Not that she'd go. And not that he cared one way or the other, beyond a selfish desire to avoid having to look at another body he had known in life. When it came to degrees of aversion, it was far easier to look at a dead stranger than a dead someone he had known. If he were allowed his druthers . . .

Aiden sighed and shook his head. God, Jules had brought him to a human low. He was sorting the world into acceptable and unacceptable victims, based on the amount of personal anguish he felt when considering their mangled bodies. His own mind was becoming as twisted as Jules's. Aiden spun on his heel and moved to the door. As he went, his gaze fell on Darcy's knife. It lay against the baseboard where it had come to rest when he'd knocked it from her hand last night. Aiden picked it up and stepped around the partition. He found Darcy standing beside her bed, looking much steadier than she'd been when he'd left her there, but still disheveled and bleary-eyed.

"Here's your knife, Darcy," he said, tossing it on the bed. "Put it back in the scabbard. Lock the door behind me. Stay here and don't let anyone in."

"Where are you going?"

"To find the messenger who delivered the package. He might be able to lead me to Jules."

"I'll come with you," she declared, scooping up the knife. "You wouldn't know Will Mahoney if he were standing right in front of you."

"Seamus was right. You look like hell, O'Keefe. Get some sleep."

She walked past him saying, "If you think you look any better than I do, you're sorely mistaken," and, as usual, left him to catch up with her.

SARAH MAHONEY HAD her nine-year-old son firmly by the ear when Darcy and Aiden left their apartment. Will was still blubbering on about the particulars of how he came to be involved in what the adults considered a very serious affair. Darcy smiled wryly as she listened to the amount in Will's story change from a halfpence to a pence. Sarah could get that truth out of the boy. She and Aiden had dragged from Will what they needed. Apparently, Jules had left the box in the hall outside the Mahoneys' door in the middle of the night, a note wrapped around some money tucked beneath the twine, asking for it to be delivered to Aiden at the Lion and Fiddle. Will had found it and scampered to the task, not telling his mother of the bounty that had unexpectedly come his way. He'd denied everything until Sarah had shaken a halfpenny out of his pocket. The rest of the truth had tumbled with it. Before the end of his tale, Will had surrendered Jules's note to Aiden.

"Well," Darcy mused as they left the building, "we should have known it wouldn't be easy."

Aiden looked at the rooftops across the street. Then he set his jaw. "Jules knew to have Will take the package to the Lion and Fiddle."

"I've thought of that, too. It means he's watching us, doesn't it?"

"If I thought you would let me, I'd send you away, Darcy."

Darcy glanced over at him. In his eyes she saw flinty resolve. "You're right, Aiden, I wouldn't go. I have obligations and responsibilities I have to see through. I can't leave them."

"I would send your mother with you wherever you wanted to go," he said softly, turning to face her squarely. "I can afford the expense."

He wanted her to tell him she'd go. He couldn't hide the hope. Darcy wished she could do that for him, but she couldn't. She shook her head. "Mother isn't my only responsibility. I appreciate your offer, Aiden." She lifted her left arm and gave him a smile. "But I've got a big knife now and I can take care of myself."

Her assurance had no outward effect on his expression. "Lovely bravado, m'dear, but that's all it is. You haven't the grit to use a knife properly."

"And how would you—" She swallowed the rest of the retort, remembering how easily he'd disarmed her the night before. Memories of the consequences flooded in after it. "Oh."

"Yes, oh," he countered with a heavy sigh. "Just stay close and don't wander off."

"Darcy, girl."

She jumped. Then, cursing herself for having let her focus narrow again, she turned to find Mick crossing the street in her direction. "What brings you out this morning, Mick?" she asked, folding her arms over her midriff.

"Ye'll be attendin' Selia's wake? Her mother asked after ye last night, an' Maureen made it a point this mornin' to tell me to remind ye to honor the dead an' comfort the livin'."

She'd thought of it yesterday, but she didn't want to go and had hoped being with Aiden would be sufficient excuse to avoid it. Obviously she wasn't going to be allowed to escape. "I will, Mick," she reluctantly promised. "Tonight, when there's little chance I'll encounter Mother. She thinks I'm on holiday with the Sinclairs, and it wouldn't do to have her meet me at the McDonough's."

"Good enough," Mick said with a crisp nod. "Just see yer duty done." He turned his attention to Aiden. "Might I have a word with ye privately, Mr. Terrell?"

"Certainly," Aiden said and walked down the sidewalk away from Darcy. Mick joined him a few seconds later.

The Irishman began without preamble. "It seems me nephew, Rusty Riordan, was carried home last night with a few less teeth than he left with yesterday mornin'. Would ye happen to know anything about how he came to lose them?"

"Your nephew's mouth slipped him into the gutter," Aiden answered blandly. "I assisted him out."

" 'Twould seem to me he had a bit of a nudge in a-gettin' there. I hear tell ye an' Darcy are sharin' one of Seamus's rooms."

Aiden met Mick's gaze squarely. "Not that it's any of your business, O'Shaunessy, but a room is all we're sharing, and it's only for the sake of expediency."

A red eyebrow inched upward. "Ye do recall what I told ye about takin' liberties with her, don't ye?"

From time to time. "In the event that it's escaped your notice, Darcy has a mind of her own and is perfectly capable of making decisions for herself. She's equally capable of defending her virtue if that's what she wants to do."

Mick studied him, his eyes hardening. "Darcy's a female, an' so capable of being led astray by a man more worldly an' experienced than she is. I promised Darcy's da to watch over her if he couldn't. Ye compromise her, Terrell, an' I'll stand for him in seein' that ye do right by her."

Diplomacy evaporated in his anger. "From what I can tell," Aiden said through clenched teeth, "you don't have much of a sense of right when it comes to Darcy. If you did, you wouldn't have sent her out to pick pockets seven years ago, and you certainly wouldn't have shackled her to me."

Mick opened his mouth to speak and then quickly closed it. A long moment passed before he finally ground out, "Just see that ye keep yer hands to yerself, Terrell."

"I'll do as I damn well please."

Aiden was furious, and Mick was crossing the street, grinning from ear to ear. Darcy quickly glanced away. She decided she didn't want to know what had been said between them.

"Breakfast might help," she said as she fell in beside Aiden. "Would you like to go see what Jack Trehune has this morning?"

"I don't want any goddamned meat pies."

"Then what do you want? Another brawl?"

It stopped him in his tracks. "You're the most irritatingly

independent woman who's ever crossed my path. Which leads me to wonder why in hell's name you allow Mick to dictate your life."

"I've never thought about it," she lied, realizing that Mick and Aiden's exchange had been about her.

"Oh, yes, you have, Darcy. You don't so much as put one foot in front of the other without having a reason for it. So, answer me: Why do you let Mick control you?"

"He doesn't control me," she responded breezily, hoping he'd believe her nonchalance. "I control me. Now, about Jack and—"

"Like hell," he said, leaning down until his flinty eyes were level with hers. His voice was the same lethal whisper it had been last night. "If you want to believe that, you go right ahead, Darcy. But you ought to know that your insistence that black's white makes you look damn stupid."

She backed up, her heart racing, angry with him. And herself. And the world for being what it was. "All right, dammit. You want to know, Aiden, I'll tell you. It's a simple enough reality. If you don't bend to Mick, he breaks you. He owns Charlestown. No one works here that Mick doesn't have a percentage of it. I have to survive, and if that means letting Mick order me about from time to time, then I accept it. I don't do it often, and I sure as hell don't do it meekly. But when there's no way out, I'm smart enough to know the value of making a strategic surrender. I don't like it, but I do it. Is that a sufficient answer for you?"

His eyes narrowed. "When you went to see Mick . . . did he threaten to break you if you didn't hold to the bargain to help me find Jules?"

"Let it suffice to say that the alternatives he offered were less attractive than being with you. The choice was mine and I made it. I'll make the best of it. Now, I'm through discussing my relationship with Mick. I'm hungry and I'm going to find something to eat. You can come along or not. It makes no difference to me." She whirled about and marched away.

Aiden caught her arm and hauled her back. "Why do you think Mick put us together? And don't give me any claptrap about you being the best person for the task. We both know it's more than that."

"You're right, but I don't know." She wrenched her arm from his grasp and faced him with her hands on her hips. "I *do* know that something Mick said to you back there stoked your stove. What was it?"

"He felt compelled to warn me again about taking liberties with you."

"Well, if it helps any, you should know I haven't said anything to him or anyone else. And don't ask me why I haven't, because I don't know that, either." He blinked in surprise and she knew that he'd assumed she had. The bastard.

"Maybe because you're not too terribly opposed to it?"

Darcy lifted her chin. "I wouldn't go so far as to say that, but it's been endurable. I don't have any lasting scars to show for it."

You will. Aiden inwardly winced, and in that instant his sense of nobility made a rare assertion. He shouldn't touch Darcy O'Keefe again. It was the only and most honorable thing to do. Darcy's life was tenuous enough already without him complicating it. Aiden didn't like the idea of denying himself something he wanted and deliberately set the issue aside, halfheartedly promising himself that he'd mull the idea over some other time. "Let's find Jack and get something to eat."

She nodded, the fire in her eyes replaced by a wariness. He preferred the brilliance of the fire, but knew caution served her better.

They navigated the streets, moving toward Jack's usual circuit, neither one of them saying a word. Only as they rounded a corner and saw him ahead did Darcy break the silence. "I'll show Jack the picture of Jules. Maybe we'll have some luck come our way and Jack will have just sold one of his pies to him."

"Which was the primary reason for making the suggestion in the first place," Aiden observed. *Nothing done without a reason.*

Darcy shrugged. "It's always better to kill two birds rather than one."

Aiden frowned as a shiver crawled down his spine. He fingered the folded notes in his pocket and decided he didn't have any choice but to show them to Darcy.

THEY'D SPENT ANOTHER fruitless day showing Jules's picture to every passerby: To tradesmen and washerwomen, sailors and dockworkers, to children playing in the street, even to a blind man before they'd realized he was blind. Aiden had watched and listened in amazement as Darcy had slipped from one language to the next, easily questioning every soul in his or her native tongue. She'd been doggedly persistent, and so readily adaptable that he'd often found himself more interested in her approach to the inquiries than in the inquires themselves.

The effort she'd expended had taken its toll. Darcy had looked exhausted that morning, and now even the moonlight couldn't hide the dark circles beneath her eyes. Aiden laid his hand on her shoulder when she paused before the doors to McDonough's Dry Goods Store. "Are you sure you want to do this alone, Darcy? I'd be glad to go in with you."

She nodded and sighed with resignation. "I won't be long. Just wait for me, and then we'll go see if George Fogarty is the one who signed that tally sheet Jules used for his note."

"Take what time you need to, Darcy," he called softly as she slipped between the doors. "If Fogarty's is like most gambling dens, they won't get into full raucous for another two-three hours."

She nodded again, but he could see that her thoughts were on the coming ordeal upstairs. Lord knew it would be difficult enough to offer Selia's family words of comfort, but to offer them knowing their daughter had died because you hadn't intervened in time . . . It was a burden Aiden had borne for eighteen months, and he wished he could have spared Darcy from it.

He stuffed his hands in his trousers pockets and ambled

down the street, wishing Darcy hadn't smiled so damn bravely when she'd read the note from Jules. He'd prefer her scared. It would keep her alive longer. A movement in the shadows against a building caught his attention and Aiden looked up, instantly wary. A man stepped forward and smiled.

"Chandler?"

"Good evening, sir."

"Might I ask what you're doing here?"

"It would appear to be the same thing you are doing, sir. Waiting."

Aiden glanced back to McDonough's, then to his valet. "Maisey, I presume?"

"If I might be permitted to say so," Chandler replied, "I am capable of interests beyond attending to your wardrobe and what passes for your domestic life."

"And Maisey interests you, huh?" Grinning at the novelty of Chandler playing court, Aiden dropped down onto cold wooden steps and motioned for the other to join him. "Have a seat."

"It's not acceptable, sir."

Aiden leaned back on his elbows and stretched his legs out. "Oh, sit down, Nathan. I'm damn sick of this *sir* business, and for the life of me I can't remember why it once seemed like a good idea to let you be my manservant."

"It was because my father was your father's manservant. Tradition mandated our adult relationship."

Aiden considered his employee, remembering. "I preferred the relationship we had as boys."

Chandler smiled ruefully. "We are no longer boys, and I no longer need you to defend me from bullies."

"Won't you please sit down, Nathan?"

"Well, when put that way . . ." Chandler said. He eased himself down on the steps beside Aiden, adding, "I must say that it's been quite some time since I've seen this side of you. I had thought it lost."

"I'm finding myself a bit turned around these days," Aiden admitted.

"And do I have Miss O'Keefe to thank for it?"

"Probably." Aiden considered the toe of his boot. "I don't want to see her hurt, Nathan."

"I would suggest, Aiden, that you could say the same of every soul in the world. Might you have some special feelings for Miss O'Keefe? Feelings that go a bit beyond a recognition of her eccentricities?"

Good God, how many years had it been since Nathan had called him by his given name? It felt good. Aiden smiled broadly. "Of course I have feelings for Darcy, but I've been thinking that I should resist my baser impulses. Darcy's life is complicated enough as it is."

"My, you are turned around, aren't you?" Nathan teased. "I can't remember the last time you exercised your conscience where a woman was concerned. Be careful or you'll sprain it."

Aiden chuckled and laced his fingers behind his head. "Damn, Nathan. I somehow thought you'd leap to your feet and congratulate me for finally being honorable. That maybe you might even go so far as to offer me some encouragement to consider adopting it as a permanent way of life."

"Speaking as your boyhood friend and not as your employee?"

"Go ahead. That's how I'm looking at this entire conversation."

Nathan took a deep breath, then said, "Under normal circumstances I would applaud your decision to deny yourself carnal knowledge of Miss O'Keefe. But I think your fascination with her extends beyond the physical, and that you've decided to be noble so that you can pretend it doesn't."

"That was as clear as mud."

"A frustrated man doesn't see past what it is that frustrates him. If you're consumed with denying yourself the pleasure of her company in your bed, then it lessens the chance that you'll have to admit that she interests you in other ways."

Aiden looked up at the stars. "I don't have any difficulty admitting that I find Darcy an interesting person. She's a talented artist, and she has a remarkably agile mind. And I can't tell you how often I've been told she's the best pickpocket in Charlestown."

"I enjoy the sound of Miss Maisey's laughter. When she looks at me, I feel ten feet tall. And when she puts her hand in mine, I feel as though I could conquer all the world."

Aiden fixed his attention on his friend, seeing him in a wholly new light. "Christ, Nathan. You sound like a lovesick pup."

"Actually, I've never felt better in my life. How do you feel?"

"Battered and weary," he answered wryly. "But I suspect I'll survive."

"Perhaps you need to reconsider your approach to life, Aiden."

Aiden's spirit plummeted. "I won't have a life to call my own again until Jules is dead," he said gruffly. "I'll search my soul for another way when that's done. It would be a waste of effort to do it now."

"With all due respect, Aiden, you didn't have a meaningful existence *before* Jules murdered your father. You've never had one. Pursuing Jules is just another way you've discovered to avoid swallowing the bitter pill."

Nathan had always had a knack for seeing through to the heart of matters. His perceptive acuity was exceeded only by his ability to cut to the quick. Aiden had never liked being on the receiving end of it. "Maybe you should go back to being my manservant now."

"I have more to say about Miss O'Keefe."

"Save it for another time."

"Very well, sir." Nathan started to rise.

The prospect of losing his oldest friend behind the mask of formality bothered Aiden. He caught Nathan's sleeve, pulled him back down on the steps, saying, "No. On second thought, say it now so I don't have to face another one of these conversations."

"I had intended to couch my observations more subtly, but I sense your patience is wearing thin, so I'll simply say it and beg you not to break my nose. If Miss O'Keefe is willing to become your lover, Aiden, I'd suggest you surrender your false nobility. I think that with Darcy you stand a decent chance of discovering what love is supposed to be."

Aiden laughed outright. "Jesus, Nathan," he declared. "As though I'd recognize love if it bit me on the arse."

"My point exactly."

"And I should just blithely dismiss any consequences my exploration might have on Darcy's life?" Aiden laughingly scoffed. "Rather a callous and selfish approach, don't you think?"

"There are times, Aiden, when I wonder if you deliberately refuse to see the point I'm trying to make. Darcy is not at all like Wilhelmina. Darcy would not deal with the consequences as Wilhelmina did."

Aiden's stomach knotted and his blood raged hot. It always did when he remembered that last night with Wilhelmina. "Darcy isn't going to get the chance to prove herself," he pronounced bitingly. "It will be a cold goddamned day in hell before I give another woman the rope I inadvertently gave Willy."

"So you're going to let the experience with Wilhelmina determine all of your tomorrows?"

"I'm not going down that road again."

Nathan glanced past Aiden and then rose to his feet as he said, "I see Miss Maisey has finished paying her respects and is ready to be escorted home. If you'll excuse me, sir?"

"By all means," Aiden granted with a wave of his hand and a forced smile. "Don't forget to duck when you go through doorways."

Love? Aiden snorted. He didn't have the foggiest notion what it felt like, and he sure as hell had never seen anything in reality that came close to the poetic expressions of the balladeers. As far as he could tell, the grandest passion was nothing more than the grandest of fairy tales. His experience had taught him that love amounted to a transaction in which the male party promised artful seduction, the female party promised breathless surrender, and both of them promised to make no demands on the other once they climbed from the bed. It was best that way.

And Nathan thought Darcy O'Keefe could show him what love was supposed to be? God, if Nathan believed that, then the man had to be even more inexperienced in carnal matters than Darcy was. Darcy couldn't teach anyone a damn thing. She was a complete novice. A novice who didn't want her horizons expanded.

Aiden felt the prickle of his conscience. Darcy had been a willing student when he'd taken the time to ease her into the newness of sensation and experience. She'd resisted and fled only when he'd pushed too hard and too fast—when he'd forgotten her feelings and thought only of his own.

His feelings. Aiden clenched his teeth and ruthlessly closed away the roiling memories. He'd learned a valuable lesson from Wilhelmina. He'd walked out the door vowing never to feel another damn thing for a woman besides a dispassionately tempered lust. It was the only sensible approach. Women were fickle at best, ruthlessly self-centered at worst. If he did end up taking Darcy to his bed, he sure as hell wasn't going to lose his self-control in the experience.

Darcy came out of the dry goods store a moment later. No, Darcy wasn't like Wilhelmina, he had to admit. At least what he knew of her so far. But, a cautious inner voice suggested, it would be best if he didn't delve any deeper. The odds were he'd only find another harsh disappointment. She saw him on the steps and waved and smiled. He watched her come toward him, noting that her step was somewhat lighter than when she'd gone in. Aiden set aside his dark musings and met her in the middle of the street.

"Was it—" He faltered, not wanting to make her relive the experience if it had been as horrible as he suspected.

"I wouldn't want to do it again, but no one pointed a finger at me and accused me of her death."

The quiet strength in her voice was so at odds with the weariness in her face . . . Aiden wanted to draw her into his arms and hold her close. Just hold her.

"I'm sorry I took so long," she said, "I had to offer up a rosary to shorten the stay of Selia's soul in purgatory. Maureen insisted, and I couldn't very well refuse. I escaped as soon as I was done and no one was looking."

It had been a very long time since he'd considered heaven, hell, and the option in between. Since his destination had been decided at birth, the particulars of earning one's way hadn't been of much interest to him. "Why is Selia's soul in purgatory? Popping in on half-dressed men in fitting rooms doesn't strike me as being such a terrible sin."

"Well," Darcy drawled, arching a brow, "it seems that popping in on half-dressed men was only the beginning of it, and that she died with a considerable number of unconfessed, rather significant sins. Father O'Hagen has been hearing a stream of confessions from men who don't want to go to their Maker with Selia as a blot on their record. He's of the opinion that she has a lot of suffering to do to atone for her earthly pleasures."

"It seems to me that she suffered enough in dying."

Darcy nodded solemnly. "That's the way you and I see it, but not the way the others do. For the next few years, Selia is going to be the example that holds all good girls to the righteous path."

Suddenly he understood so much about Darcy that he hadn't before; the will it took for her to stand on her own, the strength needed to smile and quietly endure the awesome pressure to conform to everyone else's idea of what she should be. It saddened him to think that she had to face the struggle at all. "There isn't much forgiveness in your world, is there, Darcy? No allowance given for being human."

"I've never let it bother me." She grinned impishly, easing his sadness. "Father O'Hagen told me when I was eight years old that my soul was weak to temptation, my faith was non-existent, and that I was doomed to be among the lost. Then, when I was nine, Joseph Kavanaugh and I got caught with the sacramental wine, and Father O'Hagen pronounced us the blackest sheep in God's holy flock. He forbade us Communion until we did penance and renounced our sinful ways."

Aiden chuckled. "How long did Joseph hold out?"

"He lasted a full week, then gave himself up and became an altar boy."

"But you never gave in."

Her eyes sparkled. "And Darcy O'Keefe will remain unrepentant to the end. How about you, Aiden? Would the priest fear for the roof if you walked into church?"

"He should. The truth is I had an appalling lack of enthusiasm for my spiritual education. I can recall thinking of the Ten Commandments as a personal challenge. And the only scripture I remember is: 'God helps those who help themselves.'"

"My favorite is 'Ask and ye shall be given.'" She reached inside her coat and pulled out her woolen cap. Putting it on her head and tucking her curls up inside it, she grinned and said, "Let's go ask George Fogarty what he knows about Jules."

CHAPTER 13

DARCY HAD NEVER been in Fogarty's before; her wages were too hard won to risk on a throw of the dice or the turn of a card. But danger was danger, and she'd sensed it the minute they'd come into the place. If Aiden had, he'd given no indication of it. Darcy inched further back into the shadowed edge of the common room. Aiden sat at a table with a cigar-chewing Fogarty and three other men. Their words didn't reach her ears, but she didn't need to know what they were talking about. It was what they were thinking that mattered. And if she read their faces, their gestures, and their quick glances correctly, they were setting themselves to empty Aiden's pockets.

Darcy quietly expelled a long breath and searched the smoky shadows, looking for a way out of the gaming den other than the front door. A tattered blanket had been nailed to the rear wall and while she couldn't actually see the door frame, she thought it reasonable to conclude there was an exit hidden behind it. Every place like this had to have an escape hole. The denizens who frequented it would be reluctant to come in if the only way out was past the bill collector or constable.

Having done what she could to ease one concern, Darcy turned her attention back to the others niggling her. There were ten other patrons on this night, all of them grizzled and drunk and looking decidedly predatory. She'd heard the whispered jabber as she and Aiden had crossed the room to the back, and knew that the gamblers had marked Aiden as a potential victim. At the moment, the debate seemed to center around whether the contents of his pockets were worth the risk inherent in taking on a man of his size. As she surreptitiously watched, one man rose from his table and slipped into a seat at another. Gazes darted toward Aiden's back and then to her. The words *molley man* were uttered. As the man who had moved between tables talked, the other men nodded and began to gather up their cards and coins.

Darcy inwardly groaned, knowing that she and Aiden would be lucky to escape with their skins intact. Aiden wouldn't take kindly to being robbed of his money, but it would be nothing compared to what would happen if he learned they thought he was a sodomite.

Darcy slipped her fingers beneath the cuff of her left sleeve, deriving only small comfort in knowing that she had the knife if things turned as ugly as she feared they would. Sensing the need to leave before the fools had a chance to execute whatever flimsy plan they were concocting, she edged forward to stand silently at Aiden's side.

"Is there a problem, O'Keefe?" he asked without looking at her.

"Not yet," she answered quietly. "Do you have what you came for?"

"Enough to satisfy me," he said, rising slowly to his feet. He picked up the picture of Jules from the table and put it into the breast pocket of his coat. When he removed his hand, it contained several folded bills. These he tossed onto the table at the point where Jules's picture had lain. His gaze skimmed around the table, touching each man. "Thank you, gentlemen. I'll bid you a pleasant evening."

The sudden scraping of wood against wood brought Darcy's attention fully to the tables at Aiden's back. Five men sauntered out the front door. The remaining five rose to their feet and ambled toward the blanket on the wall. Fogarty chuckled and leaned back in his chair, folding his hands over his considerable girth. Darcy quietly swore.

"Your choice of exits, O'Keefe," Aiden said evenly. "Which way do you want to go?"

"The front," she said, backing in that direction. "We'll have more room to maneuver on the street."

Aiden watched her, marveling at her cool reserve and deliberate approach to their situation. But would she be able to maintain it amidst a flurry of fists? he wondered. Would she be able to escape a brawl unscathed? If Darcy hadn't been with him he wouldn't have bothered to seek a peaceable way out of the situation, but he owed her his protection in the same measure she had given him hers since they'd entered this place. Aiden smiled thinly at Fogarty. "I'll be sure to mention your hospitality to Mick O'Shaunessy."

The tip of the cigar snapped upward, the quick motion flicking a circle of ash into the gambler's lap. The man made no move to brush it away, his attention fixed solely on Aiden. "You didn't say you were a friend of Mick's."

Aiden heard the telltale catch in the other man's voice and inwardly smiled. "I didn't see the necessity of it, and you didn't ask for references. My money seemed to be all you were interested in. Life is certainly full of surprises, isn't it, Fogarty? I'll give Mick your regards."

Fogarty considered him for a long moment and then his gaze slid to one of the men at the table. "Joseph," he said, jerking his head toward the front door of the establishment.

Joseph rose and sauntered in the direction commanded, casting Aiden a dour look as he passed. Aiden, trusting Darcy to warn him if one of the others attempted to attack him from the back, turned and followed Fogarty's henchman across the room.

A genuine smile lifted the corners of Aiden's mouth as he saw Darcy waiting by the door, her right hand tucked inside her left sleeve. As he'd expected, she watched the others behind him. Joseph deliberately knocked her shoulder as he passed her, but even as she found her balance again, she didn't waver from her self-appointed task. How odd it was,

Aiden mused, to have a woman protect him. It was even odder to find that he believed her capable of it, and that he was grateful for it.

"We'll let Joseph have a moment for a word with his friends," he said when he reached Darcy's side.

"And what if his friends are too drunk to listen to reason?" she asked quietly. "There are five of them—if you add Joseph, six—and only two of us."

"We do have sobriety in our favor."

"All that means is we're going to feel the fists and they won't."

It struck Aiden that it was a curious thing for a woman to know. But, he quickly reminded himself, Darcy O'Keefe wasn't like any other woman. "If it comes to it, keep your back to mine, Darcy. Don't let them separate us." He glanced between Fogarty and the door, then said, "Joseph's had all the time he needs. Are you ready?"

She nodded and pulled the knife from her sleeve. "I'll back out after you to be sure the rest don't come at us when our backs are turned. I'll be right behind you."

Her intensity stirred something deep within him and his chest tightened in response. "Why do I have this sudden urge to kiss you, Darce?"

"Well, for God's sake, don't!" she whispered heatedly. "They already think—" Her eyes widened, and then she breathed a curse as she yanked the hat from her head. Her hair tumbling over her shoulders, she shoved the hat inside her jacket and mumbled, "Sometimes I have mush for brains."

Aiden had only a scant second to puzzle her actions and words. From behind him came a low murmur. Aiden cast a quick look over his shoulder. Something had apparently caused a dilemma for the men at the table. Those blocking the rear door seemed equally disconcerted. He didn't understand, beyond the fact that their sudden quandary gave him and Darcy an unexpected opportunity. He grabbed her by the arm and pushed open the door, dragging her with him into the cold night air.

The six men stood in a knot on the walkway in front of the gaming house. They turned as one and began to form a half circle. Then they froze, their gazes darting between Darcy and him. Aiden stopped, facing them as he tried to move Darcy behind him. She planted her feet, and rather than struggle with her in front of their attackers, he let her stay at his side.

Aiden watched the men shift uneasily, watched them glance wordlessly at each other, and waited, sensing that the fight was draining out of them by the second. He had no idea why, but he wasn't about to challenge them when waiting might well produce a safe passage. There wasn't the slightest doubt in his mind that he could take care of himself, but Darcy's presence made matters a bit more complicated and too uncertain for his comfort.

"It's a beautiful night, isn't it?" Darcy asked lightly, breaking the taut silence. She lifted the knife and angled it so that the blade glinted in the moonlight. "Who's for a flimping with Terrell and me?"

The men shuffled their feet and looked among themselves. No one answered. Four of them flung angry glares at the man who had apparently devised their original plan. Joseph cast a longing look toward the door of Fogarty's.

Darcy chuckled. "Oh, I see," she said, sounding quite compassionate. "Matters have changed a bit, haven't they? You thought you were waylaying a boy and a molley man. Since that's obviously not the case, we'd understand if you'd like a moment to discuss amongst yourselves this unexpected change in the situation, wouldn't we, Terrell?"

Aiden seethed and fisted his hands, not quite believing that he'd been accused—even indirectly and erroneously—of such unnatural tastes.

"No offense intended," one of their assailants offered meekly. "What else was we to think?"

Aiden stepped toward him, wanting nothing more than to take the man's head from his shoulders. The man squeaked and scrambled away. His flight triggered the survival instincts of the others and they, too, darted for the nearest shadows.

Darcy laughed and slipped her arm around Aiden's as she called after the fleeing men, "Cowards!"

"A molley man," Aiden growled quietly. "A goddamned molley man."

"Well, what else were they to think?" Darcy teased, smiling up at him.

Aiden's thoughts tumbled chaotically one over the other, all of them pushing him in a single direction. He pulled Darcy hard against him and crushed her lips with his. He dimly heard her knife clatter against the walkway at their feet. In the next instant her arms came up around his neck and her lips parted in invitation. Aiden tasted her as he wanted, the possession wondrous and heady. Then, with a groan of deep regret, he resolutely set her away from him.

"That should have corrected any lingering doubts they might have had," she offered, tugging her jacket back into place and managing a tremulous smile.

It had been one of the jumbled thoughts that had led him to act on impulse. But it hadn't been the one to weigh most heavily. "I didn't kiss you for their benefit," he retorted, bending down to scoop up Darcy's knife. He handed it back to her, adding, "They can think whatever they like."

"So if not for them, why?"

"I don't know," he lied. "I suppose that if you must have some sort of explanation, you can consider it an expression of my appreciation for your willingness to stand by me."

"You could have just said so. Or shaken my hand. Or clapped me on the shoulder."

"I'll remember that next time."

She looked up at him and smiled again. And again the moonlight caressed her face as mischief brightened her eyes. His arms ached to hold her again. He turned away, determined to resist the impulse this time. He wanted much more than kisses from Darcy O'Keefe, and there was no point in torturing himself with beginning something he couldn't in good conscience finish. He jerked his head in silent command as he started down the walkway. Darcy quickly came to his side, her long legs matching his stride. He edged away from her, from the temptation to take her hand in his as they made their way toward the Lion and Fiddle.

"You were right, Darcy," he offered, hoping conversation would distract his mind from the pain of self-denial.

"A first," she countered with a chuckle. "May I ask what it is that I'm right about?"

"Jules won a large stake two nights ago. They haven't seen him since. We'll go up to Boston in the morning. We'll get rooms and—"

"Boston's a world you can navigate on your own, Aiden," she interjected quietly. "You don't need me."

He snorted. "Nonsense."

"I'm quite serious, Aiden. I'm not going with you. My task is done."

He caught her by the upper arm, pulling her to a stop. "Your task is to help me find Jules," he reminded her with far more calm than he felt. "We're closer, yes, but we don't have him yet."

She shook her head slowly. "There's no point in arguing about this. I'm not going and you can't drag me. Let's not part on angry words, Aiden."

He heard the sadness in her voice and knew she didn't, in her heart, want to be left behind. The realization warmed him. "Why, Darcy?"

She gave him a rueful smile. "Considering the animosity with which we began our . . . association, I'd say we've taken great strides toward civility and acceptance. I'd rather like to walk away with that sense of accomplishment intact."

"That's not what I'm asking. Why are you saying you don't want to go?"

"If Jules follows true to form, he'll find his way into gentlemen's clubs and the upper reaches of Boston society."

"And?" Aiden asked, folding his arms across his chest and widening his stance.

"Aiden, I know Charlestown. The streets, the alleys, the

pubs, the people. Boston might as well be London or Paris for all I know of it. I'm not going to be of any use to you there."

"You know what Jules looks like. You're another set of eyes for me."

She sighed. "I can't go there with you, Aiden. At best, I'd be useless. At worst, a hindrance."

"Why can't you *go there?*" he pressed, not seeing the line of her reasoning.

Her chin came up. "I'm not lace-curtain, Aiden. If I'm in tow, they'll bar you from the places Jules is likely to be."

Understanding dawned. It was hard to imagine Darcy daunted by any circumstance. She had been prepared to fight her way out of Fogarty's, but she paled before the thought of navigating Boston's social circles. Aiden suppressed a chuckle. Lifting her chin with his thumb, he brought her gaze to his and said, "I'm not particularly experienced in drawing the fine distinctions between lace-curtain and shanty, Darcy, but, by God, I know a woman of quality when I see one. With the right wardrobe, you can hold your own against any female in any drawing room in Boston."

"Thank you for your faith, Aiden, but—"

He put his fingertips over her lips and said gently, "No buts, Darcy. If I have to go to Mick and ask him to bend you again, I will. I need you with me, and you're going to be there."

She stepped beyond his touch, her eyes flashing. "You *don't* need me. And I don't appreciate your quick willingness to use heavy-handed tactics to bring me around to granting your whims."

"Then don't force me to do it, Darcy."

She glared at him for a long second and then abruptly spun on her heel. Aiden caught her again and pulled her back, saying, "And just where is that you think you're going?"

"Home."

She tried to wrench herself free but he refused to give her the opportunity to run. "No. I'll give you a choice of three destinations. To the Lion and Fiddle, the Presidential, or Mick's. Choose."

Darcy suspected she had no real choice. She could plead and bluster until she turned blue, but the odds were Mick wouldn't release her from the task until Jules was caught. He wouldn't be any more sympathetic to her concerns about going over to Boston than Aiden was. Men didn't understand the subtleties of social snobbery. They didn't feel the cuts in the same way women did.

"The Lion an' Fiddle," she answered curtly pulling herself free from Aiden's grip. Determined to salvage what dignity she could in the situation, she pulled her jacket back into place and added, "But I'm going to go see Bridie first. I've never been away from my mother for this long, and I have a responsibility to see if she needs anything before I'm dragged over to Boston."

Aiden cocked a brow. "Then let us go see to your mother's needs."

"You don't have to go with me. I'm perfectly capable of attending to them on my own."

"And Jules is perfectly capable of killing you on his own," Aiden countered evenly. "You don't go anywhere without me, Darcy. Accept protection with the same grace you give it."

It pained her to admit that Aiden's protection might be necessary and his insistence on it a sign of his wisdom. But she wasn't going to give him the satisfaction of hearing her admit it. Darcy shrugged and said, "Do as you please."

A smile slowly spread across his face. "I'd suggest, Darcy, that you might not want to grant me quite that much latitude. Especially where you're concerned. It would please me a great deal to do much with you."

His words swept over her like a seductive caress and her heart thrummed in response. Appalled by her reaction, Darcy retorted, "Well, it wouldn't please me."

"Would you care to bet on it?"

The sparkle in his dark eyes was breathtaking, the certainty in his voice unnerving. She chose to evade the issue rather than find herself drawn into a contest she suspected she might well lose. She glared at him and stomped off.

Aiden followed after her, letting her have the distance she needed at the moment. He'd seen the twin sparks of curiosity and desire in her eyes. He'd also seen the wariness that had come in their wake. There wasn't a doubt in his mind that if he gently pressed her, the wariness would be set aside and the passion given free rein. Caution reminded him that his own passion would have to be curtailed to a certain safe degree. Memory countered by serving up Nathan Chandler's pointed advice. Aiden considered all of it again, and then the woman marching ahead of him. His mind filled with images of her hair falling over naked satin shoulders, the taste of her lips, the feel of her skin. He imagined her long legs wrapped about him and her hands holding him to her.

Aiden expelled a long breath. Cool rationality was one thing; desire was altogether another. Darcy O'Keefe had a way of stirring the two into a swirling torrent that left him powerless. He didn't like not knowing what he would do, wasn't comfortable with living in the moment and accepting whatever life cared to give. Experience had taught him that it seldom gave anything but difficulty and regret. What little pleasure there was to be meted out was always fleeting and came with a price. He'd never had a particular problem with balancing the scales in making his decisions. The pitfalls of the pleasures he'd sought or accepted had always been apparent well before he'd acted, and he'd gone forward with clear vision and a plan for dealing with the consequences. Only once had he seriously misjudged. . . . The lesson was all he cared to keep in mind.

He narrowed his thoughts to Darcy. He couldn't see what lay ahead with her. He could easily envision himself surrendering to desire and taking her to his bed, but beyond that moment in time there was nothing but a grayness that gnawed at his insides and clenched his chest.

Irritated by his inability to impose order and clarity on his course, Aiden resolutely set the entire matter aside. Of one thing he was absolutely certain: he had spent entirely too much time following Darcy around Charlestown. And while the view of her trouser-clad backside was certainly a wondrous sight to behold, he'd seen quite enough of it dressed. The next time she thought to let him marvel at it, it had damn well better be naked.

Aiden lengthened his stride and caught up with her a half block from the door of the building in which her mother lived. She glanced over at him, but he couldn't read the expression in her eyes. He said nothing. Neither did she. And the silence quivered between them as they entered the apartment house and stealthily climbed the stairs to the second floor.

Darcy froze at the top, her gaze trapped by the large cardboard carton leaning against her mother's closed door. Dread formed a heavy knot in the pit of her stomach, and she gasped for breath as her blood went cold. Aiden paused beside her, but only long enough to see the package for himself. He squeezed her shoulder as he slipped passed her, saying, "Stay here, Darcy."

She ignored him—and her fear and her hammering heartbeat—and followed him down the hallway on leaden feet. She was only halfway to him when she saw him pluck the note from beneath the string binding the package, saw him open it, and heard him swear softly.

The string fell away with a quick pull as she inched closer. Aiden lifted the lid from the box, and the coppery scent of blood slammed into her gut. Instinct screamed for her to close her eyes and turn around. She obeyed, but too late. Aiden's coat was in the box. The one he'd given Timmy. And with it, Timmy's eyes.

Darcy gagged and doubled over, clutching her arms across her midriff. Timmy. Jules had killed Timmy. Tears streamed down her cheeks and her knees buckled beneath her. The world spun and her stomach lurched again. She couldn't control any of it, and she sobbed as the contents of her stomach heaved upward.

"Darcy."

She felt Aiden's arms come around her shoulders and she surrendered to the sureness and strength of his touch. She let him turn her and gather her against his chest. "Don't you dare tell me it will be all right," she quietly sobbed, pounding his shoulder with weak blows.

"I won't," he said, gently stroking her hair. "I'm not sure that it will. But you've got to find your feet, Darcy. We have to deal with this and quickly."

Darcy nodded numbly; her only thought was that Aiden was right. "There are r-rags in the c-cellar," she stammered. "I'll get t-them and c-clean up the m-mess I made."

"Good girl," he responded, easing her to her feet. "I'll take care of matters here." He hugged her close and then set her away. With his thumb he lifted her chin until she looked up to meet his gaze. "Are you all right, Darcy?" he whispered, his eyes soft and dark as they searched hers.

She swallowed and nodded as best she could.

"Be careful between here and the cellar and back. Scream loud and long if you need to. I'll hear you."

Darcy nodded again, her blood cold at the prospect of meeting Jules. "I'll hurry," she managed to say around the lump in her throat.

Aiden kissed her on the forehead, and then took her by the shoulders and turned her toward the stairs with a quiet, "No heroics, Darcy."

If her insides hadn't been so tightly coiled, she would have laughed at the idea she could manage anything close to bravery. It took all she had within her just to breathe while putting one foot in front of the other. She paused at the top of the stairs and looked back. Aiden stood at her mother's door, the package held against his side with one hand, his other hand slightly fisted, his knuckles resting on the door. He held her gaze gravely until the door inched open. He turned, spoke through the crack, and then looked back at Darcy in silent question.

She nodded and raced down the stairs, frantically determined to return to the safety of Aiden as quickly as she could.

Aiden stepped across the threshold and stayed Bridie's hand when she went to close the door behind him. "Leave it ajar," he whispered into the darkness of the unlit apartment. "I want nothing to stand in my way if I need to go to Darcy."

"What's happened?" Bridie asked, drawing her wrapper close about her slender body.

The decision was instant and easy. Bridie had no need to know. "Have you embers in the stove?" he asked.

"Yes, a few. Are you hungry? I can fix something quickly if you are."

Aiden doubted he could keep anything down for the next fortnight. "No, but thank you, Bridie," he said, moving into the cooking area. He took a thick cloth from the shelf above the cast-iron stove and used it to shield his hand as he opened the coal box door. Bright red light glowed within. Aiden set the cloth aside and forced the box through the opening and onto the embers. It barely fit within, and it took considerable effort to close the door on it. When he'd completed the task, he opened the damper wide to quickly fuel the fire.

"Where's Darcy?" Bridie asked from behind him.

"She'll be here in a moment or two," he reassured her. "She's fine. We came to check on her mother before we go up to Boston tomorrow."

Bridie nodded. "Her mother has been more lucid than usual the last few days. She's still knitting socks, of course, but I think it's more to preserve her dignity than for any illusion she has of General Jackson's army needing them."

"Has she asked after Darcy? Is she worried at all over her absence?"

"She's not as worried as I'm sure Darcy is. Mrs. O'Keefe is finding a great deal of satisfaction in imagining what might come of Darcy's holiday with you."

Aiden knew just what the older woman hoped, and he found himself strangely saddened by knowing she would eventually be disappointed. "Does she have any suspicions about what Darcy and I are really doing?"

Bridie giggled quietly. "I've been surprised more than once by what activities she thinks you and Darcy may be sharing with one another. I never would have suspected her to be so accepting of—" Bridie's hand went to the neck of her wrapper. "My, the stove certainly has made it warm in here, hasn't it?"

Aiden nodded and moved away from the heat, knowing that Bridie's discomfort came more from the nature of her thoughts than anything else. To spare them both an awkward situation, he changed the subject. "When was the last time you had the door open today, Bridie?"

"Just after seven," she replied. "Rusty brought us a pie from my mother."

"Did you hear anyone pause outside the door after Rusty left?"

Bridie shook her head. "Why do you ask?" Her gaze fell to the stove.

"The package was left outside with a note asking that it be delivered into my hands," he supplied. "I won't discuss the contents of it, Bridie. You'll have to accept that my decision is for the best."

She nodded solemnly. "Do you know who left it?"

"Yes." Aiden considered the young woman for a long moment and then decided he had no other recourse but to be blunt. "Bridie, the fact that he brought the package here doesn't bode well. I think you and Mrs. O'Keefe are both in grave danger."

"I keep the door locked at all times," Bridie assured him.

"That's not good enough for me, Bridie," Aiden countered. "Preserving Darcy's story for her mother makes the logistics a bit more complicated than I'd like, but we'll manage. Would your parents be willing to take Mrs. O'Keefe into their home until Darcy and I are done with our work?"

"Certainly," she assured him, her tone emphatic. "My mother and Mrs. O'Keefe have been friends for many years."

"Good. Darcy has mentioned a Mrs. Malone who lives down the hall. Is she at home tonight?"

Bridie blinked and frowned, clearly puzzled by the new direction of his questioning. "She rarely goes out. I'm sure she is."

"Then I want you to go knock at her door and ask if you and Mrs. O'Keefe may spend a few hours with her. Just long enough for me to find your father and have him send several brawny men to escort you and Mrs. O'Keefe to his home."

Bridie waved her hand dismissively. "I appreciate your concern, Mr. Terrell, but I don't think it's at all worth the inconveniencing of Mrs. Malone at this hour of the night. Can't it wait until the morning? And surely Mrs. O'Keefe and I can manage to get ourselves a few city blocks without incident."

"With all due respect, Bridie," Aiden said firmly, "you'll do as I say without argument or question. You have no inkling of how angry your father would be if you resisted me on this. Now go awaken Mrs. Malone. Apologize profusely and then come back here for Mrs. O'Keefe. Darcy and I will wait in the shadows to see you bolted behind Mrs. Malone's door, and then we'll go to your father."

Darcy would have fought him, but Bridie simply nodded and slipped silently into the hallway. From the doorway Aiden watched her approach another door along the hallway and knock. His attention shifted when Darcy bounded to the top of the stairs and stopped to grab a shaky breath. Aiden went to take the rag from her.

MARY O'KEEFE STUDIED her apartment through the keyhole of her bedroom door. The words had been muffled by the wooden panel itself but she'd watched intently, trying to make sense of the events in the darkened room. Mr. Terrell had come in and put something in the stove's coal box. He and Bridie had exchanged a few words, Mr. Terrell doing most of the talking and Bridie doing the nodding. Then Bridie had slipped out, and Mr. Terrell had done the same a few moments later. It was all very odd.

She was about to straighten and give up her spying when Darcy silently came into the apartment. Mary O'Keefe shifted the nightgown under her knees and watched her daughter look around. Mary smiled. Darcy thought she didn't know about her boyish clothes, that she didn't know about what she did for Mick O'Shaunessy and the food on their table. Letting Darcy have her illusions had been the only thing she could do for her brave and beautiful daughter once their courses had been sealed. If only her mind worked clearly all the time, Mary silently lamented. If only she could know when clarity would come and for how long it would stay. The moments were so brief, and had come much too late to keep Darcy from the path she had had to follow. The unpredictable wandering of her awareness had made such a sad fiction of their lives.

Mary had also known the holiday was just as much an invention as the Sinclair family, but the knowledge that Darcy was out and about Charlestown with Aiden Terrell had been an answer to a long-whispered prayer. Bridie had told her much. Mick had apparently seen the potential for a match between them, and seen that they had no choice but to be together. To Mary's way of thinking, God's benevolent intervention in their lives was plain, and she had let Darcy go with hope and a silent blessing.

When Darcy's gaze settled on the doorway from which she watched, Mary understood her daughter's intent. She used the doorknob to pull herself to her feet and then quickly regained her bed, pulling the sheets up beneath her chin and willing her breathing to slow. It wouldn't do for Darcy to know that she had been watching, that she knew Darcy's secrets.

The door opened quietly, and Darcy crossed to the side of the bed. Mary kept her eyes closed and her breathing deep and even, as her daughter bent down and pressed a kiss to her cheek. "I'll be home soon, Mother," she whispered, straightening. "I love you."

Memory washed over Mary O'Keefe. *I'll be home soon. I love you.* Those had been the last words her beloved John had spoken to her. He had kissed her and left her that morning. And when he had returned that evening, he had been waxen and forever still and silent, borne on a litter carried by Mick O'Shaunessy and Patrick Riordan. Her world had collapsed in that hour, and her only thought had been to join John as quickly as she could. Later, so much later, she'd realized that Darcy was too young to be left alone in the world. That obligation had been all that stayed her hand many times in the years since John had gone before her. But now . . .

Mary O'Keefe peeked through her lashes and, finding herself alone and the door once more closed, she pushed aside the covers and made her way back to the keyhole. Mr. Terrell and Darcy stood before the cookstove, both of them staring at the closed coal box door. Then Aiden Terrell reached out and slipped his arm around Darcy's shoulders. Mary O'Keefe's daughter stepped into the embrace and wrapped her arms around his waist, burying her face in his broad chest. Aiden kissed the top of her head and then nestled her beneath his chin.

The sight pleased Mary Reilly O'Keefe. She rose to her feet again and turned toward her bed. The rosary she'd had since First Communion lay on the table beside the bed, and she picked it up to press a reverent kiss to the crucifix. Then she knelt to offer her thanks.

Chapter 14

AIDEN HAD SHOWN her the note from Jules on their way to Mick's house. *I'll see* you *in Boston.* Short, sick, and numbing—so numbing, in fact, that she didn't have the wherewithal to protest when Aiden insisted they spend what few hours remained of the night at the Presidential. He said he didn't want them to be where Jules expected them. Or something along those lines. Somewhere in the midst of their conversation with Mick, she'd stopped paying attention to anything anyone said. Her brain heard the words, but it took so long for her to understand the meaning that it simply wasn't worth the effort.

Mick hadn't been pleased about being called out of his bed in the middle of the night. He'd been even less pleased by what Aiden had to tell him. Aiden had made his requests concerning Bridie and Darcy's mother, and Mick had rousted one of the servants to see that men were immediately dispatched to Mrs. Malone's. It was after the conclusion of the more pressing matters that Darcy had made an attempt to extract herself from the sojourn to Boston. All she'd accomplished was to get Maisey drawn into the affair with her. Mick would speak with Patrick Riordan at the first respectable hour that morning, and Maisey would be delivered to the Presidential to serve as Darcy's personal maid. Mick deemed it only proper that Darcy have a chaperone while in Boston.

Darcy thought it the most ridiculous concern, and she also had her doubts as to Maisey's suitability for the task. She was certain of it once they reached the Presidential and Aiden explained everything to his drowsy manservant. Nathan Chandler was clearly pleased that Maisey would be joining them, and retired to his bed humming a little ditty. Darcy sank down on the settee, wondering why she was the only person in this entire fiasco who seemed to border on physical and mental exhaustion.

Aiden sat in the chair opposite her with his long legs extended in front of him. He'd tossed his jacket over the back of the chair, his boots on the floor beside him, and had the collar of his shirt slightly loosened.

"Get comfortable, Darcy," he said. "It's almost dawn, and you'll have precious little time to sleep. You might want to make the most of it."

She nodded and rubbed her hands over her face. She didn't have the wherewithal to unbutton her jacket, much less take it off. Bending over to untie her boots had all the potential of happening as did her flight to the moon. Darcy looked at Aiden and said wearily, "Go to bed. I'll be fine right here."

He pulled himself from the chair and came to stand in before her. She looked up at him, her only coherent thought that of how handsome he was. It was while she was remembering the warmth and hardness of his chest that he reached down, took her hands in his, and drew her to her feet.

Too tired to protest, she could only watch as he unbuttoned her jacket and slipped it from her shoulders and arms. He tossed it on the back of the chair with his own and then opened the top three buttons on her shirt. He fingered the thin cotton fabric for a moment, his eyes narrowing. He didn't say anything, but instead took her shoulders in his hands and eased her back down onto the small sofa.

Darcy managed to cock a brow when he knelt at her feet and began to open the laces of her boots. Her mind drifted to wondering if Aiden was as good at undoing corset laces. It was a shame she seldom wore a corset, she mused. She'd never have the answer to her question. Not that she truly needed proof, she decided as Aiden slipped the boots off her feet. He had such gentle hands and quick fingers, he couldn't help but be very good at freeing ladies from their laces. She noticed he was frowning and she followed the line of his sight.

"They're the best pair I have," she explained, pulling her foot from his hand and her undarned sock from his vision. "They serve their purpose well enough."

"I'll buy you some new ones tomorrow."

"You will not."

"Darcy, I'm too tired to deal with your stubbornness at the moment. You need some decent socks so your feet aren't cold."

"And I'm too tired to deal with yours," she countered. "I'll not be beholden to you for a pair of socks."

He rose and went to an armoire in the corner of the room, returning a moment later with a decanter of brandy and two glasses. He sat down beside her on the settee, filled both glasses, then handed her one, saying, "Then fortify yourself, Darcy, because in the morning you and I are going to have one helluva fight."

"Over a pair of socks?" Darcy asked, sipping. The warmth trickling down her throat felt heavenly. She took another sip.

"I'm buying you a complete wardrobe. From the chemise out."

Darcy choked and managed to sputter a protest. "I don't need more than what I already have."

"You're going to Boston with me, and you need a suitable lady's wardrobe. Consider it a necessary cost of our task."

"I don't see a single reason why it's necessary. Why should I have to dress like a lady?" Her brain finally seemed to awaken and offered her an effective counter. "Besides, I have proper lady clothes in my trunk at the Lion and Fiddle."

Aiden was silent for a long moment. He took a deep drink from his glass, and then turned to face her squarely. "A simple truth, Darcy: Men are odd creatures. We'll say things to our mistresses and other men's mistresses that we would never so much as hint at to our wives, sisters, and mothers. Mistresses are a special class of women with special privileges. They're granted a far greater latitude in conduct than . . . well, so-called proper women. You have the sense to know how to use that to your advantage. To our advantage in finding Jules."

Aiden caught the glass as it slipped from her numb fingertips. As he put it back into her hand, she whispered, "You expect me to go to Boston as your mistress?"

"My artist mistress. You'll fascinate them on two counts."

"No." Darcy edged forward on the settee, determined to find the strength necessary to rise and run away.

"It's a simple matter of practicality, Darcy," he said, chuckling as he drew her back and against his side. "Sit still and hear me out."

She didn't have any other real choice. Her body suddenly had all the vigor of an overboiled potato. Darcy was acutely aware of how comfortably her curves wrapped around Aiden's planes, how warm and pleasant it was to be within the circle of his arm and pressed against his side. She took a sip of her brandy, hoping the warmth of the liquor would distract her from the other pleasures her body was experiencing.

"When Jules was in Dublin and Edinburgh," Aiden began, "he managed to worm his way into the outermost edges of privileged male society. Given time, he might have gained a greater degree of inclusion, but he didn't give himself that opportunity. Anyway, I'm wagering that he'll do the same here. All that I'm asking is that you play the part, Darcy. *Play* it. That's all. Hell, you don't know anyone in Boston. What harm is it going to do?"

A thought formed in the back of her mind, suggesting that something wasn't quite right about Aiden's planned approach to their hunt. Darcy frowned and tried to bring it into sharper focus, but it eluded her exhausted brain. She sighed and fastened her attention on the clearest and most immediate of the dilemmas facing her. "I don't know how to be a mistress," she murmured. "The closest I've ever been to real ladies, proper or otherwise, is to cut their reticule strings."

"I distinctly recall your telling me that one of the subjects you taught the Sinclair darlings was deportment." He tilted her face upward and smiled. "And don't expect me to believe any drivel about that being a lie. You also told me that you kept your yarns close to the truth so that, if your mother had a lucid moment, you wouldn't get caught in a lie. Deportment is the art of conducting oneself as a refined person, Darcy. I suspect you were schooled in it as a child, and that's why your mother expects you to ably teach it."

She was drifting away on a haze of exhaustion and warm brandy. He had the most wonderful eyes. He could melt her with just a look. "It's been a very, very long time since I put any of those precepts to practical use," she heard herself say. "I'd make mistakes, and then—"

"We'll practice and you won't make mistakes." He traced her lower lip with the pad of his thumb. "You'll do fine, Darcy. Trust me. I won't let any horrible fate befall you."

The sense of there being a flaw in Aiden's plan gently reasserted itself. And again she couldn't identify it. Instinctively, she said, "We should talk about this again in the morning."

"No, we won't," he declared gently. "It's decided and done. In the morning we go up to Boston. As soon as we arrive, you and I are off to a dressmaker. Finish your brandy."

Aiden might well believe the matter had been settled, but Darcy knew differently. Come morning, she'd be rested enough to see the defects in Aiden's strategy. And she had no intention of going along with a plan doomed to fail. With the resolution came lassitude. She stared down at the brandy, unable to get her hand to lift the glass to her lips.

"Have you had very many mistresses?" Darcy started, first at the realization that she'd spoken aloud, and then at the wholly too personal nature of the inquiry. Her mind came wide awake, but before she could collect herself enough to apologize and call back the impertinent question, Aiden answered.

"Only one," he said, his voice flat and emotionless. "I found the situation overrated, and abandoned it after three months or so." He shrugged and then added, "But if you're asking me if I know the rules of conduct, the answer is yes. They're part of every wealthy boy's informal education. You select a woman of independent spirit, good background, and attractive appearance. You provide her a place to live and adorn her as befits your own social station. You go to her when you like, but not often enough for either of you to risk an emotional attachment. When the flush of excitement fades for you, you give her a parting purse and arrange to pass her to another man."

"How horrible."

Aiden took a sip of brandy. "Mistresses are often very wealthy women in their own right."

"I don't think the money would adequately balance the rest of it. To be passed on, from one man to another, like a—a—" Darcy shook her head as best she could within the confines of his loose embrace. "How that must wound."

Aiden chuckled and hugged her. "Darcy, sometimes I think you were brought up in a cloistered convent. Darling, the cardinal rule is not to invest anything other than your body in the relationship. It's physical and financial and nothing more. If you keep it that way, then no one is hurt when the relationship is dissolved."

The cool, matter-of-fact description bothered her. Darcy eased away from him just enough to look into his eyes. "It sounds like a form of prostitution designed by rich men who don't want to be bothered by having to work for their pleasure."

He barely shrugged. "It is."

"And how do mistresses conduct themselves outside the bedroom? Are they allowed out into the light of day?"

"Don't you know any kept women?" he asked.

"I suspect there's a great deal of difference between a woman being kept in Charlestown and one being kept in Nob Hill," she countered. "This was your idea, Aiden. If you're finding it difficult to speak of it, then perhaps you ought to consider that a sign of a mistake being made and abandon the course."

"The only difficulty I'm having is in choosing the right words, so that I don't bludgeon your gentle sensibilities."

"I don't have any gentle sensibilities." Darcy sagged back against him wearily. "Just say what needs to be said, Aiden."

Aiden finished his brandy and set the glass aside. Drawing her against him with both arms, he said softly, "A proper mistress conducts herself publicly as any lady would. Generally speaking, she associates socially with other mistresses. Men have certain places they take their wives, and certain places they take their mistresses. To confuse the two is considered a significant social gaffe." He paused to turn himself so that his back angled into the corner of the small sofa and his legs lay along the length of it. He adjusted Darcy so that she rested between him and the back, her head propped on his shoulder. "Perhaps this might be easier if you asked me questions."

"I wouldn't know what to ask," she admitted. "Perhaps you'd like to reconsider the wisdom of the entire notion."

He ignored her suggestion and continued with her education. "I suppose the most consistent characteristic of mistresses is their openness to opportunity. They're always watching and listening. They can sense when a man is tiring of his current mistress and searching for another. If he presents a chance for her to elevate her social position or increase her wealth, she'll find subtle ways to convey her interest."

Darcy took a drink, contemplating Aiden's words, and then observed, "I'd think the man presently supporting and adorning her would take offense to her shift in allegiance."

"There is no allegiance, Darcy. Mistresses enjoy the most egalitarian relationships mankind has ever created. If she wants to leave, there's nothing a man can do but let her go and find himself another to take her place."

She looked up at him. "Just that easily?"

"Just that easily," he answered with a nod.

"I don't think I can do this."

"Yes, you can," he assured her with a smile. "You're simply going to pretend to be my mistress, and genteelly accept the well-mannered advances of other men who hope to lure you away from me. If you play your part well, there will be a flood of social invitations. The men will knock each other over in their effort to sample someone new. The women will want to get the measure of their competition. And somewhere in the ordeal, we're likely to encounter Jules."

"You're throwing me into a dog pit as bait." She'd intended for the accusation to have far more force than it did. Darcy stared back down at the brandy and cursed herself for having succumbed to the false comfort of it. She was being lured down the road of temptation, and she couldn't muster even a halfhearted resistance.

"I'm going into the pit with you, Darcy. All you have to do is pretend that the other mistresses are a wary crowd, and you've a mind to pluck a purse from their pockets if you find one that looks fat enough to be worth the bother."

"I don't want to pluck a purse. I don't want to be a mistress."

"I know that. But no one else should."

She sighed, knowing that she didn't have a hope of winning the contest between them, but not wanting to let him win without some sort of struggle. "I feel obliged to tell you that one of the first rules of reefing is to be sure you don't get so involved in your work that you let yourself get reefed."

"Darcy!" he exclaimed, struggling to control his laughter. "Are you afraid I'll find myself a real mistress?"

"I don't care what you do or with whom you do it. I'm talking about me. I might find someone who truly interests me, and leave you to find Jules on your own. I'll choose a wealthy enough man that I won't have to worry about answering to Mick."

"A degree of independence is considered good in a mistress, but you . . ." He drew her closer and kissed the top of her head. "Just keep in mind that men cheat on their mistresses just as they cheat on their wives, and be careful that you're not lured into a one-night dalliance."

"Men are loathsome creatures," she muttered.

"I'm afraid that I have to agree with you."

"You can't imagine how sorry I am that I decided to reef your pocket."

"You can't imagine how very glad I am that you did." After a pause he added softly, "It will be all right, Darcy. You'll see. I need you to do this for me. I'll take care of you."

I'll take care of you. They were such simple words, but they offered sweet salvation amidst a storm of fear and confusion. Darcy saw them for the false promise they were. Countless women before her had heard them, believed them to mean far more than they did, and trustingly surrendered. And once they'd surrendered, there was no going back to who they had been before. She could understand why they made the choice they did. When you were tired enough, and scared enough, a pair of strong arms around you and gentle whispers became a tempting, soothing elixir, a potion far more powerful than the best of brandies.

She would take only a small taste of it tonight. It felt good to have Aiden hold her. Just for a little while she'd let herself pretend she was safe in the haven of his arms. *Just for a little while. Just for a little while.*

Aiden gently took the brandy glass from her fingers, tossed the remainder down his throat, and set the glass aside. He inched his feet off the settee and then angled the rest of his body after them, taking care not to jostle and awaken Darcy. When he sat beside her, he turned, eased his free arm beneath her knees, and then rose with her in his arms. She curled into him, draping her arm around his neck as he carried her across the parlor and kicked open his bedroom door.

Depositing her gently on the bed, Aiden released her and stepped back to work the coverlet down from beneath her. She sighed and lifted her hips for him, then curled onto her side as soon as the task was accomplished. Aiden covered her, and then glanced back through the open door, considering the settee. Good judgment said he should let Darcy have the bed and find what comfort he could in the other room.

"Good judgment be damned," he muttered, striding toward the door and closing it. He went back to his bed and slid under the coverlet. He reached for Darcy, intending to make sure that his movements hadn't pulled the covers from her. He touched her shoulder lightly, feeling the warmth of her skin through the threadbare fabric of her shirt.

"Aiden."

It was a whisper from the realms of sleep, a soft sound full of acceptance and wonder and happiness.

"I'm here, Darcy," he whispered in reply.

He wasn't expecting her to inch her way against him, to curl into him and bury her face into the curve of his shoulder. His chest ached and his throat thickened, as she nestled her hips against his and draped her arm across his chest. Aiden wrapped his arms around her and closed his eyes, breathing deeply the sweet scent of her hair. God, what he wouldn't give for Darcy to come to him like this when awake. What he wouldn't give to know that every day of their time together would end like this, with Darcy sleeping in his arms.

But it was a fool's dream, and he knew it. In the morning, they would awaken and scramble to their respective corners, each uncertain what they wanted from the other and too wary to ask for what they needed. If only it could be different for them. If only there was a way for them to forget about the pasts that had made them who they were. Aiden laced his fingers through Darcy's, surrendering his turmoil to sleep and his hope to another day.

THE SOUND OF muffled voices awakened Darcy. In another room, she decided. Nothing she needed to worry about, nothing that needed to pull her from the wondrous cocoon of warmth in which she was wrapped. She snuggled deeper, and the warmth drew her closer to itself. It was a hard warmth she thought, almost as if made of sinew and . . .

Her eyes flew open. Bronzed skin lay under her cheek. Darcy raised her head for a clearer, wider view of her pillow. Aiden. His hair was ruffled, and his shirt had come fully unbuttoned. It was in that moment that Darcy fully understood the definitions of wanton and wicked and tempting. Even asleep, Aiden was all three. Her blood warmed and sang through her veins. Darcy drew in a shaky breath and touched her tongue to lips that had suddenly gone dry.

Her gaze flicked up and she noted the ornately carved headboard, the heavy brocade bed curtains. She shifted her hips and felt the linen brush against her skin. Had she walked into Aiden's bedroom and climbed into his bed on her own? She thought back to the night before. No. She had been too tired to move, had fallen asleep on the settee wrapped in Aiden's arms. If he hadn't carried her in here, she'd have spent the night in the parlor with him. Darcy lowered her head and closed her eyes. She'd decided to cross the line last night. She'd had reason enough. It was too late to worry about it. What difference did it make where they slept?

Aiden's skin was warm against her cheek, his body solid and comforting. His heartbeat thrummed a gentle lullaby, and she drifted back into contented sleep.

A VAGUE SENSE of having lost something brought her from sleep the next time. She opened her eyes and focused on the strip of white linen that stretched between her and the bronze wall of Aiden's bare chest. She tilted her head and found Aiden lying on his side, his head propped in his hand. He looked at her with a quirked smile on his lips.

"Scream and I'll kiss you," he said quietly.

Her heart raced. Darcy smiled. "And if I don't scream?"

"I might very well kiss you anyway," he countered, his smile broadening and his eyes darkening. "You're terribly delicious looking, Miss O'Keefe."

"So are you." Darcy flinched as she heard the words tumble out of her mouth. Aiden's smile faded.

The truth hung between them for a long moment, and then Aiden reached out and traced her lips with a gentle fingertip. "You didn't intend to say that, did you?" he asked, his voice a bare whisper.

Darcy suddenly knew there was no point in trying to lie about anything. He had to be able to feel the quivers his touch sent through her body. With that secret revealed, none of the others mattered. "No, I didn't," she answered quietly. "But now that it's said, I don't regret it. It's the truth. You do look delicious."

Aiden's expression was wondrously surprised and yet wary, too. He coiled a tendril of her hair around his finger as he studied her face. He gave her a faint smile. "Aren't you going to be angry with me for carrying you off to my bed? For not being gentleman enough to sleep elsewhere?"

"I think it would have been very uncomfortable for both of us if we'd spent the whole of the night on the settee," she answered, feeling liberated by being so truthful. "I also think it would be very selfish of me to expect you to sleep somewhere else while I claimed all the comfort of your bed." She grinned as she added, "And it would have been damned unchivalrous of you to leave me on the settee while you took the bed."

"You're not angry about waking in my arms?"

"There's a definite comfort to be found in waking in the same place where you fell asleep."

He cocked a brow. "Are you going to fight me about going up to Boston?"

"No."

"About going to the dressmaker today?"

"Would it do me any good?" she countered.

"Probably not."

"Then I don't see much point in resisting, do you?"

He slowly unwound the hair from his finger, his expression sober as he watched her face. Darcy arched a brow in silent question.

He hesitated, then reached out to trail his fingertips along the curve of her jaw as he asked, "Would you resist if I wanted to make love to you right this moment?"

Her body ached for more of the pleasures he'd given her in the past . . . even as her memory reminded her of the fear that had come with them. She gave Aiden what she hoped was an assured smile. "I don't know," she admitted. "I suppose we could try and see how matters progress."

She saw the wariness come into his eyes, saw his features

harden. He pulled his hand away from her and silently studied her face. Darcy's chest tightened with dread, and it took all her pride not to reach out and draw him back to her.

"Why the sudden change of heart, Darcy?"

Telling herself that she'd started the conversation with honesty and that it was the only way to go forward, she drew a shaky breath and gave Aiden the whole of it. "I've discovered that I have little control over how my body reacts to yours. My best efforts to resist you have come undone every time you've touched me. I can continue fighting the temptation, but I doubt I'm going to win any more of the battles than I have in the past. I think it's probably wiser to negotiate for terms of surrender than to be left sifting what I can from the ashes."

"An approach rather like the one you take with Mick?"

"Surrender is surrender. If it's any consolation, I'm not angry about having to negotiate with you. I usually am with Mick."

"What terms do you want?" he asked. The softness of his voice didn't hide the bitterness of his thoughts. "A house? Furnishings? A monthly allowance?"

His assumptions hurt. Deeply. Her anger thrashed in the pain of being so misjudged. She'd given him her truth, and he'd seen it as an attempt to extort a fortune from him. The unfairness of it finally freed her anger. "I *don't* want a child, Aiden," she replied evenly, meeting his gaze squarely. "I want to be able to walk away from you when the time comes without any ties. That's all I ask of you. Nothing more, nothing less."

Aiden felt as though Darcy had put a knife in his gut. His mind reeled between bitter memories, anger, and crushing disappointment. When the initial shock of it passed, he resolutely set aside emotion and focused on the practical aspects of her words. Aiden knew that she meant what she'd said, recognized that she'd simply insisted on a degree of common sense and restraint he'd intended to exercise for his own protection anyway. But he knew that he'd blundered, and blundered badly, in dealing with her honest approach to the matter. He should have known better. His words had not only wounded her pride, but had also utterly destroyed the ease with which they lay together. Aiden reached out, intending to cup her face and offer her all the words of apology he could find.

She caught his hand and stayed it well away from her. "Can you guarantee my freedom, Aiden?" she asked, her voice tight with hurt, even with determination.

"Yes," he answered simply, sensing that even the most earnest of his pleas for forgiveness would fall on deaf ears. He took her hand in his, lacing his fingers through hers. "I'll see you protected. You have my word."

She nodded her acceptance of the vow but he saw the reserve in her eyes. The distance bothered him and he knew he had no one to blame but himself. Perhaps with time she'd lower the barriers she'd erected against him. And if she didn't . . . Aiden knew that he'd always be haunted by the knowledge that he could have had so much more, that his blindness had cost him a glimpse of a rare, unbridled giving.

"Are you hungry, Darcy?" he asked, suddenly desperate to escape the confines of the bed and his responsibility for the shattered moment.

"A little."

"A little, my eye," he scoffed, shoving down the coverlet and dragging her with him out of the bed. "You're always ravenous. Let's get something to eat."

CHAPTER 15

DARCY LET AIDEN hold the door open for her to enter the salon before him. One step across the threshold and she regretted it. Maisey sat on the settee, her eyes wide and her mouth gaping as she blindly tried to find the saucer with her teacup. Nathan Chandler, sitting a circumspect distance from Maisey, looked past Darcy's shoulder and frowned.

"Good morning, Chandler, Miss Maisey," Aiden offered breezily, pulling the bedroom door closed.

Chandler rose to his feet, clearing his throat softly. "If it wouldn't be too much of an imposition, sir, a small bit of decorum would be both welcome and appreciated."

Darcy glanced over her shoulder and winced. Aiden's shirt was untucked and unbuttoned, not only exposing the sunburnished expanse of his chest, but also the rippled muscles of his abdomen and the sleep-twisted fit of his trousers. Darcy glanced down at her own clothing. Her shirt wasn't as open as Aiden's, but that was the only difference in their state of dress. Heat flooded over Darcy's cheeks as her mind saw the tracks Chandler's and Maisey's minds were traveling. Her first impulse was to shove her shirttail into her trousers and assert her innocence. A suspicion that the effort would be perceived as a tacit admission of guilt stopped her.

Aiden laughed, fastened two buttons in the center of his

shirt front, and stepped around her, saying, "Do your sensibilities feel better now, Nathan?"

"It is not for my benefit," the manservant countered. "I ask that you have a modicum of respect for Miss Darcy's feelings. And that you respect Miss Maisey's presence."

"Fair enough, I suppose. What time is it?"

Darcy didn't like the casual dismissal Aiden's response implied. He could have at least offered some sort of defense of her virtue. Her conscience reminded her that she'd promised to surrender it and that there was nothing for Aiden to defend. She tucked her shirttail in.

"It is a quarter before twelve, sir," Chandler was saying. "And lest you think that Miss Maisey and I have earned our wages by drinking tea this morning, I assure you otherwise."

"Oh, really?" The amusement in Aiden's voice was transparent. As was his innuendo.

Chandler drew himself up and replied coolly. "We have only within the last half hour returned from our errands, sir. Your bag and Miss Darcy's trunk were removed from the Lion and Fiddle and transported to suitable lodgings in Boston. I took the liberty of inquiring after a couturier, and then securing an appointment with the gentleman for this afternoon." He stepped forward, drawing a white card from the breast pocket of his coat. Chandler handed it to Aiden, adding, "He will see you at two."

Aiden glanced down at the card and cocked a brow. "François? The man has no surname?"

"I believe a surname is viewed as unnecessary. He comes highly recommended."

"An'," Maisey offered, "he was only available after Nathan assured him that you would be terribly generous with your funds."

Aiden grinned. "You bribed him?"

"Indirectly," Chandler admitted without batting an eye. "I suggest that it would not do to be late for the appointment."

Darcy looked down at herself again, and the misgivings of the night before returned, multiplied a hundredfold. "I can't go to a dressmaker looking like this."

"I thought of that," Maisey assured her, rising from the settee. "I took the gray wool suit from your trunk an' brought it along for you to wear. As well as your—" She blushed and swallowed hard. "Your other things. I've put them in Nathan's room, where we'll have your bath placed when it's brought up."

Darcy ran her fingers through her hair, wincing when they encountered snarls. "I'm sorry to have dragged you into this, Maise. It wasn't my intention at all."

"Oh, I think it's goin' to be the grandest adventure," Maisey breathily assured her, her eyes bright. "It's been a wonderfully interestin' mornin' already. Certainly more so than sellin' eggs in the market. An' who knows . . . If you'll vouch for me being a suitable lady's maid, I might be able to turn this experience into something larger."

Darcy found her friend's enthusiasm daunting. Aside from Chandler's concern for Aiden's lack of decorum, no one but her seemed to dread the coming days. Darcy shoved her hands into her pockets and struggled to put a smile on her face. "I didn't know you aspired to being a lady's maid, Maise. I'm afraid I'm going to be a rather poor first experience for you."

"We'll manage. An' I'm sure you'll surprise yourself, Darcy. We'll have so much fun!"

"Two o'clock will be cutting it close," Aiden observed. "We'll have to go to Mr. François directly from here."

"Indeed, sir," Chandler responded. "I have hired a carriage for the duration of our stay in Boston. It will arrive here at one to transport you and Miss Darcy to your appointment." He paused and cocked his head toward the door leading into the hallway. A moment later there was the unmistakable clang of a copper tub denting woodwork. "Ah, your baths have arrived on time."

Aiden offered his manservant a quirked smile. "You're very efficient, Chandler."

"It is my job to see to such things, sir," he replied, moving toward the door.

"And if Darcy and I hadn't emerged before the baths were ready for us?"

Chandler stood with his hand on the knob waiting for the knock. "A dilemma I am grateful I did not have to contemplate."

"Did you happen to think about anything for us to eat? It was a long night, and we're starving."

"A cold platter is to arrive thirty minutes after your baths." Chandler looked at his watch. "Twenty-eight minutes from now." The knock came as expected.

"You didn't leave much time for leisure," Aiden observed dryly.

"I rather thought you'd already taken your time for that, sir." With that comment, Chandler opened the door and stepped aside to admit the parade of housekeeping staff. He indicated the two bedrooms with a broad sweep of his hand.

As Chandler followed half the tub and bucket brigade into Aiden's room, Aiden fell in behind him, saying, "Chandler, when we get back to St. Kitts—remind me to fire you."

"Very good, sir. I'll make a note of it."

Darcy and Maisey, left alone in the salon, looked at one another. From Nathan's room came the sounds of Darcy's bath being prepared.

Maisey's gaze went to the room into which Aiden and Nathan had disappeared. "You don't think he really intends to dismiss Nathan, do you, Darcy?"

Darcy chuckled and headed for her bath, assuring her friend as she went. "I get the impression that Aiden fires him on a regular basis. I wouldn't worry about it, Maise."

"You look tired," Maisey observed, passing the departing servants as she joined Darcy in the bedroom. "Nathan said you an' Mr. Terrell didn't come in until almost dawn. You mustn't have gotten much sleep." Her eyes widened and she quickly pressed her fingertips to her lips. "Oh, dear. I didn't mean that in the way you might have taken it. 'Tis really none of my business what you an' Mr. Terrell—"

"All we did was sleep, Maisey. Nothing else. Despite appearances to the contrary."

"Well, drat. I was hoping . . ."

Darcy paused in unbuttoning her trousers, suddenly aware

of some of the more delicate aspects having a lady's maid might entail. "Don't you have something you can do other than stand there and watch me, Maise?" she asked in what she hoped was a diplomatic way. "Maybe you should get the table ready for the food that's supposed to arrive."

"I think a lady's maid is supposed to help with the bath." Darcy lowered her chin and knitted her brows. Maisey's eyes widened again and her mouth formed a tiny O. "Then again," Maisey said, hastily retreating to the far side of the room, "I could be wrong. I'll sit over here an' look out the window an' keep you company."

Saying, "Let me know if you see a dark-haired man loitering about and watching the hotel," Darcy quickly stripped and climbed into the steaming tub.

Beyond the sensation of the heavenly, luxurious warmth Darcy heard Maisey say, "Mick told us—Ma an' Da an' me— what you an' Mr. Terrell are tryin' to do. Do you think his brother is watchin', Darcy?"

"He has been," she supplied, rousing herself from the envelope of comfort and reaching for the sea sponge and soap. "Jules has known precisely where to send or leave packages for us. As to whether he's still watching . . . His note last night said that he'd *see* us in Boston. I don't know whether he's gone already, or if he's waiting for us to lead and he'll follow."

Maisey's voice quivered slightly when she ventured, "Mick said there had been another murder, but he didn't say who."

Darcy's stomach clenched at the memory of the box left against her mother's door. But it wouldn't do to let Maisey know how frightened and guilty she was feeling. There was no point in Maisey being any more scared than she already was. "Jules killed Timmy the Rat last night," she supplied matter-of-factly. "If there's anything good about Jules going to Boston, it's that I'm not likely to know the next victims."

The callousness of the words struck her the moment she uttered them. Darcy leaned back into the curve of the tub and pressed her hands over her eyes. "Sweet Mary," she whispered, "how can I even think something so awful?"

"It's understandable, Darcy," her friend offered gently. "You've always mothered everyone; it's got to be especially hard for you to know that you haven't been able to protect them from Mr. Terrell's brother."

Darcy grabbed the drying sheet and rose from the tub. "I just wish I felt as though we were getting a bit closer to finding Jules. I don't see how it's going to be any easier there than it's been here," she admitted, drying herself briskly. The activity seemed to help her think more clearly.

"I keep thinking that Jules is playing a grisly version of blindman's buff with Aiden," Darcy supplied, quickly dressing. "But I don't understand the why of it. If I could fathom what Jules wants from the game, I'd have some idea of what it would take to bring him out of hiding. I can't sort any of it out. I can sense the pieces of the puzzle being there, Maise, but I can't for the life of me see what they are or how they go together."

"But you'll figure it out eventually, Darcy. I have faith in you."

"I'd like to share your sense of confidence."

"Speaking of confidence," Maisey said brightly. "Let's do something special with your hair. Ma always says that if your hair is done right an' pretty, you feel better 'bout the whole world."

Darcy knew that an intricate arrangement of curls wasn't the solution to any of her present troubles, but she didn't have the heart to burst the bubble of Maisey's illusions, and so she acquiesced without complaint. And as Maisey muttered and fussed, Darcy silently let her mind drift through the maze her life had become so suddenly.

Aiden certainly had confidence in his strategy for finding Jules in Boston. Darcy chewed the inside of her cheek and considered the reasoning he'd offered her the night before. The nagging sense of something being awry returned. But where fatigue had clouded her vision at the time of Aiden's explanation, she was now rested enough to see the problem instantly and clearly. Aiden's hope of catching Jules rested entirely on the element of catching his brother unaware. And

Darcy knew that the chances of doing that were negligible. Jules had dared them to come to Boston after him. He knew Aiden would follow as he always had. He knew Aiden had no other choice. And so Jules was waiting, and watching. That guaranteed that they had no hope of surprising him. Why hadn't Aiden seen the weakness of his scheme?

The answer came swiftly and clearly. Because Aiden was blinded by the frustration of failure. Because he so desperately wanted the game to end that he was willing to grasp at straws, no matter how flimsy and weak. And mostly because Aiden was just as emotionally and mentally exhausted as she was—probably more so, given how long he'd been chasing Jules.

Darcy turned the basic elements of Aiden's strategy over in her mind, carefully considering it from all angles, knowing that Aiden wouldn't abandon it unless she could provide him a more workable alternative. By the time Maisey had finished dressing her hair and smoothing the last wrinkles from her skirt, Darcy had made fair progress in finding one.

THE FIRST SIGHT of Aiden dressed as a true gentleman had been breathtaking. When she was no longer fascinated to distraction by the breadth of his shoulders and the narrowness of his waist, she'd found herself horribly conscious of the dowdiness of her best dress. Dread had filled her at the prospect of being seen in public with him. It had utterly destroyed her ability to consume a decent portion of the luncheon brought up for them.

And so now she sat across from him in the hired carriage, her stomach rumbling and her thoughts just as chaotic as they'd been when she stepped from Nathan's room and found Aiden waiting for her in the salon. Thankfully, the carriage was hard-roofed, and the window curtains had been dropped to provide privacy. At least she needn't worry about embarrassing Aiden as it bore them over to Boston. No one was likely to peer inside and offer scathing comments on the prince and his pathetically plain pauper.

But the lowered curtains were a devilment, too. She couldn't seem to keep her thoughts from wandering to wicked fantasies of what such seclusion might permit. And surely they had to be possible. There had to be a valid reason why all good mothers admonished their daughters to avoid finding themselves alone in hacks with men. When she found herself wondering if Aiden had ever seduced a woman in a carriage, and if he were entertaining thoughts of introducing her to the possibilities, she took her imagination firmly in hand and shoved it behind the door of self-discipline and decorum.

"Aiden," she said, breaking the silence between them, "I've been thinking."

His mouth curved up into that wicked smile that melted her bones. "So have I. You share first."

Her heart skipped a beat. She knew precisely what he'd been thinking. The same wanton things she had. Aiden's imaginings were probably more detailed, she admitted; his experience with the circumstances were considerably broader than hers. Not that she had any at all. This was only the second time in her life she'd been in a carriage, the first being when Mick had taken her over to see her grandmother's house.

Darcy took a deep breath and deliberately stepped away from both her thoughts and Aiden's invitation. "I've been mulling on two separate lines of thought, but both concern our hunt for Jules and what—in the clear light of another day—is your rather flimsy plan for finding him."

The smile faded from his face. His brow inched upward. "Flimsy?" he repeated softly.

"Honestly, Aiden," she rushed to say, "it's not much of one and you might as well admit it. I was past reasoning last night, but in looking at it this morning, I can see that it doesn't offer much more hope of us catching Jules than showing the picture around Charlestown did."

He leaned back into the corner of the seat and crossed his arms over his chest. "And I suppose you have a better idea?"

"Not quite yet, but I do have some questions that might

lead us to one." She edged forward on her seat. "The first of my thoughts relates to Jules's likely response when he learns we've accepted the challenge in his last note and moved up to Boston to search for him. What do you think he's going to do?"

"I'm loathe to think about it," Aiden said, "but if he continues his patterns of the past, someone will soon discover a mutilated body. Followed shortly thereafter by the delivery of a gruesome package to our hotel room."

"Precisely," she countered. "Perhaps we stand a better chance of catching him if he doesn't know we're there."

"Would you care to explain more fully?"

She heard the stiffness in his voice and knew that she had only one chance to get him to see her reasoning. She plunged into the explanation, determined to give him no opportunity to cut her off short. "Last night you said you wanted certain circles to practically buzz with news of our arrival in Boston. The general idea being to garner invitations and socialize, with the hope that someone has had contact with Jules and is willing to point us in his direction.

"And if Jules is part of those circles—even peripherally— then he's going to quickly hear that we've done as he expected, and the game will be on again. Once he knows we're there, we won't stand any better chance of catching him than we did in Charlestown. The game is the same. The only thing we've managed to change is where we're playing it. But what if we were to go to Boston under assumed names, Aiden? He might not realize it's us, and give us an inadvertent—albeit short-lived—advantage."

Aiden looked at her for a long moment, his eyes slate gray and unreadable. Finally he said, "You're assuming that he wasn't watching Chandler and Maisey move our belongings this morning?"

"It's a possibility," she admitted, adopting some of Maisey's blithe optimism. "The tiniest bit of luck might have fallen on our side for a change."

"True." Another long moment passed before he added, "But there's another consideration, Darcy. Wealthy men tend to investigate each other with a thoroughness that should inspire constables around the world. Aiden Terrell has the credentials to impress them. It would be in their own self-interest to admit me and my lady to their social circle. Using an alias would place obstacles in our path. Besides, Jules is going to be waiting and watching. Once he even suspects we've come after him, the usefulness of an assumed identity is gone, and we've nothing left but the negative consequences. My plan may be flimsy, but it's still stronger than yours."

The last comment stung even more than the truth did. Darcy collapsed back against the seat cushion and groused, "Well, the gentry—of Dublin, Edinburgh *and* Boston—can't be too particular about who they admit to their precious circles. If they were, one would think Jules Terrell wouldn't pass muster."

Aiden bolted upright. "Sweet Jesus. You're right!"

"That makes twice in two days," she remarked dryly. "And again I'm afraid I have no idea what it is that I'm right about."

"Jules has no credentials," Aiden declared. Darcy had the distinct impression that had the carriage been bigger, he'd have been up and pacing as he continued to explain. "If he's gaining entry into elite circles, then he's masquerading as someone other than himself. Jules hasn't randomly picked an assumed name in the past as I've thought; he's chosen with a careful eye to the man's reputation!" Aiden made a strangled sound and shoved his hands into the air above his head. "God Almighty! Why didn't I see this before now?"

Darcy turned the idea over in her mind and quickly found the potential flaw. "I'm going to play devil's advocate here for a moment, Aiden. The identities Jules has chosen in the past—James Packer, Liam Steward, and . . . Joseph Ryan, wasn't it?—have been common enough names in those parts of the world where he was playing his grisly game. How is it that no one's known the men he's presumed to be?"

Aiden's explanation came fast and with firm conviction. "Perhaps they were Scotsmen and Irishmen who made their reputation and fortune in other parts of the world. God knows the clans have scattered their people to the far corners of the earth. Purporting to be one of the clan's own would tend to overcome some of the traditional hesitancy of accepting outsiders. The geographic distance of the man whose identity he's using would make it unlikely either that anyone would know Jules to be an impostor, or that they'd be able to verify that he isn't who he claims to be."

Darcy sighed and nodded in acceptance of the rationale. "But," she observed, thinking aloud, "if Jules really has so carefully chosen his facades, then it's hardly the reasoning of an insane mind."

Aiden shrugged, his mind clearly on another course. "Do you have any idea of who he might pretend to be while in Boston?"

"Unfortunately, not a one," she confessed. And fearful that she might lose her chance of influencing his plans, she went boldly ahead with the rest of her proposal. "But our difficulty in finding him leads me to my second line of thinking. Actually, the credit goes to Maisey, who suggested it. You've got to admit that we haven't been having any luck in searching for Jules. And if you're being honest with yourself, you'd also have to admit that the Boston plan depends heavily on that luck we don't seem to have. But if we could lure Jules into a trap . . ."

His eyes instantly narrowed. "With what as bait?"

"That's where the line of thought crumbles."

"A rather crucial juncture," he retorted wryly.

"Well, I think it's something worth giving additional thought, don't you?" she demanded.

They sat in silence and the carriage rocked through the streets for a good distance before she took a deep breath and said, "Why is Jules playing this game of tag with you, Aiden?"

He wedged himself back in the corner again, his arms folded over his chest. "I don't know."

"Then speculate," she gently pressed. "Consider it a gruesome parlor game if you'd like."

"Don't you think I've spent sleepless nights trying to see

the reason for it, Darcy? Christ! It's not as though we shared a childhood from which Jules could recall playroom slights. I was fourteen and Jules was ten when the paths of our lives crossed in the same house. I was stepping into the world of adult responsibility, and Jules was still a child. Aside from his two attempts to maim or kill me, we had no common experiences."

Her heart aching for him, Darcy continued as gently as she could. "Was there ever a time when you thought you might eventually share the bonds of brothers?"

"No."

"Why?"

"I don't know."

"Aiden, it's long been apparent that you didn't have a loving relationship with your father and that you don't find the least bit of pleasure in remembering it. But I can't escape the feeling that Jules's actions are driven by the past, by the way he saw things as a child. Our chances of finding him, of being able to draw him to us, will be much improved if we can understand the why of what he's doing. And I'm afraid that in order to puzzle it out, you're going to have to step past your own bitterness and look objectively at what happened within your family. I think doing so would give you a sense of peace, as well. I'd like to help if you'd just let me."

And as the last words tumbled from her lips the damn carriage slowed and angled to the side of the roadway.

Aiden smiled and sat up, reaching for the door handle as he said, "We've no time for it at the moment. We've arrived."

"And you've been saved by fortuitous circumstance." She caught herself as the carriage came to a final stop. Aiden flung open the door and quickly stepped down onto the walkway. "But only momentarily," she added as she put her hand in his and let him help her alight. "We'll come back to this subject later, Aiden."

"Not if I can prevent or avoid it."

"It's a shame that no one ever taught you that the primary responsibility of adults is to step up to unpleasant realities and face them squarely."

"I'm perfectly capable of facing unpleasant realities, Darcy." He closed the carriage door, then took her elbow in hand and turned her toward the storefront. "A man must be able to do so if he's to succeed in business. And I'm a very successful businessman."

"There's a great deal of difference between facing ugly business situations and facing ugly personal ones, Aiden. It's my guess that you've poured your life into the former in a determined effort to avoid looking at the latter."

She was absolutely right. It had been a conscious decision since the first day he had been capable of making one. It had served him well in the past and he had no intention whatsoever of abandoning the strategy at this point in his life. And he sure as hell wasn't about to spend the next carriage ride with her discussing the twisted roots and limbs of his family tree.

CHAPTER 16

WITH HIS HAND on the small of her back, Aiden guided Darcy through the elegantly carved glass doorway. From there he almost had to push her forward.

A young woman sat behind a gilt table in the center of the opulently appointed foyer. She rose from a satin upholstered chair with a rustle of silk, demurely lowered her chin, and said in softly accented English, "Welcome to the House of François, madame and monsieur. How may I be of service to you?"

Darcy went rigid beneath his hand. Aiden stepped to her side, saying to the Frenchwoman, "I am Aiden Terrell and this is my lady, Miss Darcy O'Keefe. We have an appointment at two."

A flash of black behind the young woman caught Aiden's attention. The slender man froze in mid-stride, his expression horrified as he looked Darcy up and down.

"Mon dieu!" he cried, all five and a half feet of him dashing forward, his hands waving about his head. "Who has committed this travesty? They should be shot! *Shot!*"

"Mlle. O'Keefe and M. Terrell have an appointment, François," the clerk said demurely. "It was made this morning for two o'clock."

"And well it is that you have come to me!" François declared, as he circled around them, his black eyes darting over

Darcy, his expression pained. He stopped and threw his hands up as though pleading for heavenly intervention. "This must be corrected immediately. It is an offense to the laws of fashion and good taste." He turned toward the opening through which he had entered the reception area, clapped his hands, and sharply called, "Magnon!"

Another young woman quickly came around the corner. She glanced briefly at Aiden and then Darcy, before offering her employer a quick curtsy and a *"Oui, monsieur?"*

"See Mademoiselle to the lavender fitting room with haste. Dispose of those"—he shuddered—"rags." His hands waved through the air about his head as he went on, exclaiming, "She will not leave my establishment as she has entered. My reputation demands protection from innuendo! And find her some suitable foundations. Surely beneath all *that* there is a womanly figure to be discovered. I am the best, but not even *I* can make magic unless I am met halfway."

"Oui, monsieur," Magnon replied with another quick curtsy. She turned sideways and said, "If you would please accompany me, mademoiselle."

Darcy didn't move. Beneath his hand, Aiden felt a tremor crawl down the length of her back. He leaned forward and pressed his lips to her ear. "It's all right, Darcy," he whispered. "Go. I'll join you very shortly." He gave her a gentle nudge forward. She went stiffly, pausing at the corner to look back at him. Aiden saw the wounded pride in her eyes. He smiled and winked in reassurance even as his pulse began hammering in his temples. She mustered a weak smile of her own, and then stepped around the corner, her shoulders squared as though she were being escorted to the guillotine.

François, standing beside Aiden, watched her go and then closed his eyes, pressed the last three fingers of his hand to the center of his brow, and offered a breathy, *"Merde!"* He shuddered and then turned to face Aiden. Clicking his heels sharply, he bowed and said, "I will do what magic I can, monsieur."

Aiden cocked a brow. "A word with you before you begin your magic, François?"

"Oui?"

"Miss O'Keefe has never been to a couturier," he said evenly. "Have a bit more care for her feelings than you've displayed so far, or your tailor will be shortening your pant legs."

It took a moment for the Frenchman to translate the words and comprehend both the implications and the threat. He gasped and leaned backward. "Ah, M. Terrell," he whispered a moment later, apparently having recovered sufficiently from his shock to dare stepping closer. "I am grateful that you have spoken to me of this. I understand completely. I will take the mademoiselle's . . . ahem, inexperience . . . into account in designing for her." He wagged his pencil-thin brow and smiled slyly. "My creations will inspire not only you, but the mademoiselle as well."

"I would appreciate that," Aiden replied coolly, knowing Darcy would have his hide if she ever guessed he'd confided her . . . ahem, inexperience . . . to this French popinjay.

François turned to look at the corner where Darcy had disappeared moments earlier. He sighed wistfully. "She is very beautiful, yes?"

"Yes, she is." *And I need to be with her. Let's hurry this along, François.* "I trust that my manservant indicated that my lady requires a full wardrobe. She will need suitable millinery as well. A large portion of the order needs to be completed by the end of the week. I've plans to take Miss O'Keefe to the theater Saturday evening."

François rocked back on his heels, gasped, and clasped his hands over his heart. *"Mon dieu!* By the end of *this* week? *Four days?* M. Terrell! I am the best couturier in Bos—"

"Then I'm sure there'll be no problem in meeting all my expectations," Aiden interjected, weary of the man's theatrics. "I trust that Chandler informed your staff of my tendency to be generous when pleased?"

"Oui, monsieur. But have you any conception of the magnitude of generosity such an undertaking will require?"

Aiden smiled slowly. "You are not the first couturier I have employed, François."

"Ah, I see."

At last, the end of the conversation was in sight. "It would appear, François, that you see a great deal."

"*Oui.* But there are none who hear me speak of it. I assure you of my discretion."

"Then we have a sufficient understanding to begin." Aiden gestured to the rear of the shop. "Shall we? My lady has been kept waiting long enough."

THE ROOM WAS octagonal, large, and made even larger by the mirrors that filled seven of the eight walls from floor to ceiling. Only the wall with the door wasn't mirrored, and it was the only place Aiden could fasten his gaze and not see an image of Darcy. It was a delightfully provocative experience at first. Darcy had been placed in the center of the room, wearing only her stockings, a fine lawn chemise, and a lace-edged corset. The elaborate coif Maisey had created had begun to come unpinned, and long ringlets brushed Darcy's bare shoulders and back. The mirrors allowed Aiden to view every delectable curve Darcy possessed. He'd instantly decided that as hedonistic pleasure went, the room had definite possibilities.

He knew that Darcy, of course, didn't see it from that vantage. She fixed her eyes on the unmirrored wall and, from their glazed look, mentally transported herself elsewhere as François's hands brushed and stroked virtually every inch of her body. Aiden tried to draw her attention to him so he could wordlessly reassure her, but he had no success. Darcy stood ramrod straight in stoic, abject misery. And being unable to do anything to relieve her distress had quickly taken its toll on him. Ten minutes into the session, the mirrors become only a torment. Aiden reminded himself that François was taking no indecent liberties, that the Frenchman was simply going about his work with devotion to detail. The knowledge didn't help much. Every time the man touched Darcy, Aiden tensed.

Some twenty minutes into the ordeal, Aiden scowled and

wondered just how much a man could be expected to endure without protest. He shifted on the lavender satin chaise, shoved at some of the fashion drawings strewn at the other end, and mentally gave the Frenchman five more minutes to complete his measurements. It would be considerably less if the man thought it necessary to adjust the way Darcy fit in the corset again. The last time, Darcy had blushed crimson and silently endured with fisted hands at her sides. Aiden had flung half the drawings to the floor and nearly strangled swallowing the rest of his outrage. He and Darcy had barely survived the assault. François wouldn't survive a second.

"Mademoiselle has the most wonderful attributes," François deigned to say at that moment, standing behind Darcy with his hands on her hips. "Truly the curves of angels."

"Now that you've thoroughly assessed them," Aiden ground out with all the civility he could muster, "perhaps we've reached the point of selecting suitable fabrics and designs."

The Frenchman reacted to the undercurrent of hostility by abruptly stepping back, clicking his heels, and offering Aiden a short bow. "Magnon, come with me," he said, clapping his hands twice as he moved toward the door.

The instant it clicked shut behind the pair, Darcy closed her eyes and let her shoulders slump. She allowed herself only a moment of relief before straightening and lifting her chin. She offered him weary smile.

"Are you all right, Darcy?" he asked gently.

She put her hands on her hips, a lovely spark of indignation brightening her eyes. "I can't breathe in this accursed thing."

Jesus, the provocative wonder of the mirrors had suddenly returned. Aiden tempered his imaginings with the certainty that Darcy wouldn't feel the same attraction to them he did. But God, it was a temptation to see if he could persuade her to feel otherwise. "I'll loosen your laces when we reach the hotel," he heard himself say.

"If I haven't died for lack of air by then," she retorted,

crossing her arms high across her chest and looking down at the carpet between them.

"Don't do that, Darcy," he protested quietly. "You're spoiling my view."

Her head came up and her eyes flashed. Her hands went back to her hips. "Well, it doesn't seem to be pleasing you overly much. You've spent the whole of this miserable experience scowling at me like a frustrated, disappointed tutor."

The sight of her, scantily clad and boldly defiant—His restraint was coming unraveled. By sheer dint of will he kept himself on the chaise. If he went any closer to her . . . Aiden smiled wanly. "Frustrated is the operative word, darling. As for disappointed—not in the least. Do you have any idea of how tempting you look?"

Her gaze went to her reflection in the mirror behind him. Her eyes widened and her breathing went shallow. A wave of heat swept through him. Had he misjudged her willingness to consider a carnal adventure?

"If François and Magnon weren't likely to walk in on us," he said softly, watching her intently, "I'd loosen your laces right now."

Her gaze darted to the next mirror panel and she pulled in a shaky breath. And through the lace of her corset he saw her nipples draw taut.

"Oh, to hell with it," he declared, coming off the chaise, the fabric of his restraint in ribbons. "Let them walk in."

"Aiden!" she gasped, whirling around and using her arms to cover as much of herself as she could. The effort was wholly ineffectual.

He stopped behind her and slipped his arms around her waist. He pressed a lingering kiss to the hollow behind her ear and then whispered, "If it would make you feel better, I could lock the door."

A tiny tremor shook her and she leaned back against him. "Do you have a habit of seducing women in fitting rooms?" she asked, her voice an intoxicating blend of defiance and surrender.

Aiden pressed a kiss to the bare curve of her shoulder, then lifted his head. Their gazes met in the mirror. He smiled at her. "Actually, while I understand that it happens quite regularly and I've certainly had the opportunity, I've never done it. You're the first to inspire me to such debauchery."

"I'm not flattered," she said, her voice husky. Her gaze slipped away from his, to take in the whole of their reflection.

"We'll get to flattery later," he offered, watching her in the mirror as he gently uncrossed her arms and drew them to her sides. "For the moment I'll settle for intrigued and interested."

"Does willing matter?" she asked quietly as he placed his hands against the flat of her stomach.

"This ensemble doesn't hide much, Darcy." He slowly moved his hands upward and when he cupped her breasts her lips parted and she melted against him. He felt her racing pulse and his own matched the cadence.

He brushed his thumbs over the lace covering her nipples. She stopped breathing. "You can plead unwillingness, darling, but your body's telling me otherwise."

She didn't protest and they both watched as he nibbled her earlobe and stroked the lace a second time. And a third.

"Aiden, please." It was a ragged, breathless plea. "I'll die if . . ."

The rest of her words drifted away on a moan as he moved his hands upward and his fingers slipped beneath the lace. Her breath was coming in short, shallow puffs. But her eyes, as she watched them in the mirror—Aiden freed her breasts from the confines of the corset. Her legs trembled and she gathered fistfuls of trouser fabric into her hands to steady herself.

"We look good together, don't we, Darcy?" he whispered, rolling her nipples between his thumbs and forefingers.

She said nothing. She couldn't have spoken if her life had depended on it. Never had she felt anything as exquisite, as wondrously overwhelming. A tattered inner voice kept telling her to close her eyes, to stop watching what Aiden was doing to her. But she couldn't obey. She couldn't resist the wantonness of it all, the heady surge of desire their mirrored image sent thundering through her. Aiden continued to pull at her nipples as he suckled her earlobe, and she struggled to breathe through the magnificent bolt of pleasure that shot into her core. He watched her eyes in the mirror, knowing. . . . Desire tightened and coiled deeper within her. The voice within her was lost beneath the staccato hammering of her heart.

Aiden's gaze slowly left hers, sliding to the reflection of the door. He expelled a long, hard breath, and then looked back to her. "We'll finish this later," he promised, his voice husky as he gently placed her breasts back into the corset.

Darcy's mind reeled, her thoughts a swirling torrent as she finally heard the gentle rapping on the door. François and Magnon were back. If only Aiden had locked the door. She should have insisted. She didn't want it to end. She wanted so much more. Aiden slipped his arms around her waist again and with a sigh kissed her cheek. Darcy looked at them in the mirror. Her cheeks were flushed. François and Magnon would know!

Aiden chuckled softly and hugged her to him. "Don't look so horrified, Darcy. We're likely the tamest couple François has ever seen."

"That doesn't help very much," she retorted. "Please get me out of here as quickly as you can."

He laughed outright. "Darling, I don't intend to waste a moment I don't have to. Now take as deep a breath as you can and let's be on with it."

No sooner had she dragged a breath into her lungs, than Aiden called over his shoulder, "Enter."

Darcy's heart lurched as the door opened and François's gaze swept over them. Too late she realized that she should have insisted Aiden return to the chaise before admitting the couturier. They were caught, and judging by the width of François's smile and the brightness of his eyes he was very pleased with having arrived in time to do it.

"*Pardon* the intrusion, mademoiselle, monsieur," the Frenchman offered. On a wistful sigh, he added, "Ah, but such a portrait of tenderness and contentment."

Darcy didn't feel the least content. Her insides were molten and aching and her heart was skittering all over her chest. Aiden's arms tightened around her, and with his chin he gently urged her head back against his shoulder.

"If you are prepared to select designs and fabric, mademoiselle, monsieur?" François lifted his arms to indicate the swatches draped over them. Then his smile widened as he added, "Or would you perhaps wish for more time alone to discuss the matter privately? It is not my intent to intrude. Perhaps you would care for some refreshments? It would take several minutes to prepare them, but I am certain you would not mind the delay, yes?"

"Let's make the fabric and pattern selections now," Aiden said, stepping back and quickly adjusting the fall of his coat front before he turned to meet the couturier at the chaise.

In the mirror, Darcy saw François's eyes widen and his lips form an O as he took in the drape of Aiden's clothing. She winced, realizing that she'd horribly wrinkled his pant legs. Aiden seemed utterly oblivious to the perusal as he scooped up the drawings and settled on the chaise.

"Ah," François murmured, laying the strips of cloth over the high-backed end of the couch, "Magnon brings the gown for Mademoiselle."

Aiden looked up from the drawings. "And how is it that you happened to have a gown ready to be worn?"

François lifted his hands and rolled his eyes. "Mme. Rodgers insisted on the green watered silk, despite my abhorrence at the very thought of it on her. I conceded only to have the satisfaction of forcing her to admit that the color is not suited to her at all. But the color will be beautiful on Mademoiselle, and so I have exercised my prerogative as a designer. I will make Mme. Rodgers look terribly sallow in another gown. Magnon, if you would see to Mademoiselle, Monsieur Terrell and I will begin."

True to his word, Aiden quickly selected the designs and fabrics. François made appreciative and breathy sounds throughout the process and, three times, clasped his hands to his heart and lapsed into poetic French. Darcy, grateful that

Aiden's attention was held elsewhere, mustered what poise she could and allowed Magnon to dress her from new stockings out. By the time Magnon was buttoning her into a pelisse that matched her new gown, François was collapsing against the chaise with the back of his hand pressed to his brow, and quietly moaning the speed with which Aiden expected miracles.

Aiden shrugged, rose from the chaise, and extended his hand toward Darcy, saying to the Frenchman, "I assume you will want my lady to return for the fittings on Thursday. Shall we say two o'clock again? If you'd care to make an estimate of your expenses, we'll settle the account at that time."

François managed a polite acquiescence as Darcy let Aiden lead her from the fitting room. Neither of them spoke as they crossed the reception area, and so it was that as they stepped across the threshold and onto the walkway they could plainly hear François's high-pitched, frantic screaming for his assistants.

Aiden chuckled, opened the door of their waiting carriage, and handed her in. He was still chuckling when he settled on the seat across from her and the carriage started forward.

"It was a ridiculous amount of money to spend, Aiden," she gently chastised. "Especially if your primary objective was to send the little man into a fit."

He was still smiling when he replied, "My primary objective was to give you beautiful clothes; so humor me and be gracious. I can well afford it."

Her pride prickled and she felt compelled to assert her independence. "I won't keep them, you know. When we're done you can have all of it back," she said firmly, "down to the last stocking and garter. Hopefully you can sell some of it and recoup the expense."

He studied her for a long moment and his smile slowly faded. Finally he said, "It's more than the clothing, isn't it? Speak your mind, Darcy."

She laced her fingers in her lap to keep them from noticeably shaking and met his gaze squarely. "From the moment I met you I've felt as though I were on the edge of an abyss, barely maintaining my balance. I've tried to step back, but I can't. Something's holding me here. And I know that before too much longer I'm going to fall. I won't be playing the part of your mistress, Aiden. It will be fact. It would be fact already if you'd locked the fitting room door."

"What do you want me to say, Darcy? What do you want me to do?"

"I don't know what I want," she admitted. "That's the worst part of the dilemma. I'm coiled tight inside. When you hold me it gets worse. But somehow more bearable, too. I've always been able to see my way, Aiden. I've always known what I needed to do, why and how to go about it. But with this . . . with you . . ."

He couldn't answer, but sat there in silence, watching her and waiting.

When she couldn't bear it another second, Darcy took a deep breath and asked, "Would it be terribly cruel or improper to ask how you left your other mistress? Perhaps if I knew how it was going to end between us, I could better face the rest of it."

His eyes grew hard and flinty. When he spoke, his tone was just as flat and cool. "My relationship with Wilhelmina was based solely on sex and money. She offered the former and I gave the latter. Eventually the balance of the exchange seemed to shift, and I chafed. Our relationship was soon done."

Darcy's heart felt suddenly heavy. "Did she cry when you left her?"

"No," he answered in the same detached way he had before. "I seem to recall that she shrugged and called for a carriage."

"Did you regret leaving her?"

"I regretted more the time I had wasted on her."

"I'm sorry it turned out so badly," Darcy whispered.

Aiden leaned forward, took Darcy's hands in his, and drew her toward him. She went without resistance, her pulse racing as he settled her on his lap and slipped his arms around her. His kiss was gentle and promissory and when he drew away, he lifted her chin with his thumb and said, "I can't foresee ever regretting a single moment of the time we've been together, Darcy."

"We've a ways to go," she offered honestly. "You well may before all is said and done."

He shrugged. "No one can see what the future holds, darling."

The casual dismissal of her concerns prodded her pride again. "You can be sure of one thing; I won't take your money, Aiden. I mean it. Not a penny beyond the wages Mick's negotiated for helping you find Jules. If you can't accept that, then we'll go no further together. I don't want any part of your fortune."

"I'm sorry for how I approached this matter this morning, Darcy. I didn't stop to think, and I should have. You're not like Willy at all. I don't feel about you the way I did about her."

"How do you feel about me?" she asked, the boldness robbing her of the ability to breathe.

He smiled ruefully. "I know the sense of teetering on the abyss, Darcy. And truth be told, I can't see the way ahead any clearer than you can."

"And it doesn't bother you?"

"It bothers the hell out of me." And then his smile transformed—to the wicked one that always so undid her. Drawing the hems of her skirt and petticoat into her lap, he added, "When I stop long enough to think about it. You have the most wonderful way of distracting me."

His hand glided up the length of her silk-stockinged leg.

"Are you trying to return the favor?" she asked, tracing the curve of his jaw with her fingertips.

His smile was as wickedly devastating as his touch. "How am I doing?"

"Very well," she answered breathlessly.

"I can do better, you know." And then he slipped his fingers beneath her lace garter and eased it down her leg as he took possession of her lips.

She vaguely felt her slippers slide from her feet, vaguely

heard them thud on the floor of the carriage. But Aiden's lips caressed hers as thoroughly and reverently as his hand did the length of her legs.

Aiden drew back slowly and looked down at her with obvious regret. "The carriage is slowing," he said. His smile was crooked as he raked his fingers through his hair and exhaled long and hard.

No one had ever touched her as Aiden did. No one had ever made her feel the kind of wild abandon he did. The power Aiden had over her was so wondrously irresistible, so achingly elemental—and yet in that moment he looked so endearingly young and vulnerable that Darcy couldn't resist the impulse to touch his cheek. "Are you all right, Aiden?"

"No," he answered with a dry chuckle. He caught her fingertips and kissed them before adding, "But I think I stand a reasonably good chance of dying a happy man."

She laughed and drew her hand back. Doing what she could to straighten her skirts, she observed, "You've managed to wrinkle my outrageously expensive gown."

He bent down, plucked her garter from the floor, and handed it to her with a roguish grin. "Given another minute or two, I'd have torn the seams apart."

She slipped it over her foot and up her leg, chiding, "You have no respect for the value of money, Aiden. None."

"There are more important things than money and what it will buy," he countered as the carriage came to a halt.

FROM THE WINDOW of the room he'd rented across the street, he watched them climb from the carriage and make their way up the steps of the hotel. His brows knitted. She was wearing different clothes than when she'd left. Aiden had taken her to buy clothes! He wasn't supposed to be doing that. Aiden was supposed to be searching for him. Aiden was supposed to be tormented and worried and haggard. He wasn't supposed to be smiling and laughing and buying dresses for a girl.

This wasn't how it was supposed to be. The plan had gone

wrong, through no fault of his own. But he had seen a way to make it come right in the end, to make everything come right. Except for that first missed step, Aiden had done exactly what he was supposed to do. Until now. Now, because of the girl. Everything was going wrong.

He couldn't let Aiden go wrong. It was too important. Aiden needed reminding. It had been too long. The comforting warmth began to spread inside him. His hands stopped trembling and he stepped away from the window, letting the drapery fall back into place. Yes, it had been too long. Aiden needed to be reminded. And reminded well, so that he'd never again forget. The next victim would have to be a very special one. And done in a more sophisticated way than before. That would take a bit more time and planning than usual. But it would be worth it. Aiden would be most impressed.

CHAPTER 17

HIGH GRAY CLOUDS had slipped over the sun, and an early, somber twilight bathed the room in soft light. Aiden threw the bolt and then dropped the key on the top of the secretary by the door as Darcy stood by the settee and tugged off her gloves.

"Where do you suppose Chandler and Maisey have gone?" she asked, turning slowly about and scanning the salon. "Do you see a note anywhere?"

Aiden sensed a tension in her that hadn't been present earlier. The ease of the fitting room or of the carriage could be found again, he assured himself. It would simply take a bit of time and patience. "Maisey needs suitable clothing for her role, too," he explained, unbuttoning his jacket. "Chandler took her out to see to its purchase. I believe he said something about taking her to dine afterward." He shrugged out of his jacket and tossed it across the back of a chair.

"So you knew we'd be here alone?"

There wasn't a hint of accusation in her question. "Yes," he answered, untying his stock.

"In fact, you made sure that we would be."

Again, no accusation at all; just a simple statement of reality recognized. "Yes." He tossed the tie atop his coat and unfastened his shirt cuffs.

She placed her gloves on the arm of the chair and fingered the lowest button on her pelisse.

"We should be out looking for Jules."

"Probably," he admitted, pulling his shirttail from his trousers. "Is that what you want to do?" He began undoing the line of buttons down the front. "There are no expectations carved in stone, Darcy. How we spend our evening is entirely up to you."

She glanced toward the hallway door. "What about supper? Shouldn't we . . ."

Aiden leaned his hip against the chair and crossed his arms over his chest. He waited until Darcy looked back at him before saying, "I had Chandler arrange for our dinner to be brought up at nine. I thought we would dine privately tonight."

A tiny smile lifted the corners of her mouth. "You've thought of everything," she observed, unbuttoning her pelisse.

"Lord knows I've certainly tried."

The short coat landed atop his jacket and stock. She kicked her slippers off and sighed softly. For a long moment she studied him and then, as though she'd come to a conclusion, slowly nodded her head. "You promised you'd undo my laces for me."

A curious mix of relief and anticipation washed over him. "I did, didn't I?" He grinned and came away from the chair. "And I am a man of my word. Come here and turn around."

She complied with easy grace, and Aiden found himself suddenly feeling an awkwardness he hadn't suffered since his first efforts at the art of seduction.

As though she sensed his uneasiness and wanted to give him an avenue of graceful escape, she said, "We could go look for Jules later."

"Tomorrow. Maybe. We'll see what it brings."

"What's happened to your sense of urgency, Aiden?" she inquired, looking over her shoulder at him. "When we first began this hunt, you were far more consumed by it than you appear to be now."

"My priorities have temporarily shifted. And I refuse to feel guilty about it." He planted a quick kiss on the tip of her nose, and was rewarded with a smile. "Jules has consumed my life for the last eighteen months and if a bit of hedonistic pleasure has finally presented itself, I'm not about to let him deprive me of it. It's a victory I'm not willing to let him have."

And with that declaration he reached over her shoulders and unbuttoned the pearl that held the lace mantle across her shoulders and bodice. What he did with the scrap of cloth after it fell away, he couldn't precisely say. Standing behind her, his height gave him an inspiring view of creamy shoulders, soft, high swells and inviting cleavage. His body responded with deep appreciation.

"So I'm merely a temporary, hedonistic diversion?"

"A very luscious one," he answered.

"May I consider you in the same light?"

"Please do." He forced his fingers to the top of the long row of buttons running down Darcy's back.

"You'll not regret it when I leave you?"

The question pierced his preoccupation with the speed and sharpness of a well-honed blade. His fingers froze, his chest tightened, and his heart slammed hard against his ribs. Aiden ruthlessly set his thoughts in another direction.

He took her shoulders in his hands, turned her about to face him, and said with gentle firmness, "Darcy, enough. If all these questions are your way of trying to delay or evade lovemaking, it's not necessary. Simply say you have second thoughts and I'll understand."

She caught her lower lip between her teeth and looked up at him, before swallowing hard and asking, "Wouldn't you be angry?"

"I think it'd be more a matter of being *damn* disappointed," he admitted with a rueful smile. "I might be unpleasant company for a while, but I'll eventually recover some semblance of good grace."

She looked away. "I always thought that making love was a

matter of being swept off your feet, and beyond making a rational decision."

"You haven't allowed yourself to reach that point, Darcy. Neither have you allowed me to take you there." He put his fingertip beneath her chin and brought her gaze back to his. "But truth be told, Darcy, I'd much rather take a woman into my bed who had both eyes open than a woman who closed them and refused to responsibly consider the possible consequences."

"You're describing the perfect mistress."

"I'm describing you, Darcy."

"I don't have much experience in these matters. My lessons on deportment were rather limited in some respects. What if I make a mistake?"

"I can't even imagine the possibility," he replied honestly, touched by her admission of vulnerability.

"Do you think you can sweep me off my feet?"

Such sweet trust, such innocent dreams . . . "I'd certainly like to try, Darcy. Are you going to let me?"

"Yes."

"Then perhaps you'd best turn around and let me at those buttons and laces."

She obediently turned and when she did, Aiden promptly swept her up into his arms. She laughed, flung her arms about his neck and pressed kisses to his cheek as he carried her into his room.

He swung her down and set her on her feet, then reached back and quietly closed the door. To his consternation, Darcy promptly sat down on the edge of his bed. Then, to his utter pleasure and amazement, she hiked her hems into her lap, and slipped first one garter and then the next down the length of her legs. He crossed his arms and leaned against the door frame, his blood rapidly heating as he watched her remove her stockings.

With a sigh of contentment, she wiggled her toes and tossed the rolls of silk onto the chair in the corner. He barely had time to wonder what she'd do next when she pulled the pins from her hair and shook it loose around her shoulders. His loins tightened and his breathing quickened.

"I'm beginning to feel like myself again," she declared happily, carrying the pins to the dressing table. They clinked in the china dish. "And," she added, coming toward him, running her fingers through her hair, "if you'd be so kind as to free me from François's torture device, I might actually be able to breathe again."

She stopped in front of him, turned around, and lifted her hair atop her head. Hardening, Aiden straightened with a grin and set about the task of undoing her buttons. "I want you to know," he said, nipping her bare shoulder as his fingers blindly worked down the row, "that your new dresses won't have as many buttons as this one does."

"Good."

His fingers found no others to open. He lifted his head, and whispered, "Let's have done with this gown." He slipped the fabric down her arms and over her lace-bound breasts. When her arms were freed, Darcy sighed and stepped away from him. She went only far enough to let the watered silk pool around her feet. She bent to retrieve it, tossed it on the chair with her stockings, and immediately reached around to untie her petticoat. It, too, went onto the chair. He held his breath as her pantilettes dropped to the floor about her ankles.

The air left his lungs in a long, slow breath when she turned back to him. Her hair tumbled over her shoulders and breasts in a riot of shimmering curls. The hem of the white lawn chemise brushed the tops of her thighs, her long and slender legs bare from there down. His gaze inched upward again, sliding slowly over the curves of her hips and waist to the swells of her breasts. She was the angel of every man's most carnal dreams. "If you had looked like that at François's, Darcy . . ."

"I did," she countered, turning and gathering her hair up again. "This is exactly what I was wearing for practically the entire session."

"Your hair wasn't down," he explained, firmly pulling the ends of the corset strings in opposite directions.

"It makes a difference?"

"Oh, yes, it makes a difference." He loosened the lacings with deft, quick strokes, working from the bottom up.

When the uppermost laces slipped loose in their eyelets she sighed in relief and let her hair fall down her back. "Oh, Aiden. Thank you. I may live."

He wasn't sure he would, as he watched her wiggle the loosened sleeve of lace and whalebone down over her hips. Impatiently he dropped down on the edge of the bed and set about removing his boots, his thoughts focused on the mechanics looming ahead. Darcy's inexperience would require vast amounts of gentleness and time. God, he hoped he could tamp down his selfishness long enough to make it right for her. She deserved all the pleasure he could give her.

Aiden's boot sailed past her to land against the baseboard with a dull thump. She turned in time to see him wrench the second one from his foot and send it flying after the other. He stripped off his socks, dropping them beside the bed, and then rose to his feet. As his hands went to the buttons on his trousers, he glanced up at her, and stopped.

Her heartbeat had begun to skitter as Aiden had watched her take off her garters and stockings. Her blood had warmed with each button he'd undone and lace he'd loosened. And now, despite being free of the corset, she couldn't draw a full breath. Aiden stood before her, his eyes dark, his shirt open, his hair falling under the collar to lie against the bronze skin of his shoulder. The glow of the lamp caressed the chiseled lines of his face and the broad planes of his darkly furred chest. It cascaded over the rippled muscles of his abdomen. A tension radiated from him, speaking of power and strength and a need barely held in check. He was magnificent, and her heart swelled.

One corner of his mouth tipped upward. "Have you ever seen a naked man, Darcy?"

She moistened her suddenly dry lips. "Once. When Mary Margaret O'Hugh's older brother caught his nightshirt on a nail while trying to climb from his window during the night."

"You never had a model in your drawing lessons?"

"We used books. And being proper young ladies, we drew only from the waist up and the knees down."

"Overlooking a rather vital section in between." His arms fell to his sides.

"Oh!" she gasped in sudden realization. "This is the part where I'm supposed to close my eyes, isn't it?" She quickly put her hands over her face. "I've heard older women whisper," she explained from behind them. "I *told* you I was going to make mistakes. Go ahead, Aiden. I won't peek."

He laughed outright. Darcy looked through the space between her fingers. Aiden lay sprawled on his back across the bed, gazing up at the ceiling and shaking his head as he gasped through his merriment. Part of her was angry, sensing she was the source of his amusement. But a deeper, larger part of her thrilled to the deep, rolling sound of his unrestrained happiness. Fighting a smile, she stomped over to the bed and climbed up to kneel beside him.

He looked up at her with tears glistening his eyes. "The part where you close your eyes? Oh, God!" He dissolved into laughter again.

"I was trying to spare you some embarrassment," she countered, grinning.

He gasped for a breath. "Spare *me?*"

"Well, apparently I shouldn't have bothered," she countered, her hands on her hips. "That will teach me to be tender with your feelings."

He sat up, his breathing ragged but his laughter under control. He looked at her for a long moment, and the light in his eyes softened. His smile eased. And then he reached out, slipped his arms around her waist, and gently drew her to him, saying, "You are a rare and precious jewel, Darcy O'Keefe."

She had never wanted a kiss as much as she did at that moment, with Aiden, like this . . . It was what she wanted, what she needed. She marveled at the gentle intensity of

Aiden's possession, willingly surrendered to the sureness of his touch. It spiraled her upward, its power reeling her into sweet abandon. She went, breathlessly and joyfully.

Suddenly, it wasn't enough. There was more to be had. She could sense it, could feel it beckoning just beyond her reach. The fullness of its promise drew her and she went, instinctively knowing that Aiden understood and wouldn't deny her.

Aiden tasted and felt her hunger the instant she gave it free rein. It consumed his senses, driving all but the need for completion from his awareness. The intent to take her gently slowly whirled away. Darcy knew, she understood, she accepted. And it was all in the world that mattered. Urgency, sharper and more demanding than he had ever known, overcame him.

He deepened his kiss in warning, and she greeted his advance with a moan of gratitude and pleasure. Blindly, he gathered the hem of her chemise into his hands and pulled it upward. Her hands slipped along his shoulders, pushing his shirt aside with equal speed and determination. Tearing his mouth from hers, he lifted the chemise over her head and tossed it aside, then helped her free his arms from his shirtsleeves. She knelt beside him, her breathing ragged and her eyes bright with untamed hunger.

He cupped her breasts in his hands and scraped his thumbs over the hard buds of her nipples. Her eyes drifted shut, as she curled her fingertips into the hair of his chest. He bent forward and took her into his mouth.

Bolts of fiery pleasure shot through her as his hands and mouth caressed her, explored her with a boldness and swiftness that acutely satisfied her yearning and yet made her ache for so much more. Aiden knew what she was seeking. He could give her what she needed and wanted. She clung to him, pulling him close, willing him to understand that she needed his help. She had to reach the elusive goal, had to find her way there.

"More."

The whispered moan tore through Aiden, slashing restraint he hadn't known existed. With every measure of his will, he forced himself to slow his advance. But slowing was all he could do. He could have no more stopped than he could have stilled his heartbeat. He kissed her as he took her hips in his hands and settled himself between her parted thighs. She moaned and arched upward, her hands pressing into the small of his back. He entered her slowly, the heat and friction so exquisite it took his breath away. And when he met her maiden's barrier there was no choice. He eased back his withdrawal, pulling his lips from Darcy's. She looked up at him, her eyes clouded with frustration, her lips swollen and trembling. The words of preparation he'd thought to offer were lost in need. Hers. And his.

He adjusted his hold on her hips, lifting her, and then he plunged forward, driving into the depths of her, filling her, claiming her. He took her cry into his mouth and went still within her, kissing her gently, waiting until the pain eased and she was ready to explore the pleasure again. When she relaxed beneath him, he drew back to look into her eyes. "It won't hurt ever again. I promise, Darcy."

She looked at him without saying a word, and he began to worry that she had changed her mind. Then she slowly, and oh, so very deliberately, moved her hips against his. The sensation rolled over him. His moan of appreciation made her smile. His deep shudder of delight inspired her to move again.

He resolutely placed the thought of needing to protect her freedom in the front of his brain and then, promising himself that the full, unbridled measure of his release would wait for another time, set about giving her all the pleasure he could.

Darcy felt herself begin spiraling again, the circles at first slow and luxurious in their winding and then growing tighter and faster and wondrously compelling. Aiden watched her face, her eyes, as he moved within her, his thrusts quickening and lengthening in perfect understanding of what she wanted and needed. There was an odd mixture of happiness and resolve in his expression, but it was the look of his certain knowing that sent a heated flutter through her loins. He plunged into it, his teeth bared and a low sound rumbling in his chest.

Darcy gasped before the flood tide of delicious sensation, and rose to meet it. A greedy hunger, demanding and undeniable, consumed her. Beyond, beneath, over, and through the rawness of desire shimmered the mysterious promise. Its beckoning whisper was wordless, but her heart and soul surged forward, refusing to be denied attainment. It flitted before her, closer but still beyond her grasp, just on the other side of sensation, on the other side of Aiden. An instinctive desperation filled her, tearing the breath from her lungs and a sob from her throat.

Aiden groaned at the fullness and pureness of the pleasure. Never had the building been so magnificent in its power. His heart raced and his body strained and quivered with the anticipation of release. Darcy rode the surging wave with him, her own hunger as intense and fevered as his own. No other woman . . . With the last vestige of restraint, he put Darcy's pleasure and protection before his own desire. The noble veil was thin and tattered, and he knew that he hadn't long before self-control would be impossible. But this time he would send her before him and then follow only as best he could allow. Resolution held him at the brink, gave him the clarity he needed to serve Darcy's struggle for fulfillment.

It was there. Her body heated and strained, fluttering with delight and the certainty that she was on the verge of triumph. And then it began to drift away, the shimmering still there, still wisping, but somehow denying her full grasp. She refused to let it evade her and struggled after it, breathless with need.

Aiden paused at the extremity of his withdrawal, waiting, feeling the fluttering within her quicken and tighten. She moaned and arched and reached for his hips and he could no longer bear denying either of them. He thrust forward, his filling swift and hard and complete. The cry came past her lips, resonant with the first sweet notes of victory and wonder. The sound of it rippled through his awareness, and then was lost, as the sweeping heat and intensity of her physical resolution enveloped his body. He pushed deeper, to that last infinite degree and held himself there, savoring the feel of her climax around him, letting her draw him to the very edge of his control. And when he teetered on the brink, he eased his possession an infinitesimal degree, then plunged deeply one last time. The wave rose molten, its release explosive at the end of his shuddering withdrawal.

Darcy let the shimmering wonder drift away with the last notes crescendoing through her heart and soul. She drifted downward, her needing sated, her body so sweetly exhausted, her mind slowly coming aware of the splendor of being held in Aiden's arms.

She willed herself past the stupor of satisfaction and opened her eyes. "Thank you," she whispered.

He smiled and pressed a kiss against her cheek. "It was a pleasure, Darcy. And thank you."

"I'm so sleepy," she heard herself answer, her eyes drifting closed of their own accord. "I'm sorry."

"Then sleep, angel. I'll be here when you wake."

It was a wonderful kiss, she thought. She'd have to ask for another later. When she could give him one as tender in return.

Aiden gathered her closer to him. His body still thrummed with desire, the release he'd attained insufficient to fully sate him. He'd fulfilled his promise to protect her freedom, and while he found some sense of satisfaction in having kept his word, there was a fundamental feeling of hollow failure in having spilled his seed outside her. He took a deep breath and decided that he could easily resolve the dilemma with a visit to an apothecary for sponges. It was a simple matter, really. Once Darcy was protected from pregnancy by more mechanical means, he needn't deny either of them the fullest measure of passion.

He glanced about the room, trying to figure the hour by the darkness of the shadow. Damn poor planning on his part, not to think of sponges in advance. And Darcy thought he'd so carefully planned her seduction.

Aiden chuckled silently. Truth was that he'd seen that they

had the privacy required, but the other practical aspects had tended to get lost in the heady visions of actually making love to her. And making love with her had been more than he could ever have imagined.

He smiled and skimmed his hand down the curve of Darcy's side, lingering first at the narrowness of her waist and then the gentle sweep of her hip. Suddenly he wanted her badly enough that the thought of curtailing his possession of her a second time didn't seem quite as endurable as it had minutes before.

She awakened at his gentle touch, keenly attuned to the ripple of pleasure that came with the stroke of his hand over her backside.

He propped his head in his other hand. "Tell me, Miss O'Keefe," he asked with a lazy smile, "do you have any specific plans for the next few months?"

She furrowed her brows and pursed her lips to give the impression that she was mentally contemplating an extensive social calendar. After a moment she smiled and replied, "Beyond picking pockets and putting food on the table, no. Why do you ask?"

"Would you mind too terribly much adding me to your daily list of activities?"

"I don't know," she playfully countered, "I'm a busy woman with so very many things to do. I've discovered that you're rather time-consuming, Mr. Terrell."

His grin turned wicked. "But think of the potential for diversion I offer." He slowly trailed his fingers along the curve of her hip, up her side, and over the swell of her breast.

Her heartbeat quickened. "I thought you had businesses to run and fortunes to amass. And heaven knows the family silver is probably in want of a good polishing. And there is that dent Jules has put in the family facade; it needs to be hammered out at your first opportunity. I'm sorry, Mr. Terrell, but I hardly think you have the time to be dallying with me."

He rolled forward, catching himself on his forearms on either side of her head. "Dallying," he said brushing his lips over hers, "implies a certain degree of whimsy and nonchalance. I'll have you know that I take making love with you very seriously."

She laced her fingers behind his neck. "Oh, you do?"

"Can't you tell?"

He seemed to truly wonder and so she gave him a quick shrug and an honest answer. "I sensed that you were holding back. Especially at the end. Perhaps you were simply trying to be gentle." His brow had inched upward with every word she uttered, and so she hastily added, "But in all honesty, I'm hardly an experienced judge of men's pleasure. Perhaps that's the way it's always done?"

He tilted his head slightly and gave her a quirked smile. "You're an observant little creature, aren't you?"

"By necessity, I'm afraid. It tends to keep me out of trouble. Pick a mark who's just lost his job or had a fight with his wife, and you could find yourself collecting your teeth up off the pavers. Keep a sharp eye was the first lesson I learned in reefing."

"What was the second?"

"Don't stand out from the crowd," she supplied. "Look common so that you're just another in a sea of faces, and another set of nondescript clothes in a throng of them. Never make a move that's out of place for where you are and who you're with. If someone glances your way, it should never cross their mind that you bear watching."

"But I noticed you that first morning. The very instant you stepped out from that stall and came after me."

"I apparently broke every rule that morning. The first in that you wanted your pocket reefed and I didn't read you right. The second, if you knew I'd marked you. And the third: Never work alone. And the fourth: Never count your take until you're well and sure away."

"What were you thinking to make you so uncharacteristically slipshod about your craft?"

"I was thinking that you cut a very fine figure in your expensive mulberry wool jacket. I was also thinking that your hair was unfashionably but attractively long and that it would feel like silk between my fingers." She ran her hands over the width of his shoulders, adding, "And by the by, you cut a very fine figure out of your jacket, too." She threaded her fingers through the hair at his nape. "And it does feel like silk. Warm silk."

"I've never known a woman quite like you, Darcy O'Keefe."

The words wound around her heart, both warming and flustering her. She quickly chose to make light of them. It was the safer course. "That doesn't surprise me. You don't strike me as the sort of man who regularly takes pickpockets to his bed. I suspect I'm your first in that respect."

"Well, you are, but that's not what I'm talking about." His eyes grew soft and smoky. "You're so openly honest and straightforward. Practical and logical. No pretenses and so delightfully unbound by convention. It's easy to be with you."

Accepting compliments had never been her strong suit. And accepting them for her performance in a man's bed was entirely too new an experience for her to be the least bit comfortable with it. "It's a bit disheartening to learn you're considered so predictable," she said.

"Predictable?" He kissed her lightly then drew back to smile and say, "Darling, you're one exquisite surprise after another."

"Then I might have a future in the mistress market after all?"

His smile faltered and there was a sudden flicker of darkness in the depths of his eyes. He recovered the smile quickly enough, but the darkness remained in his eyes when he lowered his head and kissed her soundly. The shadow was still there when, only a heartbeat later, he released his claim to her mouth, pushed himself to his knees, and said, "Wait here. I'll be right back."

She sat up and watched him disappear around the screen in the corner, wondering what she had said or done that had so suddenly changed his mood and darkened his thoughts. She wished that Aiden would consider adopting more of the straightforward honesty he claimed to so admire in her. It would make his life much simpler. Not to mention hers.

Aiden picked his razor up from the silver tray and the sea sponge from the china dish on the other side of the wash basin. With deft strokes he whittled a piece of the sponge to the appropriate size and shape. He'd be damned to hell and back before he took to the road of celibacy again, double damned before he broke his vow to protect Darcy's freedom, and triple damned before he'd hold back one more time. Darcy was going to know precisely what it felt like to be loved thoroughly and well. *A future in the mistress market!* Over his dead body.

He strode around the screen and back to the bed. Darcy glanced at his clenched fist but she didn't say anything. He slipped beneath the covers with her and then showed her the sponge, saying, "The age-old method of preventing pregnancy. A rather impromptu and makeshift version, I'll admit, but it should suffice until we can visit an apothecary. I assume you know how to . . ." His words and hope for a delicate transfer of responsibility died at the sight of her lower lip caught between her teeth. "No, of course you don't." He gathered her into his arms.

"This is going to be awkward, isn't it?" she asked, her cheek against his shoulder.

"We only have to get through it once, darling. It will be ever so much easier after that. But the question at this point is: How much do you trust me?"

"I haven't run away screaming, have I?"

He chuckled, his heart suddenly insanely light and his spirits soaring. God, what had he ever done to deserve the wonder of Darcy O'Keefe?

DARCY HAD NEVER been both so irritated and so relieved by an interruption as she was by the knock announcing the arrival of their dinner. Aiden kissed her in quick reassurance before sliding off the bed, grabbing his dressing gown, and seeing to the servants setting their meal in the salon.

She scrubbed her hands over her face and took a deep

breath. Lord help her. Aiden's gentle explanations as he'd carefully fitted the sponge into place had sent her pulse racing and her desire soaring. She had made a practical decision to become Aiden's lover. She had clearly seen it as the unavoidable eventuality it had been. But the rationality of making love with Aiden had evaporated somewhere in the first minutes of the experience, and she had emerged from the other side of it utterly and absolutely shameless. She could only image what Aiden thought of her. Actually, she didn't want to dwell on it. She still had to face him over a meal, still had to help him find and stop his brother.

Vowing to exercise some modicum of self-restraint in the hope of preserving what little she still possessed of her dignity, Darcy rose and searched for something that would effectively cover her nakedness. Finding Aiden's discarded shirt on the floor, she slipped into it, buttoning it and then rolling up the sleeves. The sound of the outer door opening and closing told her that her reprieve was at an end. Squaring her shoulders, she opened the bedroom door and sauntered into the salon as though she had trysted and dined every night of her life.

Aiden watched her come toward him, and congratulated himself on the wisdom of having ordered platters of cold food. Darcy, her hair loose and tousled from their lovemaking, and wearing only his shirt, was a stirring sight. If he managed to choke down three mouthfuls before taking her back to bed, he'd count it a leisurely meal. The food would still be there later, none the worse for having been largely ignored.

In an unspoken decision, they elected to simply stand beside the table and sample the fare casually. Aiden was on his fourth scoop of caviar when Darcy took her first taste of smoked pheasant. She made a breathy sound of pleasure and then quietly moaned, "Lord, this is so good."

God Almighty, but watching Darcy nibble and listening to her moan was a carnal pleasure in and of itself. And then she licked her fingertips, and what little interest he'd had in food was gone. Blindly, he put the bread crust and dollop of caviar back on the plate.

She frowned at his action, then looked at him, her dark brows knitted. "What?"

"I'm very hungry."

"The smoked pheasant is delicious," she countered, her smile innocent and so inviting. "Try some."

"That's not the kind of hunger I'm talking about," Aiden murmured, taking her hand. He slowly licked the tips of her fingers. Her eyes widened, anticipation flickering in their depths. He licked the tip of her first finger again, and then slowly took it into his mouth. Desire flared in her eyes as her heartbeat thrummed in the delicate hollow at the base of her throat.

When he traced the underside of her finger with the tip of his tongue, she closed her eyes and swayed toward him with a breathy "Jesus."

He led her into his bedroom, pressed her back onto the bed, and made love to her with an intensity that sent her careening wildly into the star-bright oblivion. And Aiden held back nothing of himself. He surrendered his control with a low, throaty cry of triumph that rippled through her and sent her soaring into the heavens a second time. Spent and breathless, they clung to one another in the fiery aftermath. Aiden kissed her and stroked her gently, apologizing unnecessarily for his roughness and haste, then slipped into the realms of deep, contented sleep.

Darcy drifted into the sated void in his wake, her last thought that nothing as wonderful as loving Aiden could be either shameful or wrong.

THE SUN WAS high overhead, its light brilliantly reflected by the island sand beneath his feet. Darcy was there somewhere. He could sense her presence. Perhaps up the path, around the bend. He went, plucking a white hibiscus blossom as he passed. He'd give it to her and then take it back to trail the soft petals over her bare skin.

But he had to find her first. She waited for him. Just a few more steps. He rounded the corner.

His father's house sat before him, the paint blistered and peeling beneath the Caribbean sun. The drone of flies filled the air. Darcy . . .

Aiden came awake with a heart-tearing start and an overwhelming need to find Jules before it was too late.

CHAPTER 18

THE SPACE BESIDE her was still warm, but Aiden was gone. She found him standing beside the bureau buttoning his shirt cuffs. "Aiden?"

"I didn't mean to wake you, Darcy. Go back to sleep."

She sat up. "Where are you going?"

"I'm off to inveigle an invitation to one or more of Boston's gentlemen's clubs and make some discreet inquiries after Jules." He reached for his coat and, pulling it on, added, "It's actually an early hour for the clubs. I'll still be able to see through the smoke."

"Give me a minute or two to get dressed, and I'll go with you. It won't take me any longer than that." She scrambled out of the bed, knowing her trousers and shirt were folded in one of the valises Maisey had packed for her.

Aiden stepped into her path and caught her by the shoulders. "You know you can't go into a gentleman's club, Darcy. They have very stringent rules about admitting women. And no, before you even suggest it, you're not going to attempt to masquerade as a young man."

"I wasn't going to suggest either course. I'll wait outside. It's my job to help you find Jules. I can stand in the shadows and watch for him."

"As Jules will no doubt be watching for you. No, Darcy, you'll wait here behind the bolted door."

"But—"

"I promise to be careful. And I promise not to be gone any longer than necessary."

"I don't like being left behind."

"And I don't like leaving you. But just this once, do what I ask instead of being stubbornly independent." He kissed her gently and set her away. "Now get some sleep. You won't have much of a chance after I return."

He might not have liked leaving her, but he did it well. Darcy watched the door close behind him and knew that the day would eventually come when he'd close it for good. Aiden had made it clear that their relationship was nothing more than physical—and temporary. She'd known how he felt, and accepted the terms before surrendering. She'd gone to Aiden's arms and into Aiden's bed fully knowing that the time would come when she would have to accept their parting with dignity and then go on with her life as though he'd never passed through it. Deciding that there was no time like the present to practice, Darcy retrieved her trousers and threadbare shirt.

Once dressed, however, she didn't know what to do with herself. She wasn't the least bit sleepy. Restless, yes. And just a little hungry. . . . If Chandler had for once been the tiniest bit inefficient, the cold supper Aiden had ordered up earlier might still be on the table in the salon. They hadn't eaten much of it before they'd been drawn to a more compelling use of their time.

She let herself into the moonlit salon. The cart was gone. Darcy sighed, and then noticed the plate of cheese and fruit on the side table. Leave it to Chandler to anticipate the need for a midnight repast.

She selected an apple, considered the small knife on the table, and decided that one wasn't bound by proper etiquette when alone with an apple in the night. Not that she'd bothered to consider etiquette or decorum at any time before that point, she admitted. Aiden had a way of making her awareness narrow to only him and the exquisite sensations of the moment. Beyond that nothing else existed, nothing else seemed to matter. When Aiden held her, there was only the rightness of it.

But now that he wasn't holding her, the world beyond crowded forward, demanding her consideration. Darcy fully sensed the myriad unconnected puzzle pieces and the shadowy danger they presented. Biting into the fruit, she wandered to the window overlooking the street below. Two hacks waited for fares in the darkness, their coach lights glowing softly. Clouds of frost rose from the horses' nostrils, and smaller clouds wreathed the heads of the drivers huddled beneath their capes in the boxes. Darcy scanned the shadows along the opposite side of the street and saw no darker ones within them, no movement. Where was Jules tonight? How long would it be before he killed again?

Darcy nibbled at the apple, staring out over the rooftops of Boston. At least her mother was safe. Maureen and Mick would see her protected, from her own designs as well as any Jules might entertain. And Maisey was safe, too. Maisey was here with her. Darcy smiled. Actually, Maisey was here with Chandler. Darcy glanced over her shoulder at the two closed doors on the other side of the salon. There wasn't the slightest doubt in her mind that Maisey slept behind one and Chandler the other. Maisey was a good girl, and Chandler was one of the last true gentlemen.

A strange sense of separation crept over Darcy. She had never been as good as Maisey, never as innocent and certain that life would provide her a wondrous and happy existence. Darcy had always been amazed and envious of her friend's ability to float serenely above the untidiness and grittiness of life. Maisey lived for tomorrow and the certainty of a happily-ever-after.

Darcy smiled ruefully and took another bite of the apple. Fate had dealt her a very different hand than Maisey had been given. Unlike Maisey, she could live only for today. Sometimes, when things were going exceedingly well, she had the luxury of looking toward the end of the present week, but never any further than that. Until Aiden had stepped into her life.

Darcy leaned her forehead against the cold window glass. Aiden. He had turned her life upside down. And yet somehow, despite the danger that came with his presence . . . Darcy sighed, unable to find adequate words to describe the effect Aiden had wrought. Her existence was decidedly more complicated than it had ever been. More tenuous, too. And yet she felt a wonderful, bone-deep sense of tranquillity and certainty.

It should have felt false; she knew that it was. Aiden wasn't a gentleman. He wasn't a knight in shining armor who would carry her away to his castle and make her his regal lady. He was a dark, battle-scarred crusader who had come to slay a dragon and had asked her to wield a sword at his side while healing his wounds in the respites. And for some unfathomable reason she felt honored by the request, pleased that he thought her worthy and able.

"Darcy," she said ruefully, "you're a pathetic fool. If by some miracle the crusader doesn't get himself and you killed, he's going to kiss you soundly and ride away. You're going to be left behind with nothing but a 'thank you most kindly, miss.' Aiden has too many dragons and too many wounds. He can't hope beyond today any more than you can."

She chuckled darkly. "Sweet Mary, don't we suit each other?" They had taken different roads to the same lonely destination. And both of them were trying to find some small comfort in a single bed at the wayside inn. "You're *both* pathetic fools, Darcy O'Keefe."

But were they really? she wondered. The comfort of Aiden's presence, of his arms around her, was temporary. She knew that. But it was a comfort her heart and soul needed. Perhaps it was the same for Aiden. Perhaps this time of being together would give them the strength they needed when the day came for them to resume their solitary and uncertain journeys.

She heard the soft click of a door latch behind her. Nathan Chandler's door latch. She straightened and waited.

"Miss Darcy? Is there anything I can get for you?"

"No, but thank you, Chandler," she answered without turning away from the window. "I appreciate the offer."

"Very good. I'll bid you a good night, and trust that you'll call if you change your mind."

"Chandler?" she asked on sudden impulse.

"Yes, miss?"

She continued to look out over the rooftops. "If I were to ask you a personal question about Aiden, would you answer it?"

"My loyalty lies with Aiden," he replied gently. "I can only provide you answers that do not violate the confidence he's placed in me."

"I understand."

"What is it that you'd like to know?"

She had to know if there was a sliver of hope. "Has Aiden ever been in love?"

"Not to my knowledge. And I believe I would have known."

"Did you like Wilhelmina, Chandler?" she pressed.

"My relationship with the woman was limited," he answered, his tone cool and distant, "but from my vantage, I saw little to recommend her."

"Aiden's voice goes flat just like that when he speaks of her. Why?"

"He has unpleasant memories of the association. I'm afraid that I can't say anything more, Miss Darcy. It is Aiden's place to tell you the details, if he wishes you to know."

"She hurt him badly, didn't she?"

"Let us simply say that she opened and deepened wounds he'd always borne. In the spirit of fairness, she probably wasn't aware she did so, but the act was done and couldn't be called back even if she had been of a mind to do so—which she wasn't."

"She must not have known Aiden very well."

"She didn't care to. Good night, Miss Darcy."

"Night, Chandler."

What had Wilhelmina done? Aiden had so many wounds. He was so easy to hurt.

Darcy looked down at the half-eaten apple in her hand, and realized her appetite had fled. Squaring her shoulders, she turned away from the window and the sadness of her thoughts.

As crazy as it was, it was much easier to think about Jules.

THE LIGHT SHINING under the door told him someone waited for him. Darcy. He put the key in the lock and let himself into the room. He found her sitting at the secretary, dressed in her boyish clothes and doodling with pen and ink. The page was covered with interlocking circles of all sizes, some filled with intricate designs, others starkly void. A sense of uneasiness crept up his spine.

"What are you doing up, Darcy?" he asked.

"I couldn't sleep. My mind has been too restless, thinking about all the puzzles. Did you learn anything about Jules?"

"We were right about his using another's identity, Darcy," he supplied, shrugging out of his coat. "It seems that Dr. Emile LeClaire, French physician, has risen from the grave and is haunting Boston. He's been seen in the gaming rooms, but no one seems to know much about him or where he's staying."

"It's a step closer than we were in Charlestown." She rose from the chair and came to stand in front of him. "I suppose we should be grateful for it." Reaching up to untie his stock, she arched a brow. "Have you been drinking, Aiden?"

It was nice to have Darcy meet him this way. He put his hands around her waist and lifted his chin to ease her task. "You can't very well go to a tavern and a gentleman's club and not drink. The second rule of reefing applies to those arenas as well. But I assure you that my brawn is still quite capable of being at your disposal."

"Made sure of it, did you?"

"Indeed." He grinned at her, slipped his arms around her, and drew her full against him. "May I be allowed to prove it?"

"Do you always ask for permission, Aiden?"

"Do I need to?"

"No."

"That's a rather extravagant gift. Is it your way of thanking me for the wardrobe?"

"Actually, it's my way of trying to make up for all I think you've been denied in your life."

The sense of uneasiness returned doublefold. He knew Darcy well enough to know that unless he diverted her attention quickly, he was going to find himself spitted on her questions. Leaving her alone to think was a dangerous thing. "I appreciate the tender sentiment, Darcy," he countered roguishly. "But fairness compels me to remind you that I'm the son of a wealthy man and a wealthy man in my own right. Not much has ever been denied me."

"Except for the love and acceptance of your father."

He groaned. "We're back to this, are we?" He seized the easiest and fastest way out of the ordeal. He smiled down at her. "Make love with me, and then we'll talk about it."

"You tend to use sex as a way to avoid thinking, Aiden. Let's talk first, and then we'll go back to bed."

She might as well have slapped him. Aiden let go of her and stepped back. "Sex as a reward for compliance," he observed sardonically. "You're getting very good at being a mistress. You've learned quickly, Darcy. It hasn't even been a full six hours yet."

"You also tend to use confrontation as a way to avoid what you don't want to face," she observed, unruffled. "I won't let you deter me, Aiden."

"So you think you know me, do you?"

"I know only what you want me to know. You've let me have glimpses of your past, Aiden, and I can't help but feel that you've done so in the secret hope I'll be curious enough to ask for more. And that I'll be determined enough to keep you from your usual evasions."

"And why the hell would I want you to know about my past?" he demanded, turning and walking away. "In all your musing, have you asked yourself that, Darcy O'Keefe?"

Yes, I have. I think you're tired of bearing the burden alone, and you want to lighten it by sharing it. But Darcy knew that such honesty wouldn't help their cause or ease Aiden's inner torment. Aiden couldn't accept compassion. For him it would be too close to pity. So instead of honesty, she gave him an answer he could accept, one that would appeal to his rational side and let him feel as though he'd escaped the issue.

"I think you know—if only deep down inside—that Jules is driven by what happened in the past, Aiden. And while I truly believe you feel an obligation to stop a murderer who's legally your brother, I also think it's far more than that. I think something pushed Jules over the edge, and you feel personally responsible for it. The past is driving both of you, Aiden. Maybe Jules knows what it is; maybe he doesn't. I can't say. But I do know that you're never going to catch him if you don't turn around, face the past, and understand how it's shaped this gruesome game you and Jules are playing."

She watched Aiden stop at the side table and pick up a brandy snifter. Then he swore and flung it against the far wall. The glass shattered into glittering slivers. Aiden stood glaring at the mar on the wallpaper, his hands fisted at his sides. Darcy glanced at Chandler's door and sensed that he wouldn't attempt to intervene. He'd let her do what had to be done.

Darcy crossed the room and deliberately stepped into Aiden's view. She picked up a snifter and handed it to him saying, "Here's another, Aiden. There are four more on the tray. If you need more, I'll send downstairs for them."

Aiden closed his eyes. "Jules," he said softly. "Our father . . ." He raked his fingers through his hair. "Christ. Where to begin?"

"Perhaps it would be easiest to remember the rumors that he wasn't really your father."

He opened his eyes and met her gaze. "Do you have any idea how confusing it is to refer to a man as 'father,' knowing full good and well that you're compounding the lie every time you speak?"

She set the glass back on the tray. "Do you know who your real father is?"

He exhaled and walked away, saying as he went. "Nathan's father, Edward Chandler, was my father's manservant. Nathan's mother died of childbed fever only days after bringing him into the world, and apparently Edward's grief was deep. The story the servants whispered was that my mother tried to comfort him and ease him through the worst of it. In the course of healing Edward, her own need came to the fore, and their relationship became more personal. I was the result."

"Did your father fire Edward Chandler when he found out about the affair?"

Aiden snorted and paced back toward her. "If he'd done that, he'd have missed the opportunity to make pointed but cryptic remarks as to how he'd been betrayed and disappointed by those in whom he'd placed his trust. As though the son of a bitch deserved the right to demand an ounce of anyone's pity. If he hadn't been such an unfeeling bastard my mother would have never sought comfort in Edward Chandler's arms. And my father drove my mother to her death, just as surely as he drove her into adultery."

"You mother ended her own life?" Her mind flitted to her own memories of watching her mother struggle to live.

"In a manner of speaking. She took a fever and surrendered her will to live. Edward died soon after her." His voice softened as he added, "At least they found peace, and were finally together without the shadow of my father looming over them."

"But they left you to live beneath it."

"As I told you before," he said, "I found my own way of enduring it, and I can't resent that which made me strong and independent."

"You also told me that you thought your father would have disinherited you at the first opportunity."

"That statement wasn't based on speculation, Darcy," he explained as she settled herself into the opposite corner of the settee. "He summoned me to his study to tell me privately, two weeks after he and Blanche were wed. His plan was to legally adopt Jules and to declare him his legitimate and rightful sole heir. The provisions of my mother's will granted me the property and wealth she had brought into their marriage as a dowry and, though it pained him terribly to admit it, he hadn't been able to break the will and deny me her estate."

Aiden leaned forward, resting his elbows on his knees, his hands together and his fingers laced in the space between them. His gaze was fixed on the carpet, but Darcy knew his vision focused on the past.

"His refusal to give up my mother's property was the only thing that kept him from throwing me out the door that day. He was quite plain-spoken about it all. I was fourteen then, and seven years lay between me and majority age and the right to exercise my own will over my inheritance. Seven years in which my father intended to exercise the full powers of his conservatorship and systematically destroy whatever he could of what would be mine."

Softly she said, "So he intended to cast you into the world penniless at majority age, and then deny you any inheritance from him."

"To scrape out as mere an existence as the mongrel who had sired me." He smiled ruefully. "But life under his roof had already fashioned my will. My mother's family had owned a small cottage on the other side of St. Kitts. They had often taken holidays there. It was on one of those holidays that her father met mine, and the bargain was struck. The house was part of her dowry and had long been vacant. The day my father laid his grand plan before me, I made it my home."

"You lived all by yourself, Aiden?"

"I took my favorite servants and my tutors with me. And I sent my father the monthly bills for maintaining my separate world. Reverend Stirling decided to take my social polishing upon himself, and he and Nathan—who had been sent to live with the good reverend when Edward died—were at my house more often than not. Actually, leaving my father's house was the best decision I ever made. I discovered that the world wasn't nearly as dark on the other side of the island."

"If you were living there, then how was it that you were in

your father's house for Jules to attack you with the decanter
and then the machete?"

Aiden chuckled darkly. "The one advantage of living with
a bastard for fourteen years is that you learn how to be a bastard yourself. I decided to excel at it. I never missed an opportunity to make an appearance and needle him. Especially
when it became clear that Jules wasn't quite the noteworthy
son he'd envisioned. Not too terribly mature of me, I'll grant
you, but I wasn't about to creep away with my tail tucked between my legs, as he wanted me to."

"Did you needle Jules, too?"

He turned his head and met her gaze. "Sometimes you're
entirely too perceptive, Darcy O'Keefe."

"Not really," she countered with a smile she hoped reassured him. "I doubt if I'd have had the strength to resist the
impulse either. I assume Jules knew of your father's plan?"

He looked back to the carpet and nodded. "And he tended
to lord it over me at every opportunity. At least at first. In
hindsight, I regret having given the verbal slashes I did. They
were neither kind nor wise."

"Most fourteen-year-olds aren't particularly noted for either characteristic. What did you say to counter Jules's
taunts?"

"I felt compelled to remind him that he wasn't as intelligent or resourceful as I was, and that while he could very well
inherit everything, I'd still have more than he did in the end.
I had sense enough to make and keep a fortune. With Jules's
limited acumen, all he could hope to do was lose what he'd be
given." He straightened and leaned into the back of the settee. "There were a considerable number of variations on that
general theme."

"Did your father agree with your assessment of Jules's abilities?"

"He'd have choked on his own bile before admitting it to
me or anyone else. But there was one central given with Frederick Terrell: The preservation of his wealth came before all
else. He couldn't face the prospect of his own eventual death
if there were even the slightest chance of his worldly goods

being squandered. The protection of his fortune weighed more heavily than his hatred of me. In a devious twist that only he could have conceived, he wrote his will leaving everything to Jules, but in my hands as conservator. He denied me the wealth but made me responsible for it."

"Perhaps," Darcy ventured, "it was more than merely the protection of his money and a desire to twist the knife. Perhaps he understood that you were just as much a bastard as he was and felt a grudging sense of admiration. If you look at it that way, it was truly a compliment."

He laughed, softly but honestly. "Thank you, Darcy. That's a unique approach to consolation."

"You're not a ruthless bastard, you know. When you're not boxed into a corner you're really a very decent man."

"You can thank Nathan for that. He seemed to have acquired a great deal of wisdom early in life—along with the will to see that I eventually developed a rudimentary conscience. I'm sure that's in large part due to his having spent all those years with Reverend Sterling."

"Does Nathan know that you're half-brothers?"

Aiden nodded. "We haven't spoken of it since we were boys. Now it simply lies quietly under our more formal and public relationship. My will grants all my possessions to him."

"Does Jules know of the terms of your father's will?"

"I'm inclined to think that he does. I couldn't find Frederick's copy anywhere in the house. And before you ask, yes, he kept one. In the center drawer of his desk. It gave him great pleasure to bring it out and gloat. I can only conclude that Jules took the copy with him when he fled the house and St. Kitts."

"Did the will specify how long you are to act as Jules's conservator?"

"Until Jules is judged completely sane and maintains a semblance of a normal existence for a period of five years." He cocked a brow. "Which, of course, means in a practical sense that I'll never escape the responsibility."

"Unless, of course, Jules can convince a court that he is sane," Darcy countered.

"And do you think butchering his way across the British Isles and America goes toward that end?"

"Probably not," she admitted. "What happens to the property held for Jules if he dies before you do?"

"I inherit, my father spins in his grave, and he'll meet me at the gates of hell to exact his final vengeance."

A thought, horrible in its twisted nature, suddenly came to her. Her heart slammed against the wall of her chest. "Aiden, if Jules does know about the terms of the will—The murders never begin until after you've arrived in a city. What's to prevent him from going to the authorities and claiming that you're the murderer, not him? He could claim that you're trying to frame him, to kill him so you can inherit the estate in your own right."

He looked at her as though he had long been wondering when the thought would occur to her. "Nothing prevents him from doing just that, Darcy," he replied easily. "Nothing at all. In fact, I expect him to take that course if he's ever apprehended and accused of his crimes."

"The terms of the will would make it extremely difficult to defend yourself against the accusation."

"Extremely. It would come down to his word against mine, and I stand to gain from his conviction and subsequent execution." He smiled grimly. "You've got to give Jules credit. He's very neatly managed to eliminate many of those who could conveniently testify to his madness. There's only Chandler, Blanche, and myself left to bear witness against him. And Chandler's testimony would be largely discounted on the basis of our relationship. The only bright spot is the rather poor likelihood that Jules will be brought in alive. By me or anyone else. If he is, though—" Aiden shrugged. "I'll have to muster a defense and hope it's good enough."

"You've nothing to worry about, Aiden. I'll testify in your behalf. So will Mick and Seamus and Maisey. If the charges are made in Charlestown, the matter will never go before a judge. Mick will see to it. I promise."

"And if they're brought elsewhere?"

"I'll be there for you, Aiden. You might well have to pay for my passage across the world, but if you send for me, I'll come." The wonder and gratitude in his eyes pressed against her heart. If she let him offer his thanks in words, she'd embarrass them both. Darcy smiled and abruptly changed the subject. "Tell me about Blanche."

Aiden drew her toward him. When he had her curled against his side and wrapped in his arms, he pressed a kiss to the top of her head before answering, "There isn't much to say. Blanche and I understood one another from the start, and there was never any private pretense of being mother and son. Publicly, we both played the parts my father decreed, but it was a very shallow performance at best."

"But the picture you keep . . ."

"I actually entertained some delusional hopes for happiness in the earliest days of my father's marriage to Blanche, in the days when that portrait was painted. I keep it to remind myself of important lessons learned the hard way, lessons I'd do well never to forget."

To mistrust? To not let yourself hope? Darcy knew better than to ask for the answers. "Where is Blanche now?" she asked instead. "Still on St. Kitts?"

"I ordered the house boarded up as soon as the bodies were removed for burial. Under the terms of the will, Blanche was provided a generous monthly stipend to see to her needs, and she returned to her family home in St. Croix the same day as the funeral."

"Let me guess, Aiden. You're responsible for seeing to her financial affairs as well."

"I'm somewhat frightened to see how well you follow my father's line of reasoning."

"Don't be. Once you see and understand the first twist in it, it's really very simple after that. Has Blanche married again?"

Aiden's chin brushed her hair as he shook his head. "My life wasn't the only one my father wanted to control from the grave. The terms of the will provide that the stipend continue only as long as Blanche remains the grieving widow. She's intelligent enough to realize the advantages in maintaining the illusion."

It was all so much. She had gathered so many new pieces to the puzzle. Some of them fit together easily. But others were hopelessly detached. Darcy sensed that she was still missing one or two simple ones, the ones that would make it all fall magically into place. She needed a bit of time to consider the new picture emerging.

"Now," Aiden said, gathering her closer, "have I sufficiently satisfied your curiosity, Darcy? Have I perhaps earned the right to be satisfied myself?"

She recognized the undercurrent in his voice, and knew where his inclinations were now leading. She also knew that she would willingly go with him. But not until after she'd made an effort to bring their conversation full circle. "There still remains the matter of devising a way to use Jules's motives to bring him to us."

"What motives?" he countered. "All I can see is insanity and blood lust."

"Maisey suggested it earlier and I think she's right. I still think there's more to it, but I could well be wrong. Jules does seem to be going about this game in large part to prove himself more intelligent than you. So far he's winning. Quite handily, I might add."

"I'm really very tired of thinking about Jules and the twisted relationships with my father. Can't we set it all aside until the morning, Darcy? I think much better when I've had some sleep."

"Oh, it's sleeping you want to do," she said, turning in his arms to grin up at him. "Why didn't you say so?"

"I'm not *that* tired," he retorted, slipping his hand beneath her shirttail. He cupped her breast and slowly scraped the pad of his thumb over her nipple. "At least not yet."

CHAPTER 19

I T WAS A beautiful autumn afternoon. The air was crisp and clear, the sun warm on her shoulders, and the slight breeze cool on her cheeks. She walked in the park at Aiden's side, her gloved hand resting on his muscled forearm, the perfect embodiment of feminine decorum. It was a wholly false facade, she knew. Getting dressed for the outing had taken a delightfully wicked detour soon after Aiden had tightened her corset lacings. Darcy felt the heat of memory infusing her cheeks and she deliberately turned her thoughts in a more publicly circumspect direction.

"What could you offer Jules that would draw him to a place of our choosing?" she mused aloud.

"My head on a platter?"

"Please try to be serious, Aiden," she countered, while returning a passing woman's nod of acknowledgment. "Would Jules be interested in the estate you hold for him?"

"I have no idea what a crazy man values." He shrugged. "But, be that as it may, I can't give it to him if he doesn't meet the criteria established in the will. And if Jules took the copy of the will, as I think he did, Darcy, then he's going to know the conditions under which he can have control of his estate. Ergo, he's also going to know that any offer I make isn't genuine. If he's capable of any rational thought at all, he'll know it's nothing but an attempt to entrap him."

"Well, damnation."

Aiden smiled at her. "It was a fine idea, even if slightly flawed."

"I'm not surrendering the notion quite yet," she quickly retorted. "Jules wants to feel superior to you. We want Jules to openly confront us. Now, it appears to me that we have to give him a triumph worth gloating over in person. The question is what?"

"And you truly think there's an answer?"

"There has to be," Darcy declared. They walked on together in silence, Aiden politely tipping his hat to passersby and Darcy mulling over what she knew of Jules and the game he played with Aiden. Despite her efforts, there were no grand revelations. If only it were as simple as Aiden deciding to walk away, she silently groused. And in her complaint she caught the faint glimmer of a possible solution.

"What do you think Jules would do if you publicly announced that you'd tired of chasing him around the world and were going on with the rest of your life?"

Aiden didn't so much as pause before answering, "I think he'd go after someone whose death would enrage me enough to resume the game."

"Chandler?" she suggested. "He's your brother."

"Or you," he countered bluntly. "You're my lover."

Her mind racing through the maze of the newly born plan, she said, "Then it would be best to send Chandler back to St. Kitts. He'll be safe from Jules there."

Aiden shook his head. "I can see the lines along which you're thinking, Darcy. My response is an unequivocal and resounding *no.*"

"You owe me the courtesy of hearing me out, Aiden. This has a chance of succeeding. A far better chance than stumbling blindly around Boston—a city, I'll remind you, that I don't know—in the dim hope that we'll conveniently trip over Jules."

"If any plan you're considering involves using yourself as a lure, you might as well save your breath, Darcy O'Keefe. I won't be a party to it."

Angry at his obstinacy, she abandoned her effort at subtle persuasion. "When you hear that Jules has butchered again, your chivalry is going to be little comfort against the knowledge that you could have prevented it and didn't."

The retort struck just as she had intended. His shoulders squared and his eyes narrowed. It was a long moment before he spoke. "I reserve the right to alter your basic plan as I see fit. Right up to and including forbidding its implementation."

If they hadn't been on a public walkway, she'd have stopped and kissed him soundly. "As I said, send Chandler back to St. Kitts, so he's out of harm's way and there's only one person for Jules to consider coming after: *me*. Your original plan to find Jules plays well into this one. We'll go out as man and mistress, publicly declaring our relationship. If Jules is watching us as we think he is, then he'll see us and think you have a vulnerability you haven't had in the past."

"And how is it that you intend to move him beyond watching and knowing?" Aiden asked warily. "What temptation are you thinking of offering him to act?"

"We'll make it known that we're leaving Boston soon; that we're going to travel the world or some such thing," she explained, her heart and mind racing with the real hope of having finally found a way to bring Aiden's nightmare to an end. "With Jules frequenting the gentlemen's clubs, he'll likely hear the news. It's even more likely that he'll be enraged when he thinks that your focus has shifted away from him. You're essentially dismissing him and the threat he poses. You're refusing to play the game any more."

"And he'll have to act to convince me not to give up the game."

"Precisely," she cried, thrilled that he understood. "And before we leave Boston, or he's the one who will be chasing and trying to find. It would put you in command, and—if we're right about his motives—that's the last thing on earth he wants."

"It's very dangerous, Darcy. If anything went awry . . ." He shook his head.

"I have faith in you," she declared, undaunted by his reservations.

If he heard her, he gave no indication of it. Instead, he turned her around and started walking in the direction from which they'd come. She could see him working the plan over in his mind, examining the mechanics of it and searching for weaknesses.

"If Chandler has any understanding of why I'm sending him away, he'll refuse," he said after a while. "His sense of honor wouldn't let him allow you to serve as the lure if there's a possibility he might do just as well for the task. And I suspect Maisey isn't going to be particularly enamored with the idea of Chandler leaving town."

"But letting Chandler stay makes our plan unnecessarily complicated," she quickly observed. "And besides, letting him stay puts his life at risk, and I suspect Maisey wouldn't be at all happy about that either. I think this is one of those situations where she isn't going to be pleased with me no matter what I do, so I might as well have her angry for my favoring the nobler of the two courses. No, I think we stand a better chance of goading Jules by using me as the pretense for your deciding to give up the chase. We can make our attraction quite believable."

He surprised her by asking, "Do you think Maisey might be interested in going to St. Kitts with Chandler?"

"I think she would," Darcy replied, "but she isn't about to go anywhere without her ma and da's approval. And they would certainly have some expectations from Chandler before they gave their blessing."

"The first and foremost being marriage, I gather."

"The Riordans are rather traditional in their thinking, I'm afraid."

He cocked a brow. "They can't be too terribly hidebound, or they wouldn't have permitted Maisey to have you for a friend, much less allowed her to accompany you to Boston."

Darcy gave him a shrug and explained, "Maisey and I have been friends as long as I can remember. The path I took seven years ago couldn't undo what had gone before. The Riordans understand that it was the only choice I had. As for letting her come over to Boston with me . . . The Riordans had met Chandler, and they gave Maisey their blessing because they saw the potential for a match."

"Just as your mother sees the potential in our being together," Aiden observed quietly.

Her heart skittered, but she knew the truth—and that she had to face it. "But there isn't any beyond what's in her imagination, is there, Aiden?"

He drew her to a halt and faced her squarely. "I'd be a very poor bet for a husband," he admitted. "Far too many ghosts, and no concept at all of what a good one should be or do. Now, if for some inexplicable reason you wanted to tie yourself to a selfish bastard, I'd be your man."

"Far better to be your mistress."

"Would you consider it?"

The lushness of his voice stroked her senses, and again her heart skittered. Again she accepted that the best course lay in facing the truth. "I'd be lying if I said there wasn't a certain attraction to the idea," she answered. "But the realities make it impossible, Aiden. Once this business is done with Jules, you have to return to your world in St. Kitts. You have your empire to tend and grow. I have my mother to care for. I can't very well move her to St. Kitts for the few months we'd be together, and you can't very well travel back and forth between Charlestown and St. Kitts every time you want your bedsheets twisted. It doesn't seem at all workable to me."

"Have I ever mentioned how utterly maddening I find your practicality?"

There was an edge of anger in his voice but she chose to ignore it. "No, you haven't," she retorted brightly, "but I have sensed it on one or two occasions. In all fairness to me, though, you should probably admit that you've just as often found it quite useful for our larger task."

"I have." The concession seemed to free him from his darker thoughts. He managed a smile as he added, "There doesn't seem to be anything for us to do but use the time we do have together as best we can. If you'd asked me when we began if I'd come to enjoy our association, I'd have said you were mad. But the truth is, Darcy, I do. Very much."

"As do I. Your pigheadedness aside, of course."

"Of course." He brushed his lips over hers, the possession brief. But his hands tightened about her waist, and she sensed his desire for her. Stopping on a public walkway was a breach of decorum in and of itself. The kiss, delicate and fleeting though it had been, bordered on scandalous. And suddenly she realized what Aiden had been about. She smiled up at him, delighted with his having tacitly accepted the course she'd proposed.

"Courting scandal, are you, Aiden?" she asked. "It's the perfect way to begin to lay the foundations of our ruse for Jules. And then, tomorrow night at the theater, we'll simply add to the illusion we're building."

"You're forgetting that I haven't agreed to the plan."

He had, but there was no benefit to backing him into a corner and forcing him to admit it. Aiden didn't respond well to being cornered. "Perhaps," she said diplomatically. "But I think you will. You don't have any better plan with which to counter it."

"I don't like it, Darcy. There's too much risk involved for you. You could be hurt."

"I told you that I trust you."

"I wouldn't," he said darkly.

She knew her body was safe in his keeping. He wouldn't let anything happen to her. She knew that to the center of her bones. Just as she knew that watching him walk out of her life was going to leave her patching an aching void. But it was far too late to worry about her heart. "Let's finish our stroll," she offered. And deciding to turn his thoughts in another direction, she added, "I can think of other things I'd much rather do with you."

He chuckled and turned them about, saying, "We'll cut across the green. It's the shortest way back."

They were emerging from the park entrance when they saw Chandler and Maisey strolling toward them. Maisey's arm was tucked around her escort's, just as Darcy clung to Aiden.

Darcy felt Aiden tense as the other couple acknowledged their presence. "Might as well get it over with now," Aiden muttered, just before lifting his chin and pasting a smile on his face.

"Chandler. Miss Maisey," he said as he drew Darcy to a halt in front of them. "Just the people we needed to see. Chandler, Darcy has come up with a possible plan for bringing Jules out of hiding."

Chandler instantly squared his shoulders. "I am, of course, willing to do whatever you require of me."

"Good," Aiden replied. "You'll be returning to St. Kitts as soon as we can arrange passage."

Chandler's brow shot up. "Are you perhaps planning to truss me up like a Christmas goose to accomplish this?"

A glance at Aiden's face told Darcy that he wasn't of a mind to cajole Chandler into graceful acceptance of the decree. Deciding that the situation required her intervention, and that Chandler's sense of honor mandated a small lie, she laid her hand on Chandler's forearm and smiled at him sweetly. "You said you'd do what needed to be done, Chandler. If you stay here, you'll weaken our plan and place yourself in unnecessary danger. We're going to let it be known that Aiden has given up the hunt for Jules, in the hope that he'll be so enraged, he'll come out of hiding and force a confrontation."

The look Chandler turned on Aiden was icy.

"There's no need for a lecture, Nathan," Aiden quickly protested. "The plan is very risky, I know. It's simplified if I don't have to worry about Jules coming after you to regain my attention."

"Darcy," Maisey ventured, quietly inserting herself in the conversation. "I don't know about this."

"Which part, Maisey?" Darcy inquired, hoping the conversational diversion her friend offered would ease the obvious tension between Aiden and Nathan. "Chandler going back to St. Kitts?"

Maisey's cheeks flushed with color, and she bowed her head

as she quietly acknowledged, "No, I'm not especially pleased by the thought of Nathan going."

Chandler patted her hand and gently said, "There is no reason to be concerned on either count, Maisey. I am not departing." He had no sooner concluded consoling Maisey's distress than he fixed Aiden with a hard look. "Might I have a word with you in private, Aiden?"

Knowing the confrontation was inevitable, Aiden turned to Darcy and, taking her hand from his arm, gently admonished, "We'll be back shortly. Stay with Maisey and don't wander off." Wishing he'd seen a lot more confidence in her eyes, he followed after Nathan. He'd gone no more than a dozen paces when Nathan turned around and stepped boldly into his path.

"Apparently you do need a lecture," Nathan began. "What are you thinking? I'm not a brick, Aiden. I can see what you and Darcy have so carefully left unspoken. You both know damn good and well Jules will come after her. To deliberately choose to put Darcy in physical danger, when you can just as well choose me for the task? If you feel the need to send anyone out of harm's way, send *her* to St. Kitts, not *me*!"

"First, I'm not about to put Darcy in harm's way," Aiden snapped. "And secondly, she won't go and leave her mother behind."

"And it's so very difficult to pack an old woman's bags and send her on an ocean voyage?" Nathan rejoined, sarcasm etching each and every word. "I hardly believe she could put up a resistance that would leave you battered and bleeding."

What had happened to Nathan? Aiden wondered. He was normally so placid. Was it the air, perhaps? Or maybe the water? "Darcy still won't go. She won't leave her task unfinished. It's simply her nature to see things through to the end, and there's something Mick is holding over her to keep her here."

Nathan fisted his hands at his sides. "Then I suggest that you need to parlay with Mr. O'Shaunessy at your first opportunity, discover whatever it is that he's using as leverage on

Darcy, and then dispose of it. Putting her life at risk is unconscionable, Aiden, and well you know it."

It was. He knew it. And yet there was rightness to it as well. He couldn't adequately explain it, but, because he felt Nathan deserved some sort of explanation, he tried as best he could. "I have absolutely no intention of placing Darcy in any danger at all. I'll keep her safe. She'll never be out of my sight or reach. Jules will have to go through me to get to her." Aiden paused and then gave Chandler the most fundamental truth of all. "Besides, I *need* to see it through with her, Nathan. I'm not ready to let her go yet."

Nathan snorted. "Have you considered that ensconcing her in your house on St. Kitts would be a large step toward keeping her for a while longer, much safer, and more within your reach than this addlepated scheme of yours?"

Aiden couldn't say whether it was Nathan's tone or the nature of the question, but the veil of distraction that had tempered his irritation began to slip away. "Hell, yes, I've thought of it," he said. "I've already told you that Darcy won't go. That bit of reality aside, it would be somewhat awkward, don't you think, to openly take a woman as a mistress with her mother living under the same roof?"

"While I have no doubt that Darcy would muster a more spirited resistance than her mother, I also have no doubt that you could in the end overpower her and neatly deposit her on board a ship bound for the islands. As for the awkwardness, might I suggest that you consider a more honorable course and ask the young woman to marry you?"

"Darcy isn't disposed to consider marriage. To me or anyone else. She's made it quite clear that she has plans for her own future. They don't include a family, or personal relationships beyond that with her mother."

"And you," Nathan observed sardonically, "being such an experienced man in affairs of the heart, believe her."

"I'm hardly a novice in these matters."

"I'm not speaking of seduction and bedding, you dolt!"

"Dolt?" Had Nathan actually called him a *dolt*?

"There are times when I could simply beat you even more senseless than you already are!"

"Senseless?" Aiden repeated, momentarily stunned by Nathan's uncharacteristic boldness. "I'm senseless?" He chuckled, suddenly more amused than angry. "And the day you think you can beat me, is—"

"I am going to speak my mind freely and—"

"You haven't been?"

"You may fire me if you like," Nathan ground out through clenched teeth. "I truly don't care. You are a *fool,* Aiden Terrell, if you believe Darcy O'Keefe doesn't in her heart of hearts want a husband and a family of her own. And you're an even bigger *fool* if you don't offer them to her!"

Offering. Memories flooded his mind, still bitter and painful. "Oh, yes," Aiden said mockingly, "There's no joy quite like knowing a woman is agreeing to marry you because she can't find a wealthier man or has no other recourse for her life. No joy quite like that of knowing she'll bear your children out of a sense of dreary obligation."

Nathan stepped closer and spoke quietly. "This stupidity of yours is shaped by Wilhelmina. Darcy would never consider the actions Wilhelmina took. Darcy is not at all like her."

Suddenly Aiden felt as though the earth was shifting beneath his feet. He didn't pause to consider the cause, but struggled to keep his focus on the argument with Nathan. "It's not just what happened with Willy, it's—"

"You buried the goddamned bastard, Aiden." More gently he added, "The anger and the mistrust should have been planted with him. Darcy O'Keefe is a gift from God—a gift you may or may not truly deserve. I'm not sure which. I do know that if you walk away from her, if you let any harm come to her, you'll never have another chance for this kind of happiness as long as you live. You'll spend the rest of your days becoming as hollow and mean as Frederick Terrell. Is that what you want?"

Christ, he wanted some peace and predictability in his world. He wanted Nathan compliant and marginally subservient again. He wanted to go back to the hotel, take Darcy in his arms, and forget that anything existed beyond the confines of their bed. He wanted Jules to stop butchering. And he wasn't going to get any of it until he resolutely committed himself to the plan to bring Jules out of hiding. Aiden met Nathan's gaze squarely and said, "I want you on a ship bound for St. Kitts immediately."

"I am not going," Nathan replied with a sad finality. "You may consider our relationship over. I will find lodgings and employment elsewhere."

Over? There was no trumpeting or brilliance to the revelation that swept over Aiden. It came quietly and with a cool, hard, inescapable clarity. They would never be employer and employee again. Words had destroyed the facade that had held their paths together for so long. Aiden saw the crossroads at which they stood, and knew that Nathan waited for him to make a decision on which way they would go.

"I'll accept your leaving my employ, Nathan," Aiden said quietly. "But neither of us can walk away. We're brothers. It's time we let that be the basis of being with one another."

"Then that is how we shall go forward," Nathan said warily. "I'll correspond from time to time, and I'll see that you receive an invitation to Maisey's and my wedding."

The idea of Nathan wedded to Maisey eased a measure of Aiden's tension. He grinned. "Then you've asked her to marry you? And she's accepted?"

"Actually, I was just preparing to do so when you and Miss Darcy joined us," Nathan replied with an abject sigh. "However, having resigned my position with you requires modifying that plan slightly. As soon as I've secured other employment, I intend to pursue my intention and ask Maisey to be my wife."

"Damn it all, Nathan. You don't *have* to resign. Ask her to marry you, get it done, and then take her back to St. Kitts for your honeymoon."

With a thin smile and cocked brow, Nathan answered, "But if I did, I would, in essence, be capitulating to your plan to place Darcy in danger. It's neither gentlemanly nor honorable. I can't place my happiness before Darcy's safety."

"Look, Nathan," Aiden said, determined to make the other understand. "I appreciate your determination to do what you think is right. But, you've found the woman you've always wanted. Now take her and your happiness and get the hell out of harm's way. Let Darcy and me muddle through this on our own. We'll be fine. I won't let anything happen to Darcy."

"For the life of me, I don't know precisely why I believe you, but I do."

"Your faith in me is boundless," Aiden supplied, grinning. "It always has been."

"Actually, I think my faith rests more in Darcy than it does in you."

Aiden chuckled. "Do you have a wedding date in mind?"

Nathan's gaze slipped over his shoulder, and Aiden turned to see what had caught his attention. Darcy and Maisey sat on a park bench, their conversation quick and liberally punctuated by hand gestures.

"It's my understanding," Nathan said, coming to stand beside him, "that the selection of a date is a matter left to the bride, and that the family often wishes for an extended courtship. Maisey and I haven't actually known each other very long, and while we're both certain of our feelings, I can see her family's possible request for a delay."

"You know, don't you," Aiden asked teasingly, "that there are sometimes extenuating circumstances that preclude waiting?"

"There won't be any," Nathan said with a good-natured albeit resigned chuckle. "I've always had more patience and restraint than you do."

"If your outburst a moment ago was an example of your patience and restraint—"

"It was the expression of years of frustration, Aiden. I've too often wanted to say things to you and have let social strictures keep me from it."

Aiden nodded. "Do you have any more notion than I do of how to go about being a brother?"

"No. Shall we sort it out as we go along?"

It was as good an idea as any he had. "Sorting as I go seems to be how I'm living all of my life these days," Aiden confessed. "Not that I like it. I simply don't have any other choice."

"If it helps any," Nathan offered, putting his hand on Aiden's shoulder, "I firmly believe it will make you a better man when all is said and done."

"You lived with Reverend Stirling far too long. It might have kept your planks straight and narrow, but it also made you entirely too optimistic."

"Well, we all have our crosses to bear." At Aiden's groan, Nathan laughed, and then, apparently deciding that their relationship had come to the point of honesty without the risk of blows, asked, "Have we reached a conclusion regarding this plan of yours to lure Jules out of hiding? I still stand to volunteer."

"I appreciate it, Nathan. I honestly do."

"I sense an approaching 'however.' "

"However," Aiden said with a slow nod. "I'm inclined to believe that Jules would be far more willing to take a risk to come after Darcy than he would be to come after you."

"Perhaps that's also something we should sort out as we go along."

"We'll only have a short while, until Darcy takes matters into her own hands. She's both impatient to be done with this and rather independently minded."

"Rather like yourself in that respect, then," Nathan observed.

"Perhaps. But she's a far better person than I am, Nathan. Far better."

"She's a far better person than Wilhelmina, too." And with that gentle broadside, his brother walked past him to rejoin their ladies.

CHAPTER 20

HAVING NEVER PAINTED her face, Darcy considered the pots, brushes, and bowls before her on the dressing table. Maisey had been so pleased with herself for having secured the magic coatings that not using them seemed to border on cruelty. Still . . . Darcy decided it was better to let her own pale cheeks suffice than risk looking like a strumpet plucked from the streets.

"Any particular reason for your frown, Darcy?" Aiden asked.

"I don't know how to use face paints," she admitted. "And I'm hoping that I can go without them."

"You don't need them," he assured her, crossing the room and coming to stand behind her. Their reflection in the dressing table mirror was captivating. God, but he was a breathtaking sight in his black tailored coat and white starched shirt. Darcy found herself wishing that they didn't have to go out this evening. For some reason the thought of sharing him with other people irked her.

"But I know something you do need," Aiden said. She watched in the mirror as he reached inside his coat and brought out a long black box. He opened it, not letting her see the contents until he set it in front of her with a sly smile.

An intricate rope of looped diamonds and emeralds winked up at her. "Aiden, they're . . . they're . . ." she stammered, unable to catch her breath or find words to describe the beauty of the necklace. "They're . . ."

"Yours." He leaned past her shoulder and lifted the necklace from the box with both hands.

"They're beautiful," she managed to say as he draped them around her neck. "And far too expensive. I can't possibly accept them." They were cool against her skin; in such stark contrast to the wondrous warmth of Aiden's touch.

"You can't possibly go to the theater tonight without them." He bent down and pressed a lingering kiss to her bare shoulder. Then he lifted his head to meet her gaze in the mirror. "Be gracious, Darcy."

"I'll wear them," she acceded reluctantly, "but only for the sake of appearance. I'm viewing them in the same manner as I do the wardrobe."

He pushed aside the emerald silk of her skirt and sat down beside her on the padded bench. "Do you remember our first kiss?" he asked, his eyes twinkling.

She'd never forget it. "The one in the Lion and Fiddle?" she asked teasingly.

"That would be the one." He grinned. "Do you remember how much it cost me?"

"One hundred and five dollars," she answered, the memory far more delightful than she would have thought at the time. "And you said I had no understanding of the exchange rate for feminine favors."

"You still don't. A hundred and five dollars for a kiss was outrageously expensive." His grin turned wicked, and the light in his eyes began to smolder. He reached out and trailed his fingers over the swell of her breast, saying, "But an emerald-and-diamond necklace is only a small, token expression of my thanks for what you gave me in François's fitting room."

"The first or second time?" she asked, holding her breath against the delicious ripples his touch sent through her.

"The second fitting, and well you know it." He leaned forward and placed a kiss in the hollow behind her ear. "We'll have to go back again," he whispered. "Soon."

"You're a wicked man, Aiden Terrell."

"I know," he admitted not at all guiltily, as he drew back and settled himself against the edge of the dressing table. He reached into his coat and brought out another black box. A smaller one.

"Another jewel case, Aiden?"

He opened it and set before her a pair of diamond-and-emerald ear bobs. "For the carriage ride back from François's that day."

"*I* should be giving *you* diamonds for that," she laughed, the memories of that long ride sending exquisite jolts throughout her body.

"I do wish you'd at least make an attempt to understand how this works, Darcy." Slipping his arms around her waist, he bent down and pressed a kiss to the swell of her breast.

Darcy arched back, powerless to resist the yearning for more. It was always this way with Aiden. And as always, he rewarded her surrender with devout attention to her pleasure.

HE GROWLED AT the unfairness of it. He'd planned so well, so carefully. It had gone awry through no fault of his own. His mind clawed for a new way to accomplish the end he sought. Aiden still needed to be reminded. The man outside didn't matter to Aiden. This was the one he'd wanted to send the remembrance of. *This one!* This one Aiden would have never forgotten. Time was growing short. He had to find another way.

She was dead. The bitch had ruined his plan. It had been tactically brilliant, too. It would have shaken Aiden to the soles of his shoes and made him forget all about Darcy O'Keefe. Aiden would have remembered what it was he was *supposed* to be doing. But the bitch had ruined it by dying before he'd gotten there.

Maybe. . . . He narrowed his eyes, considering the still form outlined by the blankets; imagined plunging the knife into it again and again so that Aiden would think she'd died as had all the others. He leaned forward and pressed his fingertips to her cheek. Cold. The blood would have settled. There would be no spurting, no satisfaction in cutting her. And when Aiden looked down at her, he would see the truth and know that the bitch had thwarted the plan.

From his pocket he took the note he'd planned to leave behind. Swearing softly, he wadded it into a tight ball, then tore it in half and pitched it at the lifeless body of the woman.

The dead guard outside didn't matter to Aiden. *This* was the one he'd wanted to send the remembrance of. *This one!* This one Aiden would have never forgotten. He'd thought everything out so well, so carefully. It wasn't his fault it had gone awry. Aiden still needed to be reminded. There had to be a way.

Maybe. . . . He considered the body again. After a few moments, he smiled and nodded. There was more than one way to skin a cat.

AIDEN GRIMACED AS the soprano missed the note. Yes, brother or not, he'd kill Nathan. Nathan knew damn good and well that he loathed opera. Even in the best of circumstances, Aiden found sitting through a performance barely tolerable. But in a building constructed not as an opera house, but as a theater . . . He glanced around the dimly lit hall, reaffirming his initial impression that a theater in Boston was a far cry from the palatial halls of London, Edinburgh, and Dublin. The soprano missed another note—by a far greater distance than she had the first—and Aiden winced. The company might well have heralded London as their home, but it was clear to him that for the general good of British culture they'd been asked to hone their operatic talents elsewhere—a far distant elsewhere. They had obviously left London in great haste, having had little time to gather together decent costuming and props. He again looked down at the program Darcy held in her lap. *The Marriage of Figaro.* Aiden was glad the promoters had thought to tell the audience what it was they were seeing. He wouldn't have recognized it if left on his own to name it. But along with the other impressions he'd gathered during the ordeal, he'd noticed that his standards of operatic excellence were very different from those of his fellow theatergoers.

Bored with what could only kindly be described as a performance, Aiden went back to studying the hall and its occupants. He'd heard European descriptions of American theater audiences, not the least of which had been Mrs. Frances Trollope's scathing observations, recently published in London. But he saw no one spitting tobacco juice or sprawled over the seats in various states of undress. There had been no shouting and foot-stomping at the end of the first act; only perfectly well-mannered applause, muffled by gloves. He had, in fact, seen none of the things that had so appalled the intrepid Mrs. Trollope. Apparently her genteelly stated disgust had wrought a hasty evolution of sorts to audience behavior across the Atlantic.

There were not as many ladies present as he was accustomed to seeing in European theaters, and none were as fashionably dressed and spectacularly bejeweled as Darcy, but at least she wasn't alone in her attendance. However, with the noticeable exception of several elderly matrons seated in boxes on the other side of the hall, Darcy was rare in the polite attention she gave to the labored efforts of the singers on stage.

Aiden smiled. There had been a noticeable ripple of commentary as he'd escorted Darcy through the lobby and to their private box. A few patrons had attempted some discretion in observing them, both with opera glasses and without, but the vast majority hadn't bothered. And the general tendency to openly gawk at his lady hadn't been diminished by the first raising of the curtain or anything that had transpired on stage since. He congratulated himself on having so brilliantly succeeded in introducing Darcy to the circle of elite. As he had predicted, the men were fascinated by the possibility of a new conquest. The women were decidedly distracted by the beautiful competitor who had so regally swept into their midst.

The end of the first act had seen a small flood of patrons rising from their seats and filing toward the lobby. Aiden had acknowledged the gazes of several men he'd met in his recent rounds of the gentlemen's clubs, but had wordlessly declined their gestured requests to bring Darcy and join them in the lobby. It was one thing to invite them to look and appreciate the wonder of the woman at his side; it was entirely another to put her within reach of their hands and their efforts to lure her away from him. It was part of the plan, of course, to eventually let them try, but Aiden had decided that it could wait until after the final curtain. Having been tempted and then denied until that point would make them all the more eager to bring him and Darcy into their private associations. The invitations would be boldly and quickly offered, lest the offerer find himself facing the dreaded rebuff of "a prior engagement."

Muffled applause brought his attention back to the present. The curtain fell to the wooden stage with a quick and none too subtle *thump.* Darcy sighed and turned to him with a smile.

"And how are you finding the opera, Miss O'Keefe?"

"I've never heard Italian accented in quite this way," she replied. "But it's a wonderful story."

"You'd enjoy it even more if the performers could actually sing," he observed dryly.

"Oh, that doesn't really matter. It's fascinating just being here. Have I mentioned that I've never been to a real theater before?"

No, she hadn't. Not that the confession had been necessary. He'd seen the wonder in her eyes as they entered the lobby. It was still there, still thrilling to see. It reminded him of the joyous way she approached their lovemaking. Pulling his watch from his pocket, he noted the hour, and groaned at the prospect of having to curb his impulses through two more mangled operatic acts.

"Are you feeling unwell, Aiden?"

"Impatient," he admitted, tucking his watch away. He

took her hand in his and raised the back of it to his lips. "I'd like to see your wonder under other circumstances."

"Private circumstances," she added, gently brushing her gloved knuckles across his lips.

He shifted in his seat, his trousers suddenly binding. "It would be considered poor manners to leave before the end of the third act," he said. "But might I hope to talk you into a graceful exit before the beginning of the fourth and final one?"

"Won't people comment scandalously?"

"They started as we came in and haven't stopped since." He glanced at the boxes on the opposite wall and grinned. "Even the matrons have deigned to look and whisper."

Darcy lifted her opera glasses to return an older woman's open perusal. She lowered the glasses a moment later, laid them in her lap, and, with a delicately arched brow, said, "I believe that particular matron is my grandmama."

It took every measure of his social training to keep from looking at the woman across the way. "Do you think she recognizes you?" he asked.

"If she does, she's undoubtedly thinking that the inexperienced scullery maid has certainly come up a great distance in the world."

"If you'd find it awkward to remain, we could damn etiquette and leave now."

The bell jangled to signal the coming of the third act, and the crowd began moving back toward their seats. Darcy smiled and squeezed his hand. "Her opinion doesn't matter to me in the least. We came here tonight to stir interest, and if hers is among the whispers we cultivate, then it is. When I leave here, it will be because I've decided that I have more entertaining uses for my time, not because I've let the possible censure of a stranger make me feel uncomfortable."

"Are you sure, Darcy?"

She leaned forward and kissed him, leisurely and surely, and in full public view. "I'm quite sure," she replied, settling back into her upholstered seat.

Aiden expelled a long breath and, as though on cue, the

curtain came up. He vaguely heard the resumption of the op-era, but the sound seemed to come from a long distance and was largely lost in the filter of his thundering heartbeat. God, Darcy never ceased to amaze him. Never. And she had a way of stirring his desire that scattered both prudence and good judgment to the wind.

He crossed one leg over the other, and adjusted his posi-tion in the chair until he could easily slip his foot beneath the hem of her skirt. She took a deep breath that had nothing to do with the performance on the stage below. Aiden smiled and devoted his every effort to thoroughly distracting her. Two thirds of the way through the third act, he decided the shadows in which they sat were sufficient to permit bolder play. He draped his arm along the back of her chair and trailed his fingertips along her bared nape and shoulder. She quietly purred, and laid her hand on his upper thigh.

He considered the height of the wooden box surrounding them, and then made a nonchalant survey of the audience around and below them. He caught a face he knew, turned upward and clearly watching them. John Jamieson, he re-called. He acknowledged the man's regard with a brief nod, and reluctantly told himself that his flirtations with Darcy had probably gone far enough.

He leaned toward her as though he intended to share a comment about the opera, and whispered in her ear, "When the curtain starts down, we're leaving."

She nodded, a knowing smile turning up the corners of her mouth. Then she eased back to press her lips to his ear. "I'll make you pay for torturing me, Aiden Terrell," she whispered back. And then she trailed the tip of her tongue over the curve of his ear.

His blood went hot and he quickly assessed their positions, realizing that his own head blocked everyone's view of what Darcy was doing to him. Smiling, he said, "Do that again and I'll make love to you right here."

"I'd prefer to wait until we got to the carriage, but if you'd rather . . ." She daringly suckled his earlobe.

Strangling on a groan of pleasure, he drew away from her.

Clasping her hand where it lay on his thigh, he held it there, determined to keep her from stripping away his last vestige of control. He stared at the stage, willing either for the actors to fall dead or for the curtain to drop. It didn't matter to him which; he simply wanted an avenue of escape. Time crawled by. Darcy sat silently beside him, her outward serenity and her knowing smile teasing him.

And when the curtain fell, signaling the end of the final scene in the act, Aiden was past caring about a graceful exit. He rose to his feet, assisted Darcy to hers, and drew her around their seats. Snagging her wrap from the hook at the entrance to their box, he guided her toward the stairwell that led to the lobby a flight below.

Despite his deliberate haste, they weren't the first to abandon the theater. Halfway down the steps Aiden saw John Jamieson and three other men from the clubs standing at the bottom, clearly trying to decide whether to go up and force an introduction or to wait until their quarry came down. At the sight of Aiden and Darcy, the men formed a phalanx of beaming anticipation. Aiden tensed at both the interest they displayed and the delay they represented.

"I say, Terrell," Jamieson began, "it would appear that you've been holding out on us."

"Oh, really?" Aiden drawled casually. "How so?"

"You haven't mentioned your lovely companion. And I should think I wouldn't have forgotten any description of such a delightful young woman."

"Forgive me the oversight. I didn't know that you would be interested," he answered, lying through his teeth. "Miss Darcy O'Keefe, may I present Mr. John Jamieson, Mr. Michael Smythe, Mr. George Rodgers, and Mr. William Brown."

Each of the men offered a polite bow as he was introduced, and when that formality had been completed, Darcy swept her gaze over them and softly said, "It's a pleasure to make your acquaintance, gentlemen."

They trampled over each other's efforts to be the most enthusiastic in expressing their delight at meeting her. While they did, Aiden draped her cloak over her shoulders.

"A group of us are planning to dine after the performance," Mr. William Brown said, obviously attempting to forestall their departure. "Would you care to join us, Miss O'Keefe?"

From the corner of her eye, Darcy saw Aiden's brow shoot up. Apparently William Brown did, too, because he hastily added, "Oh, you, too, Terrell. Of course."

"Our attendance is entirely up to Aiden," Darcy offered, trying to diffuse the tension in the situation. Then she looked up at Aiden, arching a brow in silent reminder that just such an invitation had been the reason bringing them to the theater in the first place. "Darling?"

His smile was noticeably forced. "I thought you had the beginning of a headache."

"Perhaps you simply need something to eat, Miss O'Keefe," suggested Mr. Michael Smythe. "It's been my experience that food has the most wonderful restorative powers."

It occurred to Darcy that Mr. Smythe's girth would suggest that he was either very sickly or very healthy. "Perhaps," she said. Again she looked up at Aiden and gave him a wordless reminder. "Might you be just a little hungry for food and conversation, Aiden, darling?"

He considered her, the men, the doorway beyond them, and then the line of waiting carriages on the street. Darcy saw the decision made. The tension eased from the corners of his mouth, and the smile he gave Jamieson and the others was genuine.

"It's been my experience that fresh air does wonders for headaches as well," he said easily to Brown. "If you'd be so kind as to tell me where you've made your dining reservations, Miss O'Keefe and I will join you there later."

The decision made and the course set, Darcy listened and watched as Brown provided the information Aiden had requested. No sooner had those details been imparted than the other men in the group thought it necessary to provide com-

mentary on the various attributes of both the dining establishment itself and its bill of fare.

Aiden was pretending interest, barely. Darcy tried to
dredge up a bit of sympathy for him, but couldn't. He'd very
deliberately set out to put them both in just this set of circumstances. He would simply have to accept the unpleasant
fruit of his labors. She let her attention drift to the other patrons milling about the lobby. A handful of people responded
to the momentary clanging of the bell and started back into
the theater. Some were clearly preparing to leave. Others
seemed to have decided that they would enjoy the final act
just as well from the vantage of the lobby. Those that had
chosen to remain where they were stood in small knots, intently conversing. No doubt making plans similar to those
Aiden and the four men were making, she decided.

"Ma'am?"

The boyish voice gave her a mild start, and she turned
toward the sound of it. A lad of perhaps ten stood behind her,
his attention focused on her. He stood with his tattered hat in
his hand and shifted his weight between his feet. His obvious
discomfiture at being in the theater lobby wrenched her
heart. "Yes?" she asked, offering him her most reassuring
smile. "What may I do for you, young man?"

He thrust a small white packet toward her, and she
glanced down at the folded piece of white vellum she'd instinctively accepted. Something hard rested inside the folds.

The boy said, "With Dr. LeClaire's compliments, ma'am,"
and started away.

LeClaire? *Jules!* Her blood went cold. She stepped after the
boy and caught him by his arm. "Where is Dr. LeClaire?" she
demanded. "Where is the man who gave you this to deliver?"

"Out there," the boy answered, his voice quavering as he
pointed to the doors. "But he's gone. He got into a carriage
after he gave it to me. It drove him away when I came inside."

"Darcy?"

She ignored Aiden's voice and the gentle hand he placed
on her shoulder. "Did you hear him give the driver an ad-

dress?" she pressed the boy, vaguely aware that her questioning had drawn the attention of the theater patrons remaining in the lobby.

"No, ma'am," the boy answered, clearly distressed by the intensity of her inquiry.

She managed a smile and released her hold on him. "Thank you for delivering it," she said. "I'm just anxious to meet Dr. LeClaire in person. He's sent me many gifts recently, and I need to express my thanks."

The boy nodded, stepped out of her reach, and then quickly made his way out onto the walkway. Darcy watched the doors swing closed behind him, and then focused her attention on the lumpy packet in her hand.

"A secret admirer, eh?" John Jamieson chortled. "Do open it, Miss O'Keefe. Let us see what it is that we have to offer to gain your favor."

"Perhaps you'd better let me, Darcy," Aiden said quietly.

His offer came too late; she had broken the wax seal holding the paper closed and was already opening the folds.

An old, well-worn rosary lay inside.

Mother's rosary.

Her world tilted and fell from beneath her feet.

CHAPTER 21

DESPERATION DROVE HER through the doors and onto the walkway. The need to find their carriage among the others lined up before the theater slowed her for only a moment. But in that fractional hesitation, Aiden caught up with her.

His hands on her shoulders, he held her fast when she would have darted down the walkway. "Darcy," he demanded, "talk to me!"

"It's my mother's rosary. Jules sent my mother's rosary. I have to go to Mick's."

He swore, spun about on his heel, and with her hand in his, dashed toward the carriage. He jerked open the door and as Darcy shoved herself through the opening, she heard him give the driver Mick's address and demand haste. The carriage lurched forward before he got the door closed behind himself.

Darcy's thoughts spun crazily. She wanted to be there now, and yet if she prolonged the trip forever, she could avoid ever knowing for sure. If they were to take their time . . . It was all a nightmare, and she would wake up before she could see her mother's body. Her mother wasn't dead. She couldn't be. Mother had always been there. Always. Mother was all she had left.

There was no reason for tears. She'd reach Mick's house and

find her mother sitting in the drawing room with Maureen. They would be having their evening cup of tea. They'd be aghast at the fears that had sent her racing from Boston to Charlestown and bursting in on their quiet conversation. Then they would pour her a cup of tea, too, and the three of them would laugh and find the humor in the situation. Aiden and Mick would go to Mick's study to smoke a cigar and drink. They'd laugh about it all as well.

Aiden slipped his arms around her and drew her against him. "It won't be long, darling," he whispered, then pressed a kiss to her cheek.

There was a wondrous comfort in being in Aiden's arms. He would see that everything came right. He would wake her from the dream and kiss her and make love to her, and the nightmare would be forgotten.

Make love to her. . . . Darcy's heart twisted. If her mother *was* dead . . . then . . . had she been dying while her daughter was accepting jewels and making love? Had she been dying while her daughter sat in a theater box reveling in her lover's touch?

She choked back a cry. Aiden hugged her closer, but the comfort of his closeness was now tainted by a wash of guilt. What had she done? Was the pleasure worth the price? She pushed against Aiden's chest, suddenly frantic to put as much distance between them as she could. He held her firmly, murmuring gentle words, not understanding that every touch, every word, deepened and twisted the guilt gathering within her.

"Let me go, Aiden!" she cried, struggling in earnest. "Let go of me!"

He did. And then he looked at her with such obvious bewilderment and anguish that for a moment she felt a pang of sympathy for him. He didn't know, and she couldn't explain it to him. The pain was too deep, too close, and if she tried to put it into words she would crumple to the floor of the carriage and never rise again. She had to be strong. To survive, she had to contain everything within herself.

Darcy clenched her hands together in her lap and concentrated on collecting her wits. Her breathing was too shallow and ragged. Her heart beat far too fast. She closed her eyes, trying to calm the physical manifestations of her fear. She couldn't arrive on Mick and Maureen's doorstep in a panic. She owed it to her mother and to the O'Shaunessys to conduct herself with dignity and poise.

But her mother couldn't be dead. She had only the rosary to suggest—*The rosary!* Darcy stared down at her hands. Where was the rosary? She'd had it in the lobby of the theater, and then . . . Darcy yanked the reticule from her wrist and jerked apart the strings. The rosary wasn't inside.

"What are you needing, Darcy?"

The gentleness of Aiden's voice only fueled her desperation. "Mother's rosary. I can't find Mother's rosary!"

"You had it in the lobby, but—"

"I know that!" she snapped. "I can't find it now! We have to go back. No," she scrambled to amend, her mind reeling, "we can't go back now. We have to go to Mick's first and check on Mother. I'll go back later."

"*I* will go back for it, Darcy. Don't worry about it. Someone will find it and think to give it to an usher for safekeeping."

He was maddeningly calm, as though he faced the death of a loved one every day and it was of no consequence to him. Darcy started. Aiden had been where she was now. He looked into the memories every day. And so would she—because Aiden had come into her life and brought the hideous specter of Jules with him.

If only she could undo the past, that she could have known on that one morning what lay ahead. She'd never have gone after his pockets. She'd have run when Mick had hired her out to Aiden Terrell. If only she'd known. If only . . .

The carriage slid to a halt, rocking on its springs. Darcy didn't waste a second in wrenching open the door and scrambling out. Her skirt in her fists, she raced up the stone steps of the O'Shaunessy home. The door opened as if by magic, and she only glanced at the butler as she darted into the foyer and past him. They would be in the drawing room. She knew the way.

She came to an abrupt halt in the open doorway. Mick sat reading the paper in his favorite chair. Maureen sat opposite him on the settee, serenely working a needlepoint. Maureen looked up, and a ripple of true hope went through Darcy's heart at the sight of the other woman's obvious puzzlement. Perhaps it was all a mistake! She had *thought* it was her mother's rosary, but she hadn't looked closely.

Mick lowered his paper to look at her. He quickly folded the newsprint and jumped to his feet, asking, "Darcy, what's happened?"

"My mother. Where is she?"

"Upstairs in her room, dear," Maureen answered, laying aside her needlework and rising to her feet. "She had the best day I've seen her have in many years. But it exhausted her and she retired early this evening."

"I have to see her," Darcy announced, running toward the stairs. Aiden stepped into her path. When had he come in?

"No," he declared. Taking her by the shoulders, he turned her and led her into the drawing room. "Mrs. O'Shaunessy, if you'd be so kind as to keep Darcy here with you for a few moments. Mick, if you'd come with me to check on Mrs. O'Keefe."

Darcy shook her head in mute refusal, determined to go to her mother. Maureen hesitated, and then slipped her arms around Darcy's shoulders. "We'll have a seat and wait," she said softly.

Darcy saw the way Mick glanced between her and Aiden. "I'll have an explanation first," the stout Irishman said.

"We were at the theater in Boston," Aiden said. "As we were preparing to depart, Jules had a packet delivered to Darcy. Inside was her mother's rosary."

Mick's chin came up and his lips thinned. Reaching for a lamp, he said, "We'll be down shortly. Get the girl a brandy, Maureen."

Darcy watched Aiden and Mick until they disappeared around the upper curve of the staircase. Time ticked by, each long second deepening the dread. If Aiden had found her mother alive, he would have immediately called out to tell her so. And when he didn't, Darcy knew. Hope withered, and the blackness of grief quietly stole over her. She heard Maureen offer her a cup of tea, and she thought she replied but she couldn't be sure. The world was going gray at the edges and her vision was seeming to narrow to a mere pinprick in the far distance. Sound came from a long way off, and she observed her own movements with the cool dispassion of her mind having been divorced from her body. It was very odd. It was also blessedly familiar. She knew there was a comfort to be found in the void into which she was drifting. It had spared her pain in the days following her father's death. It would spare her this time, too.

AIDEN SAID NOTHING as he and Mick stood just inside the doorway of Mary O'Keefe's bedchamber. Even with the distance and the shadows cast by the lamplight, Aiden knew that Darcy's mother was dead. He could feel it in the stillness of the room, could feel it in the coldness that went beyond the crisp night air eddying through the open window. Mick, standing beside him, slowly crossed himself. The sharp edge of cold deepened as the lace curtain fluttered and then billowed full.

Aiden walked to the bed and gently placed his fingertips on the side of Mary O'Keefe's neck. Her skin was cold, the spark of life long extinguished. "She's gone, Mick," he said, leaning down to draw the bedcovers up and over her face.

Mick set the lamp on the secretary and strode toward the window, saying, "There's a man who guards the rear." Pulling aside the lace curtain, he peered into the blackness of the night. "Not a sight of him to be had. I'll kill him when I get me hands on him."

"Jules probably saved you the effort," Aiden observed darkly, knowing his brother's methods all too well. "He wouldn't have taken the chance of being caught climbing up here."

Mick came to stand at his side. Softly he said, "Praise the saints he didn't butcher her."

Aiden nodded, the practical considerations slamming into him with all the force of a well-aimed and brawny fist. "Which isn't like Jules at all. Why didn't he carve her up?"

" 'Tis a cold-blooded bastard ye are, Aiden Terrell," Mick snarled. "A-standin' over a woman's cold body an' a-wonderin' why she's been left whole. Be properly grateful for the mercies given."

"Jules doesn't dispense mercy," Aiden replied, ignoring Mick's censure. "If he didn't butcher her, there was a reason."

"An' ye think there's a point in a-knowin' the answer to it?" Mick asked with obvious exasperation. "Perhaps 'twas only that he took pity on an old woman. Or, if ye're right about his a-killin' me guard, then more's the likelihood he had no stomach for another butcherin' in the same night. Or have ye considered that he might have found his sick satisfaction in simply holdin' the pillow over her face an' snuffin' the life out of her? 'Twould have a been a quiet way of a-doin' it."

Again Aiden shook his head. "He's never spared anyone for their age or sex. He's killed in multiples before, the savagery of the second and third no less than that of the first. And Jules enjoys letting blood. He'd not have chosen to smother her. It's not his way. Besides, look at the bedcovers, Mick. Mary O'Keefe didn't struggle."

Mick quietly retorted, "Jules could well have straightened them after the deed was done. 'Tis simple enough."

"No, he wouldn't have. He'd have left them rumpled as proof of his having triumphed over resistance."

"Well," Mick declared, clearly frustrated, "the sendin' of the rosary to Darcy proves he was here. Ye can't deny that."

"But that's all it proves," Aiden countered. "Jules was here, yes, but nothing else speaks of his having been the hand that took Mrs. O'Keefe's life."

As soon as the observation fell from his tongue he saw the truth. Mick must have seen it in the same instant, because the Irishman groaned and then whispered, "Sweet Jesus, Joseph, and Mary. He found her already dead."

"Does Maureen keep chemicals in the house?" Aiden asked, his gaze sweeping over the tabletops in the room. "Laudanum? Opium? Arsenic?"

"I have no idea. But even if she does," Mick hastened to add, "she wouldn't have allowed Mary anywhere near it. Maureen knows of Mary's two attempts to take her own life. It's been a handful of years since the last, but still, Maureen wouldn't have taken the chance."

Aiden dropped to his knees beside the bed and lifted the skirt. "Is there any way Mrs. O'Keefe could have sent one of the servants out to purchase poison for her?" he wondered aloud as he scanned the floor for a telltale bottle.

"She might have. We can ask Maureen." He sighed heavily. "But if yer're a-thinkin' that Mary slipped away by her own hand, then 'tis possible that she's been a-hoardin' the means for some time."

Aiden climbed back to his feet. Scrubbing his hand over the stubble on his chin, he considered the small body lying beneath the covers. God. What relief there had been in realizing Jules hadn't murdered Darcy's mother was rapidly evaporating in the face of another equally unpleasant possibility. Why had Darcy's mother chosen now to end her life? Why hadn't she waited until Darcy had finished her work and come home again? Hadn't she thought of the guilt Darcy would bear forever?

"Maureen said Mrs. O'Keefe had had a good day," Aiden posed, blindly searching for an understanding that would help him make some sense of it for Darcy. "Did you see her before she retired?"

"Aye. She took dinner with the family. She was keen an' bright, a-talkin' about her Darcy an' you, a-sayin' how pleased John must be, a-watchin' down on ye both from heaven."

Understanding brought no comfort. "Do you think she would have chosen to join her late husband without saying some form of good-bye to Darcy?"

" 'Twould be most unlikely."

"Then there's bound to be a letter or something of the sort.

Check the secretary," Aiden instructed. "I'll search the drawer in the night table." As Mick crossed to the other side of the room, Aiden eased open the drawer and carefully began to survey the contents. A prayer book, a dried bit of palm frond, a leather-bound book of poems.

" 'Tis here," Mick said from the desk. "Sealed." He sighed. "Holy Mother of God. 'Twon't be much easier on Darcy to know her mother's passin' wasn't by Jules's hand. But, be it the small comfort it is, I hope 'twill someday make a difference to her."

Aiden pushed the drawer closed. As he did, his gaze drifted to the floor between the night table and the leg of the cast-iron headboard. He bent down to retrieve the crumpled bits of paper.

"What is it ye've found, Terrell?"

He gently opened the wrinkled wads, instantly recognizing the handwriting. "My guess it's the note Jules intended to leave after killing Mary O'Keefe. Finding her already dead must have enraged him. From the looks of it, he balled it and then tore it before flinging it away."

"Would that be blood on it?" Mick observed, coming back across the room.

Aiden nodded and fit the two halves together. "My guess would be that it's your guard's. It's clearly not Mrs. O'Keefe's. If we looked, we'd probably find more blood on the windowsill where Jules climbed through."

"What did he write? Can ye read it clear enough?"

" *'The price of your forgetfulness.' "*

"Forgetfulness?" Mick repeated. "What do ye suppose he meant by that?"

Tucking the halves into his coat pocket, Aiden replied, "I haven't been pursuing him in the dogged fashion he thinks appropriate."

"Have ye been pursuin' other things, Terrell?"

Mick might as well have asked him if he'd taken Darcy to his bed; there was no subtlety in his tone. Aiden met his gaze squarely. "It's none of your business, Mick."

" 'Tis indeed," the other man countered sharply. "Yer

brother has brought his madness into me home an' deliberately tried to visit it upon the heart of Darcy O'Keefe. 'Tis
Darcy's mother he thought to murder, an' well he would have
done it had Mary not cheated him of the sick pleasure."

He pointed toward the door as color flooded his cheeks.
" 'Tis only by the grace of God that I don't have to go down
those stairs an' tell Darcy that her mother lies up here in
bloody pieces. 'Tis clear that he meant Darcy to pay the price
of yer forgetfulness, an' *that,* Terrell, would lead me to think
that she's been the object of yer pursuit, rather than yer
brother."

St. Kitts would be a frozen wasteland before he discussed
the full nature of his and Darcy's relationship with Mick
O'Shaunessy. "We've been playing our own game with Jules.
It was our intention to make him think he was being ignored, and thus draw him after us in blind frustration. We
didn't expect him to come after Darcy's mother. We thought
her safe under your protection."

The last words had precisely the effect Aiden intended.
Mick rocked back on his heels as his gaze went to the body of
Mary O'Keefe. Unable to deny his own failure in the death of
Darcy's mother, Mick's bluster eroded.

After a moment, he expelled a long breath and said sadly,
" 'Twould appear that we've both underestimated the degree
of yer brother's madness."

"It would," Aiden agreed. "But there's nothing to be done
now except for comforting Darcy as best we can."

"Aye. Ye'd better let me tell her, lad. Ye stand ready to
catch her when she falls."

Aiden followed Mick from the room, quietly closing the
door behind them. The constables would have to be summoned if, as he suspected, Mick's guard lay dead in the rear
yard. Would they have to view Mary O'Keefe's body as well?
Would Darcy insist on coming up here? A leaden mass filled
his chest. Yes, Darcy would. She'd kneel beside the bed and
cry. She'd beg her mother to return, offer God any bargain
He cared to name. And it would change nothing.

He and Mick entered the drawing room in silence. Maureen crossed herself at the sight of them. Darcy simply looked at them with bland recognition, the light in her eyes gone. The weight in Aiden's chest increased.

"Darcy . . ." Mick began.

"I know, Mick," she said softly. "There's no need to say it."

" 'Twasn't by Jules's hand she left us," Mick supplied, stepping toward her. He held out the note Mary O'Keefe had left for her daughter. "This is for ye, Darcy."

Darcy accepted it without really looking at it. She murmured her thanks, laid it in her lap, then folded and rested her hands on it. She caught her lower lip between her teeth and stared straight ahead. Aiden knew that she didn't see anything, that all of her vision was focused inward on the pain of her loss. He wanted to take her into his arms and hold her. It was the only comfort he knew how to give.

"Darcy, sweetheart," Maureen whispered, touching her shoulder, "I am so very, very sorry."

"Mr. Terrell," Mick said, the normal briskness returned to his voice, "if ye'd stay with me wife an' Darcy, I would appreciate it. I've matters that must be tended immediately."

Finding his missing man. Notifying the constabulary. Aiden nodded as Mick started out of the drawing room.

Maureen quietly called after him. "Summon Father O'Hagen, Michael."

Mick stopped, then slowly turned around. "Would ye have a priest know the truth of her passin', Maureen?"

"I would have Mary O'Keefe's soul given pardon and peace. I have absolutely no intention of mentioning the letter she left for Darcy," Maureen countered firmly. "I would have spiritual comfort given to Darcy. Send someone for Father O'Hagen."

Mick shrugged and departed. Aiden had a sense that over the years Mick had surrendered to his wife's expectations and demands far too many times to count. It was a side of the man he'd never imagined.

"Darcy will stay with us, Mr. Terrell."

Aiden considered Maureen. She sat with her arm around

Darcy's shoulders, clearly claiming her as her responsibility, clearly expecting him to obey her edicts just as Mick did. Something deep inside his gut clenched.

"Surely you can understand that Darcy needs to be here," Maureen went on, certain of her right to decree. "We are all that she has of family now."

And Maureen clearly didn't consider him part of Darcy's family. She was drawing a circle around Darcy, and deliberately leaving him outside it. He knew he could assert a claim for inclusion, but it would require, if not an outright confession, then at the very least an allusion to a degree of intimacy that Darcy might prefer Maureen not know. The decision was properly Darcy's to make.

"Darcy?" Aiden said, kneeling before her and placing his face squarely in the line of her vision. When she blinked in recognition, he asked, "Darling, do you want to stay here? Do you want me to leave you?"

"I should have been here," she whispered tearfully. "I could have stopped her."

His heart aching for her, he cupped her face in his hands and gave her the only truth he could. "You don't know that you could have changed the outcome, Darcy. And all the shoulds and coulds of hindsight bring us nothing but groundless guilt. Please don't do this to yourself."

"She needed me, and I wasn't here for her." Tears welled along her lower lashes and then spilled down over her pale cheeks. "I was with you," she choked out. "I was thinking only of myself. Of my own pleasure. My selfishness cost—"

"No," he said, pressing his thumbs gently to her lips. "I won't hear it, Darcy. You are not responsible for what your mother chose to do. Your happiness didn't cause this."

She closed her eyes, then took his hands in hers and drew them from her face. "Yes, please go, Aiden," she said, her voice cracking. "I don't want to remember."

"Darcy—"

"She's distraught, Mr. Terrell," Maureen interjected, rising from the settee and reaching back to draw Darcy to her feet. He could only watch as Maureen swept past him with

Darcy in tow. As they went, Maureen added, "I'll take her upstairs and do what I can for her. Father O'Hagen will be here shortly, and he will see that she's comforted. If you need to see my husband again, please feel free to wait here for his return."

"What help is a priest going to be to her?" Aiden demanded. "Darcy doesn't give a damn about religion."

Maureen froze, jerking Darcy to a halt as well. Darcy didn't seem to notice. "Faith goes deep, Mr. Terrell," she said coolly. "Darcy will find the solace she needs and be better in the days ahead. But perhaps you should wait to call until she is prepared to see you again. I will have her send word when that day comes."

Aiden watched Mick's wife lead Darcy up the stairs, and struggled with a volatile mix of impulses. Part of him wanted to charge up the stairs and tell Maureen in no uncertain terms that Darcy belonged every bit as much to him as she did the O'Shaunessys.

A greater part of him cringed, knowing that Darcy's loss and suffering had been brought about by his presence in her life. Mary O'Keefe had made no particular secret of her hopes that he and Darcy would wed. He didn't need to read the letter she'd left Darcy. He had a fair idea of what it said. Mary O'Keefe had seen the marriage as destined, and thus her role of mother completed. She had seen Darcy's well-being as having passed into his hands, and had finally felt free to join her husband in death. Darcy had lost her mother. And no hope of a husband glimmered on the horizon.

Aiden raked his fingers through his hair. A third impulse suggested that he needed a drink. A good, stiff drink. With enough whiskey, he might be able to drown his own sense of culpability. He might even be able to escape the sense that he had abandoned Darcy in her need. And with any luck at all he could eventually wash away the feeling that he'd just forfeited any claim he might have ever had to her heart.

He turned on his heel and strode toward the door.

CHAPTER 22

T HE VOID IN which she drifted had a tendency to unexpectedly clear from time to time, and when it did she always found herself staring into a crowd of people and wondering how she came to be among them. Now was another one of those brief moments of clarity. Darcy looked from one black-draped person to the next, naming each, and vaguely recalling the words of sorrow and comfort they had offered her during the three days past.

She replied as expected, of course. It was a most amazing thing, really. Her mind only vaguely heard the sympathies extended, but somehow the appropriate responses rolled easily off her tongue. At least she presumed they were appropriate. She heard her own words no more clearly than she did the words of others, but the things she said seemed to please those patting her hands and touching her shoulders. And as long as they were happy, they tended to go away and leave her be.

They always came back, though, she admitted with a sigh. And they invariably brought a plate of food with them. For some unfathomable reason, they thought she would be hungry. And those that nodded at her protests otherwise countered by saying she needed to eat to keep up her strength. How much strength did one need to sit in a chair, stare at a coffin, and mutter replies to whispered condolences?

She ate only to silence them. Darcy stared down at her hands, folded demurely in her lap. Tomorrow would be the funeral mass and then the burial. They would give her until the morning after to finish her grieving, and then she'd be expected to give some sign of the course she intended to take for the rest of her life. No one had felt hesitant to make suggestions.

Most of them, thankfully, had come while her mind was swathed in a deep layer of cotton. She'd listened, her lethargy apparently being taken for rapt interest, and nodded at each and every idea presented to her. Mrs. McDonough had offered her a job in the store. Mick and Maureen had assured her repeatedly that she could remain under their roof for as long as she wanted. Mrs. Malone, Mrs. Grady, Mrs. Riordan, and a host of other women dressed in black, had all thought to tell her that it was high time she found a young man of solid reputation and good prospects to marry.

And every time someone tried to push her in that direction, she thought of Aiden. And she remembered the sound of his laughter, the way the light changed in his eyes to tell her of his moods, his generosity and the depth of his conscience. And she remembered how wondrously exquisite it felt to be in his arms, to be his lover.

Invariably, in the midst of remembering Aiden, the one who had thought to encourage her toward marriage would deliver what they obviously considered the coup de grâce: *It would make your mother happy, Darcy. You should do it for her.*

And the warmth of the memories would be washed away on an instant wave of remorse. A sharp-edged hollowness would consume her, and the only way of escaping the pain and desperation that came with it was to burrow deeper into the void.

"Darcy, my child."

She sucked a deep breath, recognizing the voice. "Father," she quietly acknowledged. She knew what Father O'Hagen wanted.

"Have you given any thought to the matter we discussed?"

Father O'Hagen asked quietly, settling himself on the chair beside her.

"No," she lied. "I can't think well at all. Thoughts drift through my mind, but I can't seem to hold them for very long or make anything of them."

"Can you tell me that Maureen is wrong?"

Darcy cursed herself yet again for having spoken so freely to Aiden in Maureen's presence. Maureen had made quick—and highly accurate—assumptions about the nature of her relationship with Aiden. Maureen had begun probing for confirmation within the hour, and hadn't let up since. And having had no success at her inquisition, she'd enlisted Father O'Hagen's assistance on the second day of the wake. They had both skirted around the issue, but their insinuations were plain enough. Darcy had committed a mortal sin with Aiden Terrell, and needed to cleanse her soul of the dark blotch. Something deep within her was disturbed by the idea. Her thoughts, however, were too chaotic to understand why and what it meant, beyond its being a manifestation of a life spent at odds with the strictures of the Church.

"I can't tell you anything, Father," she replied, sighing. "Except that I am so very tired and that I would give anything to be able to sleep." *And to make you go away.*

"That would lead me to believe that your soul is troubled indeed, Darcy."

"No more so than it's always been, I suppose," she replied, thankful that fatigue dulled her voice and concealed her growing irritation.

"Perhaps if you were to confess your sins and offer penance . . ."

"I could confess, but I doubt you would absolve me, Father. The truth is that I have moments of regret for my sins, but they come only after I've fully remembered the pleasure I found in them." Father O'Hagen quietly gasped, just as he had when he'd caught her as a child sampling the sacramental wine. Darcy managed a smile, remembering a conversation she and Aiden had had on the street outside McDonough's. "My resistance to temptation hasn't gotten any stronger over the years. And as for penance, I don't think it would be sincere."

"So you would willingly know this man again?"

She saw the trap he'd laid. Under other circumstances it would have angered her. But the precious cloud of oblivion was settling over her again and she didn't struggle against it. "Again?" she said, letting her eyes drift closed. "You presume, Father."

She heard him say something else, but the words were only a low, indistinct hum. Where was Aiden? Why hadn't he come to see her? She missed him terribly.

And in the way that her mind seemed to work these days, it supplied the answers to her questions with cool detachment. Aiden was out looking for Jules, his thoughts focused on the hunt. Circumstances had sent her on another path, and he couldn't afford to wait until she had collected her wits and had the strength to rejoin him on the quest. He had, by necessity, gone on without her. She had lost him. But she had the memories.

She wouldn't surrender them to Maureen or to Father O'Hagen. What regret came with them she could bear in the solitude of her heart. And if her path ever crossed Aiden's again, she would love him again. She would always love Aiden Terrell.

MAUREEN O'SHAUNESSY HAD managed to block his entrance to her house for three consecutive days, but, by God, she hadn't been able to bar the door of the cathedral. Aiden sat in the last row of pews, watching the mourners rise and kneel. He listened to the Latin incantations of the priest, heard the choral response of the dutiful parishioners. He sat immobile, physically present but scowlingly nonparticipatory.

Darcy sat in the first pew, flanked by Maureen O'Shaunessy on her right and Mick on her left. Maisey and her family sat in the pew directly behind. Nathan sat with them.

Aiden growled and glared up at the stained glass windows.

His gut ached and his head pounded with the need for a drink. He'd managed to exercise a modicum of restraint that first night. He'd been sober enough when he'd returned to the theater to retrieve Mary O'Keefe's lost rosary as he'd promised he would. No one there had known anything about it, and while they'd been more than pleasant in helping him search for it, he'd been forced to admit defeat.

In hindsight, and in a rare moment of relative sobriety, he now recognized that not being able to take the precious keepsake to Darcy had been the beginning of his downward slide. He had taken a second step in that direction when he'd allowed Maureen to block his entrance to her home the next afternoon. She had stood in the foyer, her arms crossed, and threatened to have him forcibly removed if he wouldn't go of his own accord. He'd seethed in rage, but for Darcy's sake, decided to avoid creating an embarrassing scene.

He'd finally flung himself over the edge when later that same day a package had arrived at his Boston hotel room. Inside had been Darcy's theater gown and the emerald-and-diamond necklace and the matching ear bobs. The note inside had been from Maureen. Short and simple, she wrote that Darcy had no further need of the things he had given her.

The second and third attempts to see Darcy had ended the same way as the first. At least he had the general impression that they had. He'd begun drinking in earnest by then, and he hadn't bothered to stop until just a few hours ago. Funerals demanded a certain degree of decorum—especially those being held as a direct result of his failures.

Considering his culpability, he couldn't really blame Maureen O'Shaunessy for disliking him. If Darcy's mother had been a stronger woman, she would have undoubtedly taken the same stance against him that Maureen had. If only someone had thought to protect Darcy from him before it had been too late. Instead, he'd walked into her life with angry strides, demanded her assistance, and rewarded her good-natured compliance by turning her life upside down and destroying everything in it. He'd taken her innocence and slowly, deliberately eroded her independence. He'd shown only superficial respect for her pride, and pulled her from those she loved and who loved her in return. As bastards went, he was one of the best.

The admission trickled through his sodden brain, and finally reached the tiny portion of it still capable of decency. He sagged back against the pew and swore softly. And bastard that he was, he'd come to the funeral, not primarily to pay his respects to Mary O'Keefe as he should have, but to find a way to be with Darcy, to beg her to come back to him and help him find Jules. There were apparently no depths to which he wouldn't sink. Disgusted with himself, he pulled himself to his feet and made his way out the doors of the church.

The sky overhead was leaden, and he knew that by the time Darcy leaned forward to toss the "ashes to ashes, dust to dust" handful of earth on her mother's casket, it would be pouring rain. She would arrive back at the O'Shaunessys wet and shivering. His chest ached, but he strode down the street telling himself that she was better off with the kind of comfort Maureen would give her. He'd only want to hold her against him, and God knew Darcy didn't need to give him any more of herself than she already had.

Maybe, after he'd found Jules, he'd go to tell her good-bye. Then again, maybe it was best to leave things as they were between them. Apologies had never been his strong suit. And he suspected that accepting them wasn't Darcy's.

He'd decide on the feasibility of a farewell later, he promised himself. At the moment, he needed to find the black-hearted son of a bitch who stood between him and escaping Charlestown.

COULDN'T AIDEN DO *anything* right any more? He wasn't supposed to be walking away from the church alone. He was supposed to be standing at the girl's side, holding her hand and making her love him. They were supposed to be together, not apart. Damn Aiden. And damn that Darcy O'Keefe, too. Both of them were too dull-witted to understand how they were to play the game. His scheme was brilliant, and it deserved to be done the way he'd planned it. He'd have patience. Yes, that was it. He'd just bide his time and wait. It would be so very, very difficult, but the end he envisioned would be worth all the trouble and frustration of getting there. Sooner or later he'd find them together and alone. But which one to follow? Which would be most likely to lead him to the other? They had to be together for the end. It was the only way he'd accept it, the only way he wanted it. Killing anyone else just wouldn't give him the same satisfaction. He smiled. Patience was a virtue.

DARCY PEELED THE sodden fabric off her arms, shoved the whole of the dress down over her hips, and then tossed the garment in the wicker basket by the door. Her flesh was chilled, but her bones pounded hot. Of all the damn days to have a funeral. Of all the times of the year for her mother to choose to kill herself. Darcy yanked off her damp petticoat and flung it into the basket.

Selfish, that's what her mother had been. Selfish. Darcy's conscience niggled at her anger. Contrition, however, was out of the question. If her mother could be selfish enough to kill herself, she silently fumed, then *she* was entitled to be selfish enough to be mad about it. *She* was the one left to pick up the pieces and tidy up the details of her mother's life.

Not that there were that many matters to be dealt with, she admitted in bitter fairness. Mother's life had been very narrow since Father's death. What pieces that had to be gathered together were those left of Darcy's life, now that her mother had chosen to go away.

Darcy reached behind herself and plucked at the strings of her corset. They were wet, and it took considerable effort to undo even the bow. She swore and tugged at the whalebone-and-lace contraption, determined to get out of it. She could wait for the maid, she reminded herself, but the need to escape the confines of it bordered on desperation, and so she continued to struggle. It was a shame that Aiden wasn't there, she groused. He'd gladly help her.

Darcy clenched her teeth and closed away both memory and hope. There was no going back, only forward. Yesterday was behind her. Tomorrow lay ahead, and it didn't include Aiden Terrell. With a fierce pull, she stripped the laces through the upper eyelets. With a deep sigh of relief she pushed the corset down over her hips. A half second later it joined the dress and petticoat in the basket.

Darcy dropped into the upholstered chair in the corner of her room to remove her garters and stockings. Tomorrow . . . Heaven only knew what she was going to do with it. Her gaze darted to the night table beside her bed and the unopened, unread letter from her mother. Perhaps she'd finally have the courage to read the letter. Perhaps not, she admitted, looking away. As long as she avoided the task, she could pretend that none of this was truly happening. Reading her mother's final words would make it just that: final. She wasn't ready to accept it all just yet.

Darcy tossed her stockings across the room. One missed the basket; the other hit the rim and bounced in. She forced herself to her feet and retrieved the one that had fallen to the floor. Standing beside the door wearing only her chemise, she sighed. What she wouldn't give to climb into her worn, soft trousers and shirt, curl up in the chair, and let sleep carry her into a world where she didn't have to do anything, say anything, or think anything. Maybe tomorrow.

Now she had to dress again and go downstairs for the mercy meal. She had to be gracious and accepting of everyone's efforts to comfort her, to provide her direction for the days that lay ahead. She would have to eat to make them happy. Hopefully, the haze would drift back over her senses, and she could make her way through the entire ordeal numb and generally unfazed. The blessed sanctuary for her mind and spirit was unpredictable though. It had a way of coming and going with a speed that she didn't remember from the time after her father's death. Then it had held her safe for days at a time. Now, at best, it afforded her only a few hours of protection. And when it lifted, she found her thoughts alarmingly clear, and always angry. It was becoming increasingly difficult to keep her anger hidden from those around her, and she knew that before too much longer someone would be handed their head for daring to offer her their sympathies.

There were far too many people in her life these days, far too many people hovering around her and touching her. She wasn't used to it. Darcy crossed the room to the armoire. By the morning after that horrible night, Maureen had somehow managed to procure four black dresses that would fit Darcy. Darcy looked at the three remaining in the armoire and knew that, from the standpoint of appropriateness, it didn't matter which she chose to wear. All were of bombazine. All were plain and acceptable for deep mourning. She looked at each, trying to remember which of them had fit the loosest when Maureen had had her try them on that first morning. The last thing Darcy wanted was to be trussed up for hours in another corset.

Tomorrow she'd lock herself in her room and climb into the comfort of her trousers and threadbare shirt. The familiar feel would help her make some decisions. Perhaps she— Darcy paused, struck by sudden realization. Her work clothes weren't here; they were at Aiden's hotel room. How was she going to get them back?

Another decision to be made. Its discovery and addition to the long list of others proved to be too much. Her mind eased away and refused to consider any of it. Darcy dressed and went downstairs, watching herself move with comfortable detachment and a vague sense of appreciation for it.

CHAPTER 23

DARCY WATCHED THE sun set through the windows of her apartment. How long had it been? she wondered. Perhaps she should try to figure it, just to be sure that her mind hadn't been completely lost. Two days had been spent at the O'Shaunessys' after the funeral. The third day, Maisey and Nathan had come to call. And then Nathan had asked if it would be all right to have her trunks of clothing delivered there the following day. He'd said Aiden wanted her to have them. Maureen had squared her shoulders and haughtily declared that Darcy would have none of them, and that Nathan could dump them in the Charles River for all Darcy cared.

Unfortunately, the exchange had occurred in one of Darcy's periods of lucidity. She'd countered Maureen's decree and instructed Nathan to have the trunks delivered to her apartment. Maureen had paled, then stomped her foot and delivered a scathing lecture on the wages and fruits of sin. Darcy had held her position against it, not because she wanted the finery that Aiden had purchased for her, but solely because her instincts said that unless she asserted her independence she would end up being Maureen's puppet for the rest of her life.

Maureen threatened to throw Darcy out of her house. And in Darcy's heart it was done. With a deep sense of relief, she'd nodded and walked to the front door, taken her cape from the peg, and walked out. Maisey and Nathan had come after her, and had been appalled when she'd told them she was going home. Maisey had offered the Riordan home as a haven. Nathan had offered to take her to Aiden in Boston. The decision to be free of Maureen's control had taken a heavy toll, and her mind was simply unable to consider the merits of their offers. She remembered shaking her head and muttering something about it being time to be alone. She'd left them standing there on the walkway and had been ever so thankful they didn't come after her again.

That sundown had marked the beginning of her vigil with the ghosts of her past. She'd wandered the apartment, remembering her father, remembering her mother, remembering all the conversations and laughter and heartache that had been witnessed by the walls. There was only silence now and she wandered through it, mindless of the chill seeping into her bones. It had occurred to her once or twice that night to light the stove, but somehow she'd never managed to accomplish the task, and after a while she became accustomed to the cold and it no longer mattered. She'd cried the whole of the night.

The next day—the fourth after the funeral, if she was recalling accurately—the trunks had been delivered by two burly hired men. She had been disappointed that Aiden hadn't come with them, and she'd spent the larger part of the day wallowing in self-pity and regret. By sundown that day, she'd muttered "if only" so many times that she'd grown disgusted with herself and heatedly declared it time to get on with living. Her battered cardboard suitcase had been placed atop one of the four trunks in the parlor, and in it she found her wonderful trousers and shirt. She'd also found the sheathed knife that Aiden had acquired from Timmy the Rat.

She'd climbed into her clothes and then slumped into the chair at the kitchen table, exhausted, the knife lying on the surface before her. And she'd passed the night remembering Timmy, and how she had been the one who'd sent him to his death. She'd cried all of that night, too.

Darcy shuddered and set those hours from her mind. The

second sunset—the fifth day after committing her mother's body to the earth—had seen Patrick Riordan, Maisey's younger brother, standing on her threshold, a plate of food in his hand. It had been the closest Maureen would ever come to offering an olive branch. She'd accepted it for what it was, politely conversed with Patrick for a few minutes, and then sent him on his way with Maureen's empty plate. She'd considered the food she'd transferred onto her own plate, and then let it sit on the cold stove, untouched. For another night she'd wandered the apartment listening to the memories. Her tears had been fewer that night, her bouts of regret and longing shorter and easier in their passing.

The next morning—the sixth day—Bridie had brought her breakfast and the letter from her mother. Darcy had stared at the folded and sealed piece of vellum, and then laid it on the table beside the knife. As she had with Patrick, Darcy exchanged pleasantries with Bridie, and then sent her on her way. She had taken the food to Mrs. Malone and declined the woman's invitation to spend the day with her. Patrick came at sundown with another plate of food. She had taken it to Mrs. Malone and declined an evening cup of tea.

Today had been the seventh, the fifth alone in the apartment. It had been just like the previous two. Bridie with food in the morning, Patrick with food at night. Mrs. Malone accepting the meals, offering her company, and she refusing it. And in the hours between the knocks on her door, she had sat at the kitchen table and thought of nothing.

Darcy rubbed her hands over her face and sighed. She was a wreck and she knew it. She hadn't eaten in five days. In a distant sort of way, she suspected that a large measure of the hollow feeling inside her was from hunger. But actually eating seemed like such a monumental effort and not really worth the bother. Except for taking the food to Mrs. Malone and twice daily trips to the privy out back, she'd accomplished nothing with her endless waking hours. She hadn't once fired the stove for heat. She hadn't even been able to light a lamp. She existed in sunlight or darkness, only noting the passing of one into another, but not caring that it did.

Darcy rubbed her eyes. Maybe tonight she could sleep.
Maybe tomorrow she'd find something of what she used to
be. Maybe she could find the wherewithal to put one foot in
front of the other and go find Aiden. Perhaps if she could put
her mind to a task beyond herself, it would help make the
world come right again. Maybe. Maybe. Darcy sighed and
picked up the letter from her mother. Maybe it was time to
face it squarely.

A knock at the door startled her. Patrick had already come
and gone, hadn't he? Could it be Aiden? Her heart jumped
and her hands trembled. What would she say to him? She
tossed down the letter as she rose to her feet. But when she
opened the door, the surge of anticipation drained away.

"Mick." She silently groaned at the sight of the towel-
covered plate in his hand. Jesus, more food.

Walking past her and into the apartment, he asked, "Did I
wake ye, Darcy girl?"

"No. I was just sitting here." She closed the door and went
back to her seat at the table.

"In the dark?" he asked, standing on the other side and
looking around.

"The lamplight hurts my eyes." It probably would if and
when she ever got one lit.

Mick seemed to consider her words for a bit and then he
lifted the plate in his hand and said, "Maureen sent ye a bit of
pie. Your favorite, apple, an' 'tis still warm from the oven."

She accepted it without rising and set it on the table beside
the knife and the letter. "That's very kind of Maureen. Please
thank her for me, Mick."

"Aren't ye a-goin' to eat it?"

"Later," she lied. "I'm not very hungry at the moment."

He nodded and again seemed to consider her words. After
a long pause, he cleared his throat and shifted his stance. "I
know 'tis soon to speak of the future, Darcy, but the quicker
ye face it, the quicker ye can be on with your life."

"And life must go on," she replied acerbically. "I seem to
recall having heard that a time or two recently."

He apparently chose to ignore her poor attitude. "Aye, indeed it must. Decisions need be made, Darcy girl. Ye've had long enough to grieve. 'Tis time to be on with the considerin' of 'em.''

Darcy took a slow, deep breath and accepted that if she couldn't make herself take a step forward, then it was probably for the best if she let Mick push her. She suspected the direction he had in mind. Mick was notorious for keeping to his intentions. "Has Aiden found Jules?" she asked.

"Not to me knowledge," he answered. "An' 'twould appear to be not from lack of tryin', either. Word is he's been a-turnin' Boston upside down an' shakin' it out. Been sweepin' through the social clubs, pressin' hard an' enlistin' all the aid he can. Nary a shadow's been left unpoked but there's been not the least reward for his effort."

Darcy nodded. "I suppose you expect me to go back to helping him."

"Nay. 'Tis done ye are with Mr. Aiden Terrell."

She looked at Mick, stunned.

"Ye've tried yer best, Darcy," he said softly, "an' I'll ask no more of ye. I've a friend in St. Louis. James O'Meara. If ye still have yer dream of goin' west an' a-teachin' school, I'll send ye to him. Jimmy will see ye set up proper-like."

It was a direction she hadn't foreseen. "Why didn't you make me this offer seven years ago, Mick?" she asked, too surprised to consider anything beyond the unexpected offer itself. "Why are you making it now?"

"Ye were too young to be on yer own then, Darcy girl," Mick supplied with a sad smile. "Too young to leave the bosom of those who cared for ye. Jimmy's a good man to be sure, an' he'd have seen no harm come to ye, but 'twouldn't'a been a father's eye he'd have been a-watchin' ye with."

"And what of my father's debt to you, Mick?" she pressed. It had been such a long time since there was anything real on which to focus her thoughts.

Mick extracted a piece of paper from the breast pocket of his coat and tore it once, twice, three times. He laid the tattered pieces on the table before her. "Paid in full. When ye're ready, I'll see yer ticket bought an' ye on a train bound for St. Louis."

With Mick's pronouncement came the numbness that mercifully insulated her when words and events came in bundles too large to bear. "Thank you, Mick," she heard herself murmur.

" 'Tis best if you get on with the livin' as soon as you can, girl. There's nothin' to be found in sittin' in the dark an' wishin' the road had been kinder. Best to face the way ahead an' take the step forward."

"I know," she whispered. "You're right."

"Good," he said. "I'll see the ticket bought for two weeks from today. That will give ye all the time ye need to tidy up yer property an' to say yer farewells. Time enough, too, for me to send word to Jimmy to expect ye." He paused in the doorway and said, "Remember to eat yer pie, Darcy girl. Ye don't want Maureen a-worryin'."

She nodded but didn't move. Mick studied her for a long moment, then sighed and left. Darcy sat in the darkness, staring at the cloth-covered plate. Mick was setting her free. The dream she'd long professed but never really hoped to achieve was within her grasp. All she had to do was get on a train. Life would be waiting for her at the other end of the rails. She could begin anew. The good memories she would take with her, and the bad ones she would leave behind.

Darcy reached out and eased the covering from the plate. Maureen's cook made the best pie crust in Charlestown. Still, Darcy gagged on the first small bite. And the second. The third and fourth went down better. Six was all she could manage before her eyes drifted closed.

DARCY PUSHED THE piece of boiled potato around her plate and thought about how those few nibbles of pie crust, eaten with her fingers, had been the beginning of a new way of living for her. Not that it was really living, she admitted. But the last week had brought her at least some semblance of normality. She was managing to eat a little without having her stomach roil at the very idea. She'd stopped crying. She also slept from time to time, albeit in short snatches that always ended with her starting from dreams too vivid to endure . . . dreams of her mother and her father, of Maisey and Nathan, of Mick and Maureen, Patrick and Bridie and Selia and Timmy. And of Aiden. Always of Aiden.

And sometimes, usually in the wee hours of the morning when she'd been awakened and set pacing by those dreams, she felt a restlessness that was somehow reassuring. In it she glimpsed the hope that she would someday be herself again, that the sense of needing to *do* would eventually be strong enough to force her to step beyond the cocoon in which she'd hidden herself. She speared the potato with her fork and dutifully put it in her mouth, hoping that both the will and the strength to move would be sufficient by the time she was to board the train for St. Louis. In some respects a week was forever, but in this it seemed too soon.

A knock on the door interrupted her thoughts and her meal. She stared at the door, thinking that she was very tired of people battering their knuckles on it. She was just as tired of having to cross the room and admit them.

"It's open," she called, laying down her fork.

She was blotting her lips on a napkin when a well-dressed, silver-haired man stepped across the threshold and announced, "Mrs. Joseph Riley."

Darcy couldn't have stood if she'd tried. She sat there and simply stared as her mother's mother swept into the apartment. Good God in Heaven! What was her grandmama doing *here*?

Georgina Riley stopped just inside the apartment and openly appraised Darcy. Darcy did the same of her in return. Darcy hadn't had a long or close enough view with her opera glasses that night, but with the woman's present proximity she now recognized that the years had been kind to Georgina Riley; kinder, it would appear, than they had been to Mary O'Keefe. Her grandmother's bombazine dress made the white strands of her hair even more pronounced. The curls arranged around her face seemed to soften the wrinkles etched around her eyes and the corners of her mouth. She was still stick thin, but smaller in stature than Darcy remembered. The five years between their last meeting and this one seemed to have shrunk her. One thing remained the same, though: Georgina Riley carried herself regally.

"Have you no coal with which to heat your rooms?" she asked, breaking the silence stretching between them.

The gentleness of the query caught Darcy by surprise. For some reason she had expected the tension of their last meeting to be the tone of this one. "There might be some coal in the bucket," Darcy replied absently, trying to collect her wits. "I haven't looked."

"Leave us, Williams," her grandmother said without looking at the man. "I shall join you downstairs presently."

As he left them, Darcy pushed herself to her feet. "Etiquette suggests that I offer you a seat and a cup of tea or something." She smiled wanly. "Fairness compels me to point out that the stove's not been fired in the better part of three weeks, and that the cup of tea could take a while."

Georgina Riley managed a wan smile of her own. "I think it best if we simply dispense with the niceties and deal with the matter at hand in a straightforward manner." She opened her reticule. "You dropped this in the lobby of the theater," she said, placing a rosary on the table before Darcy. "My escort retrieved it after your departure."

Darcy recognized it instantly. Blinded by the tears, she scooped the keepsake into her hand and held it tight. "Thank you for bringing it," she whispered. "I've missed it and am glad to have it back."

The other woman waited until she'd pocketed the treasure and blinked the tears from her eyes. Then she said, "Returning your mother's rosary is not my sole purpose for this visit, Darcy."

Darcy waited, not trusting her voice to be as steady or as strong as she wanted.

"How much did Mary tell you of her early life?"

"Very little," Darcy said, seeing no reason to lie to the woman. "It didn't seem to matter to her."

Georgina Riley squared her shoulders and took a deep breath. "My late husband was a strong-willed man. He set his mind to achieving wealth and social prominence. It was all that concerned him, and it guided every decision of his life. By God's will, Mary was our only child, and so it was that all of my husband's aspirations came to focus on her. When she refused to marry the man he'd chosen as suitable for furthering his goals, he was very angry. And when she defied him by running off with John O'Keefe, a lowly born Irishman, a common bricklayer whom my husband had hired to repair a chimney . . . Joseph turned his back on his only child and forbade her name to be spoken."

"And you accepted his decree," Darcy pronounced, fully knowing the truth of it.

The older woman's shoulders went back another notch. "I had come to regret my marriage to Joseph Riley, and Mary's escape from his tyranny was a victory for my own battered spirit. Yes, I let Mary go. I did not try to find her, fearing that in doing so I would lead her father to her. He would have destroyed her happiness for the mere satisfaction of forcing her to bend to his will. I wanted Mary to be happy above all else. She'd had so little happiness in her life until she met John O'Keefe."

They stood on opposite sides of the table, but suddenly the piece of furniture was all that separated them. Darcy felt a deep sense of compassion for the woman who had always and yet never been her grandmother. "John O'Keefe was my mother's world," she assured the other woman. "They were very, very happy together."

"And you? Did you have a happy childhood?" Georgina Riley asked.

"Yes. I wanted for nothing and my parents loved me deeply."

The older woman looked toward the window for a long moment and then asked quietly, "Why did you come to the house all those years ago seeking employment?"

"I didn't want employment," Darcy replied, seeing no reason to hide her motives. "I was already working for Mick

O'Shaunessy. I just wanted to see what you looked like, and the house in which my mother had spent her childhood."

Her gaze still on the window, Georgina asked, "Do you know why I didn't hire you?"

"You said I didn't have sufficient experience to scrub your pots."

Her grandmother's gaze came back to her, and a sad smile lifted the corners of her mouth. "You were too beautiful, my dear. You would have turned the servants' quarters upside down within the first week of your arrival." A shimmer of tears blurred the blue of her eyes. "You cannot imagine how often in the last weeks I've wished that I had looked closer then," she whispered, "how I've regretted that I didn't see the shadow of your mother in you. So many years lost, so much heartache that could have been prevented. If only you had told me who and what you were to me."

"I'm afraid that pride wouldn't permit it."

"Your grandfather's legacy, that pride," she countered, the bitterness that tinged her words belying the smile on her face. "Do you make a habit of letting it lead your judgment?"

"It's served me well, more often than not," Darcy replied honestly.

The older woman nodded and then straightened her shoulders in the way that Darcy had already come to recognize as her way of preparing to make a bold step. "I've come here to make a proposal, to reach across years and mistakes to offer us both a new beginning. Joseph Riley is dead, thirteen months this past week. I lost my daughter to the tyranny of his ambitions, but I will not allow him to reach beyond the grave to deprive me of my only grandchild. I would build with my granddaughter what relationship is possible in the years I have remaining."

Darcy had anticipated something bold from the woman, but *this* . . . She could only stare at Georgina Riley, dumbstruck by the words and all they meant.

"I want you to come live with me, Darcy," her grandmother went on. "I will confess to having had your circumstances thoroughly investigated before coming to my decision. I hope that you will allow me to offer you the material comfort and security your life has lacked in recent years."

Recent years. *Those* words and what *they* meant jolted Darcy out of her shock. "If you've had me investigated," she said, with a quirked smile, "then you well know that taking me into your home is going to invoke scandal. Perhaps you'd like to reconsider."

"I care not that you have earned sustenance through petty crime," the other woman instantly said. "No one need know about that part of your past."

"Picking pockets isn't the worst of my crimes, and it wasn't what I was referring to," Darcy rejoined just as swiftly. "There would be no hiding my relationship with Aiden Terrell. It's public knowledge."

"He's a very handsome man," the older woman said, a knowing smile spreading over her face and brightening her eyes. "I can see why you are attracted to him." Her smile turned slightly rueful and she shook her head. "I cannot believe that I am about to say this. . . . Your grandfather would have been very pleased by the match."

"It's not a match," Darcy declared. A horrible feeling of loss and sadness came with the declaration.

"It is over?"

"Yes, it's over," she said flatly. *God, how I wish it weren't, but it is. Aiden has gone on in pursuit of his demons.*

"In time you will not feel as deeply the heartache of the loss, dear child," Georgina Riley said gently. "Just as people will forget the details of your association with him. Until then, I won't permit their whispering to stand in the way of my plans. There are far more important matters than public opinion."

The gray tendrils of oblivion were starting to snake around her. It had been days since their power had been as potent or undeniable as she found them now. Then, too, it had been days since anyone had thought to lay another path open before her. "May I have time to think on it all?" Darcy asked, feeling the edge of her reasoning begin to slip. "It's an idea which had never occurred to me as possible. I've lived by my own wits for so long that I'm not sure I can be the grand-daughter you dream of. I'd rather be honest than disappoint you."

"I understand, Darcy. Take what time you need to reach your decision. When you have, send word and I will dispatch footmen to fetch you and your trunks. But I beg you not to take overly long to ponder. There has been so much lost already, and I am anxious to have the waste come to an end."

"I'll send word soon," she heard herself promise.

"Have you need of anything at the moment? Food? Clothing? Shall I have Williams fire the stove? I don't like that you are sitting here in the cold."

Darcy shook her head. "I'm fine. And I don't seem to feel the cold."

"Very well, my dear. I shall leave you to your deliberations now." She turned and glided toward the door.

"Grandmama?" The woman turned back, a broad smile on her face and tears brimming along her lashes. "Thank you for coming," Darcy said, mindful of her manners.

With a quiet sob, Georgina Riley nodded and left.

Darcy sank down on the chair as the door closed. What was she supposed to do now? She and Georgina Riley were all that either of them had left of blood family. Could she board a train for St. Louis and leave the old woman alone with a lifetime of regrets? Could she start a new life out west without seeing what a new one here could offer?

She was so tired. So very tired. Maybe, she told herself, the answer would be easier to find if she slept for a little while.

CHAPTER 24

HE SENSED A movement in the gray shadows of dawn. Aiden squinted in an effort to bring the face hovering above his into clear focus. "Rusty Riordan?"

"Aye."

Rusty's face floated up and back. Aiden was midway through the process of sitting up before he even vaguely realized that's what he was doing . . . "Sorry about knocking your teeth out that night," he offered, finding that things didn't move around quite as crazily with a wall propped against his back.

"Seamus tells me if'n you hadn't a taken the swing at me, 'e would've," Rusty said, sitting on a crate. " 'e says I deserved it, an' so's no hard feelin's I bear. I've learned to chew on the o'her side."

"Where am I?" Aiden asked, staring at the red brick wall some distance beyond the toes of his boots. He'd seen a lot of red brick walls lately, and there was nothing either familiar or distinguishing about this one.

"You're a-lyin' in the slop in the alleyway behind the Lion an' Fiddle," Rusty supplied with a degree of matter-of-factness that implied that Aiden had spent a great deal of time there recently. Aiden, of course, didn't care. That was the point of it all.

"Nathan Chandler's a-lookin' to find ye."

Now that scrap of news he did care about—but only insofar as to think about how to avoid being found for a while longer. "Nathan Chandler can go to hell and take his sanctimonious sermons with him." He felt a pressure on his left shoulder and though it took considerable concentration, he turned his head to see what it was. Rusty's hand.

"Chandler's a-marryin' me cousin Maisey in a few days," Rusty drawled, "so bear in mind what ye're sayin' o' me family."

A few days? That was all? Aiden felt himself smile. He'd successfully managed to lose a substantial block of time. Then the pressure on his shoulder intensified. Rusty was trying to right himself on the crate. He gave the man a shove. "Are you drunk, Rusty?"

"Not nearly as drunk as ye've been for the better part of the last few weeks," Rusty protested. He wrinkled his nose and fanned his hand before his face. "And sweet Jesus, Terrell, you fair to reek. If'n 'twere summer, even the flies would be avoidin' ye."

"Sorry," Aiden offered. "I haven't noticed." And he didn't notice then either, because he refused to look down at himself.

"Seems to me ye've been in no condition to notice much o' anythin' o' late," Rusty observed.

Aiden snorted. "That's been the general idea."

"So why ye a-tryin' so hard to drown yerself? Would it be 'cause ye're a-missin' Darce?"

Darcy. He missed her more than he would have ever expected. Drunk or near sober, it didn't matter. A thousand times a day he remembered the sound of her laughter, the way the sunlight shimmered in her cinnamon gold hair, the stubborn tilt of her chin, the way she doggedly pursued what she wanted. And, probably because he was a selfish bastard, what he missed most was the man he had been with Darcy at his side. The advantage—the attraction—of being drunk as a lord was that while the memories of Darcy still haunted him, they didn't hurt as badly and he was absolutely incapable of doing anything to cause her further heartache. Aiden inched himself further up on the wall and decided his thoughts were entirely too focused for comfort. It wouldn't be long before they drifted to his failure to find Jules. That tended to eat at his gut only slightly less than his wanting to put his arms around Darcy again. He let his head fall back against the cold bricks. "You didn't happen to stagger out here with a bottle in your hand, did you, Rusty?"

"Seamus took it away from me," Rusty answered petulantly. "Said I'd be apt to fall an' break it, an' 'e couldn't bear the waste of fine whiskey on his conscience."

"I'm entirely too sober," Aiden declared.

"I beg to differ."

He knew that voice, that dry censure. Aiden clenched his teeth and thought about finding something to throw at it. A rock or something.

"Oh, 'twould be Nathan Chandler," Rusty exclaimed happily. "Top of the mornin' to ye, cousin." And then Rusty lurched to his feet saying, "Give me yer hand, Terrell, an' I'll be a-helpin' ye to yer feet."

Aiden stared at the hand swaying before his face. Then it disappeared as Rusty sank back down on the crate with a rolling laugh.

"You son of a bitch," he heard Nathan say. "I've spent the last two weeks looking everywhere for you."

Aiden looked up to find his half-brother standing over him, as always immaculately turned out, one foot on either side of Aiden's legs. "You've found me. Happy?"

"Not in the least."

Aiden cocked a brow and closed his eyes. "I'll give you a hundred dollars to slit my throat and have it over and done." He felt a slight impact near the center of his chest. And then with a sharp tug the world went from under him. His legs protested the sudden bearing of his weight and he sagged back against the bricks for support.

"You sorry son of a bitch!" Nathan growled. "How dare you wallow in self-pity! Have you even seen Darcy since her mother died?"

"Maureen has barred me from her home." Aiden opened his eyes. The lapels of his coat were fisted in Nathan's hands.

Nathan shoved him closer to the wall. "Darcy isn't at the O'Shaunessys' any more, you ass. She's at her mother's apartment. And has been for almost three weeks now."

"With Maureen encamped in the hall outside?" Aiden asked sardonically. "Or has Mick taken over the role of her protector?"

"She's all alone."

His knees buckled. "Darcy shouldn't be alone."

"My point exactly," Nathan rejoined, hefting Aiden's weight back up the wall.

Aiden steadied himself by grasping Nathan's shoulders. "You need to go to her, Nathan. Make sure Darcy's eating and sleeping and isn't doing anything to harm herself."

Nathan shoved him hard. "It's not my goddamn responsibility, Aiden. It's yours."

"She doesn't want to see me," he heard himself say. He'd cost her too much already.

"Not in your present condition; no one would." Nathan yanked him away from the wall and spun him into the center of the alley. "We'll sober you up first."

"An' give 'im a bath, too," Rusty piped in from his crate.

Everything around him was moving at crazy angles. He had to get back to the wall. "You don't understand," Aiden said, trying to loosen Nathan's grip on his coat. "Darcy doesn't need me."

"How the hell do you know what she needs?"

He knew. He could offer her nothing but more pain. The price she'd already paid for having him in her life was too high. He'd fully earned every last bit of her hatred. "Blow off, Nate," he growled, planting his hands against his brother's chest and pushing with all his might. Nathan stumbled back. Aiden turned in the direction of the wall and blinked to bring Rusty Riordan into focus. And when he managed the task he said, "Rusty, let's find a bottle. I'll buy."

"You're done drinking, Aiden." Nathan declared from behind him. "I'll not watch you destroy yourself."

"You're welcome to try to stop me," Aiden challenged, staggering around to face his brother. "Or you could just go away."

"Aiden, I would prefer not to have to strike you."

Nathan? Strike him? That would be a first! As if Nathan even knew how to throw a fist! He supposed Nate could try, not that—Aiden had a vague sensation of pain in his jaw and then there was nothing.

DARCY CLIMBED FROM her bath thinking that life was wonderfully back to normal. She sensed that the reason for it lay in Georgina Riley's visit the day before. She wasn't alone; she had a grandmama who regretted the past and wanted to make the future happy for them both. Darcy nodded to herself, knowing that somehow the decision had been made. She also knew there was no point in delaying acting on it. Deciding she would dress herself in one of the gowns in the trunk, so that she wouldn't embarrass her grandmother by showing up on her doorstep dressed in urchin's rags, she quickly crossed the room and lifted the lid of the smallest of the four.

Inside were undergarments, neatly folded and nestled in thin tissue paper. She stood there, feeling the world tremble beneath her feet as memories washed over her. . . . Aiden threatening to loosen her laces in François's fitting room, the ease with which he'd actually accomplished the task later that same afternoon, the way he'd laced her in the next morning and then taken her back to his bed to make love to her again. She remembered the sparkle of mischief in his eyes, the wonder of his touch. And his smile . . . that wicked smile of his that always, always made her willing to throw caution to the wind.

And all she had left of him were the memories.

Darcy reminded herself that she had known from the beginning that she and Aiden would be together only a short while, only until they'd found Jules and stopped him. And then her mother had died, and her time with Aiden had sud-

denly come to its end. Aiden could no more have waited for
her to finish grieving than she could have found the strength
to go with him. It wasn't the end for which she'd prepared
herself, but it had to be accepted as the one that had come.
No one knew better than she that life seldom turned out as
you planned.

Deliberately setting her heartache aside, Darcy focused her
attention on the matters at hand. A few minutes later she
came from her bedroom and looked around the apartment
one last time. The trunks . . . She'd ask Georgina Riley
how to best deal with the contents. The rest of it she would
decide about later. Her gaze passed over the items lying on
the table—the destroyed promissory note, the knife, her
mother's final letter. Darcy reached out and picked up the letter. It was time to begin again, time to read the words and
seal the past.

She broke the circle of wax and opened the single page.

> *My dearest Darcy,*
>
>   *Where to begin, my darling daughter? In my heart, I
> believe you understand how very much I love you and how
> proud I am of your strength. How often I have watched in
> awe from the window as you strode down the street in your
> tattered boy's clothes, making your way in a world so fre-
> quently harsh and unkind. And every evening when you
> returned home, I marveled at the brilliance of your smile
> and your brave determination to shield me from the ugli-
> ness of the world in which you made a way for both of us.
> Darcy, my darling, please know that no mother ever had
> greater proof of her daughter's love and devotion.*
>
>   *I beg you not to see my decision to leave you as a be-
> trayal of your love. I have prayed to the Blessed Virgin
> Mary only for the two greatest wishes of my heart: that
> you find a love as wondrous as the one that bound your
> father's heart and mine into one, and that, when you
> found that love, I would be released from the earthly
> realm to rejoin your father.*
>
>   *I have heard the gentle flutterings of the angels' wings,*

*Darcy, and I am soon to have my heart made whole. I go
happily, for I know that the Holy Mother of God has seen
to intercede on behalf of my prayers. The Lord God Our
Father has sent Aiden Terrell to you and granted me the
mercy of seeing the tenderness and love that has grown between you. Love your Aiden joyfully and with all your
heart, Darcy. Protect him and cherish him as he does you.
Waste not a moment of your lives together, and cling to
one another through all things. Nothing is more powerful
or enduring than love.*

*It is with all my love that I pledge to you that your
father and I will keep watch over you and Aiden, keeping
you both, and the precious children of your love, always
safe.*

Mother

Tears splashed onto the vellum and created inky pools.
Darcy folded the letter to protect it from the ravages of her
anguish. It had been a false peace that had borne her mother
heavenward. God might well have answered her mother's second prayer, but He hadn't answered her first. Aiden didn't
love her daughter. And though Darcy loved Aiden with every
measure of her heart and soul, she knew the offering of one
heart wasn't enough. There would be no joyful tomorrows
with Aiden, no precious children, no enduring together.
Their time together was done. A ragged sob broke past
Darcy's lips and her knees buckled beneath her. She felt herself falling and went without effort to catch herself, swept beyond caring by the pain of her broken heart.

DARCY STARED INTO the gathering twilight. She had
been so close to moving forward, only to have it all come
crashing back down around her. If only she could have seen it
coming; she could have braced herself so that the pain
wouldn't have rendered her so weak. But she hadn't, and she
had cried tears she hadn't known she had left in her and when

she thought the well at last mercifully dry, another had sprung open and flooded forth.

She had a bare recollection of Patrick pulling her up from the floor and dragging her to her bed. She had a clearer memory of Mick and Maureen murmuring words of comfort and telling her they were going to take her back to their home. God forgive her, she'd lashed out at their kindness and concern and driven them from the apartment. Maureen had been in tears. Mick had looked both pained and stoically resigned to letting Darcy have her way.

And when they'd gone she'd crawled back into her bed, pulled her pillow tight against her, and offered the Virgin Mary every bargain she could think of for the chance to have Aiden back again. And as always, the Blessed Mother had ignored her.

Darcy rose from her chair at the kitchen table and wandered to the window that overlooked the street below, the window from which her mother had watched her leave every morning for the better part of seven years. She leaned her forehead against the windowpanes, finding the coldness of the glass wonderfully soothing against her skin. Perhaps she was trying too hard to find her way, she thought. Perhaps the easiest way ahead lay in keeping to the path she'd always walked. She could go back to reefing until enough of her world came right that she could rationally choose another way to go. Surely the St. Louis of Jimmy O'Meara wouldn't stop if a teacher failed to arrive on a train. And if she made sure to visit Georgina Riley regularly, her grandmother would be content to let her go her own way for a time.

And with time, immersed in the familiar and comfortable predictability of the life she had always known, she would come to accept in her heart that her mother's passing was the blessing her mind knew it to be. And in time she would also accept the loss of Aiden Terrell in the same way.

"Darcy? May we come in?"

Maisey? Darcy hadn't heard the knock, but her senses were too battered to be capable of surprise. She turned away from the window saying by rote, "Please do."

Nathan Chandler closed the door behind them. "Is there anything we can do for you, Miss Darcy?"

How had she never noticed that Nathan and Aiden had the same eyes? Her heart ached at the shadow standing before her. "I'm fine," she lied. Forcing a smile she added, "But thank you for offering. It's most kind of you."

Maisey fingered her reticule nervously, glanced at Nathan beside her, and then on a rush of breath said, "Darcy, we came to tell you something."

Nathan slipped his arm around Maisey's shoulder and took up the conversation. "Maisey has honored me by accepting my proposal of marriage. Her parents have approved of the match, and we're to be married in three days."

Maisey looked close to tears. "We would have come to tell you as soon as Ma and Da approved, but it was too soon after . . . We didn't want you to think that we didn't care about . . ."

Darcy willed one foot in front of the other and crossed the parlor. "I'm very happy for you, Maisey," she said sincerely, taking her friend's hands in hers and pressing a kiss to Maisey's cheek. Then she squeezed Maisey's hands before releasing them and turning to Aiden's brother. "Congratulations, Nathan. You've managed to win the best girl to be had in Charlestown."

"I know."

The smile he bestowed on Maisey was radiant. If only Aiden were to look at her like that.

"Nathan's taking me home to St. Kitts," her friend said happily. "We'll sail the morning after the wedding."

"I'll miss you so much, Maisey. You'll write to me?"

Before Maisey could offer her obligatory promise, Nathan said, "We're hoping that we can talk you into coming with us."

Darcy met his gaze, more startled by her ability to be surprised than by Nathan's proposal itself. Perhaps she wasn't as dead inside as she'd thought. "To St. Kitts?" she finally managed to say. "Why would I go to St. Kitts?"

Maisey answered. "Darcy, Aiden needs you."

Such earnestness. Darcy smiled ruefully. "Aiden can easily find another to replace me. I'm sure they'll be lined up three deep on the docks to welcome him home."

"Aiden . . ." Nathan faltered and sighed. "Darcy, Aiden has always teetered on the edge of self-destruction. I'm afraid that he's now closer than he's ever been to toppling over. He's been drinking again. Heavily and constantly."

She knew then that the nightmares had returned to haunt him. For a while he'd slept free of them, and he hadn't needed to escape them through whiskey. "He can't very well find Jules in that state."

"Jules hasn't so much as crossed his mind in the last fortnight. Under other circumstances I would be pleased by that. However . . ." Nathan raked his hand through his hair and the gesture sent a pang of remembrance through Darcy's heart.

"I've managed to at least bring him back to the hotel," Nathan continued. "At the moment, he's thrashing his way toward some semblance of sobriety. Not happily, mind you. I've tried to appeal to what little judgment he hasn't pickled, but nothing I've said has gotten through to him. For his own protection, I feel compelled to use whatever means necessary to get him back to St. Kitts. While the employment of thugs to truss him and carry him aboard ship remains an avenue of recourse, I'd prefer to use a gentler form of persuasion."

Maisey laid her hand on Darcy's shoulder and said, "Aiden would come willingly, Darcy, if he knew you were going to St. Kitts, too."

"Maisey tells me you have dreams of being a teacher," Nathan quickly added. "There are children on St. Kitts in need of one, I'm sure."

"There are too may ways to go already," she said. "Mick has offered to find me a teaching position in St. Louis. My grandmother has found me and wants to bring me into her home. And a part of me just wants to pick up the pieces where they fell and go back to the way it's always been."

"But you can't help Aiden if you're anywhere but St. Kitts, Darcy."

Something deep inside her snapped. The heat of anger spread through her veins. Why should she feel duty-bound to help Aiden any more than she already had? Mick was right; only by the grace of God had her mother been spared Jules's butchery. Jules would have never known Mary O'Keefe existed if Aiden Terrell hadn't stormed into her daughter's life. And when he and his accursed, black-hearted brother had upended it, and Darcy had been left battered and trying to find her way, had Aiden thought to hold her in his arms and ease her pain? No. He had let his demons exercise their power over him, and he had gone away. And while he might have continued the search for Jules, in the end he had abandoned it. Had he come to her then? No. He had thrown himself into a well of whiskey. She couldn't save him from himself. She had tried and failed. Darcy took a deep breath and turned back to face Maisey and Nathan. What was—or had been—between her and Aiden was none of their concern. She wouldn't batter them with her anger. And her pride wouldn't allow her to admit how deeply her heart hurt.

"What about Aiden's quest to find Jules?" Darcy asked stiffly. "The madman's still out there, isn't he? Or has he been caught?"

Nathan considered her at length and then replied, "Jules hasn't killed again, and he's overdue to strike. But he's properly the concern of the constabulary. He always has been, but I've never been able to make Aiden see it that way. Now I have an opportunity to take matters into my hands. If I can get Aiden back to St. Kitts, I stand a good chance of saving him from both Jules and himself."

"Please consider coming with us," Maisey pleaded, not bothering to hide her desperation. "If not for Aiden's sake then for your own, Darcy. You need to go on. You can't sit here forever and grieve. Come with us so that you have something to take your mind off all that's happened. You need to smile and laugh again. It isn't going to happen as long as you stay here."

"I'll think on it," Darcy answered, knowing it for a bold

lie, but also knowing it was the easiest way of getting Maisey and Nathan out of her apartment.

"All you have is three days, Darcy," Nathan pressed. "The ship sails this Friday, and we have to know your decision well before then so I can make the arrangements and maneuver Aiden."

Darcy nodded. "Maisey, you know I won't be able to come to the wedding, don't you?"

"I understand, Darcy. You're in mourning." Maisey looked close to tears again. Nathan took her hand, as his bride-to-be bravely added, "But your thoughts will be with us, I'm sure. And your best wishes."

Again Darcy nodded. "What would you like for a wedding present? A fine piece of silver, perhaps? Or crystal?"

Nathan said bluntly, "Only your agreement to come to St. Kitts with us."

"If you don't receive word from me by the day after next, you'll know I've decided to go another way."

Nathan left frustrated and angry. Maisey left wringing her hands and casting beseeching looks over her shoulder. And Darcy closed the door behind them, very irritated with having to deal with emotions other than her own. No one seemed to understand that pushing her in the direction they wanted her to go cost her dearly. She understood that they were all trying to help, but they only made matters worse. And so much more complicated than they already were.

First Maureen. Then Mick. Then Georgina Riley. Her mother's dying wish. Now Maisey and Nathan. The only one who hadn't told her what she should do had been Aiden Terrell. She had to be grateful to him for that.

And for so much more. He had given her so very much more.

Darcy sank onto the wooden chair. She had two days to decide what course she was going to take with the rest of her life. And she knew instinctively that there was no solution to be found until she came to terms with how she felt about Aiden Terrell. And how much she was willing to risk in following her heart, how much of her pride was worth saving.

HAVING BEEN DRAGGED kicking and swearing back into sobriety only two days before, Aiden looked out over the revelry of Nathan and Maisey's wedding reception and decided he had absolutely no tolerance for merriment. A solitary celebration seemed more in keeping with his mood. He turned, grabbed an unopened bottle of whiskey off the bar, and made his way toward the door of the social club. Nathan, he knew, was far too preoccupied to even notice he'd left the party, much less come after him in an effort to hold him to a straight and narrow path.

Besides, he hadn't promised to stop drinking altogether; only for as long as it took to fulfill his role as best man. He'd done that. Because Nathan had not yet converted to Catholicism, the wedding had been a civil one, and the social club had been transformed into a makeshift church with an aisle down the center. The guests had been seated in chairs on either side with a clear view of a beribboned arch under which the bride and groom had stood. Aiden had stood at the front of the assemblage, too, and handed Nathan the ring on cue. He'd offered the couple the expected congratulatory toast at the first of the luncheon reception. He was now done. And so was his promise to Nathan.

Now he needed only to find a cab and make his way back to his Boston hotel room. Aiden spied a hack coming at him on the opposite side of the street. He hailed it and crossed, reaching into the breast pocket of his coat for his fare. A folded half sheet of vellum came out with the folded currency. He extracted and then handed the driver a bill, gave him the address, and climbed inside the cab. Nathan had handed him the money that morning as they were dressing for the wedding. Had Nathan thought to write him a note of soberly encouragement and brotherly love? To be found later, of course, when it wasn't likely to embarrass either of them. Aiden chuckled darkly. Yes, it would be just like Nathan.

He opened the note. His brows instantly knitted. It was from Darcy to Nathan. He checked the date, noting it as the previous day. Darcy politely but firmly and without explanation declined to accompany Maisey and Nathan to St. Kitts. *But if Aiden plans to take up the search for Jules again, I'm willing to help him any way I can. He need only ask me.*

Aiden sagged back against the seat. Darcy would help him? An immense weight suddenly lifted from his chest and shoulders, making him light-headed. He tamped down the urge to laugh. There would be conditions and limitations on their relationship this time, of course. Darcy was far too intelligent and prideful to blithely fall into his arms and give him a hero's welcome. But if he could get near enough just long enough, then maybe he could make sufficient amends so that, once the business of Jules was done, he and Darcy could part company as friends.

Aiden rapped on the roof of the hack. Only after he'd announced his change of mind and the driver had turned back toward Charlestown did it cross Aiden's mind that Nathan had expertly manipulated him. Recognition of the fact didn't bother him in the least. He suspected that's what brothers did to each other. But the possibility that Darcy might have been a knowing party to the manipulation did bother him. Why was she willing to help him? After all the heartache and pain he'd brought into her life, why was she willing to risk letting him do it all over again?

He hadn't found an answer by the time he climbed from the hired cab. He still didn't have one as he strode down the hallway toward Darcy's apartment door. Lost in thought, he didn't pause, but simply turned the knob, opened the door, and walked in.

She sat at the kitchen table, dressed in her trousers and worn cotton shirt, her hair tumbling in a brilliant riot over her shoulders. Her eyes widened at the sight of him, and she instantly came to her feet. For a second he thought she might bolt, then she squared her shoulders and gripped the edge of the table in front of her. She said nothing, but looked him up and down with those huge, soft brown eyes of hers.

There was so much he wanted to say, so much that needed to be said, but he thought that perhaps it was too soon for heartfelt explanations and apologies. So instead of inviting her to agree that he was without doubt the world's greatest ass, he closed the door and asked, "Why isn't this door locked?"

"It saves me the effort of admitting the parades of people."

She didn't move but he thought he saw her catch her lower lip between her teeth for just a second. He threw the bolt on the door, walked over to the table, and blindly set the whiskey bottle down.

Closer now, he could see the dark circles under her eyes and the redness of her cheeks. And her face had grown so much thinner than he remembered. Suddenly he wanted nothing more than to take her in his arms. Common sense stopped him from acting on the impulse, and then, as though exhausted from effort, allowed him to say, "You look like hell, Darcy."

She arched a delicate brow. "I've seen you look better, too."

Christ Almighty, he was making a mess of this. Aiden sighed and raked his fingers through his hair. "Sobriety isn't all it's touted to be. My gut's throbbing and my head's pounding. I ache in places I didn't know I had. The sacrifices one makes for his brother's wedding—"

"It's done, then?" she asked quietly. "Maisey and Nathan are married?"

"Quite happily, it would appear," he supplied. "I left them

at the reception surrounded by revelers, and enough food to feed all of Charlestown for the next week. Which is good, since all of Charlestown is there. When was the last time you ate?"

If his abrupt question caught her off guard, she didn't show it. "Maureen sends something with Bridie every morning," she answered smoothly. "Patrick Riordan, Maisey's little brother, brings the evening meal."

God, he knew her so well. Aiden shook his head, unwilling to let her evade the matter. "I didn't ask who's providing your food. I asked when was the last time you ate any of it."

She offered him a tiny shrug. "I don't remember. Yesterday, I think. Maybe the day before. One day tends to be very like all the others, and I can't keep them straight any more."

"And when was the last time you slept, Darcy?"

"I don't sleep much." Then, as though she knew he'd press for a better answer, she added, "I can't. Dreams come quickly and I awaken restless. And you, Aiden? Are you sleeping?"

He smiled ruefully. "I've made the sad discovery that there simply isn't enough whiskey in the world."

"Nathan said you were trying to drink yourself to death."

He clearly heard the ire edging her words, but he wasn't sure what the source of it was. "Are you disappointed that I haven't succeeded?"

"That's not fair, Aiden," she calmly retorted. "You know I don't wish you dead."

Did he? He'd given her reason enough to wish him into the fiery depths of hell. If she didn't want him there, then something had gone terribly wrong in her mind during the past weeks. "What *do* you wish for, Darcy?"

She looked at him for a long moment, and then down at the articles on the table. He had almost decided she wasn't going to answer when she lifted her head, and blinking back tears, said, "I wish my world would come right again. I wish the tears would stop. But more than anything, I wish that this horrible emptiness inside me would go away."

His chest tightened as he watched her brush away the tears. He wanted so badly to reach out and touch her, to tell her she didn't have to be brave for him, to tell her he understood how she felt and how much it hurt. But he couldn't be sure Darcy trusted him enough to let him comfort her that way. "The emptiness is easier to endure if you don't stare into it," he offered somberly. "It helps if you look past it to something else."

She closed her eyes and laughed without making a sound. Aiden inched around the corner of the table, watching her and worrying that she had come unhinged. She was easily within arm's reach when she sobered and moistened her lips with the tip of her tongue. Aiden froze.

Her eyes came open and the words came softly. "It's very easy to stand on the other side of this table, Aiden, and tell me what I should do. Mick has stood there. My grandmother has stood there. Maisey and Nathan have stood there. The whole goddamned world has stood where you are and told me what I should do with my life."

"What do *you* want to do with it?"

A bittersweet smile lifted the corners of her mouth. "Oh, Aiden. You're the only person who's asked me that."

"Is there an answer, Darcy? Do you know what you want?"

She nodded slowly. "I want a purpose for getting up in the morning and a reason to walk out of here. I want a reason to put one foot in front of the other and do something with my day besides cry for what I've lost and what I can't have. I want to start searching for Jules again. Can we?"

He understood her need for purpose. But the questions that had nagged at him since he'd read her note to Nathan returned, begging answers. He had to know why, contrary to all logic, she wanted to be with him again. He took the note from his pocket and handed it across the table, saying, "I found this in my pocket after the wedding."

She opened it, winced, and sighed. "Nathan put it there?" she guessed, handing it back to him.

He tossed it down on the table. "I'm assuming so. Just out of curiosity, why did he and Maisey want you to go to St. Kitts with them?" He cocked a brow. "Nathan's far too traditional to be attracted to the notion of a honeymoon for three."

She grinned, the first true expression of unguarded emotion he'd seen from her since he'd walked in. It thrilled him, and even after she brought it back under control, he sensed that his Darcy O'Keefe had survived her ordeal intact. And then suddenly he knew the answers to his questions. Darcy would never attempt to manipulate him. She had never been anything but charmingly honest and unflinchingly direct with him.

"Nathan wanted to use me as a lure for you, so that you would go back to St. Kitts without a fight."

"Why didn't you accept?" he asked, propping his hip on the edge of the table and folding his arms over his chest. "Is something—or someone—holding you here?"

"Would you have gone with us, Aiden?" she countered.

"Honestly?" He shook his head.

She smiled and her eyes brightened. "I didn't think you would, either."

"So why have you offered to renew the search for Jules?"

"Does there have to be a reason?"

"With you, there always is," he told her. "It's that wonderfully logical mind of yours. Is it that Mick O'Shaunessy wants you to?"

"No, Mick's declared me free of obligation."

"So why, Darcy? I'll have an answer eventually, so you might as well get it said."

"There are a lot of reasons," she began hesitantly. "Some I don't understand at all and others only vaguely."

She paused and studied him. Seeming to have reached some decision, she took a deep breath, met his gaze, and said firmly, "But I know with absolute certainty that neither one of us has done well with the last few weeks of our lives, and it's because we've lost sight of what we need. You need to defeat your demons. I need to have control over my life. The only way we can have what we need is to put ourselves back on the path we were walking before Jules stepped between us. We need to finish the task as we began it, together. Neither of us is going to have peace until we do."

Such a logical, thoughtful mind; always arrowing to the

essence of the matter. But Aiden knew that an intuitive reason always lay beneath Darcy's cool logic. "That would be the reason you understand clearly," he observed, watching her face intently. "What's the reason you only vaguely grasp?"

She swallowed hard and looked away. "As foolish and childish as it may be . . ." Her voice broke and it took every measure of Aiden's restraint not to reach for her.

"As foolish and childish as it may be," she began again, bringing her gaze to meet his, "I seem to believe that everything will be better if you would just hold me."

His heart slammed hard against his ribs and his pulse shot like lightning through his veins. He refused to allow himself to blindly accept, to hope for something he didn't deserve. He stood and faced her squarely. "I don't think I can *just* hold you, Darcy."

"Yes, I know," she said with a gentle smile as she came to stand in front of him. "You're a selfish bastard who can't resist an opportunity for hedonistic pleasure. And I wouldn't have you any way but the way you are."

He cupped her face gently in his hands and traced the delicate arc of her cheekbones with the pads of his thumbs. "I've missed you so much, Darcy," he whispered. "I'm sorry I haven't been here for you. I should have—"

She pressed her fingertips to his lips. "All things in their time, Aiden. Right now . . . hold me."

He had no right to it, but he accepted the most precious gift anyone had ever given him and gathered Darcy O'Keefe in his arms. She felt so small against him, so vulnerable, so in need of his strength. He gave her all he had to give, touching her, pressing little kisses into her hair, and murmuring promises to be there for her as long as she needed him. When she looked up at him, the wonder and happiness in her eyes stole his breath. He kissed her tenderly, with a reverence he'd given no other woman. And when her lips parted beneath his, inviting him to take what he pleased, he knew to the center of his soul that nothing else on earth mattered as much as loving her as she deserved to be. Aiden bent, slipped his arm behind her knees, and lifted her into his arms. Cradling her, he carried her from the parlor to her bedroom.

Whether her world had come right or not, she couldn't say. There was nothing beyond Aiden and the slow, delicious potency of their coming together again. There was no haste in their union, and yet no leisure either. They loved with deliberate exhilaration, savoring every touch, every tremor, knowing their bond for the rare and magnificent treasure it was. And together, as one, they claimed as their own the exquisite realm of completion. Body and soul whole, Darcy lay in Aiden's arms and drifted toward deep, sated sleep. It was as it should be.

SHE BLINKED AND frowned. A noise? She strained to hear through the darkness. No, she told herself. Nothing. She wiggled closer to Aiden's side and was rewarded by the tightening of his arms around her.

The sound came again, and this time she recognized both it and its import. She kissed Aiden's shoulder and then whispered, "Patrick's here with food," as she gently extracted herself from the warmth of Aiden's embrace. He blinked the sleep from his eyes as she hurriedly pulled on her trousers. Darcy smiled and bent down to kiss him. "I won't be long. Wait right here for me."

"I wasn't planning to go anywhere."

"Good man," she said, chuckling as she drew on her shirt and padded out of the room.

Patrick actually took a half step back when she opened the door and extended her hand for the plate. "Give it over, Patrick," she demanded with a grin. "I'm starving."

He surrendered it with a look of utter amazement on his face. It was still there when she closed the door and carried the plate into the kitchen. She took two forks from the drawer and then headed back to Aiden.

She found him sitting on the side of her bed, clad only in his trousers. She dropped down beside him, handed him a fork and said, "I hope Mrs. Malone wasn't counting on my bringing her supper tonight. I'm famished."

She pulled the cover off the plate to reveal what could only have been a wide sampling of the fare at the wedding reception. Two dainty, perfectly golden meat pies, potatoes and onions and peas in a cream sauce, deviled eggs, pickled relishes, dollops of no fewer than four salads, and a large, lavishly buttered roll. "Oh, God," she whispered, "and you walked away from all this, Aiden?"

"It didn't look as good then as it does now."

She laughed and, with the plate still in hand, scooted back on the bed. Turning so that her back was to the footboard, she crossed her legs and set the plate on the rumpled sheets in front of her. "Come share," she offered, waving her fork. And as he settled himself across from her, she managed a slightly restrained attack on the creamed potatoes.

Bliss. Pure bliss. It was the best food she'd ever eaten, and she abandoned herself to appreciation and wonder. She had done justice to the better part of her half when Aiden chuckled.

"What's amusing you?" she asked, licking meat pie crumbs from her fingers.

"You." He grinned wickedly. "You take such sensual delight in eating. Do I give you even half the pleasure?"

"Twice as much," she admitted freely. "Maybe more. I forget all about food when I'm making love with you."

"Really?"

"Really," she assured him. "Although it escapes me how I might actually prove it to you. I suppose you'll just have to take my word for it. Do you want that last half of the roll?"

"Go ahead, darling. You need to eat. You've gotten too thin."

"You've lost a bit of weight, too," she observed, taking the roll.

"Drinking has a way of killing the appetite. At least in some respects. There are some hungers that simply won't be ignored."

She knew what appetites he hadn't lost, and it pleased her

to know that she had that small power over him. She polished off the roll and dusted the crumbs from her hands over the plate. "I've had enough food for now," she declared. "But those other appetites you're referring to—Do I stand any chance of talking you into satisfying them for me?"

He smiled and turned away to set the plate on the night table. When he turned back, his smile broadened and he watched with naked desire as she unbuttoned her shirt. And then he blinked and his smile began to fade.

"Darcy?" he asked, bringing his gaze up to meet hers. "There's no sponge, is there?"

The troubled expression on his face stilled her hands. She let them fall into her lap. "I wasn't expecting you to come through the door," she said, "and then you didn't give me time." Darcy gave him a rueful smile. "Not that it ever crossed my mind."

"Is there a chance of there being a child?"

"You know more about these matters than I do. Is there?"

Darcy watched his skin pale, saw the quickened trip of his pulse along the side of his muscled neck. The eyes that looked back at her were haunted. "If you should find yourself . . . that way," he said tightly, "I'll accept the decision you make regarding it."

"Decision?" she repeated, her own heart skittering at the sight of Aiden's obvious fear.

"When and how to be rid of it."

A shiver raced down her spine and her hands went cold. "Be rid of it?" she asked, desperate for him to deny he'd suggested such a thing, desperate for him to deny that he thought her capable of it.

"You said you didn't want to be encumbered with a child. There are physicians. . . . I'll make inquiries so that you're in the hands of a competent one."

She could barely breathe. Her heart was in her throat. But the iciness of her limbs was no more. "And if I don't want to be *rid* of it?"

He tilted his head to the side and studied her with something akin to suspicion. A flood of true anger swept over her.

"Not to worry, Aiden," she said, clenching her hands into fists. "I wouldn't make any demands on you or your bank account. Neither would I use a bastard child to threaten your precious social facade. You can walk away without looking back. I'll not follow and plead with you to acknowledge your child. I don't need you. I'm perfectly capable of providing for us on my own."

He only blinked in the face of her heated diatribe. Then he cocked a brow and asked warily, "Is this an expression of your feelings on motherhood in general?"

Afraid she might actually swing her fists at him, she shoved them under her legs. "I've never had any thoughts on the matter, general or otherwise," she retorted, her voice quavering with barely suppressed rage. "It's never been a possibility, near or remote, until you came into my life. I'm talking only about you and me and *our* child. That there might be one was a risk I accepted in stepping into your arms and tumbling into your bed. Yes, I asked you to protect me, but I haven't approached the matter blindly. I know that sometimes even the best of precautions can fail. If there is to be a child from our lovemaking, Aiden, I'll have it and keep it and cherish it as a gift from you, far more precious than gowns and jewels."

She saw surprise replace his wariness. And then surprise was replaced by disbelief. "You might want to try rephrasing that, Darcy," he said softly. "You're sounding as though you actually *want* to have my child."

A long-considered piece of the puzzle suddenly fell into place with startling ease and clarity. Her heart ached with the fullness of understanding, leaving no room for anger. "That's what Wilhelmina did," she whispered, knowing with all her heart the truth of it. "She rid herself of your child, didn't she?"

He shrugged with artful indifference. "It was a long time ago."

And the wound had been so deep that it had never healed. A lifetime of not being wanted had been compounded a hundredfold by a heartless woman's act of selfish ignorance.

"Aiden," she said gently, "Wilhelmina is the world's greatest fool."

"Actually, she showed very sound judgment," he countered, still presenting his facade of casual detachment. "I came at the matter determined to be incredibly noble. Wilhelmina, on the other hand, knew I wasn't suited for marriage any more than she was. She exercised uncommon good sense and spared us both a disaster."

His determination to pretend it didn't matter made her want to cry. She drew a shaky breath and changed her tack. "If I were bearing your child, would you be bound by honor to ask me to marry you?"

He nodded slowly. "I apparently don't learn from my mistakes."

She ignored the backhanded insult. "And if I accepted?"

He snorted and answered derisively, "I'd wait until you came to your senses."

"And if I never did?" she pressed.

Hope flashed across his face for just a fraction of a heartbeat, and then it was gone, replaced by a sad, stoic resolve. "Your life would be a living hell, spent with a man who didn't know the first thing about loving you but who would manage to have you always suckling one babe while another clung to your apron. Is that what you want?"

"I want you to have a bit more faith in yourself, Aiden."

"I'm a realist, darling," he declared, climbing off the bed. "I'm not about to promise you what I know I can't give you. You'd be wise to summon your practicality and accept it."

"Are you leaving?" she asked.

"Not hardly," he answered, heading toward the bedroom door. "But all this talk of babies and marriage has me in want of a good stiff drink. I'm going to get the bottle. And while I'm out there, I'm going to rifle the trunks and find the damn sponges."

Darcy watched him disappear into the darkness of the parlor wishing with all her heart that she could make Aiden see the man she did. He was good and honorable. He was a man of strength and gentleness, kindness and determination. But most importantly, despite his staunchly maintaining otherwise, he knew how to love her. There had to be a way to make him see through the ghosts and failures of his past, to make him understand that his heart and soul were not only worthy of love, but capable of giving it.

A dull grunt and then the tinkle of glass brought Darcy abruptly from her musing. There was a heavy thud that set the windowpanes rattling.

"Aiden?" she called, scrambling off the bed. Silence. She raced toward the door. "Aiden! Are you all right?"

She stumbled to halt just inside the parlor, searching the shadows for him. And then she saw him, lying curled on his side between the table and the kitchen, shards of glass glittering in the moonlight around him. The smell of whiskey permeated the air.

"Aiden!" she cried, starting forward.

Her head snapped back as pain shot through her scalp and her feet went out from under her. She was righted almost instantly, and by a power beyond herself. Heat pressed against her back, wrapped like steel around her waist, and a wave of pain shot from the roots of her hair to the pit of her stomach. She tried to pull away and then there was only the cold sharp edge pressed to her throat. Her heart slammed upward and she froze, consumed with fear. Warm air caressed her ear.

"At last we meet, Darcy O'Keefe. Allow me to be so forward as to introduce myself; I am Jules Terrell."

CHAPTER 26

WHAT HAVE YOU done to Aiden?" she demanded hoarsely.

He eased back so that his breath no longer traced her ear. "Rendered him momentarily unconscious and bound his hands behind his back. The whiskey better serves my purpose over his head than in his gullet. He's spent entirely too much time drinking recently. I've grown very frustrated in waiting for him to sober enough to come to you."

She looked at Aiden lying so still on the floor, and choked back a sob.

"Oh, don't worry about Aiden's head," Jules said. "It's thicker than a teak hull. He'll come around soon enough to play the game with us. I wouldn't have it any other way."

Darcy closed her eyes and struggled to silence the chatter of her chaotic thoughts. She had to think. She had to find a way to escape Jules's hold. The knife pressed closer to her throat, and her breath hissed between her teeth. Instinctively she arched back against her captor as she clamped her hands about the thick forearm lying across her chest, trying any way she could to put even the smallest bit of distance between the blade and her skin.

"Pay attention and do what you're supposed to," Jules growled. "You're supposed to ask me what game we're playing."

"What game are we playing?" she dutifully offered. Aiden groaned and rolled halfway onto his back, his bound arms preventing him from going over completely. He thrashed his legs once, just briefly, then went still and silent.

Jules chuckled. "I'm going to kill you, girl. Of course. But this time, Aiden's going to watch me do it. That way he'll know, and he'll have to admit it. I'll make him admit it."

Her stomach lurched and twisted. Fear, stark and cold, crawled up her spine. Jules viciously tightened the arm around her waist. "Pay attention!"

"Make Aiden admit what?" she hurriedly asked. *Oh, dear God, Aiden, wake up!*

"That my intellect is superior to his."

She gasped at the words, at the admission that she had been right. "If that is what this is about," she offered, desperately clinging to the thread he'd offered, "I'm sure Aiden would be willing to accommodate you. Killing us isn't necessary."

"Oh, the blood is purely for the sport of it," he taunted, lightly drawing the blade down the side of her throat. "And I don't want to just hear words tumble from Aiden's lips. I want to see the absolute certainty of it in his eyes."

Aiden wouldn't look at Jules in submission and acceptance. Never. She knew that. Aiden would look at him in cold-blooded rage. "Aiden will kill you," she said, her voice strong with the courage of conviction. "You know that, don't you?"

"I'll kill him before he even has a chance to come at me." Jules chuckled and drew the knife up the side of her throat. "After I'm done with you, and while he's puking up his guts."

"But if you kill Aiden," she countered, rising to her toes and arching her neck even more, "then you'll have to abandon the game. There'll be no one to chase you. No one else to convince of your brilliance."

"I won't need to play the game any more," he replied in singsong measure. "I'll have what is mine."

She accepted her cue. "What will you have?"

"My father's estate. All the wealth, all the property, all the respect that goes with being a rich and powerful man."

"But the will says—"

His arm tightened viselike around her waist. "I have the will!" he snapped. He tightened his grip another degree and Darcy couldn't swallow back the cry of pain. The sound made Jules laugh. "It says that when Aiden dies, my father's estate passes into my mother's control. Mother will give it to me. She promised."

"Promised?" Her mind reeled past her pain and fear and in a direction it had never considered.

"It was a good plan." She felt his chest, pressed hard to her back, begin to rise and fall in rapid cadence. "Except that Aiden went wrong, and sailed off on one of his ships that day," Jules growled. "He was supposed to be at dinner with everyone else. But I couldn't stop just because he'd wrenched it. Mother would have been so disappointed. So I went ahead with what Mother wanted, and then made my own plan to kill Aiden. A brilliant plan. A much more entertaining plan."

His breathing didn't slow, but he eased the arm clamped around her waist. "Now I'm tired of playing," he said with cool finality, "and it's time to go home. Mother's waiting for me."

Again she picked up the cue and responded as she should. "Blanche knows you're on your way?"

"I wrote her," he said in the tone of an obedient and dutiful child. "I told her how I'd been playing with him, and how I was going to finish it as soon as he came to you. She'll be most impressed. Aiden will be impressed, too, don't you think?"

"I'm sure," she choked out.

"Let's see, shall we?" Jules pushed her forward, calling, "Aiden! Big brother, wake up and see what I have! Aiden!"

Darcy made Jules work to move her toward Aiden's prostrate form, dragging her feet and making him use his own legs to move each of hers in turn. Anything to delay the end

Jules sought. Ten feet from where Aiden lay on the floor, Jules snarled against her ear, "Far enough. You call him."

"Aiden," she said softly. "Please wake up."

"Louder," Jules demanded. She felt the sharp, short sting of his knife, and then the warm trickle of blood slide over her skin.

She obeyed only because she had no other choice. "Aiden! Please, Aiden!"

His eyes came open slowly, his eyelids fluttering once, twice, three times before he looked up at her. But they weren't the eyes of a man just struggling from a stupor. They were clear and focused with solemn promise. And Darcy knew in that split second before he closed his eyes again that she wasn't alone against a madman. There was hope. Aiden wouldn't let Jules kill her.

"Wake up, Aiden!" Jules commanded. "See what I have!"

"Jules," Aiden said. His eyelids drifted open again.

"In the flesh," Jules sneered. "Are you happy to see me?"

"You son of a bitch," Aiden groaned, struggling to bring himself awkwardly to his knees. He twisted his arms and shoulders, clearly testing the strength of the rope that bound his hands behind him.

"Now, now, now," Jules chided. "Control that temper of yours, or your love will get her throat slashed prematurely."

Darcy watched Aiden slowly shake his head. Bits of glass showered the floor around him. A thin line of blood ran down his neck and onto his bare chest. He lifted his head and swayed as he blinked his eyes. "Jesus Christ, Jules," he said scornfully. "My love? She's nothing but a hot romp in bed. There's no need to carve up another innocent. Let her go. The game's with me."

Darcy felt the pressure of the knife to her throat ease. It fell away completely as Jules laughed and said, "Yes, it is, isn't it? Let's begin."

The movement was quick, the pain white-hot and long, slashing across her upper left arm. It went too deep and came too fast for her to keep from crying out against it. She saw

Aiden surge to his feet, and then there was only the brilliant red wall of pulsing pain.

"Let her go!" Aiden snarled, stepping toward them. He fixed Jules with a deadly glare and twisted his shoulders to hide the frantic efforts of his hands. The glass shard cut his fingers, but severing the rope was all that mattered. Blood poured from the gaping slash across Darcy's left shoulder. She had gone deathly white, and her injured arm hung limply at her side. Her teeth were clenched and bared as she choked back whimpers of pain. "Let her go!" Aiden demanded, advancing. "The game's with me!"

Jules dragged Darcy back, laughing. "Is the sight of blood making you unsteady on your feet, big brother?"

"You goddamn bastard," Aiden growled, following, twisting his shoulders, hacking at the rope. "I'll rip your heart out with my bare hands."

"That would be rather difficult to do with them tied behind your back," Jules taunted. He stopped and put the knife back to Darcy's throat. She didn't react, but stood motionless in Jules's hold.

Aiden's heart lurched and tore. "You're going to die, Jules," he said, still inching forward. "For Darcy alone, I'm going to kill you."

Jules smiled. "Stay where you are, Aiden," he said brightly, "or you'll get splashed. The arteries tend to spurt, you know. It makes the most wonderful patterns on the walls and ceilings and floors, but it does tend to be a bit messy."

Darcy's knees buckled. Jules jerked the knife from her throat, and with the arm around her waist hauled her back up and against him. "Stay awake, bitch," he snarled. "We're not near done yet." And then with a quick flick of the blade he cut her arm again, opening a second long gash just above the first.

It all happened in a single heart-wrenching second—Darcy swearing viciously and clawing at the arm around her waist with both hands, Jules arching his back, jerking Darcy from her feet, lifting the knife over his head and shifting his grip. Aiden bellowed, his rage and desperation parting the last strands of rope as he threw himself into the arc of the blade's downward plunge.

He felt pressure and heat in his back, felt the impact of his body against Darcy's and his hands slipping around Jules's throat. The force of his lunge staggered Jules back and drove him down. They hit the floor locked together, Darcy pinned helplessly between them.

Jules gasped for a breath. A searing heat flashed along the edge of Aiden's awareness. He felt rather than saw Jules's knife hand come up. Aiden instinctively released his grip on Jules's throat and swept his left arm out until it met Jules's right, blocking the downward thrust. Straining against Jules's determined resistance, he rolled to his left just far enough to take his weight off Darcy. With his right hand he dug into Jules's fingers that curled into Darcy's waist. Bone snapped and Jules howled, yanking his broken, useless hand away from Aiden's grasp. It was all Aiden wanted. He snatched Darcy's shirt front into his right fist and then, with all his might, he jerked her up and pitched her away like a rag doll, out of the range of Jules's blade. That she was safe was his last conscious thought before surrendering to the blindness of his murderous rage.

Darcy struggled through the pain and the dizziness, a deep sense of desperation demanding action. She rolled onto her side and pushed herself to sitting. From the darkness came the sounds of feral snarls and scraping and thudding. Aiden. Aiden and Jules. She had to protect Aiden. A simple wooden chair swam into focus before her eyes, and she threw her good arm over the seat and leveraged herself to her knees. The edge of the table got her to her feet.

She leaned against it as the shadows spun and tilted around her, as the pain throbbed through and consumed her. Her stomach heaved and she fought the nausea down, gasping huge, deep breaths. Aiden. She had to help Aiden.

Timmy's knife.

There was no conscious moment between the recognition of the weapon and it's being in her hand. No conscious thought between that and pinning it against the edge of the table with her thigh. It came from the sheath in the same half second that she whirled toward the sounds of struggling and started forward, focused on the dark shapes grappling on the floor in the inky shadows cast by the trunks.

Darcy stumbled to a halt, the knife in her hand forgotten as she watched Aiden roll Jules beneath him and lean forward, throwing a forearm across his brother's throat and ramming his free hand upward to seize Jules's chin. Jules arched and twisted to throw him off, pummeling Aiden's left side with his fist. A tiny bit of moonlight flashed over bare skin as Aiden's shoulders bunched and then flexed. There was a long hard snap and then a low, rumbling growl of triumph and satisfaction. Aiden heaved himself to his knees. Jules lay silent and still beneath him, his eyes open but unseeing, his head twisted at an unnatural angle.

Aiden took a shuddering breath and then reached down to press his hand to his side. He drew it back to stare down at the dark stain covering his palm. The knife clattered to the floor as Darcy raced to him.

"Damn, but that hurts," he whispered as she dropped to her knees beside him. He looked at her, his eyes glazed. "Sorry it took so long to get my hands freed."

"It doesn't matter, Aiden," she assured him. Even in the wan light she could see the color draining from his face at an alarming speed. "Can you move a little so that I can look at your side? You're in deep shadow."

He gave her a tiny smile and nodded. Then his eyes rolled back into his head and he slumped forward, sprawling over Jules's body.

The whole left side of his back was covered with blood; the waistband and left leg of his trousers soaked with it. She didn't know precisely how she did it, but panic gave her the strength to pull Aiden off Jules and roll him onto his back. The left side of his chest was smeared with blood, the front of his trousers drenched with it. Frantically she searched for the wound, her hands skimming over him. She found not one, but two; a large oval hole in his back, the other a smaller version of it in the front.

"Aiden!" she cried, pressing her hands to the wounds, desperately trying to hold back what blood he had left within him. "Aiden! You can't die, Aiden!"

His eyelids fluttered open, but the awareness in his eyes was only a tiny flicker. "I didn't mean it, Darcy," he said, his voice raspy and weak.

"Didn't mean what?" she asked, trying to keep him talking, trying to keep him from slipping back into unconsciousness. His blood flowed between her fingers and she increased the pressure she held against the wounds.

"You're not a hot romp. Didn't want Jules to know . . ." His eyes slowly rolled backward again, and he sighed.

"Aiden! Aiden, I have to get you to a doctor but I can't move you if you don't help me. Aiden, wake up!" He didn't move, didn't open his eyes, didn't acknowledge her frantic demands.

"Oh, please dear Mary," she sobbed, holding him as tightly as she could, her tears splashing on his chest and mingling with his blood. "Please don't let me lose him. Anything you ask. Please."

"Darcy, are you awake?" a voice called sweetly. "We brought you a piece of our wedding cake."

Her heart leapt at the distant sound. *Maisey! Maisey was at the door. And where Maisey went*—"Nathan!" she shouted. "Nathan, help me!"

The door flew inward and crashed back against the wall. In the very same second, Nathan came charging through the opening, his hands fisted and his jaw set. He got no more than five feet before his gaze had swept the scene and he comprehended the gist of what had happened. He kept coming, jerking open the front of his dress coat even as he commanded, "Maise! Dr. Maguire's at the social club. Get him here! Hurry!"

Maisey flung the cake away, whirled about, hiked her skirts to her knees, and started running.

Nathan knelt beside Darcy on the floor and quickly pressed his fingertips to the side of Aiden's neck. "Alive," he said briskly. "Let's keep him that way, shall we, Darcy?"

"He's lost so much blood. I can't get it to stop."

Nathan stripped off his coat, his gaze passing swiftly, keenly over her. Asking, "Does Aiden have wounds other than these two?" he shoved one double-folded sleeve under Aiden's back and against the wound.

Darcy pulled her hand free. "I d-don't know. I didn't look any further."

Nathan quickly folded the second sleeve in half and pressed it over the upper wound. "I've got these, Darcy," he said, tensing his shoulders and exerting greater pressure. "Can you check him for more?"

She nodded and quickly set about trailing her fingers over Aiden's upper extremities. The fingers on his right hand were deeply gashed and his right arm looked like it had been flayed with a cat of nine tails. Darcy clenched her teeth, angry with herself for not having noticed the wounds before that point. "His fingers are cut," she told Nathan. "And his right arm."

"They look relatively minor," Nathan replied, blessedly calm. "Check his legs."

Her left arm throbbed at the slightest movement and so she simply laid her forearm across her thighs and worked with her right. She traced the corded muscles of his legs beneath the fabric, praying she would find no jagged edges of flesh. "I don't feel anything," she declared, relieved. "I don't think I've overlooked anything, either. The cloth of his trousers is whole."

Nathan looked at her long and hard and then asked, "What about his shoulders and head? Can you check those, Darcy?"

She nodded again, the gesture less controlled than it had been before. "Jules hit him with a whiskey bottle," she supplied, as she began carefully working her way around Aiden's feet and up his right side. "Aiden shook his head once and I saw bits of glass shower out of his hair. There was a trickle of blood that ran over his shoulder."

Cradling her injured arm, she slipped her right hand along the underside width of Aiden's shoulders. There was blood, but she could find no wounds to account for it. She ran her fingers gently through his hair. Tears rimmed her lashes as she wondered if this were the last time she would ever get to caress the dark strands. "Oh God, Nathan," she moaned as her fingers found the ragged, sticky edges just above the nape of his neck. "He's got gashes in his scalp, too. They're bleeding."

"Head wounds always bleed like a son of a bitch, Darcy. They look a lot worse than they usually are," Nathan explained with a firmness so startling that she blinked hard enough to banish the threat of tears. "Was Aiden coherent after the blow to his head?"

She nodded and quickly pressed her hand over her face to keep her head from falling off her shoulders. "Aiden knew what he was doing," she said, remembering how he'd looked up at her from the pool of whiskey and shattered glass. Such determined devotion. "I saw his eyes," Darcy whispered. "He looked at me and promised me. He didn't say a word, but I saw. He promised he would save me."

"The doctor's coming, Darcy," Nathan said sharply. "I can hear him at the top of the stairs. Can you hear him?"

His tone said it was important, and so she struggled to focus her awareness so that she didn't abandon his efforts to help Aiden. "Yes, he's in the hall now," she said. "I'll get the door." With a deep breath she began climbing to her feet.

"It's already open."

Nathan's words didn't register in her brain until she was standing and watching the room sway. "Oh." Her knees buckled and she instantly locked them to keep herself upright. Her muscles trembled in warning. "Nathan?"

"What, Darcy?"

He was such a long way off. She hoped he could hear her. "Would you think poorly of me if I fainted?"

"Catch her, Mick!"

Mick was here? Her legs gave out and the room went black.

CHAPTER 27

THERE WAS A world on the other side of his eyelids. The realization puzzled him for a moment, and then Aiden remembered with stunning clarity. Darcy. He forced open his eyes. A whitewashed plaster ceiling wasn't what he'd hoped to see.

"Good evening. Might I be the first to welcome you back among the living."

Nathan. Somewhere to his right. "Where's Darcy?"

"She's with her grandmother and Maisey. She's fine, Aiden. You had the worst of it."

Aiden slowly turned toward Nathan's voice, gritting his teeth when a sharp edged jolt shot through the back of his head. "Her arm . . ."

"Stitched and bandaged, and her only significant injury," Nathan supplied from the overstuffed chair by the window. "The doctor said she'll heal well and quickly. You're going to take a bit longer, though. The wound in your side was deep. A fraction of an inch in any direction, and you'd have had a very nice funeral."

Aiden decided to make his own assessment of his injuries. His head hurt. He felt his heartbeat in the fingertips of his right hand. A dull sense of tightness wrapped around his right arm. And his side . . . Damned if he didn't feel as if he'd been kicked by one very mean mule. "How long have I been lying here?" Aiden asked. "And where the hell am I? O'Shaunessy's?

Nathan chuckled. "Not O'Shaunessy's. Darcy put her foot down about that. You're—we're—in Mrs. Georgina Riley's home in Boston. We brought you over two days ago, when the doctor thought you could be safely moved. Darcy's grand-mother insisted on it. And between the time here and at Darcy's, you've been lying abed for a full six days. You were thrashing so badly the first night that the doctor prescribed a sedative to keep you from tearing yourself open again. You've had a fair number of moments of semiconsciousness, though. Do you remember Darcy alternately feeding you tepid broth and milk bread?"

Aiden thought back. "No," he admitted finally. But one memory did come to him; a very, very old one. "I *hate* milk bread."

"Are you hungry?"

He considered the sensations in the general region of his abdomen and found his stomach to be the least demanding portion of his anatomy. "Not at all."

"That's because Darcy's been religious about seeing to your stomach and your strength," Nathan said in the tone he always used when explaining what he thought to be the obvi-ous. "Your lady's very determined to bring you out of this whole and hale." He paused, and one corner of his mouth quirked up. "And you ate milk bread. A lot of it."

Aiden frowned. Milk bread wasn't the only thing he couldn't remember. He could recall most of that night, yes, but there were fragments of time and events lost to him. He'd known the instant the pain had exploded in the back of his head that the reckoning with Jules had come. In the same heartbeat that he'd realized Jules was there, he'd thought of Darcy and how defenseless she would be against Jules's sav-agery. It had been his desperation to protect her that had kept him from fully surrendering to unconsciousness. And then he'd heard Jules telling Darcy what he was going to do, and he'd seen the knife held to Darcy's throat.

Two certainties had struck him in that crystalline moment;

that he loved Darcy and that Jules was going to die. An odd calm had come over him then, a kind of lethal patience that had let him think past his rage. He'd feigned stupor and rolled onto his back, searching for a glass shard to use to sever the rope and free his hands. And as he'd worked, he'd listened to Jules's cruelty and Darcy's fear, and with every second that passed his hatred had deepened. He'd turned over in his mind all he knew of how Jules went about his terror, and when the time at last came for him to join the game he had been coldly ready to kill.

The memories after Darcy's cry of pain were the fragments—the flash of the blade, the certainty that Jules intended to plunge it into her chest. He'd thrown himself between the knife and Darcy, and then there was only the memory of tossing her beyond Jules's reach. Then nothing at all until he found her hovering over him, begging him not to die. He'd known then that it was over. Darcy had been covered with blood but the fear in her eyes hadn't been of Jules. It had been a fear for him. And under that fear had been a love so deep it had soothed all the pain from his body. He'd tried to tell her that he loved her, but the words—and consciousness—had slipped beyond his grasp.

"Are you all right, Aiden?" he heard Nathan ask softly.

"What happened to Jules?" Aiden asked his brother. "Is he dead?"

"Quite. I gather you don't remember breaking his neck?"

"No," Aiden admitted. Then he gave Nathan another truth. "But I wish I did. Just to savor the satisfaction."

Nathan nodded slowly. "The Charlestown constables are going to be asking you questions about it all, Aiden. Darcy and Maisey and I have already taken our turns, telling them what we know. They've been patient in waiting for you to heal, but as soon as we send word, they'll come around with their pens and notebooks."

It was to be expected and endured. "Is there anything in particular I should keep in mind while telling them the tale?"

"Nothing beyond the truth of how Jules came to be in Darcy's apartment and eventually dead on her floor."

"That shouldn't be all that difficult."

"You'll have to decide for yourself what to tell them of Blanche's apparent involvement in the murder of your father and Dr. LeClaire and his wife. Darcy discussed it with me—since you were unavailable for rational discourse—and she decided to say nothing of it to the constables. She felt it was your decision to make on how the matter was to be pursued."

Oh, yes, Blanche—and Jules's claim that the first murders had been the result of her plotting. How crazy was Jules? How much of what he said was truth? How much the product of his twisted mind? And did any of it really matter? "Believe it or not, Nathan, I don't give a rat's ass about Blanche."

Nathan drummed his fingers on the arm of the chair and then asked, "You don't think Blanche would come after you in another attempt to gain control of your father's estate?"

"My father was Edward Chandler," Aiden said, meeting Nathan's gaze squarely. "My father and yours. It was the estate of Frederick Terrell that I inherited, and it's well past time to make the proper distinction. As for Blanche . . . let her try to kill me if she's so inclined. If she's not, then I don't care. I'll let the sleeping dog lie. I'm tired of murder and the needs of justice. I want to go home and be done with it."

A long silence stretched between them. Nathan finally broke it by saying, "Perhaps this is the point where you'd like to apologize for having disrupted my honeymoon?"

Aiden started, only then realizing that he'd been selfishly consumed with his own concerns. "I am sorry, Nathan," he offered sincerely. "Did they have to call you off the ship?"

"Actually, we never made it that far," Nathan replied. "Maisey had thought to take Darcy a piece of wedding cake on our way. We happened along apparently just after you'd killed Jules. Darcy was weak, nearly unconscious herself, but struggling to do what she could for you. She's an incredibly valiant woman."

Aiden recognized the tone of his brother's voice and

smiled. "You don't need to preach, Nate. I'm a member of the choir."

Nathan snorted and hauled himself out of the chair, saying, "That will be the day."

"Would you tell Darcy I'm awake?" Aiden asked, seeing Nathan move toward the door. "There are some things I have to say to her."

With the door open and his hand on the knob, Nathan turned back. "Might I suggest that the first thing you say be some decent profession of your love for her?"

"Think it ought to be said first, huh?"

Nathan grinned. "I'll get Darcy for you." He paused just before closing the door behind himself and looked back to say, "And Aiden? Try to physically restrain yourself just a little. You've more stitches in you than a crazy quilt."

Aiden smiled. "I'll try."

Nathan laughed, said, "I'll see that you're not interrupted," and closed the door.

And as soon as the latch clicked into place, Aiden began the process of seeing how much pain moving caused, and how much range of motion he could manage. His joints and muscles had stiffened with disuse, but they quickly remembered how to work and it wasn't long at all before he felt very much like himself. His side ached, but if he were to exercise just a bit of restraint as Nathan had so kindly suggested. . . . Aiden flung aside the bedcovers and eased his legs over the side of the mattress. It was high time to take up his responsibilities as Darcy's lover. And the first steps in that direction lay in getting rid of the damn nightshirt, and a quick version of his morning ablutions.

DARCY FORCED HERSELF to halt in the hall and take a deep breath. She adjusted her arm in the sling, quickly smoothed her skirts, and then moistened her lips. There was nothing she could do to slow the beat of her heart or ease the anxiety coursing through her veins. She would just have to endure it until she got said what needed to be said. As

344   ᴏ LESLIE LAFOY ᴏ

though she hadn't spent the last six days thinking of the matter, she ran the course one more time in her head. She would tell Aiden that she loved him—in a logical, rational way, of course. No wringing or fluttering her hands. No breathless declarations of eternal devotion. Just a simple "I love you." With a firm admonition that her offering required no return declaration on his part.

And once that had been accomplished, she'd calmly tell him that she was willing to formally be his mistress. If he wanted her to go to St. Kitts, she would. If he wanted her to remain as his mistress in Charlestown, she would. And when he tired of her, she would decide then what to do with the rest of her life. And if Aiden declared that their relationship had ended with Jules's death, she would accept it without flinching. She wouldn't cry; at least not in front of him. She and Aiden had always been honest with each other. It was the only way to face the crossroads at which they now stood.

Lifting her chin, she took another deep breath, pasted a confident smile on her face, grabbed the doorknob, turned it, and boldly walked in. Her hard-fought resolve melted at the sight of Aiden, propped up with pillows and leaning back against the headboard. He looked at her and smiled, and she knew that little needed to be said between them. The larger answers were there, in the way he drank in the sight of her and yearned for more. She didn't know where they were going, but they were going together. If he hadn't been a mass of stitches and bandages, she'd have raced across the room and thrown herself into his arms. Her heart thundering and her hands trembling, she blindly closed the door.

"How are you feeling?" she asked, moving toward him with what she could only hope looked like a serene and graceful glide.

"Slightly sore and stiff, but I'm alive and that tends to compensate." The corners of his mouth twitched. "And how are you feeling, Miss O'Keefe?"

Miss O'Keefe, was it? Darcy smiled. Aiden knew her too well, knew that she was knotted with the effort to maintain a sense of decorum, and he was deliberately trying to prod her past it. She so enjoyed the little contests of will with Aiden. They always went somewhere interesting, and always ended delightfully well.

"I understand what you mean about sore and stiff," she said, smoothing the bedcovers beside him. "The doctor said there would be scars, but I'll eventually have full use of my arm. Did Nathan tell you about the constables needing to question you?"

"He did," he answered cavalierly. "Not to worry, Darcy. I'll answer their questions just as you and Nathan have, and nothing further will come of it. It's over." He patted the place beside him on the bed and with that wicked, tempting smile of his, said, "Come keep me company."

She wasn't going to let him win that easily. Darcy pursed her lips and put her hand on her hip.

It took him some obvious effort to wipe the amused smile off his face. "What troubles you, Darce?"

"First, I was *nothing more than a hot romp in bed,* and then I wasn't?" she asked, arching a brow. "I'm not certain of the logic, Aiden, but I'm fairly sure that—one way or the other—I've been insulted."

He looked so innocent, so stunned and confused, that for a second she thought it might be genuine. And then he gave himself away by chuckling. "I'm sorry. But the next part of what I said should have more than made up for it."

"There wasn't a next part," she countered, hiking her skirt and climbing up on the bed. He reached out his uninjured hand and helped her to his side. Arranging her skirt and settling herself on her knees facing him, she asked, "And the only good your passing into unconsciousness accomplished, Aiden Terrell, was to save you from a second bash on the head."

"I didn't say it? I would have sworn that I did."

"And just what is it that you think you said?"

"That I love you." Every word was deliberate and full and woven with conviction.

And with those words the game between them became a

different one entirely. "No, Aiden," she said softly, "you didn't tell me that. I would have remembered."

"Probably just as well," he said teasingly. "I thought at the time I was dying, and I decided there wouldn't be a price for telling you what you wanted to hear. I considered it my last act of earthly kindness."

He knew full well how desperately she had hoped for those words, and the knowledge that he could see into her heart so clearly filled her with a sweet, deep wonder. She leaned forward and pressed a lingering kiss to his lips. Easing back to meet his gaze, she whispered, "I don't care if you never tell me that you love me, Aiden. It's not necessary. I can see it in your eyes. I can feel it when you make love to me. It's enough."

"Not for me." He brushed the back of his hand over her cheek. "I can't remember when it happened, Darcy, but I think it was at the first. I just didn't know it for what it was. But when I heard you and Jules . . . When I saw the knife at your throat . . . Darcy, nothing in my life has ever been clearer or more important. I love you."

"And I love you, Aiden." Tears welled along her lashes. "So very much."

"Please tell me those are joyful tears."

She could only nod. Aiden slipped his hand to her nape and gently drew her lips to his. He kissed her with the same deep reverence that had marked his return to her life, and in her heart she knew that all the struggle, all the pain and doubt, had been worth enduring. When he ended their kiss, she eased around so that she curled into his uninjured side and she laid her head on his shoulder, wanting nothing more than to spend eternity in the circle of his embrace.

For a long moment they lay together in contented silence, and then Aiden pressed a kiss to the top of her head and quietly asked, "When did you know, Darcy?"

"It came in tiny pieces," she answered, "like the puzzle of Jules we were putting together. With every moment we were together, I gave you a bit more of my heart. But I didn't realize how much I had given until you were gone from my life.

And when you finally came through the door again I thought I'd burst with happiness."

"You didn't look happy."

"I was also afraid you'd turn around and walk out again."

"I was afraid you'd throw me out on my ear."

Darcy shifted so that she could see his face. "I've never regretted anything more than sending you away the night Mother died, Aiden. It was a mistake made in a terrible moment of self-doubt. I won't suffer from it ever again."

"You sound as if you're expecting me to stay a while longer."

He spoke lightly but she saw the tension at the corners of his mouth, the deepening color of his eyes, and knew that the observation hadn't been as casual as he wanted her to believe. They had reached the crossroad she had resolved to face squarely and with her heart.

"No one can make you do anything against your will, Aiden," she began. "I'm simply saying that I'd like to go on together for as long as we can make each other happy. When you decide to go, even if it's tomorrow, I'll find the grace and courage to accept it."

He was silent, watchful. Unable to bear his searching scrutiny, she burrowed down and nestled her cheek against his shoulder to wait for his decision.

"What happened to the woman who needed to know what tomorrow would bring?" he finally asked. "The one who had to control her own life and her destiny?"

"I think she grew up and learned that some things in life have to be accepted on faith."

He pressed another kiss to the top of her head and then asked, "What if I never want to leave you, Darcy?"

Happiness and hope flooded through her. "I'll find the grace and courage to accept that, too. Not that being with you is all that difficult to endure."

"So you're willing to be my mistress?"

"I thought I already was. But if I need to submit my credentials again, I'll be willing to do so. Although," she added, looking up at him and smiling, "if I were wise, I would place some conditions on the nature of the relationship this time."

He cocked a brow as a smile played at the corners of his mouth. "Conditions such as . . . ?"

Aiden watched her order her thoughts, and wondered how he had ever had the good fortune to walk into her life. Sweet, determined Darcy. So logical, so practical. So innocent and impulsive. And she had completely forgotten the first rule of being man and mistress. It was going to be a delightfully interesting contest, getting her where he wanted her.

"Well," she said in the tone she always used to preface her arguments, "I'm fully aware that it would be going against common practice, but I've never learned to share very well, and so you'll have to promise that you won't openly court another woman while we're together."

"I think I could keep that promise easily enough," he replied, knowing there would never be any other woman who fascinated him as she did. "Anything else?"

"You'll have to agree to let me wear my trousers and shirts when the mood strikes me. I'll have a care for scandal, but I don't think I could stand to be a lady every hour of the day and night."

God, he loved her unpredictable, impish disregard for convention. "Who would want a straitlaced lady all the time? Consider the request granted." A thought suddenly occurred to him, and he quickly added, "Well, except for one proviso. At night, in the privacy of our bedchamber, I'd prefer that you wear nothing at all."

"With pleasure," she acceded.

He grinned. "That would be my hope."

"Then I may consider myself hired for the job?"

"Perhaps," he countered, sobering. The next step was the most important one he would ever take. He took a slow breath to steady his nerves. If Darcy could take a leap of faith for love, then he could, too. "I've been wondering . . . Would you consider becoming my wife?"

Her eyes widened, the happiness in them so brilliant and full that he knew the answer. And because Darcy never gave in without making him earn the victory, he wasn't the least surprised when she suddenly knitted her brows and pretended to give the notion grave consideration. He knew that when all was said and done, she would kiss him and happily agree to marry him. All that was left was to enjoy the getting there. Aiden waited, wondering what path she was going to take, and how he might best use his gambits.

"I thought you were opposed to marriage," she said after a moment. "You've always maintained that you would be a horrible husband."

"I was enlightened while lying on the floor of your apartment," he supplied. "Since then it's occurred to me that perhaps I might do fairly well at it, if I entered into it with the right woman and if I treated her as I would my favorite mistress. I might be able to keep her reasonably happy for quite a long while. What do you think?"

"It sounds like a rational approach. It could well work."

"Would it be sufficient to attract you to the idea?" He tossed his first gambit by quickly adding, "And before you give me your answer, darling, I'll remind you that we've violated the cardinal rule governing the relationships of men and their mistresses. We've fallen in love."

"I tried to resist, you know, but you're a most tempting man."

She could teach *him* about temptation. Aiden grinned. "And, of course, if you were to be my wife, all the agreements we've reached on your being my mistress would still apply."

"I have one more condition," she instantly countered, her eyes sparkling. "As your wife, I'd want lots of your babies. Maybe a dozen or so."

He cocked a brow. "A dozen." Striving to achieve that goal was going to make him a well and often satisfied man.

"Maybe more," she amended. "A dozen is just a nice even number to start with."

And suddenly he wanted the contest done and his heart complete. He traced her lips with the pad of his thumb, saying softly, "We'll have however many you want, Darcy. Are these children of ours going to be known as O'Keefes or Ter-rells? Are you going to marry me or not?"

"Of course I'll marry you," she answered, her smile daz-zling. "You knew what my answer would be the minute you asked me."

"But, as always, I thoroughly enjoyed the challenge of get-ting you to say it."

He drew her to him and kissed her, offering her everything he had in him to give. She accepted it and returned his pas-sion in equal measure. As it always was with Darcy, his need quickened and intensified, the urgency of loving her over-whelming all else. Feasting on her kisses, he found the pins in her hair, pulled them loose, and threaded the fingers of his good hand through the silken strands. She sighed and reached to slip her arms around his waist. And then moaned in clear frustration.

Aiden released his claim to her lips and eased back, his brow cocked in silent question.

Darcy raised her slinged arm, saying, "Speaking of chal-lenges . . ."

"We'll manage," he promised. "We're very good at figur-ing puzzles." And to prove he was perfectly capable of hold-ing up his end of the effort, he reached behind her, and with one hand began nimbly undoing the buttons of her bodice. She burrowed her fingers through the curls on his chest as he worked.

"Someone could come in," she offered sadly.

"Nathan's guarding the door for us."

She smiled, and when he'd finished undoing her buttons, she took the sling from her arm and tossed it away.

"If there's to be a dozen babies—or more," he mused, eas-ing her bodice off her shoulders and carefully down her arms. "There wouldn't ever be any need for sponges, would there?"

She grinned and rose to her knees. "Probably not," she said, pushing her dress down over her hips.

"Did you happen to think of one before you came in here?"

"No," she laughingly admitted as the dress joined the

sling somewhere on the floor. "I thought you'd be too weak to be dangerous."

"Well, obviously you were wrong." He helped her get rid of her petticoat and pantilettes. And when they, too, were on the floor, he pushed back the bed coverings, put his hands on her corseted waist, and drew her toward him, saying, "And if you want a dozen children, we need to get started now."

"Aiden, please have a care for your side," she gently admonished, not resisting at all. "You'll pull open the stitches."

"You have the care, darling," he countered, settling her astride his hips. "But there's no need to be too gentle with me. I'm much tougher than I look."

And more vulnerable, too, Darcy knew. She would have a care for that as well. He had entrusted his heart and soul to her, and for as long as she lived she would protect those most precious gifts. Come what may, they would triumph together. There was nothing more powerful or enduring than love.

THE ST. KITTS CLARION

Saturday, May 5, 1859   Basseterre, St. Kitts

TERRELLS TO DEPART FOR GRAND TOUR

Mr. AND MRS. AIDEN TERRELL, long-time residents of Basseterre, St. Kitts, have announced plans to spend the next year extensively touring Western Europe. They will be accompanied by their twelve children: eight sons and four daughters, all of the home.

Mr. Terrell, a native of St. Kitts and a well-known and highly respected member of the international business community, has indicated that he intends to see that all of his children make use of the experience not only to broaden their cultural awareness and appreciation of art, but also to deepen their acquaintanceship with the principles of commerce, finance, and political representation as practiced in various regions of Europe. Mr. Terrell confided to this reporter that he has recently concluded negotiations to purchase four steam-powered vessels from a Bristol, England, shipyard, and that his family's tour of the Continent will conclude at Bristol, where he and his three eldest children, John Aiden, Mary Georgina, and Edward Michael, will accept delivery of the aforementioned vessels and accompany them to berths at various ports in British possessions throughout the Caribbean.

Mrs. Aiden Terrell, a native of Charlestown, Massachusetts, America, is well known and highly respected among local residents for her unstinting patronage of the arts, and as the founder of the St. Kitts Academic Academy for Boys and Girls, and the St. Croix Academy for Advanced Studies. The former occupies the island home of Mr. Terrell's late father, Frederick Terrell. The St. Croix Academy is sited in the home of Mr. Terrell's late stepmother, Blanche Terrell, who died by her own hand soon after Mr. Aiden Terrell and his wife, Darcy, arrived in the Leeward Islands.

Although equally well known for her unflaggingly independent spirit, plainspokenness, and frequent defiance of convention, Mrs. Aiden Terrell has indicated that she will neither confirm nor deny rumors of an August exhibition of her own drawings at a Paris gallery. Anonymous sources report that the exhibition features pen-and-ink studies decidedly inspired by and reminiscent of classical Italian sculptures of the male form. Mr. Terrell was not available for comment on the subject.

In the absence of Mr. Terrell from St. Kitts, the affairs of his mercantile concern will be ably managed by his half-brother and business partner, Mr. Nathan Chandler. Mr. and Mrs. Chandler will host a farewell reception for the Terrell family the evening of Saturday next at their home. Mrs. Chandler, mother of seven and a childhood friend of Mrs. Terrell's, has advised this reporter that frequent island visitors Mrs. Joseph Riley of Boston, the genteel grandmother of Mrs. Terrell, and Mr. and Mrs. Michael O'Shaunessy, also of Boston and Mrs. Terrell's godparents, will be in attendance.

ABOUT THE AUTHOR

LESLIE LAFOY grew up loving to read and living to write. A former high-school history teacher and department chair, she made the difficult decision to leave academia in 1996 to follow her dream of writing full time. When not made utterly oblivious to the real world by her current work in progress, she dabbles at being a domestic goddess, and gives credible performances as a hockey wife, a little league Mom, and a cub scout den leader. A fourth generation Kansan, she lives on ten windswept acres of prairie with her husband and son, a shetland sheepdog, and Sammy the cat.

IRIS JOHANSEN

Spellbinding, intoxicating, riveting...

Elizabeth Thornton's

gift for romance is nothing less than addictive

DANGEROUS TO HOLD

___57479-5 $5.99/$7.99 Canada

THE BRIDE'S BODYGUARD

___57435-6 $5.99/$7.99 Canada

YOU ONLY LOVE TWICE

___57426-4 $5.99/$7.99 Canada

WHISPER HIS NAME

___57427-2 $5.99/$8.99 Canada